# Acknowledgements

This series of books is dedicated to Pamela my wife with my thanks for her infinite patience as I deserted her, to go play in my imagination or with what she calls 'the mistress on my lap', my Laptop.

Also to Charlotte my clever and patient daughter for all the time she took out from her busy life, to design the covers for my books and to help me in my battles with stubborn and perverse software.

With two such helpmates what can you do but give heartfelt thanks and love?

More wholehearted thanks go to Jo Field that patient and hardworking editor who has erased mistakes and ironed out wrinkles to help me produce something I can be proud of. Jo can be found at http://www.newwritersuk.co.uk/jofield.html

Finally I would like to give thanks to Helen Hollick, www.helenhollick.net/. She is a busy, successful, historical novelist and UK Reviewer for the Historical Novel Society. Out of kindness she took an interest in this book. By introducing me to her editor she has facilitated a step change in its quality.

# Contents

AD 1685 Somerset ................................................... 1
AD 462 Thiatmaresgaho, Germania ......................... 37
AD 435 - AD 447 Germania, Gaul ........................... 75
AD 447 - AD 455 Africa, Carthage, The Middle Sea..... 169
AD 455 Rome, the Bat Cave ................................. 229
AD 463 - AD 464 Thiatmaresgaho, Germania ........... 331

**Maps in Germania**
Gewis' Tale – The Road to Africa ........................... 133
Gewis' Tale – The Middle Sea ............................... 170
Gewis' Tale – Gateway to Rome AD 455 .................. 230
Gewis' Tale – AD 455 Italy, the road home ............... 256
Gewis' Tale – AD 455 The Return to Colonia ............ 298
The Homes of the Hearth Companions ..................... 318

**Author's Note** ..................................................... 415

**Place Names** ..................................................... 419

**Weapons in use in the 5th Century** ......................... 423

IN SEARCH OF ANCIENT
FREEDOM

# THE AXE
# THE SHIELD
# AND
# THE TRITON

## James M. Hockey

**Wyrd Sisters Publishing, Bristol, UK**
www.wyrdsisterspublishing.com

WYRD
SISTERS
PUBLISHING

The Axe the Shield and the Triton,
Copyright © James M. Hockey 2010.

All rights reserved. No part of this book may be reproduced in any form or by any electronic or mechanical means including all information storage and retrieval systems without permission in writing from the publisher, except by a reviewer, who may quote brief passages in a review.

Image Credits

Front Cover: Dirty Design / dirtydesign.co.uk
Copyright Charlotte Hockey-Berry 2010

Maps: Copyright James M. Hockey 2010
Maps produced by Luisa Wells

**ISBN 978-0-9566871-0-4**

**Published by Wyrd Sisters Publishing
Bristol, UK**

WYRD
SISTERS
PUBLISHING

First Edition 2011
Revised January 2012
James M. Hockey, all rights reserved

**The Heathen Calendar --- The Festivals and Months of the Year**

| | |
|---|---|
| Christmas | Yule. Mothers Night |
| January | After Yule |
| February | Mud Month |
| March | Hreth Month |
| April | Easter (Oestre) Month |
| May | Three Milkings Month |
| June | Before Mid-Summer, (Aerra Litha) |
| Mid-Summer | Litha |
| July | After Mid-Summer, (Aefterra Litha) |
| August | Weed Month |
| September | Holy Month, (Harvest Festival) |
| October | Winter Full Moon, (Start of winter) |
| November | Blood Month, (Winter Cull and Offering) |
| December | Before Yule |

**Roman Currency in the 5th Century AD**

Follis Bronze, Miliarense Silver, Solidus Gold
15 Bronze Folles = 1 Silver Miliarense
12 Silver Miliarenses = 1 Gold Solidus

What is the power of a curse?
Know this.
That which is not in the weaving of the Wyrd has no power.
It is as the crying of a child in an empty house.
It is words of anger borne away on a rushing wind.
Know this. Even the Gods must bow before the three.
Even the end of all things is patterned in the weave.
What is woven is what will be, the sum of all that has been.
Gæð a Wyrd swa hio scel! *

*Edda of Wodanaz*

* Fate goes ever as she shall

To Charlotte & Rob,

At last the final version.

With Love & thanks to my patient Charlotte.

Read & Enjoy Rob.

James M Hockey (Dad)
xxxx

# AD 1685 Somerset

# Chapter 1

**AD 1685**

**Jo's Tale, the Treasure**

When I was a child I loved the hill, for I knew nothing then of its blood-drenched soil. It was my playground and my playfellow.

The final climb to the top, worn to bare earth by much use, was nearly vertical. When there were other boys present, we would challenge each other to slide down this slope on our arses. Sometimes this led to torn breeches and a good hiding at homecoming, but the fear and joy of casting off caution and care, of the rush down the slope, the landing and the laughter, was worth it. This was the reason my breeches were now of cow hide, hard and chafing when new, but well worn now, softened by a boy's hard use and almost indestructible.

I loved the hill best of all when great clouds billowed bright gold on top, silver blue underneath. I daydreamed they were the hills and valleys of some giant country. Here, in my imagination, I found adventures and riches in each shadowed valley or over each shining hill.

Later, of course, I learned about the blood that had seeped into the soil I so joyfully and unknowingly hurtled down on my leather-encased behind. The blood that fed the roots of woody cover that softened the hill's steep outline, but until that day it was unspoiled and it nurtured my daydreams.

When I tired of adventuring in the clouds I would turn to scan the land for anything that moved and might take my interest. Today, a light drizzle fell from the overcast sky, neither heavy enough to send me to shelter nor cold enough, on this mid-September day, to make me seek the comfort of the kitchen hearth. There were no valleys to see in the clouds and no giants to dream about today. The ground being wet, I stood and searched the misty horizons.

I looked west, along the old Roman road towards Taunton. When I had left the house this morning, my father and the preacher were in grave debate at the door. As they saw me they fell silent and turned to walk away, but not before I overheard the preacher say, '... he is hanging them in Taunton this morning; and worse ...'

This was a mystery to me and I probed it in my mind. I knew there had been much excitement in recent days and that some of our men who worked about the farm, constant in my life as far back as I could remember, were missing. I knew too that there had been gloomy faces and sobbing women around the village for days. I asked questions, but they were all unanswered.

Now, as I looked west, I saw something strange. There, just near enough to make out through the misting drizzle, was a hooded cart of the sort that pedlars use. It was a small cart, drawn by a single horse between twin shafts. As I watched, the horse ambled for a while then, as if spying a patch of rich grass, it stopped and lowered its head to eat. After a time, as if bored with eating it ambled some more before again stopping to graze. It came to me that the cart was untended and the horse, without direction, was pleasing itself. The strangeness of this, added to the weather that made my playground so bleak, led me to begin a rapid descent.

Whilst I slid and slithered downwards, sullen cloud bases pushed in from the west, darkening the overcast. Thunder rumbled in the distance, lightning flashed and the drizzle turned to rain. By the time I reached the road the rain was so heavy it bounced when it hit the ground; raining crocuses, as they say. Lightning forks were all around me, angry, sun-bright spears, and crashing thunder boxed my ears so I jumped and ducked at each clap.

Although I now started to shiver as the water soaked into my jacket and trickled down my neck, I welcomed it. Any walker on the road, not seeing what I had seen, would take shelter and I would get to the cart first and solve the mystery of what it contained, and perhaps even - and here my heart beat faster for this was the stuff of my hilltop dreaming made real - claim abandoned treasure!

I saw myself, thirteen years old, surrounded by riches, telling others what to do instead of being told; doing as I wished, not at the beck and call of all. I increased my pace to a steady jog trot, so determined was I to get to the idling horse and its burden before some adult should beat me to it and, in the way of grownups, dispossess me of it.

The more soaked I became, the faster I ran and in very short order the cart appeared out of the sheeting rain. The horse, a mare, short of leg and fat of belly, was not eating now, but danced on shuffling feet, head up and eyes rolling. Fearing it would bolt, dragging my cart and its treasure with it, I seized the reins gently pulling the beast's head down, letting it see me, speaking as softly as the wind and thunder would allow, stroking and patting to take its attention from the tumult around us. It ceased its dancing and I judged it calm enough to leave. Longing to get out of the cold raindrops beating on my head, I jumped on the shaft nearest me and climbed up onto the driver's seat. Swivelling round I swung my legs over the seat and slid through the opening and under the hood.

And nearly died from fright.

My tongue, tingling, tasted of sour apples and my stomach rose into my chest. I farted as I heard a hoarse scream - and knew it was mine. I crouched, muscles tensed, preparing to spring back the way I had entered. Why I did not flee in panic as though the Devil himself were after me I do not know, except that I heard a croaking voice and it brought me back from the quivering edge.

'Help me,' came out of the mess of body and blood and bedding, cutting through my fear. Here was someone suffering harm, not some demon about to harm me.

My only reward for the cold and wet I had suffered lay on a mattress, a cloth bag stuffed with straw, covered by a coarse blanket of un-dyed wool, though dyed now with black-red stains spreading on its upper width. The air smelled foul, of sick flesh and vomit, a privy bucket stench that hinted at unseen soiling.

The creature, whose life blood seeped into and coloured the bedding, lay on his side, half in and out of the blanket. His face, above the beard and luxuriant moustaches of fair shading to grey hair, was also grey. Both eyes were blackened and swollen; crusted blood from his nose smeared the skin on either side of his nostrils and caked in his moustache. Lumps the size of hens eggs already turning black and blue and yellow, stood out from his temple and cheek on the left side and his jaw on the right, giving his face a lopsided look. His shirt was just a torn, blood-soaked rag, held on by the collar, still secured at the throat with a bone toggle. Under the shirt was the mischief that caused the blood to flow.

The marks of a savage whipping crisscrossed the man's upper body back and front. From these wounds blood oozed. I knew little of matters of life and death but my instincts and commonsense told me that this man would die if not given care soon.

He uttered no sound, as if the one cry for help had exhausted him. He had made his try and now he awaited his doom or salvation, yielding all will to fate, much as I did when in play I careered down my hill on my leather-encased backside.

I knew I must first attend to the horse, for the cart moved jerkily, as if the mare, again bursting to get away from the storm still crashing about our heads, could not, as yet, decide where to run. I also knew that when she made up her mind, the little jerky motions would become a headlong gallop to disaster. I slipped ferret-quick out of the stink. Relishing, the sweet, rain-scented air, I leapt from the cart and took hold of the bridle then, softly, the mare's upper lip. The iron chain traces jingled, becoming tight then slack as the beast shuffled to and fro.

I spoke low; calling her good girl, telling her all was well. Her quivering stopped, although it came back at each thunderclap and returned as rain turned to hail. When I felt I had her under control, I climbed back into the seat, grasped the reins and started her walking.

By the time I had reached the gates to our front yard, between the two massive and ancient cedars that flanked them, the storm had passed. Only the puddles, the sprinkling of ice across the road and the occasional sparkle of water from the bushes, bore witness to its progress.

Getting down from the cart I grasped the bridle and led my treasure through our gateposts. I drew to a halt, afraid now at the boldness of my actions. I waited, with heart hammering, for someone, anyone, to come and rescue me.

# Chapter 2

### AD 1685
### Jo's Tale, the Gleeman

The pounding of my heart eased as, holding the bridle, I stood before the house: two broad storeys of honey-coloured Ham Stone. I waited by the cart, drinking in the familiar sweet smells of cow and sheep dung, clearing my head of the stink of sickness. I knew that my entrance would have been marked and at any moment help would arrive.

As if conjured, my mother and Beth, our cook housekeeper, turned the corner of the house from the side-door to the kitchen, at that very moment.

'Josiah!' cried my mother, grey eyes inspecting me. That's me: Josiah Hacking, although, unless I'm in - or likely to be in - trouble, my family and my friends call me 'Jo'. It sounded as if I was in trouble now.

'Mother, mother, 'lizabeth, come quick, there's a man inside and he's sore hurt, fit to die.' My mother and Beth exchanged wide-eyed unhappy glances, and then my mother hurried towards the cart whilst Beth, one hand clutching her pinafore front, the other patting her greying hair as if afraid it would fall off, turned and ran towards the kitchen door.

'I'll fetch Jedediah,' she shouted over her shoulder, 'he'll know what to do.'

My mother, short, matronly, made no attempt to enter the cart, but stood stock still, listening silently, her arms clutching each other across her chest while I laid out the details of my story. When I reached the part about the wounded man her face became thin-lipped, grim, her left hand pecked, bird like, at her right sleeve.

'Have I done wrong, Mother? Have I brought trouble to our door?' She looked at me and her gaze softened with a smile.

'No, Jo, you have not done wrong, it can never be wrong to reach out with merciful aid to any of God's children. As for trouble, we will have to see. Your father is with the harvest, we will send for him and he will know what to do for the best.'

With that, Jedediah, our 'John-do-it-all', came stumping around the corner. An ex-artilleryman, he had lost his left leg beneath the knee at Bothwell Bridge. He put his right foot on the shaft, heaved himself up and looked in over the seat. He stayed still for a moment, nose wrinkled, examining the interior, dropped feather soft onto his peg leg then, once firmly on the ground, turned to my mother.

'By your leave, Mistress Hacking, I will send Sarah to bring the Wise Woman. Also, if you please ma'am, send Josiah to bring the master, for there are things here that only he should decide.'

I looked at my mother; she met my gaze and nodded. 'Father is in the west field, tell him I want him, but say nothing else where others can hear.'

I nodded back in understanding and set off running. Reaching the lane, where deadly nightshade and preacher-in-the-pulpit grew in the verge, I clambered over the stile set in the hedge and ran towards the tall, lean figure of my father, swinging his scythe amongst the confusion of windrowing and sheaving. Despite the recent rainfall the air was filled with the dust and biscuit smell of ripe grain.

When I reached him, I could tell he was thankful for the excuse to pause: his rheumatism made harvesting hard for him, but so many men had gone missing he had no choice if the grain was to be gathered in.

'Wassup lad?' he asked.

'You must come back at once, our Dad, Mother wants you. It's urgent.'

I moved smartly away and my father, dropping his scythe followed me at a limping run. 'Tell I then, is Mother all right?'

I slowed and retold my story. My father stopped, his lips compressed into a thin line and his blue eyes narrowed in his ruddy, weathered farmer's face, his gaze darting about, looking all around us.

'Have I done wrong, Da?' I asked anxiously.

'No lad, you did right and I am right proud of you, but we live in harsh times and I must think careful upon what to do.'

I looked sideways at my father, 'Da?'

'Yes lad?'

'What's happening? Why is everyone so scared?'

My father paused and turned to look at me as if searching for something he was not sure he would find. He reached out, put his hand on my shoulder and sighed.

'Two months ago, Jo lad, James Scott, the exiled Duke of Monmouth, came back from across the sea. He landed in Dorset and led a rebellion against his uncle, King James. Some of our men from the village and even some who work on this farm went away to join him.'

'Why did they do that, Da?'

'Because like us, the Duke is Protestant. We are all Protestant Parliament men round here, Jo, or were. King

James is Catholic and we none of us want his Papist ways forced on us. Jedediah would have gone too, if he hadn't lost his leg when he fought in Scotland with the Duke years ago. And just as well he did, otherwise he too would now be swinging at the Assizes along with the rest of the men. The rebellion failed not far from here, at Sedgemoor. The King's judges are in Taunton to punish all who sustained it in any way. It would go bad for us if the attention of Judge Jeffries and his marauding provosts should come this way. And so we must be very careful not to attract it.'

As my father spoke, all the mysteries, the overheard whispers and anxious glances of recent times became clear to me. He turned to walk on, his hand rested warm on my shoulder. I was grateful for it, for, like a blow to the stomach, I felt fear strike into my carefree life and I shivered, although not this time from my cold, damp clothes. I had heard the village boys whispering fearfully of Jeffries, the hanging judge.

We hurried through the gate into the farmyard. My father had a few words with Jed, whispers I could not hear. He looked to my mother and they exchanged glances I could not read. Again, I had the feeling that much churned beneath the surface that I did not understand.

My father turned from looking inside the cart. 'Jed, get Tom and Alb to carry'n inside. Make up a bed in the cellar and take a mat to cover the trap door. We could all face the rope or the lash if he's found yer.'

'And Jed ... make sure someone watches from up on the slope at all times, if'n the King's men are seen on the Taunton road, warn the house in plenty of time so we can hide'n in the cellar. Ask Beth to send young Sarah for Mistress Alice, the Goose Mother.'

Jed nodded, 'That has been done, sir, and she should be on her way now.'

My father nodded in turn. 'Prepare the carriage. We must send Mistress Hacking and the children to Bessy in Ivelbridge.'

He turned back towards my mother and took her hands in his. 'You must visit with her, Dear Heart, and say nothing of this until I send for you.' He paused; his brow wrinkled in thought, his clenched fist covering his mouth and then, with a sigh, added, 'Do not be afraid, my dear, these are but the actions of the careful man. They would not have released this injured man, hurt as he is, if they thought him a rebel. It is not the way of the Assizes to release rebels with a whipping. If he has not received the drawing, the rope or transportation there must be some other reason for his wounds. There are no goods or possessions with him. With luck he may only have been beaten and robbed. The King's men are out of control in the County and there is much robbery, assault ... and worse, so I have heard.'

He turned to me, 'You should go with your mother and the children to Aunt Bessy.' He raised his hand as I started to protest, 'When they are safely in Aunt Bessy's care you must remain and watch over them and come for me at need.' He gripped my arm and murmured in my ear, 'Do you understand, Josiah? You will be the man of the family at Bessy's.'

I nodded, wide-eyed, hiding my uncertainty.

'While your mother packs, take this,' and he waved his hand at my cart. 'Put it out of sight in the plough shed then take the horse to the stables, and make sure it is fed, watered and stalled.'

My mother was already gone, without protest, to start her packing, and that in itself was alarming. My father turned and entered the house. Jed stumped off to carry out my father's instructions leaving me standing in the yard with the cart and the patient horse.

When our men had gently unloaded the wounded stranger and, with noses wrinkled against the smell, had carried him into the house, I took hold of the bridle and with a word of encouragement led the now docile beast towards the plough shed.

When I had completed my tasks I hurried to the hall. My mystery stranger, washed, his boots drawn off, now lay covered by a clean sheet on the table. Awakened from his swoon, his head propped forward by cushions, Beth was spooning soup into him.

The stranger's eyes peered at me between bruised lids; blue splashes in pools of blood. He swallowed and then spoke in a hoarse whisper, 'My rescuer! Thank you young sir. May the Lord, who loves charity, bless you.'

'What is your name, sir?' I asked, embarrassed.

'Hush,' said Beth, 'leave the poor man alone, he needs rest not questions.'

The stranger waved his hand in disagreement. 'My father named me Bowdyn, and his name and his father's name before, and so on into ancient times, was Galan. So, I am Bowdyn Galan or if you wish Bowdyn Galanson, I am happy if you call me Bowdyn.' And with that he attempted to smile then winced and placed his hand to his jaw, gently working it from side to side.

'Not broken anyway,' he said.

'Then open up and get some more food inside you, food heals; hunger kills,' said Beth.

The sound of feet shuffling on the boot scraper and a mumbling of voices came from outside the door. It swung open and Sarah tumbled through. She saw the lash marks and the blood on the man on the table and gave a small shriek of horror.

'Out, foolish girl,' said Beth. 'Where is Mistress Alice?'

'Here, here, give me time.' The Wise Woman of the village followed Sarah through the door, an apron tied over her skirts, her head and shoulders swathed in a shawl. She dragged a clinking bag behind her.

The man, Bowdyn, stared up at Mistress Alice as she removed a glass bottle and a large earthenware tub from the bag. 'With what are you about to poison me, Leech Hag? I have enough pain from my wounds for today, without more from your pig dung poultices.'

Mistress Alice cackled. Old and bent, she had the liveliest blue eyes, as if the soul peered through, ever youthful, while the body aged around it. These eyes were inspecting Bowdyn steadily from their corners as she placed the bottle and tub and a roll of linen, also from the bag, onto a bench by the table.

At last she spoke in her slow, old, cracked voice. 'No Cunning Man you, or you would know me, and so you would know my leechcraft, for I am well enough known. So what are you, Maker?'

He grimaced, twisting his mouth into what I took to be a smile. 'No Maker or Shaper me, I but sing or tell the words of others.'

'Well, Teller,' she said, 'What can your word hoard tell me of the Happy Plains?'

'The Land of Oats, say you,' he said. 'Why Mistress, more than you have ever heard before, of it and the Council of Mothers, of peace and plenty.'

I did not really understand what they were talking about, but I could tell she was testing him in some way, for she nodded as if satisfied, finished her fiddling with the liniments and salves she had brought and looked him full in the face with her speedwell-blue eyes.

'I do believe you are a true Gleeman, so I will tell you with what I will poison you. These are the days when our fates twist and change in the wind, Wise Women and Alices have met the rope and the flames often enough these days. You, I know, forget nothing, and so I will give this knowledge to you and perhaps, through you, it may not be lost.'

She paused and picked up the green glass bottle and held it out for him to smell. He put his nose to it, a dog sniffing a morsel, nodded approvingly.

'You see,' she said, 'not even the essence of pig dung. This is first, for your lumps. Second, for your lash wounds I have a salve.'

And she told him the secrets of the remedies.

'Truly you are a Wise Woman, I am in good hands,' he said. 'I am grateful.'

Taking her soup bowl, leaving her patient in the care of the Goose Mother, Beth sped out of the room, eager to feed the gossiping in the kitchen.

'So, who did torment you?' said Alice, as she started to dab the liniment on his temple, cheek and jaw.

He winced at her touch and then spoke; his voice sad. 'In Chard and Taunton they are hanging and drawing poor folk and the King's men are let loose upon the countryside. It was they who beat and robbed me.'

She shook her head. 'I shall remain the Goose Mother of Bishopston. None have had their necks stretched for keeping geese … yet.'

She finished mopping blood from his face and applied the liniment to his swellings and bruises. 'Now Master, what did you say your name was, Bowdyn? Well Master Messenger, sit up, I shall now salve your lash wounds, this will no doubt hurt more than a few dabs on bruises, but will in time much ease the soreness and banish fevers - and improve your smell.'

She dipped her hand, twisted and knobbed with rheumatism, into the earthenware pot and came out with a large brown dollop of salve, which she proceeded to smooth into the whip stripes, back and front. Master Galan neither spoke nor cried out during this process, but at times his flesh quivered declaring its hurt.

When she had bound him round with linen she secured the end with a pin. 'There you are, my singing messenger, done up like a parcel, all you need now is rest,' she said, putting the bottle and tub back inside her bag.

My father entered the room, Beth trailing behind, and took in the scene before speaking. 'And rest you shall have,' he said, 'but in the cellar, I fear. 'Tis dark, but dry; cool but not cold. You shall have a mattress, blankets and candles and I trust you will join us in the kitchen for meals. We'll keep a good watch on the road and if any strangers come, then back into the cellar for you.'

Master Galan hung his head and when he raised it at last his eyes were moist. 'Sir,' he said, 'you know me not, yet these lash marks put you and this good wife in great danger for me. It would be best if you placed me in my wagon. I could stop a few fields away with your permission, but you could deny me at need. Also, sir, I have nothing with which to repay this good woman for her care, nor you for food and drink.'

'Nonsense,' said my father, ''tis my Christian duty to help those in distress. As for payment, if you are a teller of tales as Beth tells me, when you are recovered you may sing or tell for your supper.'

Old Alice chimed in. 'Aye that he may, for I think he knows many a tale from times gone by, and I myself would like to be at these Tellings.'

'Well, that you shall be,' said my father. 'When our song bird has his voice, can sit comfortably in front of the fire and can clearly see his audience, then he shall sing for us for as long as he wishes to stay. The harvesting is nearly over. As the winter nights draw in we will relish some entertainment to take our minds from our troubles. So that's the end of it. We shall send for you, Mistress, when the entertainment starts.

'Now, for the time being, Beth, show our guest to the cellar and Jo, prepare the trap and take your mother, sisters and yourself to Bessy's. I will send for you when it is safe to come back.'

'And Jed is to come with us?' I asked.

'No, Jed has other work to do and with his leg may draw attention. I think you are now man enough to drive the trap in safety. Tom will go with you to bring it home.'

I left the room with great reluctance, until I saw my mother with my two sisters standing by the door with her bags packed. Margaret, one year younger than me and quite the young lady, stood beside my mother with quiet dignity, but Ann, nine years old, rocked back and forth, face flushed with excitement. I loved my mother, always the kindest of all to me and I felt the importance and the burden of my duty to her and my sisters and my need to keep them safe.

'Please wait, Mother, I will be back presently.'

I went to the stables where I found our carriage already rigged with the pony between the shafts. I drove it briskly to the front door of our house, loaded the bags on board and helped my mother and then each of the girls to step up and into the seat behind the bench.

My father came to the side of the trap and looked up at my mother. He leaned in and kissed her and then both of the girls. 'Be safe my loves,' he said, 'I will send for you when I think it is well to do so.'

He looked up at me. 'Go then, Jo, take good care of them, you will all be home soon.'

I flicked the reins and spoke to start the pony moving. Heavily laden as we were we moved slowly out through the gateposts and turned left onto the road, heading towards the market town of Ivelbridge, three miles away, with old Tom, the labourer, balanced and bobbing on the back step, holding tight to the hand rails.

# Chapter 3

**AD 1685**

**Jo's tale, Ivelbridge**

Turn right onto the old Roman road outside our farm and it runs west through Taunton and does not stop until it arrives at Exeter. Take a left turn, however, and after three miles it enters Ivelbridge. Here are houses, one of them Bessy's, which line the road for about two hundred paces before it widens into a square. At each of the four corners, streets run off to the north and south. Opposite the west road, by which a traveller comes into the town, is the Market Cross: an ancient monument dating from before the coming of King William the Norman. From here the road runs downhill to pass over the River Ivel, for which the town is named. From the bridge it continues east to Shaftesbury, although, at a fork further along the road, a right turn leads eventually to Dorchester.

The first day with Bessy, in her little Ham Stone cottage, cramped but cosy, passed calmly enough. There were only two small bedrooms. My mother and Bessy shared one, my sisters the other and I curled up with the dog on a makeshift bed in the living room. Bessy's husband had died from a fever years before; from my point of view a fortunate circumstance since had he not, I would doubtless be sharing the tiny floor space with both him and the dog.

Bessy survived, partly, I had heard, on the charity of my father. She should indeed have lived with us, but being of an independent turn of mind, preferred her own little terraced house on the edge of the town.

In the corner of her living room was the pile of sheep leather and linings that she daily cut and sewed into gloves for gentlemen and gentlewomen. From this she made the balance of her income and maintained her independence. She had taken us in without question and suffered the inconvenience cheerfully, saying she was glad of the company. She and my mother shared grave-faced conversation in the tiny kitchen. The girls, busy as two misers, turned out her button box and with 'oohs' and 'aahs', polished her brasses, pretending them gold.

I for my part was in a constant state of anxiety with what I knew of the happenings not ten miles from us, and the day after we arrived, our circumstances worsened more than I would have thought possible.

At about midday on the day after our arrival, we were all in the Market Square. Mother, always a careful needlewoman, had offered to help Bessy with the making of gloves and needed some supplies. Also, as we were already eating poor Bessy's larder bare, my mother had prevailed upon her to be allowed to stock it for the length of our stay.

So we went from stall to stall. First to the haberdashers for thread, where my sisters fussed like squabbling starlings around the ribbons and laces on display, and then to the grocer's and butcher's where, quiet and melting as snowfall, the two girls wandered to one side while I, poor brute, was laden like a pack horse with vegetables and bread, cheese and meat.

As we turned to part from the butcher there came the

sound of a disturbance, many voices calling, some angry, some strident, together with the sound of horses' hooves. The noise was coming from the Taunton road where Bessy's little house stood.

I saw three horsemen entering the Square: soldiers in red and green, followed by men on foot carrying muskets and pikes and wearing the same bright uniforms. As they crossed the Square, the full nature of the procession revealed itself. Three files of ten musketeers followed the three men on horseback, whom I took for officers. Behind them, drawn by two horses, came an open wagon in which stood eight hooded and tied prisoners, swaying with the movement over the rough road. This was followed by another; a smaller, one-horse wagon covered with a dirty tarpaulin. The end of the procession was brought up by a further thirty men, the last four ranks of which were pikemen.

As the column entered the Square, at a barked order from one of the officers, half of these pikemen broke away and sealed the road by which they had entered, whilst the other half, at a jog trot, ran to close the road to the bridge. On a second order the rest of the rearmost platoon broke and jog-trotted to block the corner roads out of the Square. We were all, shoppers and stallholders, gentlefolk and ragamuffins alike, trapped inside the Market Square.

'God protect us,' said the butcher, ''tis the Tangiers; best try to get the children away from yere, Marm.'

My mother looked around at the soldiers as if assessing our chances of leaving. 'What happens here, Master Butcher,' she said in a low voice.

'I know not, Mistress,' murmured the butcher, 'but these soldiers are from the Tangier Regiment, they are brutal, schooled in the Moorish lands. Whatever they do 'twill be ugly and unfit for children. I fear we are witnesses to an execution.'

While we were speaking the column had drawn to a halt. With the exception of six men and the officers, the remainder of the troops threw a loose cordon around the wagons and the Market Cross. The six remaining men hurried to the second wagon and taking off their red and green coats to expose green waistcoats and breeches underneath, they drew from the back of the wagon grey coats with green cuffs and donned them. They then unloaded what appeared to be a brazier on widely spaced tripod legs, which they placed in front of the Market Cross. They followed this with a small table on which they placed some things of metal, for I could hear the clash as they laid them down. They then fetched a rope and threw it over the Cross and from where we stood I could see a noose hanging down. With rough force, soldiers dragged one of the prisoners from the wagon and thrust him, moaning, towards the Cross.

My sisters were watching the activity in front of us with interest. With a gasp of understanding and horror, our mother quickly pulled them round and hurrying us away, headed for the road home. 'Quick Jo; quick Bessy; we must get the girls away from here.'

I looked back over my shoulder as we scuttled from the Square and saw the brazier piled high with what appeared to be charcoal. As I watched, a soldier unclasped a powder horn from his belt and poured gunpowder onto the brazier, which ignited with a flash. Another stood by with a blackened pitch-barrel by his side.

I turned back to find my mother was pleading with a pikeman who blocked our way. 'Please,' she cried, including my sisters and me with a wave of her arm, 'they are only children, what good will it do to steal their rest?'

The soldier regarded her steadily, swept his glance over my sisters and rested on me for a long moment. He nodded reluctantly and my mother brushed past with me and my sisters, but as Bessy started past, he barred her way with his pike.

'Not you,' he said. 'You will stay, Mistress, and watch the penalty for rebellion against the King.'

Bessy looked at us with appeal as if we could somehow help her, spare her the coming ordeal, but we could not. My mother shook her head and Bessy turned and head down, went back to rejoin the now silent and sullen crowd.

As we hurried away, the first screams of that afternoon of screams rang out in the Square.

'What are they doing?' cried Anne.

My mother had her hands cupped behind my sisters' heads as she hurried them along, preventing them from looking back. Glancing warningly at me, she tutted, 'Oh, tch, it's just an ugly game that soldiers play to see which one can scream the loudest to frighten the enemy when they charge them.'

'I would make a good soldier, I can scream very loud,' said Ann.

'Well don't,' said Mother, 'or they will press you into the Army and you will never see home again.' And that shut them both up until we were at Bessy's door. We let ourselves in and with hearts pounding, shut our ears to the noises from outside.

Mercifully, the thick walls and small windows deadened the sound of the work of the knife and brazier. I knew what the sounds meant. Village boys at school had relished telling us farm folk the details of this savagery. Their tales had given me nightmares that I was sure were now being enacted for real in the Market Square. The house did not shut out the sound entirely. Eight times the screaming started, fading to hoarse cries then falling to silence after what seemed endless minutes later.

Towards the end of the afternoon there came a feeble knock on the door and my mother unbolted it to let Bessy in off the street. Her face was whiter that a boiled sheet and she sobbed as she stepped over the threshold and into my mother's arms. Together they went upstairs, but my mother reappeared almost instantly and went into the kitchen, returning and climbing the stairs with a bottle of rum in her hand.

There was the sound of retching and then silence, followed by the murmur of soft voices and more sobbing, which trailed off into silence again. We children sat hushed and fearful, afraid to make any noise.

It was a long time before mother came down. She carried the chamber pot and went into the long garden at the back of the house to empty and flush it with water from the rain butt. Coming back into the house with the clean pot, she returned to the bedroom. When she next came down, she started to prepare a simple meal of bread and soup from the cauldron that simmered on the hob.

'How is she,' I asked, thankful it was not me who had been forced to witness the horrors of the marketplace.

'She is somewhat the worse for strong spirits now,' said my mother, 'but it has dulled her mind and she is sleeping. I do not doubt that when she awakes she will be sick at heart, but time will cure.'

At dusk we heard the clatter of hoofbeats outside in the street, then the rumble of wagons and the sound of many hobnailed boots. And they passed, fading away into the distance as we sat holding our breaths with fear. The Tangiers were leaving town and going to camp before marching back to the Bloody Assizes.

The next day they were gone. In the morning we peeked out of the door and all was silent. Before my mother could stop me I slipped out and ran on tiptoe into the Market Square. It was still and empty with a stink of pitch in the crisp dawn air.

Apart from stains on the rough gravel in front of the Cross there was no sign of the previous day's cruelty, until I got to the monument itself. There I found the reason for the reek. I looked down the slope to the bridge and saw, lined along the sides of the road and mounted on wooden stakes driven into the ground, eight glistening, black heads. On the bridge, where there had always been spikes from beyond mans' remembering, were an assortment of impaled, pitch-coated, arms and legs.

We did not see the hanging, though we heard the drawing. Here was evidence of the quartering. The sentence had been duly carried out to remind the good folk of Ivelbridge not to rise up against their master the King, no matter whether he governed according to their souls' comfort or not.

I ran home to tell my mother what I had seen and so it was she confined us to the house.

The next day, Bessy arose from her bed and joined us in the living room. She was quiet and subdued and at times her eyes filled with tears, but she contained herself and, too upset to work that day, sat with us around the fire and talked of the happier days of childhood with her sister.

We were sitting thus, that evening, shoulder to shoulder, huddled together for mutual comfort around the fire, with its blackened beam studded with gleaming brass work, when a knock came at the door. I confess my heart leapt into my mouth and I felt sick as I went to answer it. The two grownup sisters exchanged worried glances and even the younger sisters, sensing the general fear, sat quietly for a change. When I opened the door a crack and saw dear old Tom, our farm hand, I threw it open wide, my relief so great I felt unmanned and could have cried.

My mother, who was on my heels, was not so relieved. 'Oh Tom,' she cried, 'what has happened?'

'Calm yerself, Mistress,' said Tom, removing his hat. 'The Master sent me, the Assoizes 'ave moved t' Wells and the Master sez you c'n all come 'ome t'marra marning.'

With that my mother, to my astonishment, burst into tears, closely followed by Bessy and the girls. I stood by the door and exchanged uncertain glances with old Tom, thankful that my own tears were under control.

Tom shuffled the broad brim of his hat through his fingers. 'Ah well, young Maaster, thas all oi've got ter tell ee, be there any message for the Maaster?'

'Tell him,' cried my mother 'that we are all well and we shall be sorry to leave Bessy, so she is coming with us, we look forward to seeing him in the morning.'

Tom replaced his hat. 'Very well, Marm,' he said. 'God bless you,' and, with a wave to all and a wink to me, left us.

The next day, as it turned out, Bessy felt much recovered and with such an urgent need to get back to her work that she did not come to the farm with us. When Tom turned up with the trap we wished her goodbye and all hugged her with such warmth, she once more burst into tears.

We climbed into the trap, waved over our shoulders and turned our faces with relief towards our home, Browan Farm. Tom looked thoughtfully at the girls and then spoke gently to my mother. 'You ad zum trouble then in Ivelbridge, Marm?'

'Yes, Tom, but we will speak of it another time,' she said

looking at the girls. Tom nodded his understanding and swung his gaze back to driving; I was happy to let him.

In what seemed very short order we were turning through the gateposts into our own front yard. I cannot explain the joy, the warmth and the feeling of the world's weight slipping from my shoulders as my father came through the door to greet us.

His face split with a great beaming smile, 'Welcome home my loves,' he said, picking up my mother and swinging her round. He put her down then turned to the girls, lifting them both up squealing in his arms before depositing them on their feet next to their mother.

He looked at me with an expression of rare approval, but did not offer to pick me up as I feared he might, instead he held out his hand to me and clasping mine shook it warmly. 'Thank you, Jo, for looking after my womenfolk. I am much obliged to you for their safe return.'

I blushed, fearing that he made fun of me, but there was no guile in his eyes. 'In truth there was nothing for me to do, sir,' I said, 'Mother made all decisions.'

'You are too modest,' he smiled. 'Mother found strength from your calm and steady support.' He shook my hand once more. 'You are a man now, Jo, and you shall be my strong right hand.'

Now, as I look back on it, I see this was his way to deal with my fear and horror and reconcile it with my need to grow into and demonstrate my manhood.

We all walked through the broad, studded front door, which was hewn from oak and black with age. I was amazed to see our Gleeman sitting up in a chair by the fire. He still wore the balm bandage and in places the balm had soaked through, staining the linen a light honey brown. It was in his face, however, that the difference was amazing. The lumps had gone, although big purple bruises remained. His eyes, while still bruised, had lost their swelling. Bright blue, they now looked with some amusement at me.

'So, my saviour,' he said, 'you are surprised to see that I am human after all. Sit down with me and tell me how you have fared in the big city.'

I looked eagerly at my parents. Father raised his eyebrow at my mother in silent query. She nodded, 'You can be doing that while the girls go upstairs and change into sensible clothes for the home.'

I sat down beside Bowdyn and poured out to him all that had happened since we saw him last. He listened quietly and then when I had finished, he nodded.

'The same as Taunton,' he said, 'the Tangiers were the executioners there. You were all lucky that no harm befell you. It was Colonel Kirke's jolly men who gave me their special treatment and left me for dead. Thank you for telling me such a grim tale, it must be hard for you to recall it, but I ... well, I am a collector of tales and know many a grim one. And some that are lighter as well.'

'Perhaps, Master Bowdyn,' I said, 'you can tell us some of your stories to divert our minds from the grim tale of Ivelbridge?'

'With pleasure,' he said, 'when your father consents.'

I bowed in thanks and moved out to the kitchen where my mother was calling me to eat, for we had not breakfasted at Bessy's house before leaving.

For the next few days I was busy around the farm, my father made sure of that. The harvest was in, late as it was, but the threshing continued from morn to night. My task was to help gather the grains and bag them. I weighed each bag to equal one bushel then stacked it ready for the mill. At the end of the threshing, when all the grain had been loaded into wagons and sent to the mill, my father called us all together on the threshing floor.

'Well my people,' he said, 'we have passed through danger and sorrow and some of our neighbours and friends have gone to their doom ...' he raised a hand as if to halt this subject. 'Tonight all are welcome to the house, there will be food and ale aplenty, and although none will feel like singing, our guest, Bowdyn Galan, will tell us tales of long ago from his store of yarns. Please come, one and all, if you can, for our minds will be rested by some diversion from these grim times.'

The men and women of the farm all cheered, for there's nothing like a free feed and drink to take folks' minds off their troubles. At a wave from my father they returned to work, but the babble of talk sounded above the scrape and rush of the shovels and brooms as the loft was cleaned of dust and bran, until all was done and they left excitedly for home to prepare for the night's entertainment.

# Chapter 4

**AD 1685**

**Jo's Tale, the Story begins**

That night it was chill. The first cold winds of October were whistling around the house and the oak, beech and sycamore leaves were laying brown and thick on the ground as our folk trudged, tired, but happy with anticipation, to our Feasting Hall, for so it had been built in older times. It is said that our house was once a brewery and that the name, Browan, stems from that and is very ancient. Certainly, the old house would have been stirred with long neglected memories that night, for the ale flowed without halt: as long as a mouth was capable of drinking, there was ale to be drunk.

My father had the first of the winter cull slaughtered and sent for butchery, but he had held back huge joints of beef rib for roasting. There was fresh bread that Beth had started whilst the Mistress was away and with that and the roast meat, the endless ale and the roaring red fire, in no time we were a very cosy, jolly bunch; although from time to time one or other would remember the sadness of the last few weeks and would look to one side, pensive and for the moment withdrawn.

Master Bowdyn sat by the side of the fire in a big, carved wooden chair. It was Welsh and very old, but he seemed comfortable and in the red firelight the bruises on his face faded from sight. After a while someone called, 'And what about this tale telling Master Bowdyn?' and the room in general took up the call, 'Yes, that's right, and what about it?'

Bowdyn smiled and held up his hand. 'I have a tale to tell, but it is a long one, we cannot finish it tonight. I have spoken with Master Hacking and he is willing for me to tell for my supper, so I will yarn each night until it is done. Tonight we are merry and I shall make a start; in nights to come we will not be merry, for even one such as Master Hacking will not feast us for more than tonight. However, if you like my story and would like to know how it progresses then we will meet tomorrow in the old Cold-Cot. It has, as you know, stone walls to provide shelter from the wind, no roof so the moon and stars can light us and if everyone who comes collects windfall branches from the woods then we will have warmth from a good fire to sit around. Those who can, bring ale and food, if they have more than they need then perhaps those who cannot will not go hungry or thirsty.'

There was silence and then a hubbub of agreement. 'Best your tale be a good one though, Master Bowdyn, or I shall make my fire and eat my victuals and drink my ale at home,' said someone.

'That shall be your choice and so we shall see,' said Bowdyn with a smile. 'Let us begin.'

The room fell silent in anticipation. I noticed that the Goose Woman was in the front; my father and mother were at the back. The girls had long been sent to bed, happy but tired from their food and a pint of ale each.

'This story,' he said, 'is old. It begins in a country east across the sea, nigh on five hundred years after the birth of Our Lord Jesus Christ. To Africa it goes and back, and crossing the sea, ends up close by here. It begins with Creoda's grim tale'

And then something startling happened. The Gleeman sank back in his chair and by some cunning art of positioning, as he did so his face disappeared into the shadow. From the dark a voice spoke and I, for my part, felt the hair stand up on the back of my neck, for it was not the voice of Bowdyn that we heard, but that of a young boy, younger than I, for his voice had not yet deepened into manhood.

# Thiatmaresgaho Germania

# Chapter 5

### AD 462
### Creoda's Tale, the Hun

Great Mother, help me! My gut clenched as their shadows loomed jingling out of the mist. I did not want to die. It was not just with the cold that I shivered as I crouched in the freezing ditch, clutching my borrowed spear. It was fear that caused my rattling teeth.

Be careful what you wish for. Cold, wet, miserable, terrified and yet impatient for something - anything - to happen, I had wished it would be over, that if they were coming let it be soon that we might finish the slaughter then warm ourselves by the fire and don dry clothes. Fool that I was.

The man next to me, Wulfgar, in charge of our puny warband of fourteen youngsters and oldsters, placed a hand on my arm and signalled for quiet. I opened my mouth to still the chattering of my teeth and listened intently. There was silence, nothing but the slight stirring of the wind in the grass. And then I heard it. First, the high pitched tinkle of metal against metal, then the muffled clop of horses' hooves, then through the mist the shadows of men on horseback, towering like giants to my eyes at ground level.

I gripped my spear and waited for the signal. Fear again

punched me in the gut, for I was no warrior. My training was to commence after Yule. I was there because the Holding had split its forces to make sure the Hun did not get to our cattle. If they did, we would starve.

We held the gate and the wooden road that led up into the Terp, to our houses. There was not much the Reavers could do there. The women and children hid on a flooded mound nearer the sea, protected on all sides by water. The boatmen had swum to shore leaving the boats behind. We had doused all the fires in the houses to stop the burning of our homes if they took the gate. Only the things we could not carry away were there, such as they were. Any precious thing, if any of our folk possessed such stuff, was with the women in the marsh.

The Huns, we knew, would steal any goods they could carry; they produced nothing, made nothing, survived by leeching the work of others. We were the smallest band, large enough only to bar the gateway into the Terp, and so Gewis had given us the task of guarding the Holding. And he, the War Leader of the East Holding, had given us clear orders.

'Do not fight the Hun, fourteen spears on foot will not do so safely, only let them know that the Terp is defended; they want cattle and grain, not pots and cloth. Most of all they want cattle to drive away.'

Looking to be sure Wulfgar, the chosen leader of our band, understood, Gewis watched him closely. 'If they challenge you and gain entry, run. They will not want to waste time in pursuit in the mist amongst the buildings of the Worth. Your warband is old men and boys, Wulfgar. They are much loved by the folk, do not throw them away.' He paused, then added, 'If you defend the gate I think they will not try you, but keep your shields up for their bows are deadly.'

So said Gewis, wise leader; ring giver; knowing in the

ways of the Hun, the Goth and the Vandili. But since Wulfgar had lost the favour of Baeldaeg, the Headman of the folk, to Gewis, he lusted to prove both wrong.

After the death of my father, Bana, Baeldaeg's eldest son, killed on the spears of the Suebi, it was to Wulfgar the Headman had turned. That was, until the homecoming of my father's brother, Gewis. Wulfgar was a mighty warrior, but he was headstrong and hasty, without careful judgement. He was over proud, and this was the weakness that was to kill him.

Now, he shut his mind to wise council so that he could seize a victory over the Huns and thereby prove himself the greater warrior. It was for this reason that I shivered, crouched in a wet ditch, instead of dry and sheltered behind the gate. The plan of Wulfgar was that we should hide at some distance from the gate, concealed in the mist below ground level, and take the column of Huns in the flank.

And so we crouched, and as the horsemen drew in front of us, moving cautiously towards the upward sloping, wooden road and the open gate, Wulfgar gave a mighty roar. Followed by the rest of our small warband, he leapt out of the ditch and cast his spear. It took the leader of the Huns under the left arm and pitched him off his horse's back. Only one more cast made good and carried a Hun to the ground, for Wulfgar's battle roar had alerted them. Ten horses wheeled as one, faster than my eyes could follow, swifter than I could believe possible.

As if with witchcraft they were all around us and standing as they rode. I could not believe my eyes. Still standing, they shot arrows at us. They rode in a circle, kept within bow range but moving at great speed, never turning towards us to give a steady target. The power of the arrows was fearful, we were mindful to keep our shields up, but where an arrow struck it pierced the board. Wulfgar gave another roar and brought his javelin from his back as with a mighty bound he leapt towards the nearest horseman, lowering his shield to bring his spear arm back to cast.

The arrow came from the front and took him through the throat. He fell to the ground and flopped about like a landed fish, his hands at his neck fumbled at the arrow, but he choked on the blood in his throat as his life's blood leaked into the ground.

I looked around for a weapon; I had thrown my spear with no effect. Five others besides Wulfgar were on the ground. Without a weapon I saw no option but to flee. I ran for the causeway hoping to make the shelter of the houses. I expected an arrow in my back at every step.

I looked back in terror over my shoulder and saw the rest of our band scattering in all directions; it was a rout. As I scrambled up the wooden slope to the Terp no arrows struck me nor struck around me. I heard the guttural cries of the Huns and then some laughter and catcalls. As I ran through the gate I heard hooves clatter on the wooden roadway and felt my terror increase. I looked behind and saw one of the Huns come through the gateway. I started to run again but he cantered ahead and cut me off.

I stopped and faced my enemy: he was hideous and stunk. He wore no armour and was dressed in jerkin and breeches made from stitched together rat skins. Downwind as I was, the stench of him and his knobby, ugly horse, made me gag. His slitted eyes bored into mine and he grinned, exposing his brown teeth.

I turned and started to edge away, holding up my empty hands, hoping that seeing me unarmed he would leave me be; the horse came alongside and nudged me towards one of the huts. I tried to turn aside, but he kept nudging, first this way and then the other until I found myself at a doorway. In my panic and confusion I could not recognize it except it was not my mother's. At least he would not steal our house goods.

He swung a leg over and slid to the ground his cow horn bow in his hand. He swung it lightning fast onto the side of my head. I saw a flash of light in front of my eyes and then darkness as I fell to my knees; his intent, it seemed, was to beat me to death, I resigned myself to it.

He hit me again, cooing, crooning pigeon-like noises as he did so. He seized me by the arm and half dragged, half carried me into the hut. Again he hit me with his bow and this time I saw nothing but blackness until I came to, to find I was face down in the dirt.

I felt his weight on top of me and a pain where there should be no pain, but could not make sense of what was happening to me. I felt him thrashing and again the cooing noise and then a grunt and he rolled off me. I felt the cold wind against the skin of my behind, for my breeches were down. The pain persisted and with sick horror I realised that he had used me as a woman. Unmanned me.

I rose to my feet and launched myself at him my fingers clawing for his throat, but he hit me in the face with the bow and again I collapsed into blackness ....

'Hey now, Master Teller!' A deep voice cried out interrupting the story.

It was the voice of my father, silencing that of Creoda, the boy. 'Your tale is too strong meat for your listeners I think, Master Bowdyn. There are children and women here.'

The face of the Gleeman emerged from the shadows. 'Well, Master Hacking, I am a Teller not a Maker or Shaper. This is the story my father taught me, told to him by his, and so on back through a thousand years. There are no children here, Jo is the youngest and he has been through more and heard worse in the last few days than he will hear here, where we talk of death but do not have to hear the pain in which some souls pass. As for women, what says the Goose Wife as the oldest one here?'

The Goose Wife smiled. 'Well, for a man, to have one's guts pushed in thus may be painful and shaming, but not so final and painful as having them pulled out, and there has been much of that in these parts in these times. She cackled.'As for women, I see no maidens here but country wives, most of them mothers. Pity I can see for Creoda, but no shock or distress, no discomfort. Women are mistresses at knowing pain and shame.'

Other wives in the room, including my mother, murmured in agreement whilst their husbands showed surprise.

My father sat with his head sunk on his chest then he raised his head and smiled.'I am overruled Master Bowdyn, pardon my interruption, please carry on.'

The Gleeman bowed his head towards my father and his face once more disappeared as if by magic into the shadow from which came once again the voice of Creoda.

# Chapter 6

### AD 462
### Creoda's Tale, the Chase

When the shadows retreated from my eyes and I could see again, I saw a figure bending over me. I roared and probed with my fingers for the eyes and found my wrists caught in a powerful grip, whilst a voice I knew, spoke.

'Easy, boy, easy.'

It was Gewis, my father's brother, but I did not know whether that made me feel better, or worse. I felt my arse bare to the wind and jerked my breeches up. Gewis put his hand on my shoulder and I pulled away, stared at the ground, shame made my face flush red.

He spoke gently. 'You are alive, many of your band are not. Your ordeal is secret with me you have my most solemn oath on it, I swear it.' He loosened his seax in its sheath. 'Come, speak, what will satisfy you?'

My shame turned to rage. 'Nothing but his death can wipe his stink from me'

Gewis nodded gravely. 'As your uncle I will be by your side. Where does your mother hide your father's sword?'

I thought then answered, 'I am not yet weapon trained; she keeps it for that date.'

'Today you carried a weapon in war, you are now a man, if

perhaps not a trained warrior, do you know where?'

'Follow me,' I said. I paused to look for any signs that might betray my shame to a watchful eye; I scuffed the earth and went at a limping run to my house.

I pushed the door, there was only one room and that empty but for the furniture and bedding. I went to my mother's couch and moved it away from the wall. A dark door was set into the wall at ground level. I pulled it open, reached inside and drew out a bundle wound about with cloth soaked in pig fat. I dropped the protective wrapping on the ground to reveal the weapon within. The sword had a hilt of leather-bound wood, unadorned and workmanlike, as was the plain, black leather scabbard. I pulled the blade from its sheath. Burnished clean, lightly coated in lard, the edges gray and honed to a fine sharpness, for my mother had been working on it and keeping it prepared for me. I silently vowed to acquit myself like a warrior and do justice to the love of my mother; to erase my shame and earn her pride.

'Come man, the sword is good, I have a spare spear, you are armed but we must hurry or he will escape.'

'There are others,' I said, 'we killed only two.'

'Fear not, Creoda, they are dead, we met them when they turned from the Terp to seek the cattle, the noise of your battle alerted us. We laid an ambush for them that they could not escape, we were many, they few, they all fell to our spears. Your foe was the only one to escape, for he was here not there. Can you ride?'

I nodded; my need for vengeance numbing the pain in my arse. I was fit to ride, although I had no horse.

Seven captured horses were now in the storm pen, swelling the numbers of our own small herd. Gewis selected two of the ugly brutes, their saddles still in position.

'Wait,' I said, and at urgent need thrust the sheathed sword and its leather strap into his hand and ran to the screened privy pit behind the house, gritted my teeth and emptied myself. I hurriedly washed, with water cupped from the bucket left there for the purpose.

As I rose to my feet my head throbbed. I thought I might puke but managed to hold it down. I hurried back to where my uncle waited. He held out the scabbard and taking it, I dropped the strap over my head and slantways across my chest, and for the first time my father's sword swung by my side.

I bent to pick up my shield from the ground where I had dropped it in surrender as the Hun had herded me to the house. As I straightened, waves of pain from my battered, swollen head again caused me to reel. I made to lever myself up into the saddle.

'Wait. Look here,' said Gewis, showing me a strap with a leather cup at its end, swinging beneath the saddle.

'This is how they stand in the saddle and how they turn so quickly. When you mount, put one foot in it to step up and then when you are in the saddle put your other foot in the cup on the other side. You will see you can stand in them, they will help you to ride more quickly and now we must do so.'

I mounted as, with a guttural cry, Gewis cantered off, my ugly beast followed him and I found that I needed give no direction as the horse followed its leader.

Gewis eyed the ground as we rode, the hoof prints of the Hun's horse clear in the soft sandy soil. He dropped back to tell me his plan,

'He is heading back the way they came, we have lost time; the only chance we have to catch him is to ride without rest. But why would he hurry? He will not expect us to follow, so our chances are good.' He paused, and then, 'You must kill him; for your sake and also for ours, for there are many more of his company he can bring to wreak vengeance on us.'

As we rode, we passed shrubby trees, their branches all grown away from the direction of the prevailing winds. Even in the mist I felt that we were moving in a great curve. We had not been long on the way when Gewis reined in his horse and dismounting, examined the ground. He straightened and stood in thought his brow wrinkled with puzzlement then he smiled and turning his horse to the north, called back.

'We have him I think, see the wind has shifted, he does not know the land and, in the fog, has become confused, he is going by the wind. With it on his right cheek he thinks he travels south to rejoin his company, but now the wind is northeast and so he travels north, towards the river. He will soon strike the Eider and will turn back when he sees the wind has made a fool of him.'

Gewis turned towards a low ridge of ground, the beginnings of the Geestland, the sandstone outcrops that increased towards the east. It was high enough for us to see the flat land approaching the river. As the wintry sun rose higher in the sky the mist had been clearing. Now, from the rise where we sat on our mounts, we could see ahead perhaps an hour's quick walk to the north.

'We will wait here,' said Gewis, 'now is the time to rest.' He tethered his beast to a low shrub. The animal straightway started to crop the thin brown grass that grew in patches between the rocks.

I watched him as he stood scanning the plains to the north, this warrior, my Uncle Gewis, my father's younger brother. When my father Bana and my mother Elwine married, it is said that on that very night Gewis left the Holding straight from the wedding feast and went south to seek his fortune. He was sixteen years in age and already a trained warrior with blood on his spear. I was seven years old when he returned, his corn yellow hair worn knotted at the side in the Suebian warrior way, a langseax made from a Roman spatha by his side, two throwing axes across his chest and a great bearded axe across his back, a fearsome sight. On his shield he bore an ancient Vandal device called, so I heard, 'the hands of the gods'.

It was said that he had travelled and fought alongside the Suebi and the Vandals, had been at the sack of Rome and had escaped with a great treasure and his own band of hearth-companions sworn to his service. It was known that when he arrived at his old home in the East Holding he had a full purse and a warband well decorated with gift rings and torques in silver and gold, but if he had any great hoard then he had lost it along the way. His hearth-companions laughed when the curious raised the topic of a looted treasure. They would keep their counsel I was sure, even their names they held close.

They were all oath-sworn to Gewis, although all were older warriors than he. All had been at the sack of Rome and had fought for great King Gaiseric in Africa. Even I had heard tales of the conqueror who had crossed from Africa and carried off the riches of fifty generations.

Our chief man, Gewis' father and my grandfather, Baeldaeg, gave his returned son a small plot of land inside the walls that flanked Bana's place, where my mother and I lived. Off the mound we had a hide and raised a handful of milk cows, four ewes and a score of egg laying chickens. On his plot Gewis raised a hall larger than ours, for he needed room for six, but smaller, out of respect, than his father's. Some gold he must have had, for his hall had no land and yet he always had goods to trade for meat or bread. His band lived at ease in his hall. A Gleeman he had amongst his company to entertain us at his father's feasts when Baeldaeg's scop stopped for breath. His band rode our land. They protected our Holding as all could see and fierce warriors they were: a Suebian, a Goth, two Vandal brothers and a dark-skinned Egyptian. Men of mystery they were, for none knew their names.

They had not come with my uncle and me to find and kill the Hun who had unmanned me, but had been with Gewis in guarding the flocks. It was they and others of the Holding who had destroyed the raiders. I supposed they were now seeing to the stripping and disposing of the Huns' bodies and seeking out the dead and survivors of Wulfgar's ill-fated band of youngsters and oldsters.

'Gewis?' I asked.

'Yes Creoda?' he spoke without turning his head away from his steady survey of the land north to the river. Alone, on a quest of honour and feeling full grown for the first time in his company, I thought to ask him a question that had galled me for long.

'Do you think my grandfather caused the death of my father?'

His expression did not change nor did his gaze shift, but he was a long time answering and I feared that I had raised his anger. At last he spoke. 'Your grandfather is an honourable man. He would not have chosen to fail your mother's man, my brother and his eldest son. Sometimes even the best of warriors make mistakes.' He paused then added, 'As well blame him for sending them to meet the Suebi in the first place.'

My uncle looked at the ground and then quickly shifted his gaze back to the far horizon. 'Algar, the leader, should not have divided the band, as it happens; and Bana should not have confronted the Suebi for they were many. Once these two things became part of the weave of their lives so then Bana became feyman. Doomed. The Fates cut the thread of his life. It is no one's fault or everyone's fault. But I hold no feud with my father or Algar.'

We watched in silence. Bored with the landscape of browning scrub nearby, greening in the distance as it neared the river, my gaze alighted on the shield that Gewis still wore on his back. Unlike my shield, his was not plain but bore a strange pattern: a cross, but at the end of each arm, facing away from the centre of the cross, was a short crossbar with five lines drawn outwards.

'Gewis?'

He answered, again without taking his eyes from the view to the north.'Yes Creoda.'

I pressed on.'What is the pattern on your shield?'

He glanced at me, paused a while, looked again at the land towards the river and then replied, 'It is a device of the Vandals, it is known as "the hands of the gods". See, there are four hands, the one reaching upwards is that of Wothan, reaching to rule the sky and then also to the left to the realm of man to guide and rule us; the one reaching downwards is the hand of Freya, reaching down to rule the Earth and then to the right, to reach out to man and nourish and support us. It is a very old symbol, one that is becoming dangerous to use amongst the Vandals for they are slaves to the new sky god and his nailed son, the Baldor of the Christians. They tolerate nothing else.'

He sighed. 'It was not always so and is one reason why I left them and returned home. Here a man can follow the old gods without fear.'

This was the longest speech I had ever heard him make. Although he was my uncle, he was so on my father's side. On my mother's side I had no uncle for her father had died when young and her mother soon after without having taken another husband, and so I had no one to teach me the warriors' ways. Gewis had taken this burden on, but my voice was late in deepening and my warrior training had not begun before this day.

He stiffened and then pointed. A dark dot was moving on the land between us and the river. 'He comes! Listen, boy ... are you listening?'

I nodded, watching him as he squatted beside me. He took the shield from his back and crouching held it in front at an angle towards the sky so that little except his feet and the top of his helm were visible from the front.

'Can you do this?' he asked. I took off my shield and copied him.

He nodded approval and then said again, 'Listen very carefully. When he sees us he will come towards us. His thieving habits will make him. He will ride towards us and try to skewer both of us with arrows so that he can scavenge from our bodies.'

Eyebrows raised he looked at me. I nodded to show my understanding, but under the surface I was quivering with fear. The horseman had dismissed me and violated me with contemptuous ease at our last meeting; his easy use of me had destroyed my faith in myself.

'Steady now,' said Gewis as if sensing my panic, 'listen to me carefully. I will stand towards him. When you see me drop behind my shield, you do the same. When he lets loose his arrows they will hit only our shields. If any do pierce you, they will not hit anywhere disabling and you must endure the pain. This is your first lesson as a warrior: battle often hurts. If you want to live you must endure the pain and never stop fighting to kill your foe, do you understand?'

I nodded.

'Draw your sword. You must not sheath it until it is wet with the blood of the creature that used you.' Gewis grasped my arm, 'Do you understand?'

Again I nodded.

'When we drop he will ride straight at us. I will be in the forefront. He will try to jump over me and will fire his arrow downwards into my body as he passes over. When I am down he will do the same to you. The horses are used to this and the Hun skill with a bow is such that this is easy work for him. When we are dead he will strip the bodies. If we live he will amuse himself with tormenting us before we die.' He fixed me with a stern stare. 'Do you understand?'

Once more I nodded, eyes wide.

'Well, we must not let that happen. When he is close enough I will throw my battleaxe at the horse's legs. The blade will slice a leg; even the handle will break a leg or at the least trip the forelegs. The horse will fall and the rider will be thrown over my head. As he falls you will rise and kill him. Do you understand? Tell me, on your oath that you understand.'

'On my oath, I understand.'

'Good,' said Gewis and walked ten paces away from me. He shifted the broad-bladed, bearded battle-axe from his back and placed it on the ground together with his shield, which he leant against his leg, then he stood facing the oncoming horseman, upright and easy to see.

He kept his gaze fixed on the enemy as the Hun saw us and changed direction, riding towards us just as Gewis had said he would. I followed my uncle's lead, I unsheathed and laid my father's sword on the ground and shifting my shield from my back, I stood it as Gewis had. I tore my gaze from the horseman and concentrated on my uncle, alive for any movement.

I felt rather than saw an arrow as it thunked into the ground in front of him. He dropped into a crouch and brought up his shield as he had shown me. Only his head and eyes, protected by his helm, over-topped the rim. I copied his action, conscious of the nakedness of my head as I peered over my shield. I had no helm, only a stout leather cap. I doubted it would turn aside an arrow and if one hit my forehead or the top of my head then there would be no fighting for me. I gave a quick prayer to Wothan and swore an oath that if I survived and killed my foe I would dedicate the death to him.

The horseman was close now, coming at a steady, confident canter, standing in the Hunnish saddle cups. He loosed again at Gewis, this one taking my uncle full on his shield and piercing the stout board. The power of the Hun bow was frightening.

Drawing close now, the Hun notched another arrow in his bow and waited, riding by leg pressure alone, standing in the saddle cups and, as my uncle had said, intending to hurdle him and fire downwards into his body at short range. I held my breath. If the Hun killed my uncle then it would be another arrow for me - if I were lucky.

At the instant this thought passed through my head, Gewis moved, fast as a striking adder. He threw himself to the right and as he flew through the air, as if all part of the same motion his arm swung and the heavy axe whirled through the air into the forelegs of the horse. It let out a scream and went down head over heels. I heard the noise of its neck breaking.

The Hun, unseated, was flung through the air, but by some evil miracle landed on his feet in front of me. I leapt up, my shield on my left arm, my fingers gripping the handle behind the boss. My sword was in my right hand. I raised it to strike

... then hesitated. I had never killed a man with a sword before; poke him with the sharp end of my spear, yes; throw my spear and kill from a distance, yes, I was sure I could do these things, but to slice into a man with a naked blade is a different thing. I hesitated one tiny moment too long.

Quick as a lightning strike he hit me on my still aching skull with his bow. Thunder crashed behind my eyes. I felt a blinding pain and once more I went down; the nightmare on the Terp was starting again. I lay on the ground, my sword still grasped in my hand. The Hun standing over me drew an arrow from his quiver. He recognized me; I could see the surprise in his dark, slitted eyes. And then he smiled, exposing the brown teeth.

He held the arrow in the crook of his little finger and then, placing his first and second finger together slowly, thrust his thumb backwards and forwards between them and made the same cooing noise he had made at the place of my shaming. He grasped the arrow, notched it onto the string and braced to draw back. Addled by the fall and intent on mockery, he seemed to have forgotten Gewis. Snail like, I raised my sword, too slow, too slow. I waited for the pain, braced for the arrow to skewer me. In a daze I wondered if I could stand it. Would I scream?

There was a shriek. Confused, I knew it was not me. The Hun dropped to his knees.

'Kill him, kill him now!' I heard my uncle's voice and snapped out of my daze. I leapt to my feet. Dropping my shield, I grasped my sword with both hands and with all the fury of shamed manhood, I swung the edge of the blade with all my strength. It caught the Hun in the neck and to my amazement and horror it sliced right through, coming out on the other side just below the jaw. His head fell off and the headless torso fell, chest down onto the ground, blood spurting in pulses from the neck.

Then I saw, embedded in my enemy's back, one of Gewis' small throwing axes. It was this that had saved my life.

There was silence as Creoda's voice ceased speaking. Bowdyn's face appeared out of the shadows, ruddy in the red glow of the fire where the deep heart cast its glow on him. He smiled at the folk sitting around him, their faces still thoughtful seeing the scene in their minds, startled perhaps that the tale had come to a halt.

'Story telling is thirsty work,' said Bowdyn, 'and sometimes thirsty to listen to around a warm fire. We will pause awhile, refresh ourselves and then continue until it is time to go to our rest.'

There was a mumble of agreement, which swelled into downright heartiness as Bowdyn raised his stone jug of apple ale and swallowed deeply. There was a scraping and a grating as many amongst the listeners reached down to their own flasks and did likewise. Some bit into the supper they had gathered from Farmer Hacking's groaning table and washed it down with the ale he had provided.

# Chapter 7

**AD 462**

**Creoda's Tale, the Murrain**

After a time, as the folk put off the spell of the story, they turned to their families and neighbours and talked merrily amongst themselves for the first time for many days. And then, as if the outside world of doom and sorrow had broken into the story world that Bowdyn had woven around them, one by one they fell silent and to thinking, and then to looking at the Gleeman as if to say: Tell us more, take us away from here, to your far off land where the problems and sorrows are those of other folk and not ours.

As if he were expecting this, Bowdyn set down his drink. His face was still flushed from the fire, but perhaps also from the frost-grown strength of the apple ale within the jug. He held up his hand until all eyes were focused upon it and then he spoke.

'That's better, I have wet my whistle, and if you are all agreed we will continue with the tale.'

All agreed with haste, for within the story was ease from their thoughts. They had not known how much they had relished this until the storytelling had come to a halt, returning them to the real world of regret and pain.

Bowdyn sat back in the chair, weaving his magic with

voice and shadow and we were all once more in a far away land, listening to the story told by the youth, Creoda.

We sat side by side on the ground for a long time. I think my uncle could see that I was shocked and he gave me the time to recover. Also he forbore to point out that in the butcher's yard of a war-hedge there would be no time for shock, but only to kill or be killed, time after time, until one side or the other broke and gave themselves up to pursuit and death, or slavery.

It was the kindness of Gewis that won me to him. I don't know what he thought. I suppose he made little of it; he was a great warrior; the survivor of many battles. For my part, all I could see, over and over in my mind, was the Hun's head dropping to the ground and the lifeblood pulsing. My feelings were only of sickness and it was with difficulty that I controlled my urge to puke. I felt nothing of triumph that my violator laid dead at my feet. Was it truly by my hand? At least the final blow was mine. That was something I would think about later. My thoughts were too full at that moment to work out the blow to my honour caused by the manner of the brute's death.

Eventually, Gewis rose and taking hold of my hand, drew me to my feet. 'First we must decide what to do with this filth,' he said. 'We will take back only the head, the folk do not need to know anything, other than that you took his head with a mighty blow worthy of Thunor.' I knew he was speaking of my near fatal hesitation that had ended in my warrior dishonour.

I was for burning the corpse and I told my uncle how I had promised the kill to Wothan. We looked around us, but there was nothing for fuel aside from wet brushwood shrubs and scrub grass, burning was impossible. Nevertheless, the torso with its shameful axe wound in the back was not something I wanted anyone from the Holding to see.

Gewis pointed to the little cluster of rocks we had used as a vantage point. In the creases between rocks there was a piling up of windblown sandy soil. 'We will bury it here, cover it with stones and in no time the wind will pile more soil on top and no one will discover it. We will give the head to the flames at the Holding to honour your vow to Wothan.'

He recovered his axe and wiped it carefully in the grass before returning it to the leather strap across his chest. Then he stripped the Hun's body of weapons and searched it for any hoard, finding a few coins of Rome, which he gave to me. That done we scratched a hole in the sandy soil, first with our spear points and then our hands, and rolled the corpse down into it. We covered it with small rocks and then scooped back the earth we had dug out.

In time the wind would carry more sand and bury the remains as deep as any grave, but I was still unhappy. For a party would set out that very day from the Holding to butcher the horse. In normal times, horseflesh is forbidden meat, but in times of hunger, such as we faced this winter, nothing was forbidden except man meat and sometimes, I have heard, even foes have been eaten when Holdings have lost all their winter food.

All of the horses that Gewis had brought in, including the ones we rode and the dead one in front of us, would end up in the pot before the spring litters of pigs and the lambing and calving came to save us; and most of that birthing must still be kept if our flocks and herds were to grow to healthy numbers again.

I stood up and looked at the mound we had raised for the

Hun beast and then I relaxed. I could not see any of our party digging the body up again. Why should they?

Gewis took strips of leather from the dead horse's saddle and the straps attached to the standing cups and tied them together. His lips twisted in disgust, he pushed them into the mouth of the Hun's head and drew them out through the neck. When knotted as secure as any prize haunch of deer meat, he hung the head from my saddle girth where it bumped against my left leg all the way back to the Holding.

'Come,' he said slowly, as he cleaned the filth off his hands with sand and soil, 'we must go. Your mother will be worried, but at least she is getting you back alive. I feared that I should be taking your body home. I know she would have killed me and it would not have been an easy death. Your mother is a woman of very strong passions. I wish to have her gratitude, not her hatred.'

This was the first small hint I had that my uncle had other motives than to rescue my manly self-esteem.

As we rode, I sat in silence, using the time to examine my feelings about my kill. There is a very old story of the Anglekin. Their great King Offa, when a boy, had fought a battle to set the borders of Angleland at the Eider River, that same river that had turned back the Hun whose head now bounced against my calf. The legend goes that until just before the battle, all Offa's kin thought him voiceless. The truth of that was thus: when young he had seen his brothers join in murdering a stranger they had challenged to single combat. The only way he could hide the truth and yet not accept the dishonour of the murder, was to strike himself dumb, until one day it became necessary to speak to save his father's life.

I feared that the slaying of my Hun would have struck Offa dumb again. I rode up alongside Gewis. 'Uncle, we must tell the folk. I cannot take credit for killing a foe you struck down from behind.'

Gewis rode in silence turning my words over in his head. At length he spoke. 'We will tell them nothing. If I had not done what I did he would have killed you. I would have acted in just the same way to save my own life. Tell the truth and scops will not sing of your kill. But the songs about heroes are not of real life; they teach children a warrior must treat a beaten foe with honour if that foe is honourable.

'In real battle a warrior must use a different set of rules to those we teach a child. In battle the warrior's only task is to survive and kill the enemy. The shield-wall which does that best on a battlefield will possess the field. If you had died, your mother would have been bereft and she would have despised me. Where's the honour in that?'

I thought about this for a while, weighing different versions in my head, testing my comfort with them.

'I will not lie and claim the kill for my own,' I said at length.

Gewis nodded. 'You're a good boy, but this is what we will say. We pursued him to stop him from telling more of his horde of the slaughter of their foragers. This is true. We worked together, which is also true. I brought his horse down; you took off his head with your father's sword. This is true statement of fact. We need not tell everything. We are not lying, only leaving out that which is private to us. Do you agree? Can you live with that story? If they praise you, let them call you a young hero, enjoy it. After all, the stroke that removed his head was a mighty stroke. There is passion in you, boy. Thunor must have strengthened your arms.'

I thought over his words, sifted them in my head. In my mind I acted out telling the story to my mother and my friends.

In the end I nodded. I could tell this story and not feel a liar. I did not always tell all of a story to my mother. There had been other times ...

Gewis leaned over and clapped me on the shoulder. 'Good,' he said, 'this is the best way, you will see.'

With this worry settled, sore and aching as I was, I was able to relax in the saddle. Although no practiced horseman, I rode well enough to be able to appreciate the greater safety and control the riding cups on my Hunnish saddle gave me when my feet were in them.

'Why do we not use these?' I asked my uncle.

He shrugged his shoulders. 'Truly I don't know; the Huns and their allies have always had them I think. The Romans did not, nor the Goths. Until they took the idea also and used it, the Huns had a great advantage and won many battles because they were so fast. You saw yourself the war-gain from standing and aiming the bow. This is another; he patted the double curved horn of the Hun's bow now slung over his back under his shield. The power is in the double curve and the use of horn instead of wood. It is a fearsome weapon in capable hands.'

Before this day I had never heard my uncle speak at the lengths he now spoke with me. I felt that I had crossed some unseen barrier between child and adult, between farmer and warrior, and was now more an equal than a child in his eyes. I cannot say that the feeling of pride that grew in me did not go a long way to wipe out my feelings of disgrace at the indignity I had suffered. Perhaps that was what he had intended.

Now we descended from the low hills of the Geest on a course running alongside the lie of the high ground. As we rode further south I saw, far off, the rise of our Terp with its piling fence and the roof of the halls and the larger of the dwellings rising above it. Smoke from the fires hung still in the air, for the god-sent wind that had delivered my enemy into our hands had dropped to nothing. The air was cold and still with a brightness on the horizon over the sea where the clouds, overcast and grey, were now giving way to blue.

My mood, after a day of moods that changed swifter than clouds - fear then shame, fear again, revulsion and shame again - now gave way to happiness. One month before, during a terrible storm like a battle between Freya, our Mother Earth, and her father the sea, Great Neorth, had come a wave tall as a tree, sweeping all before it. It had flooded the land. Many of our beasts had drowned and been washed away to the sea; all of the unharvested crops were lost. Only our being inland in the Holding, atop its Terp, had saved us and some of our beasts. Now, at least the livestock that escaped the flood was safe and I had played my part.

Between porridge and horsemeat, and even some salted or smoked cattle meat, some sea fish and marsh eels and maybe some seal meat, we should not starve this winter. At last I had passed into manhood: I had killed my foe and could wear my hair long, in a knot like my uncle's if I chose.

When the Weird Sisters have chosen a design for the tapestry of a life then even the gods must obey. My happiness, through much of my life, was often ill judged or untimely, as I was to discover.

When we reached the wooden slope into the Terp, my mother, back from the island of refuge and alerted to our arrival, was already waiting by the gate. I was afraid she would rush down the ramp and throw herself at me, pitching me headlong into childhood again. I should have known her to be too wise for that.

At that time I did not know my mother as well as I came to

know her later. To me she was just Mother: tall, strong, a blend of strength and tenderness, of wholehearted love, a fierce and terrible smiter of the wrong doer. An object of love and pride, as she swept through the Holding with her long-legged stride, her corn-coloured hair caught back and bouncing as she walked, like the tail of some fine, high-stepping horse.

She clasped me tightly whenever I did something foolish, was hurt or in trouble and let me know that I was safe and everything could and would be put right. The giving of justice and punishment, if needed, would come later. It was this enfolding that I feared. But my mother in her wisdom sensed that I had passed some barrier to adulthood and she merely reached up and laid her hand on my arm.

'Welcome Creoda, welcome Gewis, we were worried for you.'

She glanced at the Hun's head without turning a hair. 'I see you were successful, you must come and tell me about it. You will be hungry. There is stew on the fire, come, eat.'

Gewis sat in the saddle, suddenly hesitant.

'Come ... come,' said my mother waving him towards the door.

'Thank you, I must pen the horses then I will come straightway. I am starving.'

He rode away and my mother's face settled into grim lines. 'Come and eat while you may,' she called after him. 'Starvation will be all our futures soon. I have foul news for you.'

I followed my mother into the house. Something deliciously savoury bubbled in the cook pot hung over the fire, the aroma mixing with the scent of wood-smoke. This was my home. I was used to its comforting warmth and appetizing odour. I was thankful that my home was untainted by my assault earlier ... could it be the same day? So much horror packed into so few hours. The familiar warmth, smell and surroundings helped me push it from my mind.

'What else has happened, Mother?' I asked.

She smiled sadly. 'We will wait for your uncle. Tell me the events of your day and I will tell you mine,' she said, reaching to the pot and ladling the wholesome smelling stew into wooden bowls.

There came the noise of shuffling feet, the curtain was pushed aside and Gewis entered. He sniffed the air appreciatively, savouring the scents of meat and herbs.

'Come, sit.' My mother indicated a bench on the other side of the fire. He sat down and took the heaped and steaming bowl from her hands.

'There is no bread,' she said. 'The elves have cast a sickness on it, the grain can only be eaten as porridge and then only when skimmed.' She smiled. 'You must sup from the bowl direct, but if you eat like Creoda that will be no hardship for you.'

He smiled in turn and in jest raised the bowl and began to gulp and slurp the liquor. Then, picking the larger pieces of meat out with his fingers, he stuffed them in his mouth. Deeming this permission enough, I followed his example and as the hot savoury food made its way into my guts I felt better than I had all day.

First, the feeling of bone-deep cold was replaced by a feeling of warmth; then good cheer pushed away the horror of the day. Even my head, which had felt as if it was splitting in two from the ill usage it had received from the Hunnish bow, felt somewhat better, subsiding to a dull ache. The elves may have laid their sickness on the bread, but in my head I thanked them for blessing my mother's stew.

We ate hungrily, telling my mother between mouthfuls the

story we had agreed. When it was finished she smiled proudly and touched my arm in praise. I felt ashamed to have misled her so.

Gewis must have sensed this, for I could see he wanted to move on before I blurted something out. He raised his bowl, swallowed the very dregs of the stew then placed it empty on the floor. 'Truly you are Elwine, for that food was a magic potion. Already I feel twice the man who entered your door.'

That was my mother's given name, 'Elf Friend', although I often thought when I felt the lash of her sharp tongue that a more warlike name would have been nearer to the truth, Gartonge, Spear Tongue, perhaps.

My mother smiled and then the smile faded. 'You are welcome husband's brother, enjoy it for there will not be much more unless we can solve the riddle the gods have made for us.'

Gewis regarded her gravely. 'Tell, then, what is amiss?'

She told us, the worry plain on her face as she spoke. 'When we feared the Huns might steal our cattle, we drove those of our flocks remaining from the flood into the common grain fields, so that they might be contained within the hedge and wall, and might feed while we defended against the raiders.'

The field she mentioned was a large one of perhaps two hides, held in common by the folk. Around the edge to keep the cattle out from the growing grain was a hedge of thorn, but at the end, so that the flocks could be driven in and out, was a wall that funnelled outwards to a gate. From the outside the wall carried on, on both sides, to form a funnel to the gate for driving in the flock.

'This morning, when the news and the cost of the defeat of the Huns was known,' said my mother, 'Baeldaeg set in hand the gathering and sorting of the bodies and the building of the balefires. He also sent herdsmen to turn out the cattle to the pasture. Half of the beasts are dead.'

She stared at the floor and then sighed. 'Dead,' she repeated. 'They have the murrain. Those not dead are fierce and charge at the herdsmen and at each other; others fall down and writhe and call out in pain, and then they die. The fields are cursed, the bread poisons the folk, the stubble the cattle.'

She looked up and her eyes spoke the tragedy as much as her words. 'We are utterly lost. There is no food. We shall all starve!'

'There are the horses,' said Gewis.

'Yes, the horses, and how long shall three hundred of the folk live on seven skin and bone and gristle horses?'

'There are the dead cattle laid to salt and those just dead,' said Gewis. 'Given time the curse may pass, some can eat them after salting or smoking has purified. If only some eat then the others will know if it is safe.'

'Of course,' said my mother 'we can eat well on meat this winter, if the diseased cow flesh does not kill us. It is clear that you have learned the warriors' trade, but have not learned anything about where comes the food you steal upon your way. Food does not just appear, it is earned with much labour and skill and maintained with much care and planning. If we eat all our meat, from whence will come the young to maintain the flocks? You cannot eat meat and then breed from it. The cattle left to us are not enough to breed and feed us all next year. If we keep all the calves, and we must, then there is no milk. If we keep all the calves there will be no slaughter in Blood Month next year and so no meat next winter.'

Again she sighed and then continued, 'If that is not enough, we have no bread and little grain to eat as porridge, the harvest was small as well as cursed. We cannot know whether the grain we have is fit to sow, but we must sow it anyway, and do it now. If we eat only meat and no bread this winter we can sow all the grain, but if it is cursed, when we harvest next year we shall not have grain or meat.'

We sat in silence thinking this over.

'We must get more cattle and we must get more grain, enough good grain for bread for the winter and to sow for next year. That much is plain,' said my uncle.

My mother laughed harshly in scorn. 'Spoken like a warrior, and what will you do? Go thieve it? From whom?' she asked. 'Will we take it from the Suebi to the south or the Anglekin to the north? Who shall we go to war with, that they may come and slip their seaxs into our men and their soft daggers into our women?'

Gewis held up his hands in surrender at her teasing. 'I was not thinking of stealing cattle and grain but of buying it, north or south, whoever is reported to have the best harvest this year.'

My mother again laughed scornfully. 'Buy with what? We know how to buy. We shall buy food with the slavery of our menfolk. We shall eat the food that they fetch and carry; the food that grows in ground ploughed by them. Women and children - women who sleep in cold beds and children with no father to protect them - must plough our own ground. Oh, we know how to buy our food, by selling our folk into slavery.'

Once more Gewis held up his hands in mock surrender. 'It may be that the Anglekin will sell us food for gold rather than slaves. Gold eats nothing and buys much; slaves eat their master out of house and hoard. If there is any food to sell or trade in Thiatmaresgaho or Angeln then I may be able to help. There may be a little gold left in my purse.'

My mother looked at him, weighing his words and then she spoke. 'You will need more than a few pieces, if you are not just boasting and mean what you say.'

'Let me be clear,' said Gewis. 'There is food enough for this winter, but then nothing left for the year to follow. So the folk will need food for that year and also cattle for milk and meat, and seed corn for the year to come?'

'At last,' said my mother, 'the warrior's head awakes. Yes, and for that you will need more than a small purse of gold, if there is any food to be found.'

Gewis smiled. 'Then please tell me what size purse will be needed?'

My mother removed a small leather bag from her waist and shook out a number of stones of two sizes, some about the size of a hazel nut and others of a large wheat grain. She laid these out in two rows.

'These are my tally stones,' she said. She started to move them around, first into one row and then into another and then into a third. Gewis watched in silence, all amazed.

After a while she looked up. 'There are three hundred of the folk, each will need meat and bread to survive and these may possibly be bought. To this we can add the horses in the pen, the eggs and chickens we still have, eels from the meres and fish from the sea. By my tally we can survive and all remain free if you can find sixty pieces of Roman gold.'

She looked challengingly at my uncle, there was a smile of triumph on her face, but underneath it, knowing her better than any, I saw also fear and hope.

Gewis returned her smile. 'Is that all? Then, if there is any food to be had, perhaps I can help. I will speak to Baeldaeg, if he can give the people hope that help may come, perhaps it will. None must speak of this or my part in it, out of this company. Any gold I have is secret to me. I do not wish to raise false hopes and I do not wish to draw misfortune on my head or those of my hearth companions. Let the folk think I go to beg food or steal it. But, on my oath, the gold is not a problem.'

My mother looked at him, then down at the floor and then up at my uncle's face. 'The gods see fit to punish us, I know not why. Then they send us you and take the punishment away. I do not understand, but if you can do this, then by your oath we are saved.'

Gewis climbed to his feet. 'I must go and confer with my war brothers, for this also touches on them. Tonight we will sleep on this. In the morning we must leave. We will take the horses and I beg that you will allow Creoda to accompany us. He is a man now, blooded and proved and he has my trust.'

My mother looked stricken, her eyes beseeching, hoping I would refuse, but she read my silence and nodded.

'Take care of him. Lose him? Then send the gold to fulfil your oath, but do not return yourself!'

My uncle and mother gazed at one another for a long moment then Gewis bowed, and turning, walked towards and through the door, speaking over his shoulder as he went. 'Creoda, tomorrow, at daybreak, bring your spear and, if your mother permits, your father's sword. I will find you a helm if I can.'

He turned back, 'Oh, and by the way, the head: I told them to put it on the balefire to honour your oath. All the other filth is there, living or dead.'

My mother made her farewells to him. She gave me a hug and then waved me towards my bed. 'Rest, you will need to be fresh.'

I hugged her in return, 'Thank you. Uncle Gewis is a

mighty warrior. I will be safe with him.'

She nodded, her eyes moist, and I turned away before the heat behind my own eyes started to moisten. I lay down, pulled the sheepskin over myself and closed my eyes on the slow steady throb of my head.

I knew nothing more until I wakened as the first light of dawn came through the edge of the curtained doorway. The fire was out and I, like a cat into water, slunk out from under the sheepskin. I looked at my sleeping mother, unsure whether she slept or, in false sleep, sped my parting. I took the Hun's coins from my purse and placed them by the side of her bed in case of need and then picked up my shield, spear and sword and walked into the cold morning air, pausing to splash icy water on my face from the pottery bowl on the wash bench by the door.

Gewis and his warband were waiting by the horse pen. They had already chosen their mounts and in addition held three packhorses on lead reins. I moved to the last loose beast and captured it.

Before we mounted, Gewis made me known to the others. I knew his warriors by sight, for they had always been a part of my growing up since they had come to our village in my seventh year, but I had never met them, they were warriors and heroes, too high for a mere child to know.

First he spoke to his companions. 'This is Creoda, my brother's son; slayer of Huns, taker of heads and worthy to join our band.'

He then spoke to me. 'These warriors are oath-sworn to me and me to them, we are brothers and have ridden over many a weary mile together.' He spoke no more, for it was well known that his hearth-companions had no names, being, or so everybody thought, outlaw.

I learned later that each one had reason to lose his name: the giant we called 'the Goth' was sought by the Huns; the Moor was sought by the wicked in Africa, and the two Alans also by the Huns, who never forgave those they trained in arms but then deserted them; the one we called the Suebi I learned, much later, was sought as a murderer. But his murders were vengeance and would only be murder to the blood kin of those he killed, and their Lord.

'Now that you have been made known to my brothers, let us go,' and with that Gewis led off and our column followed. I moved towards the front until I could speak to him.

'Where are we going?' I asked.

'To the entrance to Hell,' said the Moor, riding close behind.

'To Hlawdun,' said Gewis, 'but 'Cave Mountain' is our name for it. We do not speak its true name. Know only that we are going to the forest and the hills to the southeast.'

The Suebi glowered at me. 'I know you are Gewis' brother's son and I know he finds you to be worthy of this company, but know this, Dungbeatle, if you betray us, or the place of our hoard, I will lay my hands on your liver.'

'Easy, easy' said Gewis, 'the lad is worthy, you have my oath on it, if he betrays my oath I will take my own vengeance and then suffer death at the hands of his mother.'

The Suebi laughed. 'That I can accept, Lord Gewis, you will hear no more from me on this.'

I felt a twinge of excitement in my upper stomach, I was in the company of great warriors and I was off to seek a hoard.

'Gewis?'

'Yes Creoda'

'Can you tell me the story of the hoard?'

'As we ride I will,' said Gewis, and so he did.

There was silence in the room. The glow of the fire lit the nearby faces, but as the flames had died and only the glow at the base remained, those further away had fallen into shadow.

'It is late,' said Bowdyn, 'time for rest, tomorrow is a working day.'

'Candles,' called my father. There was movement as someone moved to light a spill from the glowing logs. He lit a candle and revealed the room and the silent feasters.

'With Master Hacking's leave we will meet in the Cold-Cot on the next dry night and I will tell you more – that is, if you wish it.'

There was a clamour from which my father's voice arose. 'You must not stop now, Master Bowdyn,' he said, amongst cries of agreement.

The Gleeman bowed his head in consent. 'Then so it shall be, the next dry night, and come all who may.'

There was a shuffling around and then, after thanks to my father and to the storyteller, the crowd filed out through the door and the hall was empty, but for mother, father, Jedediah, the Gleeman and me.

'I am afraid,' said my father, 'that you shall still be quartered in the cellar until we are certain all the King's men have left the county.'

Bowdyn smiled. 'Your cellar, sir, is ease indeed compared to life on the road. You have my heartfelt gratitude for such a lodging.'

With Jed's help to lift and lower the hatch, Bowdyn retired to his bed in the cellar, and we retired to ours, no doubt to review in our minds the story just told and to try to foretell what was still to come. And in so doing I fell fast asleep.

# AD 435 – AD 447
# Germania, Gaul

# Chapter 8

**AD 440**

**Lothar's Tale - the Killing**

The next Saturday night, as luck would have it, was dry, clear and cold. There had been showers during the day, but the great billowing clouds had blown away to the east and the sky was dark blue-black and glittered with stars edging the moonshine. There was a gibbous moon casting its cold light upon the ground and lighting up the inside of the Cold-Cot, and by this light the great pile of brushwood, branches and logs could be seen.

'Damned if I can afford to feed and ply the county with ale,' said my father, 'but there are still woods aplenty and at least we shall not be cold.'

At darkfall we lit the fire and it flared into life, leaping and twisting and covering the walls with glowing movement.

The first of the crowd started to arrive as the fire sprang up and none came empty handed. There were logs and branches and bundles of faggots to feed the flames; there was a clinking of bottles and jars, for some had brought ale, others home-brewed cider and perry, beer of all sorts, elderflower and berry, nettle and plum. The beekeeper had plundered his stock of mead; food also was on show, pies, pasties, sausages and tiny loaves of fresh bread small enough to be handed around, one for each person. It soon became plain that more were in the Cot than had ever been in our hall. Word had spread to the village and folk who did not belong to our farm were also coming, in hopes of a free show.

All who came brought something to eat or drink and benches or cushions to sit on. They shared these with their neighbours, so my father welcomed them all.

The hubbub died down and the crowd sat in quiet expectation, munching and supping in a half circle around the fire. The Gleeman appeared out of the shadows of the doorway. The old carved chair had been carried from the hall and was against the wall. Bowdyn had fussed with its placing until it satisfied him. He dropped easily into it, giving his greetings and receiving a chorus back.

Old Tom piped up from the back, 'So where be this place, Germania, Gleeman. Who rules there? What be the law?' He paused, as if regretting his temerity, 'You don moind oi astin ee Zir?'

'No, Tom,' said Bowdyn, 'in another time, another place it might be me asking questions of you. In another time, another place we would do what we are, instead of being what we do. This will always be so until we find once more our ancient freedoms.'

'Hmm!' My father cleared his throat loudly, 'No sedition here, friend Bowdyn,' he said warningly.

'You are right, sir. No sedition intended. I am sorry,' Bowdyn smiled. 'I was thinking of my answer to Tom's question.' He turned back to the villagers and to Old Tom.

'Much of Germania had been ruled by the Romans, but Rome was failing at this time. In the east there was warfare between the tribes. Also in the east were the Huns, spreading across the land like a plague of rats; men clad in rat skins.

Wonderful horsemen and bowmen they were. They made nothing, grew nothing and consumed everything. Gold they needed to buy Roman weapons and artefacts in the West and the East. Everything else they stole. Where there was nothing to steal then they took slaves to sell for gold.'

He paused and looked around at us all before continuing. 'Where they had to fight to conquer, the vanquished were rewarded with tortures that would sicken all here. Where they ruled but did not enslave they took the men to fight for them and the women to serve their needs. Times were hard in the East of Germania in these times. I will tell you a sad tale, of Lothar, a Goth who lived in lands ruled by the Huns. I will call it Lothar's tale and it fits well enough into our greater tale. Do you all agree that I should take this side road?'

He smiled at the chorus of assent. With that he worked his magic with light and shade and voice, and the deep-chested words of a giant man came from the shadows.

I was born on the east bank of the Tisia River, five hours' walk from the great river to the south of us. I was always a big boy. My mother raised her hands in horror when talking to other women about my birth. From the age of five my father found me work to do about the place, on the bank with the skids leading down into the water. Here he built and launched anything that was wanted that would float. I was a happy child. I loved the water that flowed past the slips. I was never happier than making rafts, using the skills my father taught me on any old off-cuts of timber or logs of driftwood I could find.

Because I was big, I was strong for my age. With the adze

and axes that I used in my work helping my father, I built strength into my arms, wrists and hands early on. The exact use of the adze and the hand axes for fine work became second nature to me. In my play I learned to throw the small trimming axes and had my father give me a pair for my work. I trimmed and shaped the handles of these until the balance was so good I could split a short log at ten paces.

One dark cloud hung over my happiness and that of my family. We were freemen, but not free, for we were the vassals of the Hun. Settled in the long length of the Tisia valley they ruled by force that we must obey if we wished to live.

Because of this my sisters could not romp in the countryside as I did and always covered their heads with scarves for safety, to hide their looks from our Hunnish overlords.

Whenever our lords wanted spears to fight for them on their raids into the west and north, my elder brothers were among those taken. My father said that in his youth he had been at war for months at a time, in the army of the great Hunnic King, Octar. Of course, the present Hun King, Attila, was not our king, but nevertheless, our own King Valamir was oath-sworn in service to him, and through him so were we. Our standing as allies of their king did not lessen the crude and insolent manners of the young Huns settled around us, and their contempt for us was obvious.

We bore their brutish behaviour with some forbearance. My father demanded that, for as he said, we had a good life and getting killed over bad manners would not make it better. And thus, although I bristled at the tone of the young Huns when they spoke to my father or me, the care my mother and sisters took in hiding themselves kept our feelings at the level of secret discontent.

The women lived in constant fear that lawless Huns would

see them. This weighed on their spirits until it became too great a burden to be borne. I must think this, for how else am I to understand what came over my youngest sister, Aefre? It is foolish and weak of me to blame her for the lapse from which all our future troubles flowed for, in truth, the fault was mine.

The day, on which my life unravelled, my last day of true happiness, began as a beautiful morning on the river in spring, at the very end of Oestremonath.

I paused in my work and listened with pleasure to the birdsong. I wondered whether I should ask my father for rest time for the water was warming in the sun and fish were just starting to jump, causing ripples that spread out in shining rings of sunshine on the water. I longed to be fishing, breathing in the sweet air perfumed with fir trees and the new leaves on the oaks, bright with dancing catkins.

I was facing the river, my trimming axe in my hand where I had straightened up from stripping the bark from a seasoned length of pine. As I drew in deep breaths of air in the sheer pleasure of the day I felt that I could never be happier. At that point the Fates cackled and changed my life forever.

I stretched my arms above my head, turned it to ease the muscles of my neck and saw, coming along the bank, leading his ugly pony at a silent walk, one of the young Huns: one that we detested more than most for his arrogance and contempt. I turned my head to look quickly to my right, checking that all was clear. To my horror, Aefre was approaching the riverbank. She had removed her headscarf and was joyously breathing in the air, shaking out her long, curling blonde hair, her head back, laughing; delighting in the unfamiliar freedom.

Seeing her, our Hun tormentor mounted his horse in a single leap and urged it to a gallop. I shouted to Aefre to get back in the house; my mother and father ran through the doorway gaping. Nothing seemed to happen as it should, everything was so slow, like a nightmare where the dreamer runs and runs but as if through waist deep mud, whilst some horror draws nearer and nearer.

The Hun reined in and in one swift movement sprang from his horse to the ground in front of Aefre, whose mouth now opened to scream. Seizing her by the hair, he forced her to her knees, his hand mingled with her curls and, laughing, he began thrusting himself against her face. She turned aside in disgust, all the while screaming.

I cannot think what made the youth, for he was no older than I, believe that we would permit his abuse of one of our women to go unpunished. I could see my father and mother running and if I had let them gather up my sister and hurry her inside then nothing worse than insult would have passed. But I didn't, I did as the Fates decreed, and caused the death of all except my own guilty self.

I have learned that there are points in time where small actions give rise to endless and mounting aftermaths. One small, quick, unthinking deed, which causes bigger action and backlash round and round in circles, like the water spreading out where a fish has jumped, until the original offence is quite forgotten.

I did not know this, of course, until much later. If I had, would it have stayed my hand? I doubt it, because my hand seemed fated to move on its own without a thought to guide it. My hand, which had made this movement in harmless practice so many times before, now made its moves with deadly skill. Before I could recall it, the axe flew through the air, splitting the head of the Hun in the same way as it had split the logs. He fell sideways, spraying blood.

My sister turned her head back to look, saw the blood on her skirt and then the body on the ground and screamed with renewed strength. Reaching her, my mother dragged her to her feet, struck her to shut her up and pushed her to the doorway and inside, whilst looking over her shoulder at the body and my father with fright in her eyes.

My father snarled at me to come and help. He levered my axe from the dead youth's skull and picking up the body by the shoulders, signed with his head that I should take the feet. We carried the corpse to the water's edge and threw it in, watching it float away towards the place downstream where our Tisia joined with the great river.

The horse, perhaps smelling the blood, was hopping from foot to foot. It tossed its head and backed away as my father tried to seize it, reversing into a saw trestle and whirling to see what was behind, kicking out as it did so.

I grabbed the flying rein and together my father and I led the beast to the riverbank and urged it in. It splashed in the water, swimming, and then, walking to the bank heaved itself out. I went to catch it again, but my father shook his head. He picked up a piece of wood and threw it hard at the horse's rump. With a shrill cry it turned and galloped back the way it had brought its ill-fated rider.

My father stamped out the marks of the horse's hooves in the soft mud of the riverbank and then turned to me. 'You fool,' he said, 'if they find him with his head cleaved you may have killed us all, they will take revenge on every family on the river. For the sake of your mother and your sisters you must go. They will seek him. If they find his body they will question everybody. Many know your skill with an axe. The Huns will come for you. When they find you gone, if our pleadings that we know nothing are believed, they may let us live.'

And so, to the bleating of my sisters and the quiet tears of my mother, I donned my cloak, packed a satchel with food, then fastened the cross belt with my great war-axe and the two throwing axes. I embraced my father in silence for I knew he could do nothing more. I accepted the purse of coins he pressed on me and set out, I knew not whither.

His last words to me echoed in my head for days: 'The Gods go with you, my son. Do not let the Huns catch you, for your mother's sake – and mine.'

# Chapter 9

**AD 440**

**Lothar's Tale, the Legion**

At the joining of the rivers I pushed a driftwood tree out from the bank and clinging to it, kicking with my feet, eased myself across the river. As I drifted down towards the east, I knew I would have to make this good later, for my chosen direction to get away from the lands of the Huns was west. The extra walk was worth it, for there was no bridge and unless they had good reason to cross the river, they would stay on the northern bank.

I squelched ashore through the mud of the south bank and followed the great river west for days until I came to another river and marsh blocking my way. For a coin I was able to get a fisherman from Colonia Mursa to ferry me across and I continued to follow the setting sun with the river on my right. After a day or two I found the afternoon sun on my left cheek as I walked along the river, showing me that it now curved north.

Where else had I to go? So I continued to follow the river, thinking about where it might lead, and cursing myself. I cursed my hand for the disaster it had brought on me and my family. I felt sick in my stomach thinking what would happen if the Huns took revenge on them. It was my fault; all my stupid fault. I thought to turn back, to give myself up to the Huns, but knew such a thing to be useless. They would kill me with great pain. Eventually I would gain the peace of death, but my mother and father would live on in dread and sorrow at the horror of my end, though I did not think they would suffer so for long. The vengeful Huns were still likely to kill my family and everyone around them to give a lesson in the rewards for harm to a tribesman. No, going back would not help. My father was right: if he, my mother and my sisters could deny they had seen or heard from me for days, they stood a slim chance of surviving the rage of the Huns. And so, sick at heart and with great self-loathing, I carried on walking beside the river and away from my home. Thinking about what I might do to feed myself as my food and money ran out changed the direction of my unhappy thoughts.

After two more days, hills rose on my left side and the riverbank began to steepen. After five more days I came to a city. Or, rather, I came to two cities. On my side of the river was a small Roman settlement and on the other side a large Roman city with stone buildings bigger than any I had ever seen. The name of this town was Aquincum. Huns infested it, so I thought it best to avoid the east bank and stay where I was. There were Huns there also, but for once the Fates looked the other way, for none took any notice of me and I was able to buy some bread and cheese, enough to fill my satchel. That evening I left the town, passing the night sleeping in a damp thicket.

The next day I went on my way with the river still to my right. By mid-afternoon I found the sun shining into my eyes and understood that the river had made another change of direction and I was now heading west. After three days of this I came to the ruins of a gate and a wall, beyond which stood a small town. When asking my whereabouts, I was told I was now inside the limits of the land of the Romans and that the last of the Romans in the district could be found in a large garrison town, just two days further along the river.

When I arrived there, it was plain to see that Roman interest was waning. Much of the town and the great camp were in a poor state of repair. There were a few uniformed men of the legions, true Romans, but most were like me, Goths or Gepids. There was the clatter and noise and smell of large numbers of horses and I guessed that this town was the real border between Rome and the Hun. I felt safer knowing this, although my heart ached that my family were not with me.

I soon solved the problem of earning my keep. It seemed that entry into and out of the Gothic forces of the Romans was very careless. I was mistaken for a recruit while standing watching a great group of Gothic warriors. I was pushed into their midst, had my name taken by an officer, was issued with a shield and a spear and told my rate of pay was four folles each day, but that the cost of the arms would be taken first.

I found myself standing next to a small Gepid and asked him what was happening, for as I told him, I had not wanted to join the Roman army.

'Don't worry,' he said, 'this is the third time for me. If you run away at night, just leave your shield and spear behind. You don't get paid the next day, the paymaster will pocket your pay and sell your arms to the next recruit and won't report you missing for a month until after payday, by which time you will be far away.'

Having found that joining up was not as binding as I had feared, I resolved to stay and see what I could learn.

I served as a soldier of Rome for two years. I learned much

from the training; we all did. I fought against the Huns in some small engagements against raiding parties, which taught me care in battle. I found that one of the favourite pastimes of bored soldiers was betting on mock gladiatorial contests fought with spear shafts. To kill a fellow soldier meant trial and death and so real weapons were not used. Except occasionally, such as sometimes in the forest, when a pair of would-be deserters would battle for a large purse before a crowd of the more serious gamblers amongst the five thousand warriors encamped at Vindobona.

For the most part the contests were in a makeshift arena and even the officers watched and wagered. I was strong and big and quick, and although I collected a few headaches, my Roman helmet protected me from a cracked skull and my leather and scale armour from a cracked rib. I became good at it and also at weapons and combat drill. I won a little money by betting on myself, and I became a well-trained warrior.

I enjoyed and profited from my time with the Gothic cavalry. Oh, and of course I learned about horses: how to ride them and care for them and spent much of my time shovelling up horseshit and dumping it in the countryside. At the end of two years I felt that my life was standing still. I wanted more than to be a Goth horseshit shoveller to the end of my days.

Making the decision to desert, I offered to fight a contest of arms for a purse. I left my spear, shield and armour behind and while it was still dark, took my axes and my money and sneaked into the woods to the south, away from the river. The contest took place in a clearing by early morning light. My adversary fought with spatha and dagger and I with my great axe - which was both sword and shield to me - held in my right hand, and in my left, the hand axe.

The contest was hard fought but short, to the disapproval

of the betting crowd. My opponent, a stocky Alemanni from the North, first rushed at me and thrust with the knife as a diversion. As I turned to the right and fended with my hand axe, so he spun to his left and aimed a cut across my left side with the sword. I already had my right foot at stretch behind me and easily drawing back my left foot I outdistanced his sword. It swung past me and across my front as I brought up my left hand axe to guard against his back stroke, at the same time hefting my bearded axe over my head to aim at his arm. Seeing this he brought his arm into the body, his sword pointing ready for the thrust as my axe swept past. But at the last moment I turned my arm so that the flat of the axe struck the sword, forcing it down. I then sliced up along the blade towards the hilt and raked my axe along the length of his forearm, spraying blood in every direction.

I stepped back, allowing him to submit, but he sprang at me, sword trailing, and coming under my left guard sliced my hip with his knife. I decided there and then to give no more chances and flicked my hand axe to fly through the air. It hit him below his helmet rim. He moved as quick as lightning and my axe flew past, but as he turned his head and withdrew his hand to guard his face, I hit him a mighty blow on the left side earflap with the flat of my axe and tumbled him arse over hairline. He flew sideways and then crashed to the ground where he lay without stirring.

The master of the ring knelt beside him and felt for a heartbeat. He declared me the winner and gave us the news that my opponent still lived. I took his purse, for he would not be going anywhere; all he could do was go back to the army and make up some story about a horse savaging him.

I collected my winnings, staunched the bleeding from my hip as best I could and ignoring the grumbling gamblers and fight followers, I picked up my hand axe. I then paid the 'immunes' boatmen, who always came to these contests expecting business, to ferry me across to the German marketplace, the Cannabae, on the north bank. From there I hurried west along the river hoping to be out of sight before the sun rose too high.

On my way upriver I took no more chances. My wound began to heal and I hung around garrisons, touting for paid contests as a Barbarian warrior. Sometimes in the ring with staves; sometimes in the woods at first light, with axes and my newly purchased leather body armour and helmet, both second hand and tight on me, but fit for duty.

I won every fight and after a year my purse was starting to hang heavy so I changed bronze into silver to lighten it. Eventually I hoped I would have enough to change into gold. The fights and the money soon became all I wished for. Over a period of four years I had gone from shipwright to cavalryman, to prize fighter and become a self-employed gladiator. As my father would have said, I had striven and struggled to climb in order to end up below where I started.

I crossed from the great river to another leading north, travelling from garrison to garrison, until I arrived at Argentarium, all the while fighting and winning, building up my money store. Until one day I fought against an ugly German sword fighter, who beat me by always knowing what I was going to do and forestalling me; who let me know what he was about to do and then, when I parried thin air, I found he had done something different. Then, when he could have felled me, for no apparent reason he lowered his sword.

Seizing my chance I hit him with the flat of my blade and laid him low. Only then did I realise what he had done: knowing I was beaten he had lowered his sword to let me submit. I was remorseful; yet again my hand had worked quicker than my brain. I hurried to help him and in time we became friends. His name was Atilec: horrible by name and, with his lopsided grimace, horrible to behold, but by nature the fount of kindness. A man of skills: warrior; singer; storyteller and a good, trustworthy companion. These were surprising qualities in a wanted murderer, as once I had his trust he confessed himself to be.

Staying together, for a year we worked the camps and halls of the Border Lands. In the former we were prize-fighters and in the latter we entertained with tales by Atilec. In both we fought, but only with staves, for to kill a henchman of a chieftain would not have led to long life. Even the staff can be deadly if wielded well. We showed great care for the lordling's dunderheads and pulled more blows than we landed.

In the end we came to Colonia Agrippina, a great, rich town, well and strictly run. The dangers of prize fighting there were too great for the rewards, so for a few days we relaxed and enjoyed the pleasures of the town from the full purses we had collected elsewhere. Then we looked for work, touting our skills in the horse and merchants' markets, but the money offered was little.

It was in the moneychanger's forum that we found our place. There we met an Egyptian, one Harith by name. He offered us the chance to be his bodyguards to and from the market at the beginning and end of each day. We bargained hard for our pay until we were able to agree a sum.

'You bargain hard,' Harith said with a smile. 'That means you will not rob me; thieves always take what is first offered, for they mean to take all in the end. But you must give oaths in front of the market Praetorian.'

We agreed and made our oaths of honest service. Once the

Praetor witnessed and recorded these, we had a job. It paid well enough for us to live well at an inn while we decided what to do next.

It was there that we heard about service in the Vandal army, the looting of Africa and the rewards of piracy. We talked and talked for days, weighing the possible rewards against the certain risks. We knew the rewards and risks of prize fighting and of bodyguarding. It was certain we would never buy our way into a hall of our own without higher rewards than we now reaped. And so we decided to go to Africa.

There was silence in the Cot whilst the tale of Lothar sank in and the folk mulled over what it would be like to live under the rule of the Huns. Some, their lives blighted by the King's judges and the Tangier soldiers, felt not much had changed.

We looked expectantly at Bowdyn, unwilling to believe the entertainment was finished for the night, for it was still early.

Smiling, the Gleeman exchanged glances with my father and at a nod of consent, rewarded us with the continuing story of Gewis.

# Chapter 10

**AD 447**

**Gewis' Tale, the Road to Colonia**

For a moment Bowdyn waited patiently until he had everyone's attention and then, without more ado, he spoke.

'We will continue where we left off before Lothar's tale. We were in the forest with the boy Creoda, his uncle and the hearth-companions, oath-sworn to Gewis. You will remember they were riding to regain a hidden hoard to feed the folk threatened with famine. Creoda has asked Gewis whence came this treasure and Gewis has agreed to tell him the tale as they ride.'

The listeners sat in silence, remembering the story. The Gleeman drew back from the bright firelight and sat perfectly still. Although there was no shadow now to hide him, by some trick he seemed to disappear. Then he moved and he was no longer Bowdyn, but someone else, and from him came a voice, not this time of Lothar the giant, but nevertheless that of a deep-voiced man, which we knew must be Creoda's uncle, Gewis.

My story starts with your mother, Creoda, and this part is hard for me to tell. Now you know me as warrior, war leader, and battle victor in Gaul, Africa, the Isles of the Middle Sea and Rome. I was not always so. At the start of my tale I was young, sixteen years in age, war trained, blooded on Wolf's Head raiders, but still a boy who had never strayed far from the East Holding.

You may have marked, being young yourself, that youths have no shortage of passion but are sorely lacking in patience. They can and do feel pain, but do not easily endure. When they hurt they act rashly, when instead they should do nothing, bearing pain in patience until in time it fades. So it was with me; and from that weakness sprang all else in my life. Do the Three Sisters use our acts or our nature as the woof when they weave our fate? In my case, if my nature had been more steadfast I would have stayed in the Holding, and my future - and that, I forecast, of our whole folk - would have been different.

Creoda, my pain was caused by Elwine, your mother: friend of elves by name and like an elf herself, tall, strong-limbed, beautiful to me beyond dreams, but two years older than I and not at all mindful of my being. I dared not do other than look from afar. And she, alas, loved my older brother, your father, Bana.

When they married I could not bear the thought of their wedding night bliss. It made my gorge rise in my throat, I wanted to be sick, I wanted to kill, but knew that would not win her. I was helpless; there was nothing I could do to alter the cause of my wretchedness and nothing I could do to take away the hurt.

So, on the night of their wedding at the end of the Month-of-Three-Milkings, and on the first day of Before-Midsummer,

I ran away. I packed a leather bag with meat and bread and I picked up the small purse of brass coins I had taken from the Wolf's Head I had stuck on my spear. Took all that was precious to me and while the wedding feast was taking place, before the dreaded moment when the new husband and wife would take their leave to the ribald cheers of the guests, I took my leave.

Throwing my shield over my back and picking up my seax and spear, I found the night watchman who patrolled inside the fence of the Holding. The bar was down on the gate. I did not want the noise and fuss of him unbarring it, so I told him I was off to see the world, as if it was the most natural thing. I did not want to make a mystery of my leaving or cause any search to take place.

I mounted his lookout step by the side of the gate and vaulted over, passing from sight into the darkness. I had no idea where I was going other than that the Roman world lay to the southwest and there, I had heard, a warrior could find a Lord and earn his hire in food, warmth and gift rings.

I will not dwell in detail on the first part of my journey. I had not known or even feared that there could be so many rivers in the world as I found in my first week of wandering. First I went south, for I knew I must be south of the sea before I could turn west. But when I could no longer see the sea in the far distance I turned west and came upon a broad river, which forced me back towards the south again.

I walked beside it until, after two days, I came to the village of Hamm, where for one of my brass coins a boatman ferried me across. From him I learned that to my west was another river. He counselled me to walk in that direction, fording or swimming any small streams on the way and then to strike south along the main river until I came to the settlement the

Romans called Fabiranum. There I would find another ferry crossing. After that, he said, I should seek other directions for he himself had never been that far.

I crossed the Visurgis by ferry, at Fabiranum, a village of substantial size. Here a ferryman advised me to head southwest. I must swim across many small streams and rivers, he said, but then there was the Rhenus, a great river, too wide and swift to swim. Follow the river south, he told me, and you will come to a bridge into a great city called Colonia Agrippina; it will amaze you. Outside this city is the Roman land of Gaul.

I followed his directions and five days later I stood on a rise looking westwards towards the bridge and the city of Colonia on the west bank of the Rhenus. Truly I was amazed, I had never seen or even imagined something so strange and wonderful. Let me tell it to you as I first saw it.

I had been making my way over many thickly forested hills, each dipping down into a valley and each with its own little stream to be forded. Hill, valley, hill, valley … I was beginning to think this country would never end, that perhaps I went in circles. My food had run out and I was hungry. I had just started to lose hope of ever finding my way from this maze when I walked into a glade - to find that it wasn't a glade at all, it was the edge of the forest. Endless trees now gave way to heathland covering a small knoll, which fell away to meadows studded with cattle reaching all the way to a mighty river.

It was what stood by the river that took my breath away. It was a city, but greater than any I could think of. Later in my life when I remembered it, I knew it to be a poor thing against the greatest of this world, but then, never having seen a stone built city before, it amazed me.

The deep voice ceased speaking and Bowdyn emerged into the dying firelight. 'Well, my people,' he said, 'it is time we went to our rest, for we have told a story we did not plan, thanks to friend Thomas here. There were chuckles. Old Tom rose to his feet and removed his brown and battered, round-crowned felt hat.

'And thank ee kindly zir,' he said. 'Now I knows what it would feel loik to live in Germania, but Oi still don know where 'tis.'

Chuckles spread around the Cot mixed with some groans.

Bowdyn smiled, 'Think, Tom, how far you might walk in a day. Think that you might then travel across the sea to France. Imagine that there you turn half left and walk for sixty days; then and only then might you come to the birth home of Lothar.'

'I'm with ee zir,' said Tom, his forehead wrinkled as he tried to picture it.

'Is there anything else that it would comfort you to know,' said Bowdyn, still smiling.

'Well, by your leave zir,' said Tom, 'you'm a storyteller. Did they 'ave storytellers in Germania?'

'Indeed they did, Tom, for there have been forty generations of Galansons leading back to Roman times and each of my predecessors has handed down his stories to his learner, and each learner has taken the name of his teacher.'

He paused, looking down in thought and sat thus for so long that a murmur of quiet talk started up between the villagers, until he looked up again and spoke.

'If you wish I will tell you the story of my Teller from the time of Gewis, for that will fit in with this story well enough.'

There was a murmur of approval and Bowdyn nodded. 'Very well, I will do so, but not now. When we meet next I will tell you the story of Atilec the murderer, for we have talked of the Huns and so we should talk of the warring tribes to add further colour to the picture of that far away land. And then, if you promise not to take me down any more side alleyways, I shall carry on with Gewis' tale.'

He smiled at the folk watching him and then bowed gracefully, describing small circles with his hands, so like some of the foppish visitors to the hall that those from the village who were in service there chuckled with delight.

'And so I bid you all goodnight, sleep well and wake hale.'

With noisy shuffling and scraping of benches the crowd rose to their feet and chorusing their thanks to the Master and Mistress and to Bowdyn, left the Cot and walked out into the cold, clear night air.

With shouts of goodnight and God bless, each party went off chattering, the farm folk to their cottages and the villagers to their houses. Each group wandered in its own direction, but all went to seek warm beds and restful sleep.

# Chapter 11

**AD 435**

**The Murderer's Tale**

It seemed that Bowdyn's weather luck had let him down, for the next Saturday it was raining. Not showers with towering clouds but steady rain, falling from a sky covered with an unending and featureless sheet of grey, the rain blown sideways by a strong southwesterly wind.

We had gathered the harvest. Only the care of the livestock remained. My father talked the matter over with Bowdyn and agreed that he would declare a half-day holiday when the weather was suitable. I am not sure why he came to this, for whilst fair, he was hard working and expected this of all others. I think perhaps that by then he and my mother were looking forward to Bowdyn's stories of far off lands as much as the other folk.

Our family had suffered no personal loss from the rebellion, but the farm had lost good men; men who were valued and who might even be thought of as friends, and so Bowdyn's stories, I believe, also provided relief from sorrow for my father and mother.

Whatever the reason, it was on the Wednesday following the rainy Saturday that my father passed the word that we would meet again.

Bowdyn and I went in the morning to gather windfall wood and, as always when the going was wet, we struggled to drag the handcart through mud-slicked fields.

By the time our listeners had started to appear we had changed into dry clothes and had built and lit a fine fire, which was already warming the Cot.

The clinking of grounded flasks signalled that whistles had been wetted, when Bowdyn, who had been sitting in his Story Chair and gazing broodingly into the fire, turned to look at the assembled village. He smiled, 'Welcome, welcome,' he said. 'When we last met I promised Old Tom ...'

Here he was interrupted by groans whilst Tom looked from side to side with hands spread wide as if to say, What? What!

'... I promised Old Tom,' Bowdyn continued, 'that I would tell the tale of the storyteller from Gewis' time, who passed on the stories of those times that have come down to me and which I tell you here.'

All sat quietly now, listening. 'You will not agree now,' he began, 'for it is a bad time, but I know many stories and from them let me tell you this: there have been many kings, some good, some bad, but a bad king is often better than no king. For a king brings law and order, but when there is no king then the Devil rules.

'The story I will tell you now, comes from the time when Roman rule had withdrawn. There was no king in the land and so the tribes fought each other, for food, for women, for slaves, and Hell spread everywhere in the East beyond the Rhine.

Those who suffer worst in such times are always the children and it is with a child, a very young child that my tale begins.'

And then began a story that will always, to me, show the greatness of the true Gleeman's art. It started with Bowdyn's voice from the shadows and as before his voice seemed to change, but now, when needful, it became that of a young child and then it aged in keeping with the story. By the end, when the child had grown, the voice was manly, strong and yet easy to listen to, for the speaker was a storyteller played by a master spinner of tales.

Thus, as Bowdyn sank back into the shadows the voice of a child emerged.

I am of the Suevi now, but was born of the Langobardi, a tragic race to the south of the Thiatmaresgaho. Twice the Romans destroyed us and our folk now are thinly spread on the land.

Our warlike past and our part in the Suevi League did not protect us from the ravages of our neighbours. I was nine years old when the Chatti killed my family during a raid on our village.

When they came I hid beneath a bench in a dark corner of our home, where my father had thrust me. I saw them spear him as he fought them. I saw them use my mother and then cut her throat like a slaughtered pig, because, one said, she was too old for the slave market. After they had sated their lusts on my sobbing sisters they dragged them, limping and soft-dagger wounded, away into slavery.

I obeyed my father. I lay in the dark and made no sound. My luck was that they didn't burn our hut with me inside it. When I crawled out after they were gone I tried to bury my parents, but they were too heavy for me to drag into the open.

I stayed inside and started to dig a grave. It was very slow and hard; I had a mattock and tried and tried, but I could not do it. Thirst, hunger and weariness overtook me.

There was no food in the village. The looters had taken everything of use or value they could carry: it was only the heavy weight of the solid oak bench beneath which I had hidden that saved my life. All that night I lay awake in the hut with the corpses of my mother and father, until daylight crept in through the broken doorway.

In the morning a small troop of warriors from the hall came past and made a huge pyre on which they burned all the folk of the village, with them my mother and father. They were kindly enough, but said they could not take me with them for they were to join a party to take revenge against the Chatti.

They told me to go through the forest until I came to the hall of the Lord of Luefana; they gave me bread and a water flask, bade me good luck and strode away into the forest on the other side of the blaze, shouldering their spears at the slope.

I gazed shocked and dry-eyed at the blaze for a long while, staring at the blackened bodies as the hair and clothes burned away, wondering at the gaping pits where mouths and eyes had been, as if screaming their protest to the gods. Dazed and numb I was sick inside.

'Oh Mama, Mama,' I wanted to cry, 'why have you gone and left me?' But I sat dumb, and after the bodies fell into ashes and could no longer be seen to be my family, I began to think over what I should do next, for I had no idea what to do other than as I was told. And so I headed for the forest.

I was alone in the world now, entirely alone: I had no uncles, no aunts, all in the village were dead; no mother, no father and no sisters. Can you imagine what it is like to be orphaned at the age of nine years? I had been the darling of my family; the only son; the brightest star in their sky.

They had been my friends and to earn more of their love I learned songs and sang to them. Around the village I heard stories of the sort that idle grownups tell children, of elves and dwarves and giants. I picked them up easily and would recite them. I was good at it: it was a gift. Even my father, who wanted me to help him with working our forestland as a woodcutter and hauler, said I was destined to be a Gleeman.

He himself told me stories of long ago warriors, of Offa on the Island and Amleth of Angeln. I remembered these and very well I spoke them, or so everyone said. But now everyone who said so was gone.

Eventually, I pushed my way through the last of the forest branches and arrived at the hall of Ætheling Wulfmur of Luefana. The gatekeeper greeted me rudely, 'Who are you child, what do you want?'

I told my tale to him and that the warriors of his Chief had sent me hither. Grudgingly he allowed me entry to the hall where the Lord and his fellows sat at board. I told my tale again to the Lord.

'Well,' he said, 'what use are you, what can you do to earn your keep if you want us to feed you? We cannot feed every orphan brat in the countryside, unless they can perform service of some sort.'

'I can sing, Lord,' I said, 'and I can tell stories.'

'By Wothan's hounds,' shouted Wulfmur,' we have an infant Gleeman amongst us. Sing up and tell up for your supper.'

I sang some songs that I knew, about brave and tragic fights. I told the tale of Offa on the Island. At the end, the warriors, more than a little drunk all of them, roared with laughter and approval, calling on the Lord of Luefana.

'Keep the lad,' they shouted.

They pressed bread and meat on me, pig meat I think. I was so hungry it was the most delicious thing I had ever eaten, and when I was full I fell asleep by the fire amidst the raucous sound of the feasters giving their renderings of the songs I had sung them.

Before I slept I think I came out of the shock and numbness in which the day's happenings had left me. There, against the merciful background of the drunken revelry, stuffed full with food, I cried for my family and for myself until from sheer weariness I fell into a sleep haunted by roaring fire and gaping eyes and mouths.

When I woke in the morning it was with the Lord's boot stirring me. He had not, it seemed, slept. I came awake in alarm expecting a blow, but I found that my rough greeting the night before was his try at humour. There in the morning light, with the drink out of him, he was kindly.

He listened again to my tale and then spoke softly. 'Well boy, you have courage. You will stay. When the travelling Gleeman comes with his new rash of tales I will give him a sack of salt to take you under his wing and teach you his arts. He has no learner and I know he searches for one. If he likes you he will teach you a trade and a living.'

His kindness touched me and I started to snivel again. He patted my shoulder and turning away spoke. 'Go to the kitchen and tell them I say they should give you food and drink then put you to work.'

With that he turned and left the room, whilst from the board came the snoring of two of the revellers, asleep with their heads on their arms.

I worked about the kitchen, doing tasks for which my age made me capable, until the Gleeman came by on his travels through the forest. He told news as well as stories and was close with the Lord for all the day of his arrival. The following day the Lord sent for me.

The Gleeman was small, dark-haired, dark-eyed and thin; the lines about his mouth gave him what seemed a permanent scowl. He was sour looking and glanced at me with gloomy disdain. My heart sank, for to be bonded to someone with such a nature did not fill me with cheer, not that there was any cheer in me for a long time; not until the sight of gaping eyes and mouths ceased to haunt my fiery dreams and daylight thoughts.

He regarded me thus for a long moment and then spoke. 'Sing me a song, boy.'

I sang, a sad air, which caused the tears to trickle down my cheek. He waved his hand.

'Enough, enough, what stories do you know?'

I told him of some I could remember, some heroic, some children's stories. He selected one, of a wicked forest elf, and asked me to speak it. I obeyed, although grief nearly overcame me. My sisters had always squealed when I told them this story. They were terrified and delighted when I came to the part where I pushed the wicked elf in the water to drown. I tried to tell it so now, through the grief.

When I was finished, the Gleeman nodded and then commanding me to listen, he started a story of his own. When he came to the end of the tale he ordered me to repeat it back as told. It was an easy task and so I did as he bade me.

When I had finished, to my astonishment his sour face lit up in a smile. It changed his appearance and was like the sun coming out from behind a cloud. I learned to do this later, for it is something all Gleemen must learn: to alter the voice, to alter the stance, to alter the face to suit the story. Of course, some years later once my face was slit, the left side ceased to obey me and I lost this skill, but by then I could put all my feeling and the story's meaning into my voice, and so I survived as the ugliest Gleeman alive.

The Lord had been watching this scene with great interest. Now the Gleeman turned to him.

'Lord, the boy may have some small talent, I will take your salt and try to make something of him, but if he proves impossible I will seek to find something he can do and pass him to a new master.'

At that the Lord nodded and I was sent back to the kitchen to return to work.

That night I slept beside the kitchen fire with orders to feed it and make sure of a red heart for the morning's cooking. Next day, the Gleeman summoned me to join him outside the hall. He was standing beside a mule laden with his goods. 'Have you anything to fetch boy?'

I shook my head. 'I should thank the Lord Wulfmur for his kindness,' I said.

He shook his head in turn. 'He is still sleeping. He will not expect it. Come.' With that he took the bridle and walked on the path into the forest. I followed, although he did not look back and would not have known otherwise.

'My name is Ahreddan Galanson,' he called over his shoulder. 'The first is my given name, the second the name of our guild, Galan, for our knowledge is secret.'

He stopped and turned to face me, his hand on the pommel of the seax at his waist. 'So now you must swear that you would sooner have your throat cut and your belly slit open than tell anyone the secrets I shall teach you. Do you so swear?'

He looked at me with a face so fierce I expected him to leap at me and start tearing lumps of flesh from my throat. I stared at him in fright and then bobbed my head in agreement.

'Good,' he said with a smile. 'What is your name?'

'My true name is Beltic, but my sisters in jest called me "Atilec the Horrible",' I told him.

He thought for a moment and then, 'In future you shall always be called Atilec, it will amuse for a winsome child to be so called. That is our work, boy, to amuse. Your name henceforth is Atilec Galanson.' And with that he carried on his way.

Now, many years later, I believe his renaming of me was his way to separate me from the horrors of the last days. New life, new name; it was my first lesson in Gleemanship, for in some way I felt a different person, free somewhat from my grief, as if that belonged to someone I had left behind. Free from everything but the nightmares of gaping eyes and mouths, of mother's beauty and father's strength turned to horror. That dream has pursued me all my life and still wakes me sweating in the night even now.

The Gleeman's life, wandering from hall to hall on forest trails, was a dangerous one. Twice he defended us and drove off thieves, three times they were too many and we were robbed, although he showed me how to hide our money in a way I shall not disclose and so only the bronze was taken from our purses.

When I had been with him five years, we stopped at the Great hall of the ruler of a township of one thousand people. We stayed for many days, playing to the hall and also in the market square.

The coins we made there and in the alehouses, my master gave to the Master at Arms of the Lord of the place, for him to give me weapons training. Here I discovered an even greater talent than for Gleemanship. I had grown in strength in our wanderings and was naturally quick, but the training that Ahreddan had given me had made me a master of expression.

Think! To be able to read the other fighter's expression and know what he is to do; to be able to put a false expression on and mislead your enemy, what an advantage in any weapon fight.

I had amazed the Master of Arms with my progress, for in no time I was beating young warriors older and stronger than I. I did not understand why either, for I thought everyone did what I did: read and mislead my foe, that is. It was Ahreddan, questioning me after my tenth stick fight without defeat, who realised how I did it. No, he told me, only the most experienced warriors could read their enemy and few had the skill to mislead.

He warned me to keep my secret to myself for to tell it would blunt its edge. Thus was my warrior training money well-spent. As a free man I could carry a sword and so my master bought me one; old, a Roman gladius, but solid, well kept without much rust. We two were now so forbidding none dared rob us. We put to flight any who tried. In the end I believe they came to know us and that we never hurt without reason. They grew to respect us and tolerate our passage without harrying us.

This stage of my life was a very happy one. My fighting skills made me confident, whilst my sorrows and my debt of thanks to Ahreddan stopped me from becoming a strutting fool. I could fight, but I took no pleasure in any hurt I gave out. Thus my nature, confident but kind, drew young women to me and I had many sweethearts in the kitchens of the halls.

The Fates give and the Fates take away. This happy life

seemed as if it would go on forever and then two things happened to change everything. The first was that I found myself led into foolishness by a deceitful woman. Her husband, the Captain of the Lord's Guard, caught me in her bed. He fought me for his honour, in the great hall before a crackling fire, under the eye of the Lord. For once I met a sword fighter more skilful and cunning than I. I parried a thrust that was not there and missed a slash that was. The blade caught my face on the left side and slit it from ear to mouth.

The fight was in the hall of the Lord of Leufana, my old benefactor. He called a halt at first blood and thus saved my life. I would still have bled to death, but for the skill of my master in staunching and stitching the wound. His skill in knitting up the outside was not enough for the inside. Something did not heal and that side of my face never moved again, which is why I am as you see me.

Strangely, this did not stop my fighting. Having only half a face tells little; it was as hard for my foes to read me as before. For my story telling I had to learn to put the story that my face had once told, into the sound of my words. That was hard and took much practice.

The next great change was that after ten years, two years after my injury, my master died one day of a fever. It was very quick, but he was not a young man having more than fifty years. Before he died, beside a spluttering fire I had lit beneath a shelter of branches I had fashioned to keep out the rain, he told me he was pleased with me. That we had been friends, that I was a good Gleeman and could tell a story as well as any he knew, but that most of all, without fault or error I remembered the stories back before the start of time.

He begged me to make new stories, but only of great and

heroic events. He asked that as soon as I was able I would pass the old stories and the new, and the skills to tell them, to a youngster of talent, as he had with me. Once I gave him my oath on all counts he fell into shivering, no matter how I built the fire, and during the night he died.

All the turnings of my life seem to have started before a fire, but at that time I could not bear the thought of his gaping eyes and mouth if I burnt him, so I used my sword and my hands to dig a grave and buried him in the bosom of the Great Mother. After that, however, each turn of the Wheel was before a fire.

So how did I become a wanted murderer? The truth is I do not know what changed in me with my master's death. Perhaps the urge for vengeance was always in me. Even when young the nearness of a Chatti tribesman made me feel sick. Perhaps it was the death of the man who had been a father to me that brought back to me the cruel deaths of my father and mother. Perhaps it was the young women of the halls set me to thinking of the ruined lives of my sisters. In truth, I don't know. But when Ahreddan died I felt sorrow, but also I felt free. He had asked me to learn great stories. I resolved to take my revenge, but not a small revenge. A great one that would make a story fit to last a thousand years: a story fit for my father, mother, sisters and the man who raised me. I resolved to destroy a whole tribe single-handed. Foolish I know, but I was young.

With these thoughts of vengeance I lay in wait for my victims. From the Chatti lands there is a road that leads to the great city. All Chatti slavers and merchants must travel by that road and must stop at the taverns along it. There I knew I could meet them, could join with them as a fellow traveller. As a storyteller I knew they would welcome me, to pass time during the cold nights along the way. I offered my company as a travelling Gleeman. I was willing, I said, to entertain, in exchange for the safety of companions on the road.

The first time was the hardest. I had injured opponents in sporting conflict, but had never set out to kill.

At the Ivy Bush, an ancient tavern by the roadside in Leufana, I took up residence and waited. I told stories to the drinkers and they put money on the board, small stuff, but together it paid for food and drink. After a week of days I thought I had made a mistake, but that night four Chatti merchants came to the inn. They listened to my stories, applauded with the rest. I spoke with them. They were going to Dorestad they said, first to Colonia and then up the river. I asked could I join them and they agreed, provided I told tales to liven their campfire, they said.

'It will be very lively,' I promised them.

And so it was. I set a pattern that pleased me and repeated it over and over with other travellers. We would stop at night, light a fire under the trees. Imagine it: the wind sighing through the treetops, the fire crackling as it grew. The Chatti and I sat around it taking our supper. Then, before we slept, someone would speak.

'Well, storyteller, tell us a tale before we close our eyes.'

'Certainly, I will tell the story of the fires and how I became a Gleeman.'

Then I would tell them of the raid and the fires that burnt my parents, of the fire at the Lord's hall where I wept for my lost family and myself, of the fire burning in the grate the night the cuckold found me in his bed, of the fire by which I buried my master and friend.

Then I pointed to the fire before us as I rose to my feet. 'This is the last fire of the tale, for it is your balefire.'

Before they could grasp my meaning I drew my sword,

jumped the fire and slew them. It worked every time. They carried weapons, but none ever drew them, they could not grasp what was happening while my sword felled them.

After I cut them down, I did as I promised: I hewed great branches, built up the fire to a roaring bonfire and pitched them onto it.

After some time pickings became lean, travellers on that road rare. Stories spread of some ogre, or bandits or evil elves spiriting away travellers. The road earned an evil name and none travelled it except in bands too big for me to tackle.

I shifted my work, from the south road to the north road, out of the Chatti lands. And then, having made my tale, a tale I told at taverns to frighten travellers, all rage went out of me. Still at night I had the dream, but now I did not know whether it was my parents or the murdered travellers that I saw gaping at the gods. And I sickened of the whole thing. Saw that what I did was mad. It came to me that the tribesmen I slaughtered were innocent of crimes against me. Guilt weighed me down; the slaughtered men had wives and were the fathers of children, children like me. And so I turned away from that path and vowed never again to murder.

As if this time of death had never happened, I returned to the life I had led with my master before he died. I carried on from hall to hall as before, but without him it was not the same, I had lost the relish for stories, at least for a while. But man must eat and so I returned to using my sword in contests for money and found it a better living than being a Gleeman, until I met Lothar that is.

It was the first time I had fought an axe man. Oh, I could read him all right. It's just that my parries were useless against the weight of the axe and the strength of the arm behind it. I could have killed him all right, for although he beat me down with ease I could have slipped my seax into him just as easily with my left hand. But I didn't want to, this was not Rome, this was to do with skill and not blood. So I lowered my weapons in surrender and, stupidly, my eyes too, just as his axe took me flat on at the side of my skull where the ear flaps of my helm hang down. He bowled me arse-over-head across the floor and when I woke up he was sitting by my side pressing a cold, wet cloth to my face.

'What are you doing,' I snarled, although my head felt as if his axe had split it in two.

'This will ease the swelling,' he said. 'I did not understand you were yielding.'

Thus it was we became friends. We toured the halls together for a while, until we heard of fortunes to be made in Africa ....

Bowdyn ceased speaking and reappeared from the shadows.

'And so, you see Tom, there were Gleemen in those days. Indeed there were many, for it was only through pedlars and storytellers that news could pass.

'But now we must return to the tale that Gewis tells. You will remember that he had begun to tell Creoda the story of how he came by his hoard. That story is long and will take more than tonight, but we can carry it a little more forward between now and the time for our rest. Are you willing or are you weary?'

The chorus from all was that they wished to hear more. In truth, I think they found the story of Atilec to be a harrowing one and they wished for a more cheerful diversion to take with them to their beds.

Bowdyn smiled. 'Very well then, let us continue.'

He launched back into the tale of Gewis and how he had come by the hoard by which he meant to rescue the folk of the East Holding from starvation.

# Chapter 12

**AD 447**

**Gewis' Tale, Colonia**

'Gewis had related, as you will remember,' said Bowdyn, 'how he had left his home and after many a hungry mile had found himself on a hilltop overlooking Colonia. There we left him and we will now have him carry on the telling from that point.'

With that our Gleeman withdrew from the fire glow and in Gewis' voice continued from where he had left off.

On my side of the river was a series of stone houses in two rows, flanking a road leading to the bridge over the great river, a stone bridge, big and solid beyond all thought. These houses, as I shortly learned, were the barracks of the soldiers guarding the eastern approaches to the city.

On the other end of the bridge there seemed to be an island and there were other stone houses. These, as I found out at some small cost, were where the tax gatherers lived and worked, collecting taxes from all goods brought to the town for sale.

Past these buildings there stood the city wall and the gate

into the city itself, which was amazing beyond all belief. It was made up of street after street of stone dwellings laid out in squares. Some of them were rows of houses where the folk of the town lived, or shops where merchants traded. Others were huge, larger than I had ever seen, so big that Baeldaeg's hall would fit inside many times over. Most of these stood around what I later learned to call the 'Forum', which was a meeting place for the folk as well as being the main market. These great buildings were those of the city rulers. I was to discover similarly large houses clustered around hot springs and enclosing great baths. Here the strong and the wealthy gathered to soak in hot water and gossip. At that time I thought this a very strange habit.

From my vantage point, I could see the city had two main roads: one ran its length between the North and South Gates dividing the Forum in two; the other crossed it, passing through the centre of the city and running between the East and West Gates.

Having looked for long enough to be sure to remember the main layout of the city, I started downward towards the road leading to the river crossing. When I was but five hundred paces from the fort that guarded the bridge, I could see that it was set behind a barrier manned by a company of soldiers. I examined the look of my clothes. My shoes and gaiters were covered with mud from the many rivers, streams and marshes I had forded, but my breeches had dried and I brushed the mud off as well as I could. I straightened my tunic, pulled my seax to where it was in plain view, re-rolled my cloak and hung it round my neck and ensured my spear and shield were in plain display on my back. My money purse, empty food sack and firelighter sack, I hung from my belt at the back. As respectable and unlike a Wolf-Head or vagrant as I could make myself, I approached the guard.

The officer in charge looked me up and down. His company of soldiers carried on talking indifferently amongst themselves. 'Slave or Freeman?' he asked. I breathed a sigh of relief; he was a Frank and spoke a heavily accented language I could understand.

'Freeman,' I said.

'Going where?' he asked.

'Across the river, somewhere to eat and then to find some Lord to employ me,' I said.

He looked at me, taking in my beardless chin. 'Little young for that aren't you?'

I paused and thought carefully, this was a question that many folk might put to me. 'I'm trained,' I indicated my spear, 'and I'm blooded. The Wolf's Head who slaked my spear's thirst did not ask my age.'

He considered for a while. 'Very well, keep out of trouble, we hang thieves and crucify killers here.' He swung the barrier to one side. 'Oh, and if you come back through the Colonia, make sure you come back with a Lord. There are armed slaves running loose in Gaul; if you are mistaken for one, the Praetor will burn you.'

I walked through the fort, between the barrack buildings and onto the bridge. The river was wide and the bridge longer than I could ever have imagined. At the other end there was another barrier, with a further company of soldiers and a civilian official of some sort in authority. He approached me as I stopped in front of the barrier.

'Welcome, traveller. What goods do you bring to Colonia?'

'Only myself, sir,' I said.

'Ah, but you also bring weapons, these can be sold in the market place; you must pay the Emperor taxes on the value.'

I protested, 'But these are my personal weapons, sir. I cannot sell them, I am a warrior for hire and without them I am nothing.'

'Even so, you must pay taxes on them before you may enter Colonia. Have you any money?'

I produced my purse with its few coins.

He looked in it and pulled a face. 'Is this all you have?' I nodded. He took one of the five brass coins left in the purse and threw it into a box of money on the table then made an entry on a wax pad.

He looked up. 'Well, what are you waiting for? On your way, and make sure you leave town before your purse is empty. We gaol vagrants in Colonia.'

I bowed slightly and walked away briskly, fearful that he would call me back for a search. I was aware of the weight of the gold and silver arm rings that my father had given me, hidden in a small leather sack beneath my tunic; the gold to celebrate my warrior training, the silver to reward my first kill. Warriors make rings from captured weapons, but my Wolf's-Head had only a stone-tipped spear and a stone axe in his belt and so my father made my loss good.

I relaxed as I walked up to the entrance to the great market without a challenge from behind. I looked in my mind at the town layout, fixed in memory from my lookout on the edge of the forest, and turned left onto the main street running north to south. Here were many merchants with stalls or shops set back from the road and let into the great building itself. Turning right, up the outside of the great market square, I could smell food cooking. My mouth started to water and my stomach hurt from the reminder of just how hungry I was. I walked across the south entrance to the market and kept on until I reached the end of the buildings on my right. I stopped at the next crossroads and looked left and right. To my left was another great building with a line of archways running along the west side of the road.

Sniffing the air, I let my nose lead me to the appetising smell of hot food. I turned left and crossed the road to find myself outside a shop, or as I learned later, a tavern. An ivy bush hung from a bracket above the doorway and the smell of roasting meat from within made my head swim.

As soon as I entered I saw fowl legs and fruit laid out on a wide bench. Sausage was turning on a spit dripping fat, flaring up and sizzling in the fire. I reached for my money and offered one brass coin for a length of sausage. The servant behind the bench pushed the sausage, a piece of bread and a flask, which he filled with ale, towards me and held up two fingers. I fished another coin from my purse, handed it over and took my food and drink to a board in a corner by the entrance. There, sitting on a stool against the wall so that I could see into the room, I stuffed food into my mouth like some wild beast. When much of the bread and sausage was gone, I washed it down with a gulp or two of ale and then paused to look around me before I finished my feast.

The room was small with space for no more than four tables, with a bench for two on each side. Two tables were empty. The other was next to me, on the opposite side of the entrance. At it sat two striking men bent over a board with coloured disks. These they moved after they each threw three dice in turns. I say striking, for one was ugly with a scowling face, his long dark hair gathered up to the left side of his head and tied in the warrior knot above his shaven jaw. Running from his ear to the corner of his mouth was a deep scar. His spear was leant against the wall and an unmarked shield rested under it.

The other, bearded and fair-haired, was one of the largest men I had ever seen. His legs were too long to fold under the table and so stretched out towards the entrance. He was dressed in a tunic and breeches, his calves cloth bound, but the tunic was fringed with rich tablet edges, putting his status above that of mere freeman. He also had a spear and shield, and an iron helm sat on the floor next to a lengthy leather sack.

With a laugh the ugly one read the throw of the dice and moved the last of his pieces from the board. The big man scowled. He pushed some brass coins across the table. The ugly one swept them up and dropped them into a purse he sheltered under his strong right hand.

The unlovely face turned in my direction, considering and judging me; even I could see that. 'Well lad,' he said, 'do you fancy your luck at Tabula.' He indicated the board.

'Thank you, sir,' I said, 'but I do not know the game.'

'I can teach you,' he said quickly.

'And I have no money, none to lose anyway, one more meal and I must leave Colonia or it's gaol for me.'

'Ah,' he said, 'a pity, there is no answer to that.'

'Honestly spoken,' said the giant. 'Think yourself lucky or this rogue would have you without an as to your name.'

I puzzled over this. 'How so, sir, I certainly should not bet my arse?'

Both men burst out laughing hugely. 'We should not want it, lad,' said the ill favoured one. 'I see your spear and will not insult you, but you should know that an as is a very old and lowly coin, no longer to be found. Do you not know Roman money?'

'I am from the North, sir. We use little money in our Holding. What I have is battle won. I hold it out and a good man takes what is needed to pay the price.'

The two warriors, for it was plain that such they were, exchanged glances.

'Well,' said the ugly one, 'come, let me show you something, for good men are rare and those who would cheat you many.'

He tipped the purse, which had lain under his hand, onto the table. I drew near and sat as he pushed a brass coin towards me.

'This bronze is a follis, there are fifteen of these to a miliarense.'

I blushed at my ignorant country stupidity, no wonder these men of the world had laughed at me. I felt the colour rise into my cheeks and sank my chin into my hands in an attempt to cover it as I recognized the brass coins I had in my store.

He pushed a silver coin forward. 'This is a milia and if I had a gold solidus, which I don't, there would be twelve of these to one of those. Will you remember that?'

I nodded and wondered how to recover my pride. I made to rise and return to my table, the ugly man touched my arm lightly to indicate I should stay.

'I am Atilec,' he said, 'and this mighty warrior is Lothar. I,' and he indicated his hair knot, 'am a Suevi and my big friend is a Goth, a subject of King Theoderic.' He paused and both of them beheld me steadily.

'My name is Gewis, I am from Thiatmaresgaho, of the Ingwines of the Seaxsen Guild.' I waited to hear if they had had their fill of my story.

'Can you tell us why you are here and where you are going?' said Lothar.

I nodded. 'I am trained and blooded and seek a warband I can join for battle, and in peace a hearth to sit by in service to a generous Lord.' I had gone over this reply many times in my head.

'We also,' said Atilec. 'Where do you seek such work?'

I blushed again, 'I don't know,' I owned.

'If you can fight you could come with us, the countryside is dangerous, the more in the company the better. We are going to join the Vandals in Africa. There is much loot to be had if you don't mind pulling an oar; and the weather is warm.'

Said Lothar, 'What horse have you?'

I had to admit I had no horse.

'Pity,' said Atilec, 'the way is long, very, very long. No horse and no money to buy one, no money for food on the road. I am afraid my big friend spoke without thought. You cannot join us.'

My head spun. Africa, a name heard only in legend. Africa, loot, sea raiding. I sat quietly thinking, trying to judge the trustworthiness of these strangers. Certainly if they tried to rob me they would succeed. I made up my mind.

'I would like to join you. How much would a horse cost?'

'Far more than you have my young friend, far more than I have, at least four solidi for a nag, eight for a war horse.'

I reached inside my tunic and pulled out the sack hanging by its thong around my neck. I undid the drawstring and pulled out the gold arm ring my father had given me when I became a trained warrior. I placed it on the table.

'Will that buy me a horse?' I asked.

Atilec and Lothar both sat motionless staring at it. Then Atilec reached out and picked up the ring, weighing it in his hand. He pulled out a small eating knife and drew the tip across the metal and looked at the groove he had made. He looked up at me and pushed the band hastily back across the table.

'Put it away. Now!' he said, looking quickly around the

room. It was still empty and the servant at the counter was busying himself with something behind the table out of sight.

'Oh yes,' said Atilec, eyeing me as I quickly replaced the ring in my sack. 'That will buy you a string of horses with saddles and gilded reins. Where did you get it?'

I explained.

'Your father must be very rich or a great warrior. We will go with you to the Forum to help you buy a horse and make sure no one cheats you.'

He tied his money purse to his belt and pushed his bench back from the board. 'You are too trusting, young sir, many men such as we would slit your throat and rob you of such a treasure, you are lucky we are not such.'

I gulped the last of my ale and we all rose together. The servant wished us good fortune and to come again and we made our way out into the early summer afternoon.

My companions turned left and walked past the head of the street by which I had come. Halfway along the great building that lay to our east, they crossed the road and passed though an entrance into a courtyard. It lay between that building and another great curved structure, which enclosed the west end of the great market place itself. Here it was that the bankers and moneychangers set up their stalls. A company of soldiers guarded the entrance. More patrolled the spaces between the stalls. They were there to protect the gold and money, of which there was much on display.

My friends stopped in front of a stall, behind which was a small, dusky-skinned man wearing a long tunic colourfully embroidered with unfamiliar designs. On his head was a scarf of similar colourful material, wrapped round and tied in a knot at the back. At our approach he rose to his feet, smiling.

'Well my friends,' he said. 'Let me guess. You have won

rich jewels at Tabula from a prince of the Parthians and you wish to change them for money?'

'This is Harith,' said Atilec to me. 'He is foolish enough to hire us to guard him on his way from the Forum to his home. He is a rogue and he would cheat you in a heartbeat, but he knows we will slit his throat if he does.'

Harith looked me up and down. 'What are you doing with these wild men? They will rob you. They would rob me if I did not pay them ten times what they are worth.'

'He is joining us wayfaring to Africa, to rob and enslave your rich relatives,' said Atilec.

'So, he needs a horse,' said Lothar, 'and would change gold into cash and you will deal fair with him or deal with us.'

Harith held out his hand. 'Horses are not cheap; your gold will need to be heavy.'

I hesitated. My father's gift was my most treasured possession. To think of selling it was one thing, to do so another. I imagined the wrench: it would be almost like selling my father into bondage to sell the band he had given me in pride. But gold was only gold, just a thing, not flesh and blood. Reaching a decision I pulled it out of my sack and placed it into the hands of the moneychanger.

His eyes widened in surprise as he felt the weight of it in his hand. He looked it over carefully then took a small knife of his own and made a deep cut inside, opposite the one made earlier by Atilec. He touched the cut with his tongue; reaching under the table he brought out a small glass bottle from which he tipped a drop of some liquid onto my band watching the progress of the drop with great care, and then, satisfied, he wiped the band on a filthy cloth and laid it on a set of scales. He reached under his counter and pulled out a small strongbox from which he started to take gold coins, solidi I guessed.

One by one he placed them on the scales in the opposite pan to the one in which my father's gift ring rested. I felt a great pang of regret seeing it there abandoned and almost snatched it back, but I could not face returning to the Holding. The thought of Elwine and Bana together still made me feel sick.

When the count reached thirty-five the two pans balanced. Harith looked at me and removed five from the pan filled with gold coins.

'This is my fee, you understand?'

I looked at Atilec, who nodded. The moneychanger scooped up the remaining thirty and pushed them towards me.

'Give him some small change, man. He cannot be bringing out gold to pay for his daily bread,' said Atilec.

The moneychanger took back nine solidi and then counted out one hundred milia from his box, shrugging as he did so.

'Eight milia I keep, for my money changing fee you understand.'

It was only then, looking at the pile of silver, that I realised what a great treasure the band had been. I felt a sorrowful love for my father and regret at what felt like betrayal. I knew my father well enough to know that given the facts of my plight he would be the first to tell me to sell the band, and that gave me comfort. I gathered up the coins and poured them into the calfskin bag that hung round my neck on its strong leather thong, concealed under my tunic.

I kept back ten of the solidi for horse-trading and ten milia for food and drink and placed these in my money purse hung from my belt. I thanked the moneychanger for his honest dealing.

He smiled. 'Thank your gods that you have two such wild

rogues with you with such sharp knives. And thank your gods that in a wicked city you have fallen in with two of the few honest men.' Harith waved a hand in dismissal and then tidied his counter and placed the box back underneath. As we left he called, 'I will see you tonight?'

'Tonight is the last, tomorrow we set out so you must find other guards,' said Atilec.

Harith waved to show that he had heard as we walked off. I was aware of and somewhat weighed down by the risks and responsibilities of my unexpected wealth as we passed out through the archway by which we had entered.

We crossed the road and continued west onto a very wide stretch of cobbled roadway. This was the street of the horse mongers and along it stretched their stables. In front of them a series of posts were sunk in the ground, a horse hitched to each one. At the foot of every post was a small manger at which the horses fed and a trough at which they drank. It all seemed very well arranged.

'So, what do you know of horseflesh?' asked Atilec.

'Nothing,' I confessed, eyeing the clattering horses, 'they all look good to me.'

He laughed, 'You speak truly of your knowledge, for to my eye they are a sickly lot. But please, leave this to Lothar, for all Goths are born on horseback.'

I nodded. 'Thank you, will you choose and bargain for me, Lothar?'

He smiled in agreement. 'But know that as usual, Atilec lies, although he would say he weaves a story. I am Goth but I was not born on horseback. Rather, I was born on a river and know more of all things that float than walk on four legs. Where there is a little seed of truth in his lie is that I did serve Rome as a horse soldier and so know more of the brutes than you seem to.'

He stepped up to the line of beasts and strode along them, first past the head end and then back past the rump end, dodging the piles of dung. Without hesitation he chose a beast of astonishing ugliness with a large knobbly head and small shaggy body.

The horse monger stood at his shoulder. 'How can I help you noble sir? I have a stallion that will carry one of even your size into battle and fight all day.'

'How much for this one,' said Lothar pointing at the ugly beast.

'Well,' said the monger, 'that is a fine, small stallion, one of the Hunnic breed, trained in battle, fearless against a shield-wall, strong and tireless, but a little small I think for you, sir.'

'How much?' said Lothar leaning close to the monger and looking down on him.

'For that fine stallion, eight solidi,' said the dealer.

'You jest surely? It is not young and we have far to go. A horse that dies of old age along the way is of no use, but I would take the chance for the right price.'

He stepped forward and looked at the mouth. 'These are the teeth of old age,' he said, 'it is also ugly beyond belief. Others will laugh at anyone who rides such a beast. No woman would ride it. It is too small for most men, and any small man will look for a horse of beauty to add to his lustre. I will offer you four solidi.'

'Do I look as if some know-nothing Goth, who doesn't know a nag's arse from its head, can swindle me out of the worth of a good horse...'

He faltered, for Lothar's face had reddened and he locked gazes with the man, his fist clenching and rising to chest height. I thought for a moment he was about to strike him to the ground. The horse monger clearly thought so too, for his gaze darted about looking for help. Seeing none, he spread his hands as if to say, Sorry, but this is business.

Atilec touched Lothar on the arm in warning. The giant relaxed his fist and smiled. I could see that whatever wild passion had passed through him had drained away.

The horse monger wrung his hands. 'Sir, you seek to ruin me and you smear this noble beast. Not a milia less than six solidi.'

'Very well,' said Lothar, turning to me. 'Give this rogue five solidi for both the beast and its Hunnish saddle and we will take this ugly dwarf creature off his hands.'

I reached into my money purse and counted out five of the ten solidi I had placed in there. I held them out to the horse monger. He looked at them, then at the horse and then, with a sigh and a grimace, he nodded and turning, walked away. Lothar and Atilec set off after him and I, mystified, followed.

'Where are we going?' I asked.

'We must go to the Market Praetor to get him to witness the sale so you may not be accused of stealing the beast.' said Lothar.

When the procedure was completed, the tax paid by the dealer and the bill thrust into my sack, we returned to claim my horse. The dealer swung the saddle onto its back and finally he grinned. 'Good luck to you all,' he said. 'This horse will never let you down. It would break my heart to sell him at such a price had he not been battle won and bought for a song.'

Lothar grinned back. 'And I would not have paid such a price did I not know that for toughness he is worth twice as much.'

We all waved good-naturedly and leading my ugly mount, I followed my two companions to the stables where they had stabled their horses. I paid the keeper and stable ward two folles for a night's lodging for the horse.

'You can share our room for tonight,' said Atilec, 'you will need to pay the innkeeper four folles, but it's cheap at the price, the straw is clean and the rats not too troublesome.'

Thus I found myself just days away from my home for the first time, with money in my purse and lying on the floor of a small room shared with two strangers, either of whom could break my back with a twitch of a finger.

It is small wonder that I did not sleep easy at first. The room was small. The sleeping pads were stuffed with clean straw and not crawling with fleas or lice, but the room smelled of stale beer and farts, which over the years had soaked into the walls and floor. My nose was used to worse smells and worse there were from the slop pale in the corner. My two new companions had spent some time before sleep swigging flasks of the inn's good beer and now used the pail in good measure. Daily emptied perhaps, but never scrubbed, it stunk.

I had drunk too, but only sparingly for I was now fearful of the company in which I found myself, but when they rose to take their rest I went with them. To sit in the tavern all night when I had paid for a bed seemed foolish.

I lay fully dressed on my pad, my cloak rolled as a pillow, my hand beneath it and my fingers clenched around the hilt of my seax. I lay there for a long time listening for the slightest movement of my new friends. There was little. They lay on their pads, each against its own wall. Rolling themselves in their cloaks, in no time they shook the night with their snores. I lay for half the night listening and wondering whether I could trust these men not to kill and rob me now that they knew I had gold.

I made lists in my mind. Could they kill me? I had little

doubt of that. Lothar was twice my size, a blond-haired Goth, but not fat, all solid muscle and strength. His manner was calm and kindly, his beard and moustache cut and combed, his hair brought back tidily in a plait; not at all a wild man in appearance. But I had seen the flash of anger at the horse trader, quickly controlled. So, a man quick to anger, but one whom life had taught to control that anger, to force it back down into the depths from which it had arisen. That Atilec had had to remind him, to caution him, told me that Lothar was a dangerous man and that Atilec watched him and his temper with care.

What if he demanded my gold and I refused him, for I must? Would his temper flare, would he kill me in a fit of rage? My grasp on my seax tightened.

What of Atilec the ill-favoured? He was thin-faced and bony-skulled, a scar running from his left ear nearly to his lips. The wound had left him with a mouth that curved down slackly on the left hand side and hung without moving. To balance this he did not move the right side, so his face was always set in a scowl. Later I could see why, for when he did laugh the right side curved upwards and he looked lopsided and worse. Never a good-looking man, the wound to his face had made him fearsome. But his eyes were kindly. I felt that his interest in me was good-natured. Perhaps someone once helped him. Perhaps he wished to perform the same service.

But a Goth, a Suebi? These were the enemies of my blood. How many such raiders had we killed; how many folk of the East Holding had fallen to their spears?

Anyway, I thought, if they wanted to kill me they could easily do so now. Lothar could hold me down, and Atilec cut my throat. That they had not already done so seemed hopeful.

And then I remembered the gate guard's words: 'We

crucify killers here.'

Perhaps buying my horse was a trick. Once clear of the city they could kill me, steal my money and my horse, and sell the horse at the next town along the road.

I thought then about the moneychanger, Harith. A man in his position would need to be very careful; he hired these men as guards, he called them honest. If he were not a very careful man he would not have lived so long and prospered. So could I take heart from his trust in his guards, or was he part of a game to entrap me?

My thoughts went round and round in circles and, with the resolve to take care and be alert eventually I fell fast asleep.

The next morning I awoke still in possession of both my life and my gold. We rose. Atilec saw my seax lying by my rolled up cloak and gave the fearsome smile that would make a blind man shudder.

'You can never be too careful,' he said. 'Now let us breakfast.'

We did so and then purchased food and drink for our wayfaring before setting off through the West Gate of Colonia.

As we rode through the gate and entered into Gaul I looked back, still amazed at the might and grandeur of the city. I did not know that the Three Sisters were already threading dark strands into the bright weave of Colonia and that within four years, the smoke and flames of that pillaged, burning place would be seen for twenty miles as hordes of victorious Huns poured empty-handed over the bridge into the city, and then drove out with carts and horses loaded down with loot and slaves, the fruits and hapless survivors of theft, rape and wanton destruction.

And the Huns, did they know what the Wyrd Sisters were weaving into the pattern? Could they even imagine their own headlong rush to destruction in the fields of Chalons? Even in Carthage we heard rumour of that great bloodletting. But that was later.

Bowdyn fell silent and held up a hand towards his listeners. 'Here we must pause, for much happens at the beginning of this journey that changes Gewis from callow youth and brings him nearer to the man he will become. Now is not the time to consider this for the hour is late and we must sleep, for there is work tomorrow. I will tell more, if the weather is good, come Saturday.'

There was silence for a moment and then a chorus of agreement, for the middle of the night was now approaching and the listeners suddenly felt tired and ready for their rest. Now, freed from the storyteller's spell, they remembered that the day was Wednesday and that the following day was Thursday and a day of work, not Sunday, a day of rest, as was usual after a storytelling.

With the usual clatter and chorus of thanks they rose and quickly departed for their own firesides and well-earned bed rest.

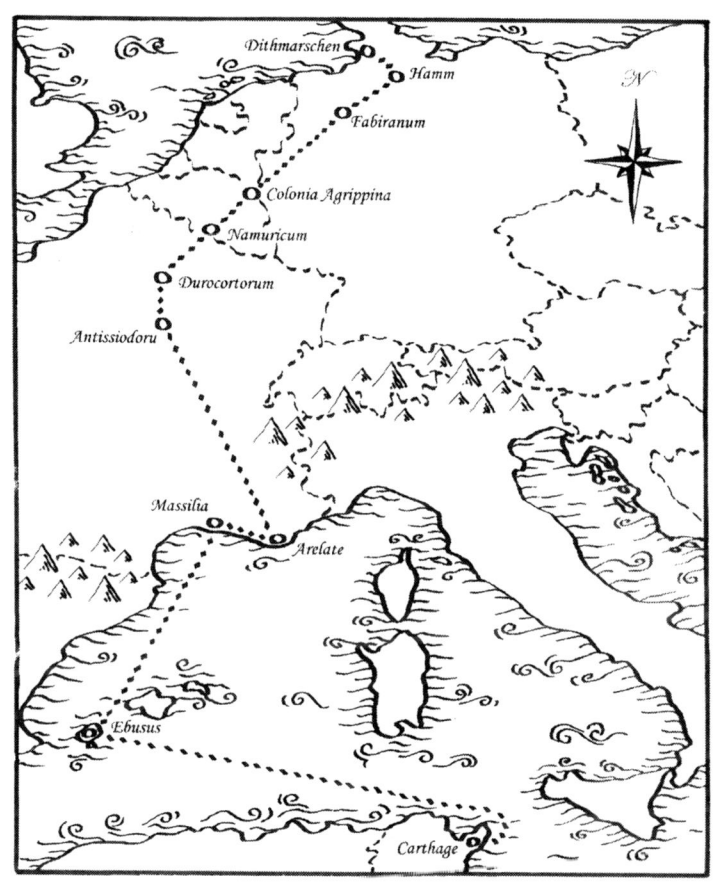

**Gewis' Tale – The Road to Africa**

# Chapter 13

**AD 447**

**Gewis' Tale, The Bagaudae**

Saturday dawned calm. It was a fine, crisp, autumn day. It was the sort of blue sky, cold air day that heralds winter but without any of its discomforts. Fires lit in the houses filled the air with the smell of wood smoke.

As the sun set and darkness set in we lit the fire in the Cold-Cot. By the time the growing audience arrived there was light aplenty and the inside was growing pleasantly warm. They sat themselves on their stools and benches with the usual clatter and buzz of chatter and there was a clinking of bottles and a quaffing of whistle wetters before the hungrier ones opened their wallets to start on their suppers.

As my mother and father entered and sat in their usual places they were greeted by all and then the noise died away in anticipation of the start of the night's entertainment as Bowdyn entered and sat in the Story Chair by the fire. He smiled at the throng and his eyes took in the room, noting, I suspect, that the numbers continued to grow.

'Welcome to all on this fine autumn evening. I am sure you remember that our story ended as Gewis and his new found companions were passing the gates of the city of Colonia and starting out on their long journey to Africa. You will also remember that Gewis, burdened by much money from the sale of his gold warrior band is fearful that his companions might murder and rob him. We will continue from there with Gewis telling the tale.'

Without more ado, Bowdyn again worked his magic - which still I could not fathom - and merged with the shadows as from out of them came the voice of Gewis.

Outside the gate, Lothar stopped and dismounted. We sat our horses, watching, I for my part with care, ready to make off as fast as my horse would carry me - if I did not fall off - but also I watched with curiosity.

He took down the great clanking leather sack and reached inside, pulling out a wide leather belt that he knotted tight about his waist, he then brought out a thick shoulder belt, which he threw over his right shoulder and fastened back and front to the belt. Then out came two small throwing axes, which he pushed into loops in the front of the shoulder belt. Finally, he retrieved a great bearded war axe. This he pushed into a loop fixed to the back of the shoulder belt so that it lay snugly against his back with its blade just behind his head. To protect his skull he wore a nose-guarded iron helm, dark grey with just a trace of rust at the seams.

When his weapons were secured he walked to look up at me and before I could move or even protest he seized my right leg and heaved, tipping me off my horse. The sky spun as I fell and my shoulders hit the ground so heavily that the wind was forced out of me and for a moment I could not draw breath. Before I could recover he rounded my horse, placed his foot on me and pressed me into the earth.

Atilec, who had dismounted and drawn his sword while I was tumbling through the air, loomed over me and held the blade to my throat. I cursed my foolishness for putting myself in the power of these two killers. I prepared to die, regretting that I had ever left my home, sold my father's gift, placed myself at risk so foolishly.

Atilec, pressing his sword tip like a mother's kiss against my throat so that I dared not move, began to laugh. From his twisted face the expression and sound was almost more frightening than the closeness of my death. And then Lothar, still with his foot on my chest, began to rumble and I saw that he too laughed.

'Now we can kill you and take your gold,' said Atilec, 'do you agree?'

I nodded my head, eyes staring.

'But you see, young Gewis, we are warriors not robbers and we are insulted by your fear and your caution. We do not wish to journey to Africa with a fellow warrior who always peers over his shoulder at us. If we journey together we must have trust, for if we must fight we must trust you and you must trust us. Do you understand?'

I nodded, 'I do.'

Lothar took his foot from me and Atilec, sheathing his sword, held out his hand to me. Shamefaced I grasped it and he pulled me to my feet. Without another word they mounted their horses and I, aching from head to foot, followed suit.

We rode off led by Lothar, with that great war-axe bouncing to his horse's gait. The way to Africa, he said, was south. First we must cross the Icauna at Antissiodorum. From there we would find the Via Agrippa, which led south all the way to Arelate. There, if we were lucky, we could take passage on a trading ship to Ebusus. This would depend on how things stood between Tolosa of the Goths and Saldae of the Vandals. If they were normal then a trading ship from Arelate or Massalia would be well. If not then there were always smugglers who would ship from anywhere to anywhere if the pay covered the risk.

'Anyway,' said Lothar, 'even if Tolosa is at war with Saldae and Carthage, men must still have salt. There will be salt Shipments from Ebusus and wine and grain back, I am sure.' He grinned, 'Once we get to Ebusus we come under the care of great King Gaiseric and getting to Carthage will be child's play if you like to row.' He made it sound so easy, as if the Via Agrippa was just around the next rise of ground.

After the fright of that first day, no further move was made to rob or kill me and I decided that I would trust them as they demanded. From that point on I slept easy - as easy as the wet weather would allow.

After ten days of hard riding we still had not come to this wonderful roadway to the south. First we had ridden west, to keep to the low ground, he said. We rode ever westward, passing north of a city that Lothar called Namuricum. We crossed a rain-swollen river by the bridge at Mosae Trajectum and finally, at a great city called Durocortorum, we turned south. Here we headed through gentle hilly vineyards skirting higher ground to the west. Although it was early in the year, great bunches of small, tart grapes swelled our food supplies.

By now the aches and the chafing of riding had lessened. I had somehow avoided falling off of my own accord and my hurts from being pitched off by Lothar had eased, so I was starting to feel more comfortable on horseback. Lothar told me that the Hunnish riding cups attached to my saddle had helped with this. To my surprise, he also told me they were not common; the Roman cavalry rode without them, he said, holding place by the pressure of their knees alone. He and Atilec both rode in this fashion. Not being a horseman ever before, I had paid no mind to their manner of riding. When I tried it I bounced like a sack of bones! I blessed the monger for throwing in the Hunnic saddle with my Hunnic horse.

We rode south for four days looking for the bridge over the Icauna. On the fifth day we sighted the towers of Antissiodorum and crossing the bridge, passed the guard and trotted through the city, stopping only to buy more food.

Antissiodorum was given over to the worship of the Nailed God and had a large Christian temple built of stone. I for one was glad to leave. Although no one bothered us, I felt that in some way my presence there might earn the disfavour of my own gods.

We rode south on the Via Agrippa and very easy going it was too. The roadway was perhaps ten foot-lengths wide, paved with stones, with wide ruts where wagons had worn through over very many years. The Wyrd Sisters had brought me to this roadway and from this place, at this time, fate directed my steps in ways of horror that changed the pathways of my life and my regard for myself forever.

As we rode, a great column of horsemen came up behind us. They shouted at us to clear the way and then cantered past. We turned off the road and stood to one side watching. First there were at least one hundred bowmen, pointed out by Atilec as Alans. Following them, perhaps twenty to thirty mounted spearmen, some Suevi like Atilec, others Goth, like Lothar, and even some who might have been of the Anglekin. As they passed, a horseman, who from his dress and the sword that hung at his side I took to be an officer or some kind of chieftain or leader, reined in and crossed over to where we waited.

'Warriors looking for work?' he asked in the Frankish

tongue.

'Maybe,' said Atilec, 'and maybe we are couriers for Great King Theodoric. Why do you ask?'

'I have work if you want it; easy work for a practiced hand. Ride with me and I will tell you. We have plenty of bowmen and cavalry, but we lack spearmen who can break a war-hedge if need be.'

As we rode he explained that much of the control and taxation of the countryside had fallen to the great local landowners. They had taken over the powers, which in the past were the mandate of the tax gatherers of Rome itself. Great Aetius, the 'Ruler of the Military' in Gaul, supported these patricians in this.

Enraged by taxes and injustice the free peasants had risen in revolt and been crushed a number of times in the last hundred years. There was now another outbreak, guided it was said, by a healer, but the rebels had no army only local bands of ill-disciplined, ill-armed fighters. We warriors were to fight for one of the great landowner tyrants, he told us, with the approval of Lord Aetius. The townsfolk within his dominion were siding with the revolt. So he had decided to make a grim example of the rebels to discourage the town from such foolish disloyalty.

'The pay for a spearman,' he said, 'is four times the normal legionary pay of one milia each day or part day. Sign up now and already there will be four milia in each of your purses.'

He looked at us. 'Well?'

With some reluctance, I thought, both Atilec and Lothar nodded and so I followed them.

'We're your men,' said Atilec, 'but only for the money. I've no great stomach for the slaughter of peasants. I'm a warrior not a Wolf's Head.'

The officer laughed. 'Fairly said, there's no honour in this and you would not make a battle ring from it, but the money is good, a dead man is a dead man whether warrior or peasant and there is no siege work to be done here so the work is tolerably safe.'

He took a wax tablet and wooden scribe from a satchel hanging at his pommel and stopped his horse, speaking our names as he wrote them down: 'Atilec, Suevi, spearman; Lothar, Goth, spearman; Gewis, Ingwine, spearman.'

He added the date and read it to us then put the tablet and scribe away. 'If you fall,' he said, 'your pay will be shared amongst the rest, that's true for everyone, so either you won't care or you will surely get more than the minimum four milias per day, agreed?'

We all nodded.

'I command the spearmen,' he said. 'I am Aster, a Gaul and Roman, schooled in letters and number and the Frankish tongue. I am a veteran commander of ten and am now overseer for Flavius Claudius Pulcher.'

He paused, brow wrinkled, thinking, before he continued, 'It is not likely you will meet him, but always stay clear of him. Pulcher is a mad dog, but very influential and a strong supporter of General Aetius. He has taken on himself the office locally of Magister Officiorum and therefore, with the General's permission, has command of the Limitannei.'

He paused and looked directly at us. 'You, however, will obey me in all particulars. Until we pay you off, you are under legionary discipline. Is that clearly understood?'

We all nodded, but I had no idea what legionary discipline meant other than to obey Aster. He waved us on and we cantered to join the end of the column; me awkwardly, for at that time I was still no horseman. Aster galloped past and returned to his position at the head of the spearmen.

We had not ridden for more than the time it takes to eat a meal when one of the scouts rode up and spoke with Aster, pointing in the direction in which we rode. The spearmen were commanded to stop and dismount. We and the leaders of the Alan cavalry gathered around Aster, who then explained the situation and what we must do.

'The rebels are drawn up ahead in a position blocking the way to the estate of our employer. It is our task to destroy them. They are many more than we, about two hundred in all. You, the spearmen, will form a shield-wall three deep but only ten across and will advance against their centre.

'Their shield-wall on the left is guarded by woodland; on their right there is an incline too steep for the horses. The cavalry will divide into two to protect the flanks of our spearmen. The bowmen will keep the rebels behind their shields and will advance if they attempt to turn your flanks. I doubt they will do that for they would then expose their own flank to the horsemen.

'The task of our spearmen is to break through their shield-wall. This should be easy for they are not trained warriors; their shield-wall is loose and will not close up quickly to fill the gaps you will create. They are poorly armed and when the front line is cut down the rear line will run; then the cavalry will pursue and kill. Is that all clear?'

We muttered our agreement.

Aster pointed at Lothar. 'You will take centre front with the shield breaker,' he pointed at the great bearded axe, 'choose your own flankers.' He then indicated another seven men in succession, 'All of you get into the front line.' He pointed at more, 'You in the second line and everyone else in the rear rank. Remember, if a man falls, close the line smartly. The man behind must step forward into the gap, and so on for the line behind him. Everyone understand?'

Again we muttered our agreement.

'Very well, you have all done this before. Let's go.'

We loosed our spears and gripped our shields and followed him.

Atilec edged up to me. 'I don't know how many times you have done this before, but we will be flanking Lothar, you on his left and I on his right. We will cover him with our shields; he will hang his on his chest and wield the axe with two hands. The beard hanging down from his axe is to hook the enemy shield, when he hooks it he will pull that shield down. Stab at the face and throat of the enemy with your spear and keep your shield high to your left. I will stab at the belly, these men will not be armoured. When our foe falls we must try to push through the gap and thrust at the men on either side, you on the left, me on the right. Lothar will push through the gap and will start to hack at the rear of the front line shield-wall. Once we make the gap we will all push through and work left and right trying to clear space for the cavalry. Once they are through the fight is over.'

I nodded to show I understood, my palms sweating.

We soon came in sight of our enemy. That seems a strange word now, looking back on it, our enmity having been bought for four milia a day or part thereof. These were strangers who had done us no harm; who threatened us in no way and whose lives we were determined to end for such a small price. Truly, when hatred is bought for small silver the world is a dangerous place with little to depend on.

Anyway, when our enemy came in sight all was as Aster said. Lothar pointed to the woods, I could see forms moving there. My guts clenched. I feared that Aster led us into an ambush.

'They will fight,' said Lothar. 'See, the women and children are in the woods.'

I could now see he was correct. What I had thought in my nervousness to be reserve troops were in fact the anxious faces of the rebels' families.

The peasant army stretched from the wood to the cliff edge exactly as Aster had said. I saw that we were facing a nervous shield-wall for there was much movement. The shields were opening and closing causing gaps between them where a spear could drive through. I did not know if they could even make a locked shield-wall.

There did seem to be many, compared to us, and I felt a loosening in my bowels. Soon I would be trying to kill these strangers and they would be trying to kill me.

I wondered what I was doing there. The sun was shining and soaked warmly into my shoulders. I didn't need to be here, I told myself, I had money, I did not need the four milias, nor did I wish to kill these men, to create widows and grieving mothers. I did not even know the full offence of these men or what actions of their tyrant master had driven them to it. Most of all I did not wish to put myself by choice where they could kill me, or worse, disfigure or injure me in some grisly way; death, after all, is not always the worst outcome.

But then there were my new found friends; they were relying on me to protect the left flank, to be left-shield man while Lothar did his work. How could I, with honour, desert them? How could I live with showing my cowardice to these men, or even to the other strangers in our tiny war-hedge?

My pride trapped me; I could not avoid this battle. I could not go back and my bowels foretold my fear of going forward.

Go forward I did though and all fell out as Aster and Atilec forecast. It was child's play. The rebels though brave, for there is nothing like the presence of women to straighten and strengthen a shield-wall, were not trained and so were easily destroyed and once broken were hunted down and gathered in like sheep. The beard of Lothar's axe hooked the shield at his front, he pulled backwards and down and revealed the man behind it. I thrust at his face and carved off a bloody flap of cheek, the man flew backwards with a cry of fear and pain, spraying blood. Atilec's spear took him in the belly and bloodily he fell. With a roar Lothar pushed forward, axe swinging, and we with him, stabbing left and right. Our shield-wall, curving back into a shallow wedge, pushed relentlessly through. Led by Lothar, the left half of our warhedge wheeled to take the line to the left in the flank. The right half, led by Atilec, did the same to the right and, in so splitting, opened room for the cavalry reserve.

With wild cries of triumph the horsemen rode through and loosed their bows on the rear ranks of the peasant army. They fled only to be hunted down and slaughtered by the Alan horsemen breaking through on the wings.

After the battle, the survivors were gathered together: men, women and children. The men we herded into a guarded enclosure where the Magister could deal with them at his pleasure. The children and girls were loaded onto carts for transport to the slave markets of Lugdunum. The mature women, having less value, were given to the victorious warriors. Us!

I confess that blissful at surviving my first shield-wall, desiring to punish those arrayed to kill me and urged on by the example of those around me, I gave way without effort to the natural lust, curiosity and cruelty of the young. There I took my first experiences of the joys of women's bodies in all their possibilities, real, rather than the imaginings of my fevered mind.

To my everlasting shame, like a wild beast I rutted on the unwilling, fearful, protesting flesh of our captives. But I found that even in lust and cruelty there are the seeds of tenderness and compassion, and afterwards I was deeply ashamed. And then horror piled on horror.

When our company had done all it was possible to do and we were sitting lost in the melancholy that follows excess, the Magister came to us and ordered that the women captives should be given to the fire. Our victorious and sated Alan companions, inured to cruelty by their early service with the Huns, took stakes - two score, sharpened and piled in readiness - and hammered them into the ground. They collected kindling and wood from heaps standing against the compound ready for the purpose, and piled this about the base of them. It was plain to me that the Magister had prepared in detail for the torment and punishment of his rebellious peasantry. I felt sure, even at my young age, that there was more of pleasure than of justice in this for him.

Some of the women, coming slowly to an understanding of the threat, tried to flee and were quickly caught and bound. Others, too stunned by what had already happened to them and unbelieving of what they saw, sat weeping until the soldiers laid hands on them.

The Alans dragged the shrieking and pleading women to the stakes and secured them, two or three together, their hands above their heads, the faggots about their feet.

From the compound that housed their menfolk there arose a frantic hubbub and the wall nearest the stakes shuddered as the mass of men inside threw themselves against it. It was too strong for their feeble weight and they ceased to try, but the voices still rose, now in begging rather than rage.

Once the faggots about the stakes were burning high, the

screams from the blackening bodies ceased. Then the Alans set light to the compound that the men might themselves suffer the agonies of their womenfolk. I saw clearly that this, the vengeance of Flavius Pulcher, was well planned and showed the face of the cruelty and evil that had caused the revolt to take place.

I could not and would not take part in this, and prayed to our Lady Freya, for forgiveness that I could do nothing to stop it.

As I witnessed and heard in sickness and horror those I had lately abused and who had, belatedly, unlocked my feelings of pity and shame, twist, writhe and scream at the stakes as the flames rose around them, falling silent as they passed into merciful shadow, something snapped in me. These had been free folk, not even slaves. They could have been my mother or the lost Elwine and, as I snapped, so the Lady sent a great rage, rising out of pity and shame and guilt. More than rage... madness came over me.

The Magister was standing in front of me at the forefront of those watching, his face lit by the roaring flames leaping high around the compound. He alone was smiling, taking pleasure from the torment of the innocent and the men's screams of grief, rage and agony.

I ran towards him, drew back my spear and drove it through him, the author of all this misery. He, whose greed and pride had caused the destruction and torment of so many, made no noise as he sank to his knees. I withdrew my spear and he fell with the blood welling out of the hole I had made and spreading in a rapidly growing patch on the back of his white tunic.

The rage ebbed out of me as he fell. I felt fear now at what I had done. The Alans, I was sure, had no loyalty towards the Magister, but he had not yet paid them and now could not.

Now they would riot and I would be the object of their anger. They would break me into pieces; it would be mercifully quick, but final.

If I escaped that, worse waited for me, for when Lord Aetius, who had launched the crushing of the Bagaudae, heard of the assassination of a great landowner, he would order me hunted down and my fate would be public and very nasty. All this fled through my mind in an instant.

The attention of the crowd was still on the burnings, although by now the screaming had stopped. Of those nearest, many were drunk and did not understand what had happened next to them, but from the cries of alarm, I knew that some did and that I had not long before they turned on me.

I ran! I ran as if Wothan's hunt was after me. I did not look around for Atilec or Lothar, I just ran to the horse lines, found my ugly mount, unhitched, mounted and set out at a gallop to the south, my still bloody spear bouncing on my back.

I rode all the remainder of that blood-soaked day and long into the night, driven by fear and the desire to be as far from my horror and shame as I could. I stopped at last only out of pity for the poor beast, afraid that my mad rush, whether from vengeance or from myself, would kill him.

I watered him at one of the numberless streams we forded and then tied him to a tree, loosely so that he could crop. Exhausted, I threw myself down on a warm grassy bank under the stars and despite the turmoil of my mind fell instantly asleep, only to twist and turn in endless dreams of guilt and dread.

I awoke to feel a sword at my throat.

The sun was shining directly in my eyes and I knew I was a dead man. I moved my head and shaded my eyes, relief flooding through me as I saw the sword holder was Atilec.

'For a wanted man killer, who the Agentes of Aetius will soon be pursuing, you are careless with your life,' he said. 'Thank your gods it is us who have found you and not Aster's Alans. You and your nag can be seen for many miles around.'

I made as if to leap to my feet, still part blinded by the sun in my eyes.

'Stay down,' said Atilec, 'if they see five they will think only that we are just another search party.

'Here,' he said, and threw a small clinking bag down beside me, 'your pay, two days, eight milia.'

I shook my head. 'I don't want it.'

'Nor should you. I doubt the dead Flavius would pay up with joy. His widow did though. It was that or have the house burned around her.' He bent and picked up the purse and returned it to his larger one.

'The bargain was that we should find you and bring you back,' came Lothar's voice. 'These fine men helped us track you.'

I turned towards him and to my sudden fear saw that two Alan horsemen stood beside my recent companions.

'So, you are taking me back?'

Atilec regarded me gravely. 'Well we thought about it, these fine eastern warriors are here to make sure we do. But, no, we think our dead employer deserved to die. He was a troll and probably now is tormented in the very worst part of Hell set aside for really bad, rich, dung eaters. He will probably torment you one day, when you meet there. Unless the Lady saves you.'

The lifting of the threat of agonising death filled me with relief. The prospect had been aching in me like a punch to the stomach. 'Thank you,' I said, with great feeling. 'I would like to keep my skin for a little longer, but what about them?' I nodded towards the Alans.

'These are your new wayfaring companions, Gunthar and Hunneric, they are Alans, but have lived with Asding Vandals so long they have Vandal names. They have also ridden with the Huns and owned Attila to be their King. They say that when their people went south some families stayed in the north with the Huns rather than follow Gaiseric. Now they are sorry. Their looting of Gaul has left them poor. They wish to come with us to Africa. To rejoin their kin and loot the Middle Sea.'

I examined them more closely: there was swarthiness about them and something about the cheekbones and eyes that cried out their eastern homeland. They were blue-eyed, however, and their dark hair had streaks of blond burned in by constantly riding helmetless under the sun. Each was dressed in breeches and tunic, but wore a sheepskin waistcoat instead of a cloak. At their waists they carried short swords and slung over their backs was the deadly double-curved, horn and wood bow. On a shoulder belt slanted left to right across their chests hung a quiver full of arrows and on their round shields was a strange design, 'the hands of the gods', as I later learned. It consisted of a cross, but at the end of each arm was a bar from which sprouted five upright short lines. This was the symbol of the gods that the Alans held in awe and bowed down to. When Gaiseric and his followers had sworn loyalty and bent the knee to the Nailed God of the Christians, many of the Vandals and Alans had clung to their old beliefs. For this reason the people of these two had left the Vandals in Spain and returned to their settled lands, even though this meant servitude to the Huns.

Five now in number, we rejoined the Via Agrippa and continued south. Atilec rode beside me in silence for a while and then he told what was on his mind.

'The next time we have a job and you decide to murder our master, let us know before you do it,' he said mildly, 'that sudden itch of yours could have cost us much.' He regarded me steadily. 'The burning was outlandish, but the rest is part of warfare, boy. Look, there is no honour in playing the beast; you know that now. For myself I take no pleasure in the abuse of womenfolk. After victory, when the shaming of the women starts, I look for a nice plump wife or widow of a certain age; someone who will forgive an ugly face or not wet herself with fright at the sight of me. I save her from the horde, we sit and talk and sometimes out of pity she will let me be gentle and friendly towards her. If not, well I keep her safe, we part on good terms and I ride away without the sort of nightmares you were having when we found you.'

I rode in silence reflecting on his words. 'What about Lothar?' I then asked.

'Lothar hates the shaming; you will not find him near it. Why, I cannot say, you must ask him yourself if you dare. You are young; you need to learn that not all warriors are beasts. It is a trade. Those good at it command trust and respect. Those who are beasts command only doubt and fear. You must decide now, at the beginning of your calling, which you will be.'

He rode on ahead and coming alongside Lothar sought his guidance on the best route to Ebussus, whether through Arelate or Massalia.

I dropped back for I had much to think on and their voices became a faint murmur barely to be heard over the creaking of the saddle harness, the breathing and thudding hooves of my brave mount. He seemed to have recovered from our headlong flight and as before, I silently blessed Lothar for his knowledge of horseflesh.

Once again, sorrow rose in my chest at the memory of the day just past and filled my throat until I wanted to release it in a great cry of pain. I loathed the evil I had found in myself. The loathing moved inside me like a sickness in my stomach and chest. Only the remembered feel of my spear striking home to draw blood payment lifted my spirits a little. Then I made an oath. I drew my seax with my left hand and cut my right palm. The blood ran from my hand as I let it hang down, dripped on the earth, into the heart of the Mother of all. I called on my Lady Freya to receive my blood and my oath. I swore that I would never again, through all my life, mistreat the helpless or weak, rather that I would uphold and help. I begged her to end my miserable life if I ever broke this oath.

I have tried through all my life to remain true to this, the oldest of all my oaths to my Lady. I believe that I always have, no matter what.

Once again, the Wyrd Sisters changed the pattern in the weave of my life, for its path was in new directions from that point onward. Where I find myself, and what I find myself doing, is a constant surprise to me, and still I do not know where I go or the entire design of my life's cloth.

As Bowdyn's voice fell silent my father was the first to speak.

'Again, Storyteller Bowdyn, I must tell you that the meat of your story is strong. This time I have kept my silence thus far, for the last time I spoke out I misspoke. But I feel that the story tonight took some folk - and he looked at me as he said this - to places and scenes they would not imagine; scenes which may haunt their dreams. Tell me, friend Bowdyn, that there will be nothing stronger than this for the future or I may need to restrict some of your audience.'

Bowdyn replied, respectful but firm. 'Sir, the story is as the story is, and is told as it was told to me, and for that reason, I believe is as it happened all those years ago. It is not a storyteller's task to bring change into a story for if he did, then how could his listeners believe in its truth?

'However, sir, I can tell you that there is no stronger meat than this as the tale unfolds. It is this shame and guilt that causes Gewis to swear the oath he will never break. It is this oath that governs his conduct all his life and which leads to the mighty changes he will bring about before he passes into shadow. For this reason it is an important part of the working of the Fates and must be told.'

My father considered this, then spoke, 'Very well, Master Storyteller, then what is done is done. I take your word that the younger members of your audience will hear no more of base and evil conduct even if followed by remorse and shame. Thank you for your stories, they are truly enjoyable, where they are not shocking.'

There was a chorus of agreement and also thanks as the villagers, realising there was nothing more to be heard, rose, picked up their possessions and buzzing in quiet debate at what they had heard from both Bowdyn and my father, set out for home.

# Chapter 14

**AD 447**

**Gewis' Tale, the Road to Africa**

As the last storytelling session had ended in some controversy and debate there had been no arrangement made for our next meeting in the Cold-Cot. This must have struck some of the villagers on their way home, for the very next morning a small party of our farm hands approached my father to enquire, respectfully, would the story continue and if so when?

My father called Bowdyn from his work and it was agreed that weather permitting, the story would continue on the next Saturday or if the weather was bad then on the next dry day.

As it turned out it rained all Saturday and Sunday and so there was a longer gap between the story, which had ended in my father's dismay, and its resumption.

On the first dry day, a Wednesday, Bowdyn and I had been to the woods to collect wood for the fire, for the evenings were now striking cold. As we worked our breath misted in the air and between lifting and carrying I pushed my hands into my armpits to warm my fingers.

'Was Gewis a wicked young man?' I asked.

'Indeed not, but as prone to sin as any,' said Bowdyn, 'but many of the best of men are repentant sinners. Ask your priest about Saint Paul and Saint Francis.'

'But what he did was evil, as my father said?'

'Indeed, and the killing of Flavius was also wrong, for it is God's right to punish the wicked,' his eyes twinkled. 'But, it is a part of the story that I like well. I for one could not but cheer a man who punishes the truly evil. That he did it partly out of sorrow and partly out of guilt I cannot deny, but I believe that even at that young age he had a sense of justice and the goddess guided and strengthened his arm.'

I did not talk further about goddesses and such, I had a feeling that neither my father nor our vicar would approve.

Perhaps because there had been a gap in the telling of the tale, we had hardly laid and lit the fire and the tip of the sun had barely dipped below the hill before the first of our audience started to appear. Maybe the village felt that by showing keenness for the telling they could ensure it continued. I think they feared that my father's disapproval might bring their free entertainment to an end.

By the time Bowdyn and my mother and father arrived, the throng was embedded and the people halfway through their refreshments. Bowdyn smiled at them. The rawness of the last part of the story had not offended the men or the women, it seemed. This clearly pleased him and still smiling, he bowed his head to my father and mother. He had said nothing to me in the woods, but perhaps he had been fearful that they, the host and hostess, would cease to attend and in so doing bring his stay to an end. I think Bowdyn took as much pleasure from having the time to tell one of the long stories from his store of tales as we did in hearing it.

'Welcome all,' he said, when it appeared that all who could come were present.

'Tonight we carry on with Gewis' tale of the road to Africa, although along the way we take a side road to hear the story of the two Allannic horsemen who have joined the company. Then we will leave the land behind and take a sea voyage.'

As usual, Bowdyn sank back into the shadows and from them we heard the voice we had come to recognise as the young Gewis.

The first night, when we felt we were far enough from pursuit, the five of us sat in a circle around the fire and ate our meal.

I regarded our new companions with curiosity and finding that their dialect was understandable to me, I asked them their story, for I knew that little angered the Huns more than the desertion of their servants and to run from them made the runner a lifetime fugitive in any of the Hun lands.

So, while we sat in warmth and comfort around the fire Hunneric told us their tale.

'We were born on the move,' he started. 'Our people were breeders of horses and herders of sheep in a land far to the East. Our race bore the name "Alans" and our forefathers fought the Huns when they came out of the Steppes from the rising sun. The invaders would have destroyed them had our fathers not seen they were beaten and made peace. And so, although my people never grew to love our conquerors, we served them and rode with them to war. They herded us as they herded their sheep.

'As their wars won them more land, first ours, then the Goths, then the Germans and then the Romans, so they moved us west with their borders. By the time we two were born, both in the same year, our kinfolk - not all the Alans, but only our tribe - had been settled on land to the east of the Albis. There we built yet another village and over many years, more and more of our people were moved to join us until we felt that one day we would hold all of the land between the Albis and the Sprewa. Some of our people joined with the Vandals as they journeyed west. Some of ours decided to part from them and return to that land.

'I am Hunneric, it is my given name, but I am not fond of it. It means that I will lead, maybe rule, Huns. I have no desire to. Destroy them yes; get away from the stink of them, always; but to join with them other than under force, never.

'My friend is Gunthar the Battler, his name at least is right for him for he always was a warrior in his heart. I prefer to think and talk rather than fight, although I can do so, and well enough at need.

'As we grew, we were friends, first as children then as young horsemen and then as trained warriors, expert with the bow as all horsemen of the Huns must be. Once they trained us we became part of the warrior share that the Huns levy from every village under their rule. Although my name seems to tie me to our masters I look like our people, fair of hair and skin and tall. Gunthar, on the other hand, looks much like a Hun: short, although not bow-legged; dark and swarthy, with eyes that tend towards the slitted; the devil-eyes we so hate. I think there is Hun in his bloodline somewhere, but as it must have entered in shame I do not bait him with it for the sake of our friendship.'

At this point, Gunthar leaned over and pushed his friend in the chest knocking him to the floor, to the laughter of both, before Hunneric continued.

'We rode with the Huns because to refuse would mean death, but such work filled us with dread and sickness. The Huns won many battles - often without fighting - cities fell from fear of their cruelty, for their main weapon was fear. This they wielded by the most awful tortures and deaths.

They destroyed without mercy any tribe, town or city that opposed them.

'We two are human, we feel pity, we feel the pain of others; such warfare sickened us. Yes, we will fight for ourselves, for each other, for our comrades, but not against unarmed women, nor tiny children. The Huns sought not only to destroy an enemy, but to create heart-stopping fear, not just in those who opposed them, but in all who might oppose them in the future.

'When we were part of a fully trained Turma, a detachment of us rode into Gaul on loan to Lord Aetius. Our task? We were to crush the peasants revolting against the harshness and the corruption of the owners of the great patrician estates of the Province. Lord Aetius, a great patrician at heart, resolved to destroy them.

'It was strange: we fought the Romans at every turn, yet here we were doing their work for them. It seemed that Lord Aetius and our master, Attila, played a game above the understanding of ordinary mortals. It would have seemed amusing were it not for the blood and pain it caused.

'And so we found ourselves, separated from our fellows, in the company of Atilec and Lothar. Where they were going was far from where the Huns could seek us out and drag us back for such punishment as would renew the fear in our fellows. To the tyrants we followed, the worst crime of all was to desert them, as if they were jealous lovers and not our hated and feared masters.'

Hunneric's tale drew to a close and we sat in silence as we thought about what he had said. Then we thanked him and having built up the fire against the early morning coolness, we slept in readiness for our journey to Arelate.

As for that journey, once we were far away from any pursuit it was without event of any great note. We arrived at Arelate but found we could obtain no passage to Ebusus from there. A salt trader had drawn his ship up on the slip for re-caulking her underwater seams. The vessel's master did not expect to sail for Ebusus until two months after Midsummer, during Weed Month. We did not wish to wait, for two reasons: the first was that it would be a drain on our stock of silver; the second was the fear that the Agentes of Aetius might be seeking us. The risk that they might stumble across us was especially high in Arelate where they had an office. So we moved on to Massalia down the Via Domitia.

Lothar was not worried. He told us that even if we could not get passage from Massalia there was still Barcino further down the Domitia and the Via Augusta. He was sure, he said, that if there were no traders to sell us passage then there were always smugglers, so long as we could pay their price. At this he looked at me and raised an eyebrow.

I pledged that I would pay for passage at any reasonable amount and would rely on them to negotiate. My relationships with my companions, which had been quiet and strained after my foray into murder, warmed much after that.

Saying little, we continued on our way and in the silence of the road I had time to mull over in my head the company in which I found myself. I knew little of them other than what had happened between us and what they had told me. On the one hand they seemed to get me into a lot of trouble; on the other they were willing to get me out of that trouble, which was all to the good.

Lothar, huge with his ready laugh and long fair hair caught back in Gothic braid was a friendly giant, or so it seemed, but I was not so sure. He had become angry and threatening when we bargained for my mount and I had seen how he quickly smothered this, replacing his anger with placid good humour. He was like a wild horse held in check by a strong rider and I would not like to be in the way if he broke free. For all his easy laughter and friendly manner, Lothar seemed to me to be a dangerous man, but perhaps a good comrade if treated with care. I thought it would be a long time before I ceased to be a little frightened of Lothar.

Atilec on the other hand looked dangerous, but behind the scarred and ugly face was the mind of a reasonable man: a warrior, yes, but unlike many warriors also a thinking man. One who would react to the facts and seek how they could best be bent to serve him. Even so, in Atilec I also saw mercy, fellow feeling, even kindness. I would trust myself to Atilec and fear no harm. I was yet to learn that this kindly man had in past madness murdered many an innocent.

I wondered what long ago events had shaped my new friends. What hand in the fire had given Lothar his caution and what act of mercy had grown mercy in Atilec?

Of the two Alans I knew nothing other than that some religious dispute had separated them from their warrior kin. I held back on judging whether to trust them or not until I knew more, deciding for the time being to keep a furtive watch on them. They kept together and kept to themselves, as if they were at all times in a strange land amongst strangers, which I suppose they were.

As luck would have it we found a salt trader in Massalia who was prepared to take us on as crew if we would help pull an oar and also pay him one milia each for the two-day passage, starting the very next day at cock crow. This being within everyone's resources each of us undertook to pay our own passage.

We went in search of a horse dealer to get the best price for our horses and saddles, and thence to find an inn to rest for the night and a taverna for hot food and cold drink.

As is always the way, we did not get for our horses what we

paid for them. We found that horses, which were in short supply when we bought them, were a glut on the market when we came to sell them. I sold my ugly nag, for which I had developed some affection during our three-week ride from Colonia, for three solidi, but felt that I had received good service for the two solidi I lost on the deal.

So, with money in our purses, good food and drink in our bellies and rested after a good night's sleep on clean straw, we arrived at the quayside to start the last stage of our trip to the kingdom of the Vandals. There, as we went upon our way on the sea, our happiness and sense of wellbeing soon ended.

However, before I tell you why, let me describe the ship. It was perhaps fifteen paces long and five paces wide. The after end was decked in way of the steering oar; there was a small deck at the bow with the rest of the vessel being open, apart from the central fore and aft walkway and the rowers' benches. Set forward of amidships was a mast, perhaps ten paces high, with a yard of five paces in length, to which a bunched and lashed sail was attached. In the deep cargo holds was wine in small amphorae, grain in great amphorae and numberless other trade items wrapped in sacking and all stowed so neatly together and so tightly interlocked that it was impossible to see the whole shape of anything but the very top layer, over which the lashing ropes formed a tight network.

Above the hold was the central walkway, to either side of which were the rowing benches with room for two rowers. The crew each took up only one space on each oar and we, the passengers who were set to help, took up the second. There were five benches on either side, so ten oars in total. We passengers split into two groups: Lothar and Atilec rowing on the steerboard side; Hunneric, Gunthar - who was small in stature - and I, the youngest, rowed on the ladeboard side. The crew also split into two parties. Each of these rowed for two hours and rested for two, so that we helped first one party then the other, and because we were fee-paying passengers, we rowed two hours and rested four. For that I was grateful.

The oars were heavy and not well balanced, seeming to twist in the hands. The rubbing of the wood upon skin new to the work soon caused blisters. When they burst I discovered that the salt the vessel carried had over time soaked into the woodwork. In no time at all also into my hands, which from the blisters and the re-opened cut were soon aflame. Atilec said they needed toughening anyway and that salt, used to preserve meat, would preserve them too. I noticed that his calloused hands were showing no sign of wear. I supposed if rowing were to be my life, which at that time it wasn't, then mine too would soon toughen to the trade. Until then I would bite my lip against the torment. As I was soon to discover, calluses, as with resistance to seasickness, take longer than two days to form.

When we sailed from the harbour there was a brisk north wind blowing, although the sky was blue and clear of clouds. The sailors said this wind, the Magistralis, was very common in the area. I was pleased because it was only necessary to row clear of the land and then the crew hoisted the square sail. We started to make rapid headway and as the land sank from sight astern of us so the sailors brailed up the sail to shorten it. There was a gentle up and down motion, which caused my stomach a little discomfort and gave me a sore head, but not unbearably so.

The wind continued brisk from the north, but the waves now topped with white grew in size from astern, passing us by. They lifted the stern and moved it from side to side in a circular motion. I started to feel sick.

By the time the land had dropped from sight the waves had

grown and overtopped us, their crests were breaking in white foam and roaring as they rushed past us. The ship started to increase its side-to-side motion so that I feared it would turn side on to the waves, which would then overwhelm us.

By then I was vomiting over the side and wished to die. It did not relieve me to see that the others of our warrior band were in the same state.

At that point the shipmaster ordered us to take our places at the oars and row to help keep the ship's bow pointing away from the sea and give him and his mate on the steering oar sufficient way through the water to prevent the ship from broaching to.

Fevered with suffering, I believed the Lady had refused my vow, for I was in Hel in the grasp of Loki's daughter. Hel: that place where those go who have not earned their way to Wothan's or Freya's hall, in the part of that icy drear realm where the wicked torment each other; where Flavius would take his revenge on me until world's end. Heaving at the oar, my hands on fire, I vomited onto the cargo below my feet until I was dry and still I vomited. Hour after hour we rowed. When the next crew of rowers relieved us, we collapsed exhausted, our stomachs still heaving.

I wished for death, for the sea to overwhelm us; to drown would be wonderful, the Hel of death would be better than this. The ship, pitching and rolling, survived and roused, we once more took our turn at the oars. This seemed to last for days and awful nights, for an eternity of sunlit days and moon-drenched nights, but in truth it was but a day and a half, for the speed from the following gale brought us off our harbour, in bright sunshine, by the middle of the following day.

The crew scrambled to drop the sail. We struggled to bring

the now rolling ship round until the bow pointed into the wind. Then we rowed and rowed and slowly, at its leisure, tormenting us to the end, the sea dropped down as we came under the blessing of the lee of the land. And so we rowed, exhausted, but with clearing heads and stilled stomachs, into calm waters off a coast of low, pine-forested hills with white beaches and deep blue water, shading to pale green in the shallows.

The vessel turned into the east and we passed a narrow wooded headland to our north before turning north again into a deep bay, at the head of which lay a small wooden pier: our destination.

We drew in our oars to the Shipman's orders. Now just the aftermost pair gently nudged us nearer. One of a crowd standing in wait on the pier caught our heaving line. This they made fast to a heavy mooring line secured to wooden cleats on the pier. We heaved this mooring line on board and secured it to the forward bits.

Drawing in the last two oars we tossed another heaving ashore. In no time we heaved the after-mooring rope on board and safely secured the ship to the pier. We helped lower the gangplank and as soon as we could, bade our grinning shipmaster goodbye and thankfully – if unsteadily on our sea legs - walked ashore. If there was any way that I could have walked to Carthage, be it ever so far, I swear at that point I would have done so cheerfully. Ships, I decided, were not for me. I was wrong of course.

The road to Ebussus started at the end of the pier and we walked through the bleak, arid landscape of the salt flats until we came under the shelter of pine trees lining and shading the road.

The town was small and although not Roman, it everywhere

showed Roman greatness through its stone buildings and decoration. We found a taverna where we started the long business of replenishing the water and food lost on the sea passage.

From the taverna, replete with the wine for which Ebussus was renowned, we, reeling, followed directions to an inn used by soldiers and sailors near the main harbour. There we slept, until the warmth and bright sunshine through the glassless and shutterless window awoke us to a sense of well being and renewed hunger.

After splashing water on our faces from the trough in the yard we retraced our steps to the taverna for a breakfast of bread, cheese and fruit and then started to enquire for a ship to Gaiseric's kingdom. At first our enquiries drew black looks, for the Vandals were not popular in Ebussus, but then we heard of a ship discharging grain from Africa, which would be loading salt for Carthage when ready.

And so we made our way to the harbour, spoke with the master, haggled and then agreed a fee and secured our passage south on a trader of sixteen oars.

Although the voyage to Carthage was longer, the weather was very fine. The Magistral had abated when we left Ebussus and the western Middle Sea was undergoing a span of settled weather. Our progress was slow but easy. The westerly breeze favoured us and was just sufficient to cool the ship. The oars stayed stowed in their inboard crutches and I, for the first time, started to believe that a life as a sea reaver might not be so bad after all.

Seven days we lived the lazy life while the wind blew us to our journey's end and on the eighth we all took to the oars, breasted the wind as the sail came down and pulled into the great, ship-crowded harbour of Carthage.

There was silence in the Cot as the crowd waited for the tale to continue and then, realising it had come to a halt, a hubbub of voices and noise arose as people spoke to their neighbours, stretched, scratched, shifted creakingly on their benches, raised flasks to their lips and generally carried out all the tasks that had been held back by the storyteller's art.

After a pause, during which the noise died down, Bowdyn held up his hand and when silence resumed, began to speak.

'Well my friends, there is sleep awaiting and work to be done in the morning. We will pause the tale of Gewis here only half done. If you wish it, we will continue on another night,' he looked at my father enquiringly.

Nodding, my father smiled and asked, 'In this place?'

'Yes,' said Bowdyn, 'in this place. Today is Wednesday, let us say, Friday. Do you wish it?'

The audience gave a resounding chorus of agreement and, with many a 'Thank you' to Bowdyn, people rose to their feet and left the Cot, only to gather outside, for some had seen the sea, but most had not. Those who had were moved to share what they had seen and those who had not, to listen. For them, whose knowledge of wastes of water was limited to the mere that lay twixt the twin hills nearby, this evening's story had been a puzzle. They stood and talked and drifted off until the very last few, overcome by tiredness, ambled away to their homes, a moving hum of conversation and calls of 'Good night' and 'God bless' gradually dying away into the night.

# AD 447 – AD 455
# Africa, Carthage, the Middle Sea

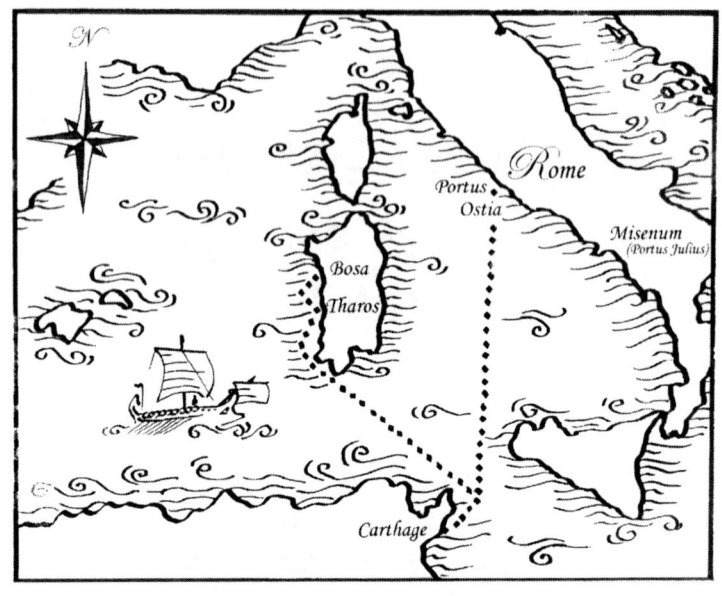

**Gewis' Tale – The Middle Sea**

# Chapter 15

**AD 447 to AD 455**
**Gewis' Tale, the Land Ship**

On Friday we all assembled in the Cold-Cot after sunset. As before, the audience brought fuel, food and drink, furniture and cushions and, for some, warm cloaks, for the nights were growing cold and while the fire warmed faces, backs grew chilled.

Bowdyn quickly took his place and without more ado, in the hush that followed his appearance, worked the magic of transformation and we were once again listening to the voice of Gewis.

I lived for seven years amongst the Vandals as a warrior, oath-sworn to King Gaiseric. Not to Gaiseric himself, of course, but to one of his Captains. There were many Captains, for the Vandal warriors who had crossed from Baetica had numbered in the tens of thousands.

Our Captain called himself Wisimar, he chose us for his band and that was our great good fortune. He was a wise and brave leader, generous in victory, forgiving in defeat. Those in his company were loyal above the needs of their oaths and united in companionship in a way that was new to me.

It was hard to become one of their company. I fought hard and I was proud of that adoption when it came. Lothar went into the first row of battle at once; Atilec the second row, but then quickly into the first. I bore my spear in the third row because of my youth, but I fought my way up until I too carried it in the forefront of the battle line. All of us were first line on the oars, however, but that was no great distinction.

When we first berthed at Carthage two surprises struck me. The first was the great size of the city, bigger by far than Colonia. The second was that it looked to be in ruins. The city walls overthrown lay piled in rubble around the outside of the buildings, but once we entered we found the houses undamaged. Only the walls of the town were ruined. I heard later that King Gaiseric, when he had taken the city nine years earlier, had ordered the walls destroyed so that no rebels or armies could capture them and hold out against him.

Before we left our ship, we enquired of the tax official who boarded how best to seek employment. He told us that the tavernas on the road girdling the military harbour were the most common recruiting centres, so we found our way into the first of many that were scattered along the stone quayside.

Here our luck turned to the good. The taverna keeper, the storehouse of all gossip here as everywhere, pointed us towards a table in the corner. 'That wealthy gentleman in the centre of the crowd is a Captain of Gaiseric called Wisimar. His ship is the Triton. I hear he is a good and fair Captain, I also hear he has lost men from his company in ambush in Sicilia and is looking to replace them.'

We thanked him and approached this Wisimar, who looked up keenly as we drew near. Atilec stepped a pace forward.

'Captain Wisimar, we are at your service. We hear you

seek good fighting men and would offer ourselves to you.'

He proceeded to name us each in turn, beginning with Lothar the Goth and reeling off a string of the battles and campaigns in which he had won distinction. Atilec then announced himself as a warrior, giving his own warlike pedigree and adding, 'I am also a Gleeman, one who can tell many a story of glory to pass a boring night or to embolden soldiers before a battle.'

My eyes widened in surprise for this was the first I had heard of this in the four weeks we had travelled together.

He then pointed to me, 'And this is Gewis, young but trained, I have fought beside him in the shield-wall and was there when he broke the line of the Bagaudae at Antissiodorum and enabled a famous and almost bloodless victory - on our side that is.'

I thought this was overstating the case by much, but Wisimar looked at me with interest and I kept quiet.

'These warriors,' said Atilec, pointing to Gunthar and Hunneric, 'are your own Alans of the Asding Vandili.'

Taking in the bows slung across their backs the Vandal Captain nodded. 'Good, I need bowmen.'

Wisimar continued to look at us as if weighing us in some balance in his head. At last he spoke. 'My company is a very select group, we are looking to make up losses, but only with the very best. I will give you a week to prove you can fit in during peace, and if so, then a month to prove you can earn a place in battle. Go to the Sign of the Ram and ask for Tzazo the Gubernator. Tell him to take you in and sign you on at standard rates on trial, he will understand. He will order and you must obey. On the Triton, loyalty and courage are well rewarded, mutiny or cowardice are death. Good luck.'

He turned back to his companions, dismissing us. We

thanked him, but he only waved a hand in reply.

Once we had asked the taverna keeper for directions, we set off as instructed for the Sign of the Ram.

The sign itself was, we thought, a mark of the wealth of the city, for hoisted over the door was a fragment of the wood of a ship's keel with the bronze tip of the ramming beak still attached. This bronze weighed as much as a large man. It was a piece of great value and any but the rich would have sold such a great treasure. Thus we discovered that this taverna was a special place. It was in fact the headquarters and property of the Tritons, as the company of Captain Wisimar, named for his ship, the Triton, were known. The bronze over the door was the mark, not of the wealth of the city, although the city was indeed rich, but of the Tritons, and was a pointer to the wealth to follow for those good enough and lucky enough to be welcomed into that choice fellowship.

The Gubernator of the Triton, was a stocky man, strong in appearance although of no more than medium height. A broad white scar from forehead to chin drew his left eye down to the left giving him a savage and aggressive look, although we found that, like all under Captain Wisimar's command, he was a fair if hard driving officer. He it was who dealt with patience and close attention to most of the tasks for preparing and fighting the Triton. He listened to us repeat the Captain's instructions and then began our questioning.

Who had been a sailor before? Who had served on a two-bank Liburnian? How much time on oars had we spent? He asked us much more of the same kind and as he listened to our answers his face became more and more grim.

'Well,' he said, 'warriors you may be, and that's to be seen, but sailors you are not. Your good luck is that we will not sail for some days. Report tomorrow at first light to Celeusta

Hoamer, Master of the Rowers, on the west quay of the centre isle in the military harbour and he will try to make you useful to us. You will stay here, this hostel is only for the Tritons and you may take the mattresses of those you replace, the innkeeper will show you.'

'What is our best way to the military harbour? We are new to Carthage,' asked Atilec.

The Gubernator walked to the doorway and beckoned us. 'You see that hill?' He pointed to a hill with large buildings on top. 'Well, that's Byrsa Hill, and there,' he pointed to a huge, long building, 'that's the Hippodrome. Go out from here and turn left and left again so you are walking with the Hippodrome behind you and Byrsa Hill on your left. At the end of the road you will find the military harbour gate. Tell the guard that Tzazo of the Triton sent you for Hoamer's amusement. When they admit you, turn right and keep the water always on your left even though you end up facing Byrsa Hill. When you get to the water that is ahead of you, you will find Hoamer, some other recruits and a wooden structure that looks like part of a ship on dry land. Follow Hoamer's directions exactly and you may come away as rich as you went. You are on pay starting tomorrow. Any further questions?'

'Yes,' said Lothar, 'may I ask our rate of pay?'

Tzazo laughed. 'That is up to you and Tyche - Lady Luck – but the pay is eight follis each day and your share of plunder. The King, who pays your wages, receives one quarter in gold weight of whatever we take. The remainder is divided amongst us thus: the Trierarchus, Captain Wisimar, gets one eighth part; the officers each get one third part of one quarter; the petty officers each get one sixth part of one eighth, the rest get one quarter divided amongst one hundred and fifty. For special bravery, the Trierarchus will also make awards from his one eighth and I can tell you that Captain Wisimar is very generous to those who truly deserve his generosity.'

With that he dismissed us with a wave and turning, stumped out of the room.

Calling our thanks to Gubernator Tzazo for his help and information we went in search of our pallets for the night.

On rising next morning we splashed water on our faces and donned our weapons. We offered to buy five bowls of some form of oatmeal stew, mostly porridge but with finely chopped meat and onions in it. It was tasty and disappeared quickly. The cook at the Sign of the Ram was also the cook on the Triton so we felt we should not starve at sea. The Ram would not take our money; it fed its residents as part of their wages. We were already beginning to be thankful for our employment, even if on trial. That feeling was shortly to change, at least for a time.

We followed the directions from the Gubernator and found our way with ease. We passed without trouble through the gate and came at last to the structure he had told us of. We were early and sat down to wait beneath a sloping roof of oars that stuck out from the side of the part ship and came to rest in a bed of tall grasses.

Within minutes another group of eight arrived, one of which we learned was Row Master Hoamer, Celeusta of the Triton.

He was a stout, jolly looking man, which only goes to show that looks mean nothing and that a man should be judged by his actions, not his looks. Folk rarely do this, however, which explains how wise men like us found ourselves under the control of a monster. He stopped, the group stopped, he stepped forward.

'Who are you?' he said with a smile, oh the treachery of it!

We named ourselves and said we had been sent by the Gubernator. Bidding us stand in line with the other seven so that we were twelve in all, he examined us with twinkling eyes and a smile on his face before he spoke.

'I am, as you know, the Rowing Master of the Triton. The Triton is a fast Liburnian Galley. She must be faster through the water than the Roman Triremes because they outman and out-oar her. In one-to-one combat the Trireme will first use its catapult to throw burning pots of fiery mix on board to burn us all to death at our oars. It will then come alongside, drop a raven or some such boarding ladder on our deck, and then heavily armoured, well trained Roman marines, perhaps as many as our whole crew in number, will come aboard and kill us until we are all dead or surrender. They will then take us to Rome or whatever shithole they are based at and there crucify and burn the survivors.'

He paused and then continued. 'I like my life here in Carthage, I am getting rich as the Celeusta of a successful galley of Great King Gaiseric; long may he reign! I don't want to end my life in any of the above ways. The Triton is successful because it is a fast Liburnian. It is a fast Liburnian because its oars make it fast and because I train every man on board to make it go fast. If you cannot convince me that you will make it go even faster, then your job on the Triton will end here. Any questions?'

There were none, we were, I think, dumbstruck by the contrast of the smiling jolly face and the harsh tale he told.

'Good,' he said, 'that's a good start, don't question; follow orders quickly and just so. What is just so? Well, it is the way I will show you over the next five days.'

With that he passed along the line touching each man on the chest in turn. The first four he named first rank, top bank.

The second four were second rank, lower bank. In the first four were included Atilec and I, Lothar and one of the other men. He pulled out the two Alans and two others, 'You,' he said, 'are archers and will row only in emergencies. Any time we meet up with a superior force is an emergency. Any time we meet up with a weaker force you will be using your bows. When you are not rowing or fighting or resting, you will be working for the Gubernator, mostly with the Faber, the ship's carpenter.'

He surveyed the results of his work: three groups of four, first rank upper, second rank lower and archers, and smiled his approval. 'This is how it works,' he said. 'There are three ways in which we row. When the Triton is cruising only the upper bank is manned. To make it even easier, the first rank and the second rank relieve each other every four thousand strokes. At the end of each thousand, half the bank rests for one hundred strokes and then the other half. When we are cruising we do not hurry, but we must make land and raid for food as we have little space for stores for one hundred and sixty men.'

He paused, 'Any questions? None? Good. When we are in battle we man both upper and lower banks, we need speed to overtake a well-driven merchantman. When a powerful enemy pursues us, that is an emergency and then both banks are manned. What is more, the upper bank is double-manned, for the rowers pull and the archers and any others, including the officers - except the Trierarchus and the helmsmen - push. If you cannot imagine that now you soon will.'

He smiled at us. 'We will now mount to the oars. Oh, by the way, these grasses are well loved by me.' He pointed to the grasses amongst which the oar blades lay. 'Take care of them when you row. You must brush through the tips to give them an airing; you shall be a breath of spring to them. But woe betide any man who strokes his oar low and breaks off any of my beloved, for he will lose one day's pay every time he does so. Any man who strikes the ground with his oar will lose two days' pay. This money will come to me, so be sure I shall be very watchful.

'Now, first rank, mount your benches, second rank mount to the deck and wait your turn. We are cruising. We man the top bank only and we change rowers at the end of one thousand strokes, we will row for four thousand and then stop.

'Then we will change to fighting stroke and you will man both banks. We will do this for one thousand strokes.

'Finally, we will change to emergency rowing when both banks will be manned with double-manning on the top bank and we will do this for one thousand strokes. When we have done all three then we will start again and the two ranks can take turns to row and to rest while we cruise.

'In the beginning the first rank will take upper oars, the second rank the lower, but every time we come back to cruising they will change. The first rank will become second rank, the second rank will become the first. Do you understand?'

There was silence as the glum rowers-to-be struggled blankly to grasp his meaning, murmured to each other and then nodded.

'Good,' said our tyrant. 'Your bodily functions you must do at the oars, there is a pail for that purpose at each bench. Upper rank be careful not to splatter the lower rank, it leads to bad feeling and even disagreements.' He said this last with a twinkle that I already found disagreeable.

And so we mounted the ladder of the structure and each found our way to an oar or the deck or the bow as directed.

The bowmen, when not helping with emergency rowing, practised their skills with the bow. To make it more practical, each bowman, whilst standing on a platform near the stern, took it in turns to loose his arrows at a soft target of painted straw on the quay. The platform rested on a central upright shaft and to the front and side on an egg-shaped wheel, which was turned by the other bowmen causing the platform to tilt and pitch in a most uneven way, thus imitating the movement of a small ship in rough seas. This severely tested the skill of the bowmen.

So it went, not for hours, but for days. First, the first rank rowed the upper oars, which pivoted through a trellis set above the upper-wale. I lost two days' pay quite rapidly before I got the true feel of the oar and swept it through the correct height without fail. The oars were easy to handle. The oarsman's end of the loom was bored out and filled with lead. This gave them perfect balance and the lightest of touches lifted them.

At the start the oars were in the air; at the command we all pulled together and the sweeps moved in perfect time once we got the hang of it. A drumbeat helped maintain the rhythm and timing. Hoamer said that the Pitulis would normally do this, although sometimes in good weather when no danger threatened then the timing was kept to the fluting of a Symphoniacus. Now, for lack of either, the Celeusta beat the drum.

At the end of each period would come the command, 'Up oars!' We would then hold the loom under our feet until the reliefs were seated. As soon as they took hold we would slide out and the orders, 'Ready,' then 'Pull together,' would be called. This system allowed both first rank and second rank to man the upper and lower oars in turn. We needed much practice at the lowers, for the oars came through a hole cut in the hull and there was little of the sea of grass visible.

Any failure to abide strictly to the drum led to a clashing of oars and loss of pay. I lost a further two days' pay before I delivered a faultless performance.

The emergency rowing was odd. Normally, rowers manned the upper and lower banks of oars with their backs to the bow. The archers, as emergency rowers, stood facing the bow and the rowers on the upper bank, slightly to one side so as not to obstruct the backs of the rowers behind. Then, without breaking the rhythm, they took hold of the oar and pushed as the rowers pulled and pulled as the rowers pushed. This gave the effect, said the Celeusta, of three oarsmen plying the two oars instead of two. A Trireme, whilst triple-banked, had only one oarsman to each oar. As we were lighter and finer formed than the larger ship, we should go faster.

The secret weapon, the Celeusta told us, was that when we were going north to raid, the winds were usually against us so we could not use the sails and must row all the way. But if pursued, our tactics were to turn back south and flee, thus taking advantage of the wind, raising the mainsail and the sprit sail and rowing with emergency manning on the oars. The Triton had never yet been outpaced by a Trireme, he said, but there were others: a few vessels in the Roman navy had three banks of oars and were broad enough to have two men to each oar. The Romans called this a 'Six'. Evidently the Triton had not yet met one - thanks to Tyche.

And so it went, round and round, to the beat of the drum. When it fell dark we expected to go to the Ram but when questioned Hoamer laughed. 'What do you think we do at night when we are raiding, drift around in unknown waters while everyone sleeps? Keep on rowing.'

We passed the oars to the next rank by the light of oil

lamps. As we lay recovering our breath and letting the aches flow out of our arms and guts, a runner came from the inn. He carried a bowl of cold, meaty porridge for the standby watch, as he called us. The rowers did not eat until the end of their thousand.

We had to make use of the pails hung below the benches for one thing or another as time passed. When half full we emptied them over the ship's side into a tun standing among the grasses.

Our contortions in trying to avoid soiling our clothes during the use of our pails showed us why it was that sailors went naked whilst at sea. By the second day we too had taken to this practice.

Even the bowmen, when not practising emergency rowing, continued their work at night. Hoamer lit two large oil lamps on the quay and so, tossing and turning, the archers continued to loose their arrows and retrieve them by lamplight.

The routine became automatic and we carried it out without thought, counting strokes in our heads until the order to change over. The practice during the day had made our handling perfect, for although it was black night, no one hit the ground with his oar. Tiredness was another matter.

The Pitulis came after nightfall when we had counted three thousand more strokes in the dark. He took over the drum and Hoamer retired to a small, but long kennel on the poop. This we found out later was the Trierarchus' cabin.

And so it went on: row, rest, eat, shit, piss, row, rest, eat… for five days, and as we tired so we lost more days' pay. I calculated that I now owed money so concentrated harder until, tired as I was, my rowing was faultless.

I grew to hate the Celeusta during that period for he was merciless, a monster at torment; driving us to breaking in order to enrich himself from our errors. Only later was I to realise that of all the men of the Triton, he it was who saved our lives.

By the fifth day we had become so used to this routine that we forgot all else. So it was that when the Celeusta called a general halt we sat in puzzlement unable to think beyond the moment. Slowly it dawned on us that our torment was over. The training period was completed.

We still needed much practice, said the Celeusta, but none were so beyond hope that they were to be cast out from the crew of the Triton. He then passed amongst us giving out bronze medallions on a chain, which he hung around our necks. These bore an image of a triton with shell horn, trident and double fishes' tails. These, he said, marked us as trained and accepted Velarii: fighting sailors of the Liburnian Triton.

'One last item,' he said, 'when the ship goes to sea, hang your shields on the upper bank trellis. They will lend some protection to the rowers from arrows and spears.'

With that he released us, and donning our clothes we stumbled away, our medallions swinging beneath our tunics.

And thus I began my seven years in the Kingdom of Gaiseric the Wise. There are many, many tales I could tell, but much would be repetition for many things happened over and over: different raids, different places, but with the same outcome and with little cause for pride in the feat.

We on the Triton were well trained, well disciplined and well led. We also had a wise leader who never committed us without first scouting to find the lay of the land. We never entered any combat that we did not believe we could win easily. We were the terror of the Sicilian and Sardinian coasts.

Of course, there were two hundred ships in Carthage and others in Leptis Magna - small wonder that after a while the people of the islands moved away from the shore and took to living in the mountains.

There were two raids when the Wyrd Sisters seemed to be working new threads into the cloth of my life, three, if the sack of Rome is counted. These most of all are worthy of telling. The first was my very first raid following the training. What happened there, I believe, altered the direction of my life once more.

# Chapter 16

### AD 447 to AD 455
### Gewis' Tale, the Triton and the Six

Two days after we received our medallions word came to the Ram that all hands should report immediately to the Triton boathouse.

We followed the rest back to the military harbour and part way round to the left. We halted in front of one of a line of great buildings that were roofed, but open under the roof to let the wind blow through. Walled at the sides and back they were open at the front. Through this wide doorway we saw our ship, resting on a gently sloping roadway leading down into the water.

On the command, ten Velarii boarded and the rest of us put our shoulders to the Triton or our hands to the tackle ropes and eased her down the slope and into the water.

As she floated into the centre of the harbour out came the oars from the crew on board and they rowed her alongside the fitting-out quay. There we made a human chain from the warehouse. We carried barrels and filled her water tuns. We loaded the sails and cordage, stocks of arrows for the archers, lead shot for the slingers. All Velarii checked that their personal weapons were with them.

Then the crew stood in line and the cook issued goatskin

bags of water and a leather sack of food: bread, cheese and goat meat. We were told to eat sparingly for the next food we ate we would need to find for ourselves.

We boarded the Triton, slung our shields from the rail above the rowing lattice; the top bank of oars were shipped, with all first rank rowers benched, oars up, ready to row. The steersman, a double-pay sailor, took his place at the steering oars with the extension bars, one in each hand, and the ship was poled from the shore. The signal 'Pull together' was given and we dipped our oars into the water. Thus the Triton pulled away into the channel, through the breakwater and out to sea.

My stomach fluttered inside with excitement, and if I am truthful, more than a little fear. This was my first trip to sea on a warship as a fighting sailor and I confess I did not know what to expect.

The sails were not rigged as we headed out into the prevailing wind, although the standby sailors busied themselves with bracing up the stays and shipping the bowsprit.

We headed north with the land to our ladeboard side, our oars dipping in time to the piping of the Symphoniacus and then the steady beat of the Pitulis, first one thousand strokes to the merry sound of one, and then one thousand strokes to the steady beat of the other. The pace was easy; I counted ten heartbeats for each stroke. Happily, my hands were now as callused as Atilec's and blisters a thing of the past, and after our five days of torment the work was not tiring. I found I was grateful to the Celeusta - and not for the last time.

This, my first harrying with the Vandals, was another turning point in my life; yet another time where the weavers of the cloth of my life changed the woof of the cloth, and changed the course of my future days. For that reason I will tell of the events in detail.

When the land began to fall away to the west on our ladeboard side, we altered course into the setting sun, about northwest. We rowed in this direction for seven full periods each of one thousand strokes, by which time the sun had again risen and it was near midday. We altered again to the steerboard and short shadows lay along the deck towards our bow, so I saw we were heading north again. During my next spell of rest I turned to the resting oarsman from the next bench, one of a number of the Anglekin in the company, and asked him where we were going.

He thought for a little and then shrugged. 'Probably to Sardinia, my guess is Tharros. We usually call there first for food and water. It is a Roman town but the garrison is small there you see. So the governor comes out, records we are a harmless merchant ship and then sells us what we need. We, on our part, don't attack and sack his town. It's a sensible understanding. Where we will go for tribute I'm not sure. Perhaps Bosa, we haven't called there for some time.'

'But,' I said, puzzled, 'isn't this Roman land?'

'Of course, but Rome can't defend every small town with a force big enough to drive us off. So they pay us taxes and we don't sack and burn the town. They have to pay taxes to Rome as well so that is their bad luck. They would probably be happier if they were part of our kingdom.'

I thought over this for a while and then fell asleep.

My oarsman roused me when he reached the thousand, and the order came to change rowers. This operation had become second nature now and was quickly completed.

I had not been pulling beyond my first half thousand when the Proreta, the bow officer, called out a warning and the order came to up oars.

The Trierarchus, the Gubernator and the Proreta stood in the bow for a while talking together and then the Captain crossed back down the walkway to the poop and spoke to the helmsman. The order came to ready the oars and then to pull together and we were on our way again.

We came around to ladeboard and I could see land to steerboard over my left shoulder as I rowed. I guessed it to be perhaps five thousand paces off; high, grim cliffs, the sort you would not like to be blown towards by the wind. We now altered our course as we went so as to keep the same distance off the land. Sometimes we crossed great bays and the land fell away, but always we met up with it on the other side. Four full periods more we rowed, until the order came to lift oars and we sat idly drifting in a great bay surrounded by a low rocky coast. The sun was starting to set behind the cliffs to the left of the Triton and so I knew we had arrived.

After what seemed a long time a small boat approached and a man of some importance, judging by the richness of his clothes, climbed through the steerboard bow gateway, where he was met by the Trierarchus.

'Lucius, my friend, how are you? It's been a long time. How was Rome?'

'Welcome, Wisimar, Rome is eternal as always and the light of the world. Sorry I am to be back. How is Carthage and when will you give it back?'

They both laughed and the Roman clasped the hand of Wisimar in the Roman way.

'Now what can I do for you? You know we are always glad to help a merchant ship upon its way.'

Wisimar smiled. 'The usual, for the usual price, cheese of course and cooked sheep meat, water to fill our tun. Stay, take wine with me and you may tell me of Rome and its beauties -

of both sorts, eh?'

'No great difficulty with the stores, but we were not expecting you and our stocks are low. We will need to send to the farms for supplies so it may take a day or two to bring together the usual quantity. I will go and see to it now; you may pay me when I return. I will not stay for wine, it is better that I set this in hand, but I will bring you a flask of something very special and we will broach it together.'

Lucius backed through the gate and climbed down the ladder into his boat. Wisimar stood and watched the boat until it disappeared into the falling darkness. He turned and beckoned the Gubernator and Proreta and spoke at some length. My oar position being nearby I strained my ears to listen and overheard the Captain say, 'I am very uneasy. Something is wrong here. Lucius was jovial, friendly, but his eyes slid away to the headland many times. The stores delay is unusual also.'

Captain Wisimar clasped his chin in his hand and stared at the foredeck as if seeing something there, then he looked up, decision made. 'Mount both sets of oars and man them, have the standby crew bring out and rig the mainsail ready for hoisting, also the split topsail. Rig and secure the bowsprit and bend on the spritsail ready. Oh, and turn around so that we are heading south. Keep the standby hands standing by ready to hoist the sails in order: mainsail, spritsail, topsail steerboard and topsail ladeboard.' He looked questioningly at them.

'All is clear, Lord,' said Tzazo. 'Shall I put fire pots ready?'

'No,' said Wisimar, 'if I am right, now will be the time to run.'

Tzazo nodded and then spoke to the bow officer, who moved off smartly to organize the sails; he then crossed to the

Celeusta and spoke.

The Celeusta called for ladeboard oars to back water and the steerboard oars to pull together. We started to turn in the water. At the up oars signal we swung to a halt and drifted, heading south. His orders then rang out to ship the lower bank and for the standby watch to man them. I was still on watch on the upper steerboard bank so I stayed where I was.

The non-rowers continued with the business of readying the sails. The steersman stood by the west side rail looking out over the poop towards the headland, whilst the Proreta attended to the rigging of the sails. Those on the bow oars gave a brief stroke from time to time to keep the Triton heading south.

For the rest of us, we just sat at our oars with the strain abuilding. We did not know what, but we knew something was about to happen. We sat there until dawn, cooled by the northerly breeze, and nothing happened. The sun was showing its first reddened arc above the hills to the northeast and I was drifting off to sleep at the oar when the helmsman shouted, 'Ship coming to steerboard!'

I jumped. Looking through the trellis and beneath the hanging shields I could see the low-lying headland and just above it the topmast of a ship moving rapidly south.

Wisimar strode to the rail and looked and then roared an order to the Gubernator: 'Raise sails,' and to the Celeusta, 'start oars, maximum speed, when the sails are up put the standby men to emergency rowing.'

The Celeusta called, 'Up oars,' then, 'pull together,' and we were off, but this time with a difference, for as we settled into our rowing pace he called for an increase and then for another until we were rowing three heartbeats to the stroke, following the beat of the Pitulis.

With a snap, the sail, which had been taking all my heed, on the way up bellied out as the wind caught it and continued to the top of its run with the crew hauling on both halyards. These were then turned up on a pair of wooden horns, stout pillars set at an angle to each other making a shape like two fingers spread apart, perhaps ten paces from where I sat. I turned my eyes from peering over my right shoulder and now looked left over the rail and under the shields.

I gasped: a massive ship, three rows of oars flashing in the light of the rising sun as they moved in perfect time, was clearing the headland. On the deck of the ship, forward of the sail, there stood a machine of war. Along the side were armoured archers. It was, without doubt, a Trireme of Rome, but broad beamed, a Six as I heard later. The first one the Triton had encountered. I put my back into rowing as never before. In my mind the flames already licked at my feet.

I heard the Celeusta cry out to commence emergency rowing and the next I knew the Pitulis was facing me standing and grasping the oar. As I pulled so he pushed and I saw that this doubling had happened all along the upper bank. The Celeusta had taken over the drum and speeded up the beat. The Triton was now moving through the water at an amazing pace, but as I looked across the rail fear fuelled my efforts. The Triton, deep within the bay, had to head west of south to clear the southern headland. The Roman warship had only to head south to reach the headland and with less distance to go would reach us at the Cape if we were not going fast enough. Only time would tell.

It was at this point that the Wyrd Sisters changed the weave of my life. As I sat rowing as if my heart must burst, my gaze rested on the horns on which the mainsail halyards were turned up. I could not believe what I saw. In places along the rope small pennants of yarn were hanging from the great halyards where wear had parted threads. One of these was creeping towards the horn. I was sure of it. I would look away, and when I looked back it was nearer. It came to me that the halyards were working loose and were starting to ride through the horns. I knew with a pang of fear that if the halyards flew, the sail would come down, rowers would be covered with the cloth and ropes, the beat would be lost, speed would come off, the warship would catch us and we would all be dead men.

All this passed through my mind in a flash. I looked around, no other had seen what I had seen; all attention was on the gap between us and the Trireme, from which a fiery ball now shot through the air in an arc, landing in the sea well behind us. They were firing fire pots at us from their catapult, just as the Celeusta had predicted. I looked at the drummer facing me.

'I am leaving, keep the oar in time,' I said.

He shook his head in fear and spoke in a high, childlike voice. 'No, they will kill you, I cannot do it.'

'You must! Keep - the - oar - rowing!' I growled and without another glance at his fear-stricken face, I let go the oar, slid from my seat and ran the few paces back to the horns set in the deck to the side of the central walkway.

I loosed rope from the coil hanging from its peg and hurled a few turns on the aftermost post of the horns then bracing my feet against it, pulled taut and thereby halted the relentless slide of the halyards. I shouted at the top of my voice. All hands were busy rowing except the Trierarchus and the helmsman. The Trierarchus abandoned his position on the poop and ran to my side.

He took in the situation at a glance, shouted, 'Hold on!' and rushed back to the poop where he took the steering oar extensions from the helmsman, releasing him to help me.

I clamped the ropes of the topmost turn together with all the strength of my hands, jamming them for now against further movement. The helmsman removed my hasty round turns from the aftermost horn and then commenced to make extra crossed turns around the two horns, finishing with a locking turn.

He nodded to me and I pulled my hands with some effort from their position in the middle of the rope-turns around the bits. Now the halyards were secured with six turns where before they had only three. A locking turn laid on in the beginning would have secured them, but someone in haste had failed to put it on and from that our lives had been hanging by a thread.

Our danger was still great. I returned to my oar, sliding myself in under the loom as the Pitulis strove to maintain time. He was still frightened at having been left in sole charge of my oar and as I took up position again, tears of relief slid down his cheeks. He understood that if he had missed the beat, got out of time and entangled with the other rowers ahead and behind, that would have led to a general loss of stroke with dire results for all of us. His tearfulness at his plight was strange for a warrior and I puzzled over it as we rowed, his plump, hairless face, dry now of its tears, bobbing in front of me.

As we cleared the headland the Trireme had closed with us and continued to lob fire pots. All fell into the water, although now they were close enough that we could hear the plop and sizzle as they fell.

'Row my lads,' called the Trierarchus, 'they are at their nearest, now we are heading due south for home and they shall not catch us for we match them at the oars and we have up all sail.'

I looked over the rail, it was not obvious that we were drawing away and yet the occasional fire pot came no nearer so we must be holding position.

All on the oars settled down for the long race. The crew that fell first from weariness was lost. Either the Trireme lost its prey or we lost our lives. We were the crew rowing with most to lose and therefore more driven to endure; also we had up all sail. The Romans, as was their custom on going into action, had all sail down and stowed to clear the decks for the marines.

Hour after hour we rowed; five heartbeats to the stroke. There was no thousand-stroke rest now, no four-thousand stroke relief. I counted seven thousand strokes and my back was breaking with weariness. I shook my head like a wet dog to clear the salt sweat, which ran into my eyes and made them burn.

We passed perilously close to the land on the ladeboard side as we kept to our southerly course and then I saw that we had land on both sides. The Trierarchus, speaking horn in hand, addressed us.

'We are sailing between the coast and Sparrowhawk Island. When we pass under the Cape to the south we will be clear of Sardinia and closer to our seas. He is clearly falling behind. Keep going brave lads, show no lessening of stroke and I think he will give up.'

And so, with new courage and hope breathed into us from his words, we forced our aching bones as we flashed between the Island and the mainland and the beat picked up. What it was in heartbeats I could not tell for my heart had been racing for so long it was probably beating six to a stroke, where before was only three. Certainly now, the gap between us had increased and the Roman had long ago given up throwing fire pots at us.

Then we saw our salvation: rather than enter the channel between the island and the shore the Trireme raised all its oars from the water and coasted slowly to a halt as its bow came round to ladeboard. And then its oars dipped once more and it turned north and sped away. Weary and breathless we may have been, but we were still able to raise a cheer.

The beat slackened slowly until we were stroking at normal speed. The order came for the end of emergency rowing and the Pitulis let go the oar with a sigh of relief, smiled at me and walked aft to take up his position on the drum.

As soon as we cleared the headland, the lower bank of rowers ceased pulling and rested on their oars and then, on the command, brought them in and stowed them in the bench side crutches. Ordered to rest, the men slipped away to lay their weary bones down upon their benches.

The upper bank ceased rowing and we rested thankfully on our oars while the sails carried us south. When it became clear that the Trireme had indeed given up the chase then the upper bank was unshipped and we joined the lower bank rowers in blissful sleep, laid along our benches, feet hanging on the walkway.

I heard the shouts and cries of the standby Velarii as they brought down the topsails, brailed up the mainsail and braced the yard round, but they faded away as I fell into sleep. Nor did I wonder for a moment what they did.

I awoke in the dark, we were heading west with the wind on our steerboard beam. A Duplicarii, one of the Bosun's mates, was shaking my shoulder.

'Come to the poop right away,' he said.

I came fully awake and rising from my bench, ignoring the

aches and cramps in my body, followed him aft to the poop deck, stepping carefully in the moonlight through the limbs still stretched from the benches onto the central walkway.

Many lamps brightly lighted the poop. I arrived in front of the Trierarchus and hastily bent my knee and bowed, wondering what wrong I had done. Had leaving my oar been some deadly sin with no excuse?

Standing beside me with hanging head was another of the Bosun's mates.

The watch woke the sleepers and ordered them to pay attention. Captain Wisimar stepped forward and spoke in a loud voice.

'This man you see before you,' he pointed to the Duplicarii, 'is called Gelimer, Bosun's mate. His job it was to secure the mainsail halyards and he failed to do this through haste and carelessness. His failure could have cost the lives of every man on board the Triton. He is sentenced to twenty lashes and to be reduced to single pay and to service on the oars.'

He turned to Gelimer. 'Do you have anything to say?'

'Yes, my Lord,' said Gelimer, 'I am in wrath with myself, I admit the fault and accept the punishment willingly. I thank you, Lord, that it is not death, which surely I deserve.'

'Well said,' spoke Wisimar. 'This man has been a good member of this crew and has not erred before. His sentence is not for life and when the time arises and there is need then I may re-make him, for he will be careful to avoid mistakes in the future.'

He turned to me and I awaited my punishment for maybe I should have called for help not left my oar.

'Here,' he said, 'is Gewis, the newest member of our crew. That we are still alive tonight is from his work in the morning of this day. His sharp eye and quick thinking saved us from disaster. He deserves reward, but gold and silver is not enough. This crew needs sharp eyes and quick thought. Thus I make him up to Learner Officer. He will take station with the Proreta when we cruise and with the Bosun when matters of seamanship are in hand. He is made up to double pay at once and when we split the spoils he will receive the rate of Bosun's mate.'

To my amazement, dazed as I was by the praise of Wisimar, the crew raised a shout of approval. The Captain turned to me. 'Henceforward you will row only when we are in danger. Take your station now alongside the Proreta. Listen and learn from him, he will release you to the Bosun at need. Learn also from the Bosun for he is the source of much wisdom in matters concerning the workings of the ship.' He paused and then, 'Can you read and write?'

'No, Lord,' I admitted.

He stroked his beard, musing. 'When the ship is in port and in store with only usual maintenance to be carried out, you will meet with the Secretarius and when he has the time he will teach you. An officer who wishes to advance in his skill and knowledge must be able to read, write and speak Latin. Now go to the prow, and join the Proreta and learn your trade.'

I bowed, gave my dazed and bewildered thanks and scampered along the walkway from the poop, whilst many called their approval. For the moment I was a hero.

When I reached the prow where the Proreta and the Gubernator stood together, I met Tzazo's cool glance and came back to earth with a bump.

'You have had the best of this night,' he said, 'now stand and watch the price of carelessness.'

I turned. Gelimer was leaning both hands upon the mast.

The Celeusta swung the lead tipped scourge from his right hand. He glanced at the Trierarchus who nodded. The Row Master brought his arm back and then delivered the first of twenty strokes, each falling with the regularity of his drumbeat. During the whole course of this punishment Gelimer made no sound, although the blood running down his back marked the harshness of the laying on. At its end he turned and on faltering legs made his way silently, amidst the silence of all the crew, to the bench so lately my home at the oar.

'Very well,' called Wisimar to all the crew, 'let that be an end to the matter. We have other punishment to dish out, but first we must deal with the Roman interloper in our sea.'

The crew roared their approval at that, amongst some laughter. As the noise died away, Wisimar added, 'That done, we must deal with the treacherous scoundrel who claimed friendship and plotted destruction. There will be plenty of plunder for all when we sack Tharros for its trickery.'

Again this was greeted by a roar of approval, for fear, so lately the feeling of choice, had given way to anger and the desire to crush our enemies in the dust.

I took my station by Hilder, our Proreta. Our job was to set the direction of the ship by sun and stars, so we might go where our Captain decided. Also, when called by the lookout or when judged timely, to look ahead and use sharp eyes and ears to spy out breaking surf that showed the position of reefs and shallows, so that the vessel could turn about to get distance and then make a wide berth. It was also our task to spot the land as soon as possible and, through experience, to tell what land it was and what course should be steered to keep off it. We must also spot shifts of wind or when storm clouds were sighted, warn of approaching squalls so that the sails could be brailed up in good time. All this the Proreta taught me over the coming weeks.

On this my first occasion in the bow station he explained what action had been decided on to destroy the Trireme that had chased us. 'We shall head north by sail as much as we can,' he said, 'or by single bank if not, for we may have to fight and the Velarii must be fresh for it.' He leaned against the rail and pointed ahead.

'To get close to the Roman we will approach from the north in two or three day's time, when the memory of the chase to the south is fading from their minds.'

My eyes widened, but he simply smiled and continued speaking. 'When we do so we will be an Egyptian trader and approach by night.'

Hilder went on to explain that in the old days, ships fought mostly with the ram, sinking the enemy by ramming. This was no longer the way and the Romans fought by boarding and using their heavily armoured marines to kill enemy fighting sailors. But the crew of the Triton had kept her ram in good order and she could use it if required, although did not do so normally, for there was not much profit in sinking merchantmen when it was their ship and cargo you want.

In the guise of an Egyptian merchant ship coming from the north, we had a good chance of getting close enough to the Roman, especially if he was at anchor, to sink him with our ram.

'Of course,' said Hilder, 'we have the dancing girls - they are our secret weapon - and an Egyptian on board to answer their hails just in case any there speak the language.' That was quite likely, he told me, for the Romans have little interest in seafaring and apart from the officers, all of the crew would be mercenaries: Greeks, Syrians, Egyptians and even Germanians.

'Are they not mostly slaves?' I asked.

Hilder shook his head. 'Slaves are too expensive to risk on board ship, although some may be there on hire from their owners, as are our Secretarius, the Symphoniacus and the Pitulis.' He laughed. 'They are our dancing girls; our secret weapon. You'll see.'

He looked in amusement at my puzzlement. 'Of course, you are fresh from some northern shithole where a poke in the mud is the height of your knowledge of the world. Those three, our hireling slaves, are eunuchs. You know? Eunuchs?'

I shook my head.

He grinned at my ignorance. 'They have their bollocks cut off, boy, so they can sing in a high voice for the pleasure of their master, especially when he pokes them, and they never, never, molest the lady of the household, no matter how much she is aching for it.'

I felt revolted, but I understood. I also now understood the smooth cheeks, tears and high voice of the Pitulis, which had been bothering me since the handing over of the oar.

The Proreta pushed his head close to mine and spoke in a low voice as if sharing some great secret. 'Molesting the slaves or any other kind of buggery is forbidden on board if that's your fancy. Not that I care where you dip your wick. It's just that it leads to disorder. We can't have the Velarii fighting over a piece of arse.'

I hurried to admit that was not my fancy.

'So, a man for the ladies eh?' He smiled at his own thoughts.

'Not even that now,' I said and then, without forethought or guile, I spilled out my experience in Gaul that still gave me troubled dreams and which seemed to have killed my desires.

The Proreta regarded me gravely. He was a rough-mouthed man and I waited for him to mock me or to make some coarse comment, but he did not. His stern gaze rested on me for some time as if considering some weighty matter and then he smiled.

'What ails you is easy to cure, my boy,' he said, 'just leave it to me I know just the thing.' And as I was later to discover, he did.

Our conversation turned back to the coming attack on the Trireme, for which I was thankful. The Proreta told me the rest of the plan. The Triton had used this tactic before and gained a victory. Those involved understood it well. They called the manoeuvre 'the Egyptian' because it imitated the careless luxury in which noble Egyptians travelled at sea.

At sunrise the Gubernator took over the bow watch to allow the Proreta some rest. The Captain had gone to his kennel on the poop and all was quiet as we ploughed west. I went to help the Bosun take in the spritsail and unship and stow the bowsprit.

There was less explanation given here for the Bosun was a dour man and I found I was just another spare pair of hands. But I observed and learned and stored in my head, until the work was finished and all was stowed away out of sight. I went then to catch some sleep until the Proreta returned to his bow watch or the sails were changed, whichever happened first.

The sail change happened first, but I had some time to lie on the deck and try to come to some grasp of my new standing and the speed with which it had happened. I started to think that perhaps my Lady had some task in mind for me.

I watched the change of sail, determined to learn. Some of the top bank rowers had to man oars and row to keep steering and hence direction. The Velarii loosed the halyards and the yard came rattling down. They loosed and pulled out the brails, let go the lacings and the sail was free to fold and carry away. The new sail was rigged, the yard hauled up and our plain old sail was replaced with one splendid with broad vertical red stripes. A sail fit for a king, or a rich Egyptian merchant.

Now we looked to ourselves. Taking my shield from the rail, I placed it where I could easily grab hold of it. If the spikes of a raven thudded into our deck and Roman marines poured over it we would be fighting for our lives with little chance of survival.

The oars were unshipped and we continued to sail west. I rested on a bench in the shade of the southern bulwark. At midday we brought down the sail, manned the upper bank oars and altered course to the north, rowing easily into the gentle breeze.

I took station with the Proreta and he explained more of the plan: we would continue to row north until our Captain was sure we had rowed at least half a day further north than the Trireme's most likely base at Bosa. When we reached that position, in the morning at about sunrise, we would raise the sail again and sail east until we reached the coast of Sardinia. The Triton would then make its way south under sail until the hills about Bosa were just in view at the setting of the sun.

When darkness fell the deck entertainments would begin with music and dancing. It was the hope of the Captain that we would come on the Trireme at anchor in the lee of the Cape and that the lookouts, posted on the hilly cape north of the Bosa anchorage of the Trireme, would pass on the news that an Egyptian merchantman was sailing close by from the north. Once around the Cape, the Triton would steer into the anchorage as if heading for Bosa. We would lower our 'Egyptian' sail when we knew the Trireme had seen it, as if we were coming to anchor to await daylight. The rest would be at the orders of the Captain.

And so it was. Everything worked as if to the design of Captain Wisimar. When he felt we were far enough south he ordered oil lights in pots to be lit and placed on the stern so that it was almost as bright as daylight. The Pitulis, the Symphoniacus and the Secretarius, dressed in women's muslins and with their heads hooded by muslin shawls made an appearance on the stern deck to the cheers of the five rowers a side on the top bank, and the standby men.

The rest of us concealed ourselves and were told to be silent on pain of death. The Pitulis drummed and sang, the fluter played some music like nothing I had ever heard before, but with a lilt and a beat that joined with the drum and had my foot, oh so silently, tapping. The Secretarius joined in the singing and started to whirl in a sinuous dance.

As we approached the Cape to the north of Bosa we saw the flicker of the signal fire at the top of the lookout tower. We rounded the Cape and wonder of wonders, there dead ahead was the Trireme. She was lying to her anchor with oars in and as inviting a broad-side as ever laid itself open to a ram.

We raised our small contingent of oars and at the same time brailed up the sail to the maximum. As we drifted closer to the warship, the officer of the watch shouted for us to identify ourselves. Our Egyptian called across for anyone who spoke his language and after an interval a voice replied. I could not understand what passed between them, but I heard later we told them we were the Luxor, come from Alexandria with a split cargo of grain, some for Adjacium and the remainder for Bosa and Tharros.

We were told we could safely anchor anywhere to the south. We swung to steerboard and continued swinging through west. The Triton by this manoeuvre concealed its south side from the Trireme. At the whispered orders of the Captain and the Celeusta, all oars, upper and lower, were run out and manned on this side. We also ran out the upper bank oars on the north side, the steerboard side, in plain sight of the Trireme. That would not seem unusual as we were manoeuvring to anchor. We swung in a wide curve until we were heading north, as if stemming the wind before dropping anchor.

And then ... we slewed back to the east, pointing directly towards the Trireme. The rowers quickly ran out and manned the lower steerboard bank and at the order of the Celeusta we rowed as if Wothan's hounds were after us.

The Triton leapt forward and cries of alarm and the beating of the watch drum calling the marines to arms could be heard from the Trireme, but by then we were only one hundred paces away.

With high-pitched shrieks our dancing troupe rushed off the stern deck, instruments tucked under their arms, their muslin dresses blowing in the wind of our speed.

In less than twenty heart beats we were into her, dead amidships with an almighty rending crash whilst the rowers came to a stop so abruptly they slid on their benches. The Trireme rolled over to her steerboard side under the press of our speed. There was a heartening cracking and rending noise from the planks, splintered and broken by our ram.

Our archers ran to the bows to try to keep the Roman marines away from the bulwarks. Being higher than our decks their archers could rain death on us. Some arrows found their way into the deck and even to the mast of the Triton, but none struck the crew.

Our slingers picked up the oil light pots from the stern by their chains then sprinted towards the bow, whirling them around their heads and casting them up and onto the deck of the Trireme. There were shouts of pain from the deck above as Romans were splashed with burning oil. The flames flickered on the masts and rigging and could be seen through the row ports at eye level as the fire spread. This now became our danger. If the Triton were caught fast by the ram and could not draw free the flames would spread to us.

The Celeusta took over, for now it was his skill we relied on to enable us to withdraw from the side of the enemy. First he backwatered ladeboard banks and then he raised those oars and backwatered the steerboard banks, and then back again and so on. The effect was to loosen the ram in the hole it had smashed, as the vessel was skewed first one way and then the other. This allowed water to pour into the Trireme and reduced the press of sea holding us against its hull.

After three repeats of this he gave the order to backwater together and we glided astern, gathering way and leaving the burning Trireme behind. The flaming deck of the Roman warship was now settling deeply in the water and there arose a great din of shouting voices and screams as her crew fought in vain to douse the flames. The cheering that rose from the Triton overwhelmed their cries.

I had been standing with the Proreta on the bow throughout, fully armed, my sword in hand and my shield on my arm. As we backed away I became aware of the swift beating of my heart and breathed my relief at the outcome of the brief battle. I could see crewmen from the Roman jumping into the water.

I pointed, 'What will we do with them?' I asked.

Hilderic raised his eyebrows in surprise. 'Do with them? Why nothing, I hope they all drown, although of those without armour, some may swim ashore, it's only about two thousand paces. Listen, my lad, they would have shown no mercy to us.

Had I a fleet of small craft I would pursue them and spear them in the water like fish in a tun.'

# Chapter 17

**AD 447 to AD 455**
**Gewis' Tale, Tharros**

The Celeusta brought the ship about to the south and we started the short row to Tharros. The Trierarchus wanted us to be there and storming ashore while it was still dark. There were gently shelving beaches near the town, ideal for the purpose.

The standby Velarii, including me, released the brails so that the vessel could sail and allow the crew to take rest. There would be fighting to do, maybe, and looting could be hard work.

Before dawn, by moonlight, we sailed around the headland into the bay we had fled from but three days before. The moon was low on the horizon now and the shoreline hidden in shadow. We brailed up the sail and drifted, awaiting the dawn.

As soon as the pale sand of the beach nearest the town came into view, we pulled on our oars by the dying light of the moon and the lightening eastern sky until the prow kissed the sand and we were grounded. The gangways went down and sailors carried ropes up the beach, securing them to saplings near the woody edge.

In full armed might the rest of us stormed past them and in moments were along the road and into town whilst the town watch was still trying to turn out the militia and the small Roman guard.

There was no fight in them when we told them how we had destroyed the naval power of Rome in the area. We locked them under guard in the guardhouse, which we thought amusing. We could have set light to it with them inside, but we did not. It was the Governor we had come to punish.

We brought him out from his bed. He was still in his sleeping clothes and did not look happy to see us, even less so when Wisimar gave the order to show the town how we dealt with betrayal. We stretched him in the shape of the Roman marking for ten and nailed him to the double door of his house.

He was a Roman of the old sort and a brave and disciplined man, he made no sound as we hammered the nails in and even after this was over there was only the sound of his shuddering breaths as he tried to fill his lungs. For all that day he hung there in the sun for the townsfolk to witness how we dealt with treachery. By the end of the day he was dead for he was no longer a young man. We took him down and gave him to his wife for burial. Severe we may have been but we still understood courtesy.

Our men drove the townsfolk from the houses in which they cowered. We brought them together in the market place. This was the nearest thing to a forum in the small town and there Captain Wisimar addressed them.

'We came here for stores, as in the past, and for which we have always paid. It was our habit to take stores here and raid further north or south. This time your Governor betrayed us and our lives were put at danger. We have sunk the Roman warship, its crew are drowned and the betrayer gasps out his life just there, as you can see. We are no longer going to raid north or south. We are going to raid here. This town has much gold in it, some of it ours. Now all of it is ours.'

His voice slowed and he spoke in a measured fashion. He was a fair man and wished to make sure there was no misunderstanding now that he was dealing with matters of life and death.

'Here are the rules. My crew will come to each house in turn. You will deliver up your gold and any other precious thing. If you say your house has nothing then we shall burn it. If you have nothing in truth then you had better borrow from your neighbours. When you deliver up your precious things better be sure there are none hidden. If you give everything, your house will be safe from insult and harm. If my men search and find hidden wealth then that protection is withdrawn. The head of the house will join the Governor on some convenient piece of wood; the rest of the household will be delivered up to my men to do with as they will. So, if you value your wives, daughters and sons then make sure you are not miserly in your giving.'

This speech worked like a charm; there was gold, silver and precious stones forthcoming from every large house and a contribution of some sort from even the poorest hovel. And so, as promised, we treated the citizens with dignity and mercy.

From that small town we collected the gold weight of ten pounds, worth, so the Secretarius said, about seven hundred solidi. The sale value of the stones he said could be as much as a further three hundred. A thousand solidi was not huge wealth, but a very good haul even so and that, plus the relief from the strains of the last three days, made some of the crew over-cheerful. They broke open the wine store and harassed the maidens of the town. We had to restrain them.

Captain Wisimar had given his word and that was gold, he said. Any further outbreaks, and the gold they had lately won would be forfeit. That quietened the riotous ones and we brought them, less than sober, back to the ship with the rest of us.

We took the anchor ropes in and with a mighty heave from all, except the few oarsmen put on board, we refloated the Triton. We swarmed on board, manned the oars and commenced the long trip back to Carthage.

This was typical of my life with the Vandals. Seven long years I was with them. All was to change once again when I went with them to Rome, but that was yet to come.

Bowdyn ceased speaking and reappeared, once more the Gleeman and not the narrator he glanced about him. There was silence throughout the Cot. The fires had burned down and the light came only from the glowing embers. Someone turned and threw faggots onto them so that they blazed up and suddenly I could see clearly the faces around the fire. All were directed towards Bowdyn as we waited in silence.

'And that is all for tonight,' he said. 'I think we need our sleep for the morrow.'

'Oh, Master Bowdyn,' said Beth, 'they were such cruel days, I can hardly bear to listen at times.'

'Well, Mistress Elizabeth,' said Bowdyn, 'cruel they were, but can you say in truth that our times are any less cruel?'

There was a murmur of agreement as, in ones and twos and threes the audience rose and thanked Master Bowdyn for his story.

'Again on Saturday then?' he asked. There was a buzz of enthusiastic agreement and then, quietly and with less chatter than the previous time, they went thoughtfully on their way.

# Chapter 18

**AD 455**

**Gewis' Tale, Carthage**

The Cold-Cot, built on our farm long ago, had just four high walls of fieldstone. As I have said before, it had a wide doorway on the south wall, but no roof. Its purpose was to provide a shelter against the wind for those of our animals we had brought in from the fields for one purpose or another and which needed better shelter than that afforded by a sheep-hurdle pen.

When we assembled early on Saturday evening it seemed to me that our open-air theatre was becoming smaller, for certainly it seemed fuller than ever before. My father noticed this also for he gave the opinion that perhaps for the future we must think of two fires, with Bowdyn sat against the wall the same distance from each. There was no doubt that those at the back were so far from the fire they would feel little heat and the nights were now getting wintery and cold. So far, however, it had not rained again; a small miracle for which we were grateful.

Our growing numbers should have been no surprise, for there is nothing country folk like better than free entertainment. To be so amused whilst sat around a fire eating solid food and in the company of bantering neighbours getting merry from good ale and country wine, was perfection.

All understood that they must bring fuel, food and drink and their own stools or benches and so my father, other than the remark about re-organising the fires for the benefit of our growing audience, merely smiled and called his greetings to each party as they arrived and added their fuel to the fires. These now started to burn fiercely with a fine crackling, casting shadows of the folk in sharp outline on the walls.

When our audience had assembled and settled, our storyteller arrived with that wonderful instinct for timing that seemed natural to him. He looked around at the growing throng and smiled with what I thought was approval.

Having recovered his health and vigour with the healing of his scars and the fading of his bruises and swellings, Bowdyn was cheerful and active. He had insisted that besides storytelling he must help around the farm to pay his way for board and lodging. After token protests such as one would make to any guest, my father had given in and had discovered yet other talents in our Gleeman. He was a handy mechanic and carpenter, something of a blacksmith too; and so he was truly useful, working with and under the direction of Jedediah in making good those failures of wood and metal so common on an active farm. So useful in fact that my father had insisted on paying him a small wage and so his status had changed from refugee to something between a guest and a handyman.

Now, Bowdyn took his place by the fire and waited until the murmur of voices, the chinking of bottles and the shifting of seats died away and silence fell.

'Tonight,' he said, 'we shall start Gewis on his journey home. With some exceptions we shall skip over much of his seven years in Africa, for the telling of them would become tedious repetition of skirmishes and battles as he grew from mature boyhood into a seasoned warrior and leader of men. So, we shall leave out the battles and pass over the seven years, briefly and in other directions.'

This drew a mixed response, for the younger men relished the telling of death and destruction, whereas the womenfolk felt there had already been perhaps a little too much.

Bowdyn smiled and leaned back in the old carved Welsh chair that everyone now thought of as the 'Story Chair', and as his voice deepened he again spoke to us as Gewis.

Carthage, you might say, furnished the soil in which I grew from a sapling to a tree. That soil, thanks be, grew a strong tree, for I needed that strength to carry the weight put on my 'branches' as I grew over those seven years. Lovingly nurtured, I in my turn gave out shelter from the harshness of the sun and the wildness of the wind. I speak of my lovely Elisia, for whom I shall always feel tenderness and loss. Why I did not stay with her, why she did not come with me, I do not know although I have spent many, many hours racking my mind for the answer to those questions. Fate did not wish it. What her fate is now I do not know, nor under whose branches she shelters. That there will be someone I am sure, for she gives tenderness and care and receives protection back as naturally as the wind blows and the sun shines .... But I am getting ahead of myself and must tell you how I came to meet her.

When we arrived back in Carthage from Tharros the first order of business was the division of our spoils. The Secretarius met with the King's third Assistant Chamberlain and together they apportioned the quarter that belonged to the King. Our

Secretarius wrote and had a receipt for the amount of two hundred and fifty solidi and the Assistant Chamberlain went away happy. In truth it was not much, for the whole amount would not pay the wages on a Liburnian such as the Triton for more than four weeks.

I was surprised the King was content with such a small share for he had two hundred ships to support. I raised this later with the Secretarius during our regular reading and writing lessons. He explained that the yield from plunder was but a small part of the King's income as he had the taxes of the whole of Africa, from Sala Colonia beyond the pillars of Hercules to Barneek, where his Kingdom met with that of Constantinopolis. To add to that, there were the cargoes from those ships taken at sea. We could take an Egyptian grain ship carrying a Roman cargo and then, through a middleman, sell back ship and cargo to the Romans. And so, whilst our gold was welcome, it was less than a drop in a bucket to King Gaiseric. As long as we gave up at least this much every month then we paid our way and were safe from changes, the Secretarius told me.

When we had completed this business I busied myself helping the Proreta and the Gubernator to strip down the Triton and return her to her boathouse. This took all of our first day back and it was a very tired crew that returned to the eating hall and pallets at the Sign of the Ram. Here we wolfed bowls of thick hot broth made from meat and oat grain and then, drained, fell onto our donkey's breakfasts in deep sleep.

The next day the Proreta sent for me. 'Go wash,' he said. 'Get the stale sweat and shit off and make yourself a clean smelling officer of the Triton. I told you I could cure what ails you. Meet me here at the count of five hundred strokes.'

Counting strokes at normal pace had become such a part of

my nature by then that I was just getting to the five hundred mark when I arrived back in the taverna of the inn.

The Proreta was waiting for me; he looked me over, noted that I wore my seax at my side and with a quick nod of approval he set off, beckoning me to follow. 'It is time you learned your way around Carthage. I am taking you to see a lady. She is the sister of my wife and a widow. Her husband died of a fever he caught on a raid in some shithole in Corsica. When we got there the whole town was dying; I was lucky, many were not. This was about five years after we got here, so about four years ago.'

I kept pace with him as he hurried through the streets, intrigued to know more.

'Her name is Elisia, she is a Moor as is my wife and she will show you everything you need to know about the city. I support her so she wants for nothing. Do not insult her or you will answer to me. Be kind and be a friend to her and she will welcome your company, although you are younger than her. How many years have you?'

I admitted to nearly seventeen years.

'Hmm, then that makes her about six years older than you; well that's about right. The last thing you need is a silly girl to show you the way when she does not know the road herself and you are lost.'

I puzzled over his meaning, but had some idea as I remembered my confession on the Triton and his claim to 'know just the thing.'

The widowed Elisia occupied a room in one of a block-long row of houses, in a street almost under the shadow of the hill of Byrsa. It was a modest room, but had a bed in one corner a bench and board, and a window with shutters that when open, as they were, gave a view onto the street. The great buildings on Byrsa hill towered in the distance over the roof of the house opposite. In the corner of the room was an angled ladder leading to a hatch, which I assumed, rightly as it turned out, opened to the flat roof of the building, a communal eating and sleeping area during the heat of high summer. The room was clean and well kept; everything neatly in its place, the board scrubbed, the mud floor trodden into a fine, almost glazed finish and swept clean of all dust and sand.

The lady Elisia was small, dark of skin and inclined to plumpness, but with merry dark eyes that seemed to create a glow of laughter wherever she went, like the light thrown out by a candle on a dark night. And yet, behind the laughter was sadness and from the eyes as they beheld me was concern and sympathy - for me; for me! Yet she knew nothing of me, except what she read, like a sorceress, at first glance.

'This is the lady Elisia,' said Hilder. He smiled at her, 'And this young man is he who saved us all from the Romans, so we have cause to be grateful. His name is Gewis and he is of the far northern German folk. He needs to learn the ways of the city as he will be here, I judge, for a long time. I thought perhaps it would be amusing for you to show him the beauties of Carthage?'

The lovely Elisia looked thoughtfully at me and then at Hilder. 'I have become more and more concerned at the behaviour of some of the crewmen in the streets of the city,' she said. 'To have a fine, young, armed warrior to escort me when I go about the town would be a great relief for me. If you could bear to be my guard as well as my companion I would enjoy that. There are many parts of our city where I no longer dare to go alone for fear of insult or worse.'

She smiled and the glow lit the room. She spoke the tongue learned from her husband, a charmingly accented Saxon dialect. It was easily understandable to me, for which I was grateful.

'M-m-my Lady,' I stammered, knowing the courtesy I wished to give, but tripping over my own tongue. 'It would be a great p-p-privilege to escort you anywhere in the whole wide world and guard you from insult with my life.'

Elisia smiled at my gruff and stumbling offer. 'And I, my Lord, welcome your offer and would be ready, whenever my sister's husband can release you, to make good use of it.'

Hilder grunted. 'There will be much time after the sun goes down and maybe even before and at least one day in every seven free,' he said. 'But if guard duty it is, carry your shield and mark on it the hands of the gods so that all know you for one of us.'

Thus began my recovery from the wreck created by my own folly. I will not detail that part of my life of which Elisia was the centre, for that is private and sacred to me. All men's days have many mingled parts, these all taken together make up a life. Mingling of some parts scratches; it is better to forget some. Others stand in solitary splendour.

Elisia was the sun to my day and the candle flame to my night. She was always in my mind, warming and lighting, even when that around me seemed at its blackest and most savage. She it was who taught me love, selfless giving and receiving. She it was who taught me gentleness. And most of all, she it was who taught me forgiving, for although she was not party to my shame she somehow forgave me for it and I was able to accept her forgiveness. I have never understood that, it was as if she were the fingertips of the Goddess herself, reaching down to give me a second chance to be the true man all men should be.

From her forgiveness I learned gentleness and mercy and

these lessons have stayed with me all my life. If sometimes I am harsh and cruel it is only because I think it best for the greater good. I do not believe I am ever so from wantonness or indulgence. I have no taste for it and always prefer mercy to cruelty, love to hate and gentleness to brutality. I try to live my life in this way. I am as drawn to those of like mind as the vicious cruelty of some others repels me. All this I learned from Elisia, as well as how to please a woman.

We talked and talked from the beginning for she was a great talker and loved to gossip. Like all women, as I found out, she was relentlessly inquisitive. She wanted to know all the details of my life, and because I would have trusted her with that life itself, I told her. When I told her of fleeing my hopeless love for Elwine she sat thinking for a little while.

'But you are over it now?' she asked. 'You have someone else you love?'

'Of course,' I said. 'I love you.'

'Silly boy,' she said. 'Love your Saxon princess. I am only teasing you.' But I could see she was pleased.

She was wise. With only a few details, without knowing the person that we spoke of, she could go at once to the core of their secret self. Many women can do this; it comes from their closeness to the goddess. Once she had sounded the depths of my feeble character she wanted to know everything about those closest to me on the Triton.

I spoke to her of Lothar; she listened and then spoke sadly. 'Poor man, there is a much sorrow there. His temper has caused great harm; inside he tears himself apart to curb it so that it does no further hurt.'

I turned this over in my mind many times, even much later, for what she said was true, although it took me long to find this out.

Of Atilec she spoke wisely. I never found fault with her judgement. 'Trust him, for although great wrong has been done him so also he has seen the good of this world. Atilec, I believe, understands love and from love springs all else of truth and beauty in our lives.'

Of course, she knew nothing of his murderous past, nor did she guess, but then, possessed as he had been by some avenging god, he had hardly been himself.

Of the two Alans I could not tell her much for I knew little myself. She listened then said, 'They are two lost children who just want to go home. As long as they stay with you they will always see you as strangers. The world holds them prisoner. They long to be with their families. Their minds can think only of that which they have lost. They do not see that which they have.'

I learned much from her wisdom. During the whole of my seven-year stay in Carthage we were together, but I still stayed at the Ram for Elisia had no taste for marriage. Having lost one well-loved husband she did not seek to risk that grief again, she said. She would not have me stay with her beyond a day at a time because, as she said, having lived alone, once she got over her grief she found she liked the freedom of movement that her own home gave her. I suppose loving friendship was what we shared.

As time passed, I wanted more and she wanted less. When I decided that I would take the chance to go home with the riches I had won, modest though they were, she would not come with me. She did not take much from me, although Hilder was dead by then and she relied on me to sustain her.

Because her needs were so simple, I was able to leave her as much of my hoard as would keep her for life, with care. We parted with broken hearts, or so it felt, but they mended. I am sure hers mended before mine, but in the end even mine healed. Regrets fade and all that is left is the pleasing warm glow of loving memory.

What of the rest of my life in Carthage? As always, some things changed and others stayed the same. Life became a routine of care for the Triton, sailing on raids in the Triton, taking cargo ships at sea with the Triton. Aside from Elisia, the ship was my life. My hoard grew slowly and I husbanded it close-fistedly. We fought no more battles with Roman warships for after the affair at Tharros, our Captain Wisimar became even more careful. We never more fell into a wonted plan, such as had nearly led to our destruction. It was as if on each cruise he rolled the dice and decided our course of action once we were at sea; certainly he knew where we were to go but no other could predict it.

There was another sailing where the Fates again wove a new pattern in my life. Hilder died of an infected wound. We were boarding a Rhodian freighter carrying Egyptian grain to Rome when a hired guard shot a dart, which took my friend and tutor in the arm.

The wound seemed not serious but did not heal; the arm grew swollen and blackened. The Captain spoke with us and we agreed it should come off. We could not seek permission from Hilder himself because he was raving by then, deep in talk with the gods. So we removed the putrefying stinking flesh and sealed the wound with hot pitch, but he never came to himself again and his spirit passed to that place in Hel where those who have lived a decent life go.

He was coarse of mouth, but true and good in his actions and as good a friend to me as I ever had. I shall always thank him fondly in my prayers for making me known to my lovely Elisia; she who salved my life and showed me my true path when so many wrong ones lay before me.

To him also I owe such mastery of my work as I have. Over the two years we sailed and fought together he taught me much. So much that young as I was, on Hilder's death Wisimar chose to make me up to Proreta and so I became a full-fledged officer, senior to the Celeusta and next in line and junior to the Gubernator. The thought frightened me, for there were men both above and below me who knew far more than I, but what the Fates determine, a man must deal with.

When we returned from that sad cruise I told Wisimar that I would bear the doom of Hilder to his wife. He entrusted to me a donativum, a gift of money, for the most part from him but also all the officers, for we had all given as we could. In addition he gave me Hilder's paid up earnings and prize money. It relieved me to see that the two together were enough to keep the bereaved wife and her children housed and in food until the children were grown and could bring a living home.

I took Elisia with me, for I knew that women are of more comfort to each other at such times than is a clumsy man. Together we delivered the hateful news and after making sure she understood how much I and all the other Tritons would miss him, and had grasped that she was not destitute, I left them to their tears and wails, drying my own eyes before I stepped onto the street.

My new rank on board the Triton wrought a change on my own group of companions. When I became Learner Officer, Atilec and Lothar and the two Alan bowmen had taken little notice of my change in situation other than to salute my enterprise and wish me well of my good fortune. I was only a trainee after all. This changed when I became Proreta. We were still friends, but there was a new deference in their manner even though I was much younger than they.

The last word on this was Atilec's. 'Our chick has become an eagle,' he said.

I noticed a new reluctance to discuss ship matters, to complain and criticize as in the old days. I spent much of my time with Elisia so they had plenty of time and space in which to behave normally when I was not with them. When I was with them we remained good companions.

I suppose, looking back, we were on the road to change. At the beginning, I was the youngest member of the band. At the end they were my oath-sworn hearth companions, I the leader, they the followers.

And so the years passed.

The doings of the Great King were far from the doings of the Triton, but sometimes gossip flew around the city and settled at our board. When I first joined the Triton many in the hall felt pressed to bring me up to date with the nature of our rulers. I learned very early on in my stay there that Prince Honeric was not the man his father was. Great King Gaiseric was wise and firm, harsh sometimes, but not cruel.

The same could not be said for his son, who had nearly brought the whole kingdom low six years before my arrival. King Gaiseric, to form an alliance between the Vandals and the Goths, had made a marriage between Honeric and the daughter of Theodoric.

The young man's conduct towards her was so disagreeable that she became very unhappy. He could accept her defiance in nothing. She, the daughter of a great king, could do nothing but defy him, the son of a pirate, or be broken in spirit.

Then the Emperor of Rome made offer of an alliance through the marriage of his daughter Eudocia, then a child, to the already married Honeric.

Amongst the Royal Court of the Vandals were sundry

Goth nobles. Rumour does not make it clear whether the princess sowed discord amongst them, from her unhappiness and her apprehension that she would be set aside, or whether she joined a plot already growing.

Rumour has it that in support of this palace rebellion she tried to poison the Great King. Whether this is true or not the discovery of the plot gave Prince Honeric the opportunity to set her aside, and being of a cruel nature he ordered it done in the most unnatural and unkind way.

He mutilated his poor, unhappy princess by removing her nose and her ears. He sent her home to her father in that humiliating condition. Theodoric, in his outrage, determined to revenge himself on the Vandals.

The King of the Goths blamed Gaiseric for this evil and he, out of royal dignity would not deny it. Indeed it would be difficult to lay the blame on Honeric, for he was in Ravenna as a hostage at that time, so maybe the King was responsible for the deed. I can only say that it was the view of all that it was extremely unlike him. He was the most diplomatic of men in his foreign dealings. Why would he deliberately seek the enmity of the most powerful and moderate ruler outside of Rome at that time?

After Eostremonath, perhaps halfway through Thrimilci, after I had been with the ship for a little less than seven years, Captain Wisimar summoned us officers to his apartment in the Ram. This was unusual, for although we often met ashore it was in the hall of the inn that we discussed business. The Trierarchus was a private man and rarely invited crew into his private quarters.

On this occasion his wife answered our knock at the door. She ushered us into a spacious room, well hung and decorated with the plunder from a score of raids. She sent the children out and invited us to sit at the board where she had laid out small food and wine for us. The Captain, she said, would be with us shortly.

Presently there was a murmur of voices, we heard the door to the outside open and shut, and then Captain Wisimar entered the room. He flopped on the stool at the head of the table and stared for a while at the floor as if gathering his thoughts. At length he looked up and smiled at us all.

'Welcome, welcome,' he said, 'I see you have food and wine, my wife has greeted you.' Then without any more small talk he launched into the reason for our meeting.

'I have brought you here to listen to rumours,' he said. 'What we say here must remain here; will you all give me your oath on that?'

We trusted Captain Wisimar with our lives and agreed to an oath of secrecy without misgivings.

He nodded his thanks. His next words surprised and frightened us. 'There is fighting between the Romans. That has changed things and may change them further. The Emperor Valentinian is dead, murdered by a usurper. His wife Eudoxia forced into marriage with the usurper Maximus and his daughter Eudocia forcibly married to the son of Maximus.

'The Empress is determined to revenge herself. She has written secretly to Gaiseric asking for aid and he now has an excuse to go to Rome, at a time when the head of the snake is amazed and bedazzled.' He paused as if to draw his thoughts together and then continued.

'The child betrothed to Honeric is a child no longer and so Maximus has broken the pledge made by Valentinian to marry the princess to Honeric. It is likely that we will go to Rome.'

He looked enquiringly at us looking for our reaction to this startling news.

Tzazo spoke up. 'Rome is not the same as Palermo, the walls are great, the forces strong, it is a long time since Alaric sacked it, plenty of time to have made provision. Never taken from the sea - Carthage failed to take it from the land, never even tried the sea.'

The Celeusta chimed in, 'The Roman fleet is in Portus Julius two days to the south, but we will need to pass them on our way to Rome. There will be a mighty battle of ships and even if we prevail, there will be the legions on land, and if we prevail there too, then there are the walls and the youth of the city. It can't be done. We will be weakened and open to a counter-stroke.'

Wisimar looked to me, waiting for my words, eyebrows raised questioningly.

I hesitated and then embarrassed at the silence, I spoke up. 'Perhaps. But what if this strife divides the people and the army? Eudoxia is an Empress and of the line of Emperors; Maximus an interloper, a usurper. If the Empress has sent for us will she not make sure the fleet stays in harbour and the legions are elsewhere? We could never hold the city; the East would not allow it. At the best, if we get in we can right the wrongs of Eudoxia and Eudocia, loot the city and run.' I sat, gasping for air, having nervously blurted out my thoughts in one long breath.

Wisimar looked warmly at me. 'I see your lessons with the Secretarius and your readings have not been wasted, you have a grasp of the truth of the times. I think you are quite right. We will go, try out how things stand, make the most of it and come home.'

He looked us over. 'In the morning you will assemble the crew and float the Triton as if we are going for a cruise in search of mischief. On no account tell them where we might be going. They are quite used to that by now.'

He stood up. 'Thank you for coming, by this time next week we will either be very rich, dead, or wishing to be dead. May Tyche, Fortuna and the Wyrd Sisters favour us, and of course, Lord Jesus. Oh, one more thing, when we return, Gaiseric wishes us all to accept the passage through the waters to the Nailed God, Lord Jesus Christ. From our return onwards we will all be Christians and will give up the old gods, at least in public. I think he waits for our return because he does not wish to upset any of our gods before so risky a venture.'

We did not respond, just looked at him, but I think he understood that if we survived, some at least of his crew would be leaving by choice from Rome. He shrugged and said, 'I am not the King nor would wish to be.'

His words were no great surprise, for the number of Arian Christians amongst the Vandals had grown like shit flies. The bitterness towards the Roman Christians both in the East and West had also been increasing and there was no place for a third group, us Heathens as they called us, in the middle. I had noticed more and more that the sight of the insignia on my shield now drew hisses and the sign of the cross where before there was only respect. Only my stature, the axes and long seax I carried in full sight protected Elisia and me from worse.

Ah yes, the axes. My friend Lothar had carried these axes. On his back the great two-handed bearded axe and on his front the two throwing axes. Fearsome weapons in a land fight where making gaps in the war-hedge is all, but of less use in naval warfare where fighting is hand to hand with no clash of shields. The one is too big, for there is little room to swing it without as much danger to friends as to foes. The others will fly into the sea if not strung to the thrower. When I say strings attached I am sure you see I am joking, for such strings would entangle and endanger the struggling battlers as if caught in a web.

Thus was Lothar forced by the nature of our tasks to lay aside his most favoured weapons and concentrate on his work with the longseax and buckler. He had a fearsome spike added to his buckler and the same smith made his longseax from a captured spatha, with all the additional weight that gives. The smith folded one edge over to give a strong back edge for guarding and that left a sharp edge for hacking and a sharp point for stabbing. Thus equipped for close quarters work he was terrifying and friends tended to cluster near him, as foes sought to avoid him.

I was a student on many fronts at this time; I had learned the basics of the Proreta's work and was still learning from Hilder. I was learning my seamanship from the Bosun, reading and writing from the Secretarius. It seemed to me that there was no better person to continue my warrior training than Lothar.

My grounding thus far had been in the use of the spear and seax, but not at all in axe work, and as my tasks were small when we were not harrying the Middle Sea, I had time to increase my skills. I begged Lothar to take me on as a student. Once he resolved the awkwardness of our changes of station - first I as his junior, then as his superior and now, voluntarily, as his disciple - he was happy to help me, for between cruises time hung heavily on all our hands. Since then, of course, he has claimed that it was a deep-laid plot on my part to deprive him of his axes. Maybe so, but I have repaid him for my cunning, he is rich enough now to have one hundred axes crafted in gold in their place - he knows he was not cheated.

First, he persuaded me of the virtues of his longseax made from a Roman spatha. It did not need much argument to show me that the thickened back edge added strength and could take sword blows without fear of fracture, while the hacking edge was ideal for work at close quarters. I looked to the market place and found a spatha with ease, for we seized much Roman weaponry and sold it on to dealers.

The same smith who had worked on Lothar's spatha nodded with approval when I produced mine and for the cost of seven folles and a few hours of work, he produced a replica of the weapon carried by Lothar that I so admired. I hung the longseax he produced at my side for hot work; my father's sword I cleaned, oiled, wrapped and laid to one side in readiness for my own son one day. Then, although Lothar warned me that they were the wrong weapons for shipboard fighting, I asked him to teach me axe work, my wish being to learn the art of the thrown axe, although, as he showed me, there is also an art to the use of the two-handed axe if the user does not wish to be gutted while he is whirling it round his head.

Lothar showed me and I practised, and practised and practised some more until, one day, I wagered with Lothar that I could beat him throwing axes at a target at twenty paces; his axes against a golden solidus. He scoffed at the folly that would surely lead to me parting with my gold. But I beat him with ease, and the axes became mine. He was sorry to lose them for they were old friends, but he did not use them and so was able to live with their loss. I was not remorseful, for in my mind was the thought that I should not stay in Carthage forever, if I survived. When my fortune was made I would go home, but until that journey these fearful weapons might save my life. Which they did and more than once. One gold solidus well chanced.

# AD 455
# Rome, the Bat-cave

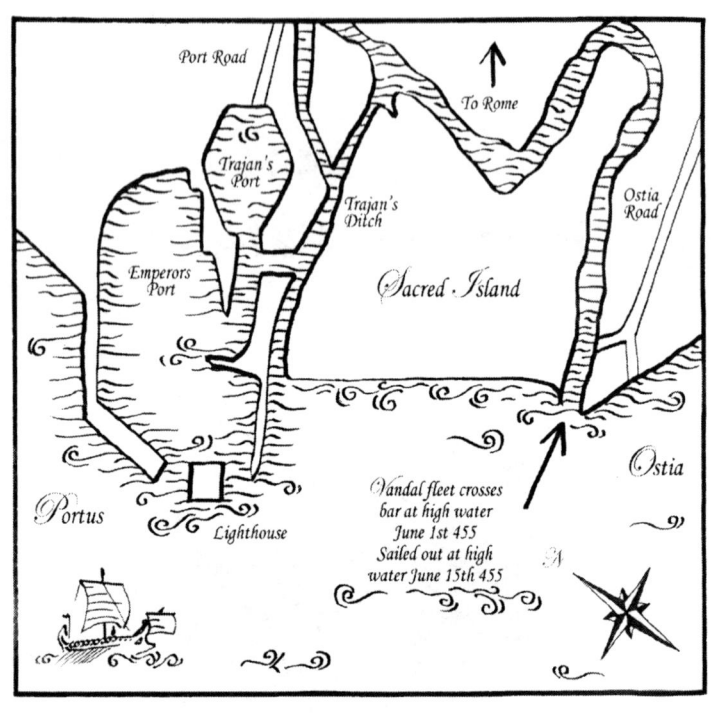

**Gewis' Tale – Gateway to Rome, AD 455**

# Chapter 19

**AD 455**

**Gewis' Tale, Invasion**

The morning following the meeting with Wisimar we mustered the crew at the Ram and ordered them to the boathouse to launch and prepare the Triton. My four companions fell in with me as we walked to the military harbour. It was Atilec, as usual, who spoke up.

'We hear we are going to Rome?' It was a question I was oath-sworn not to answer and so I said nothing.

'We understand that you cannot speak, but there is something we need to say,' he continued. 'If we land on the mainland we wish to leave the ship. We have enough gold for comfort, perhaps a few hides of land and some families to work it. We have been here long enough.'

I was surprised to hear this for although my thoughts had trended in exactly the same direction I had always thought my companions were the professional soldiers and I the odd man out, the inept, the exile; the homesick.

'So what do you want from me, if what you say happens?' I asked.

Atilec, Lothar and the two bowmen exchanged glances, this was something they had already talked about, that was plain.

'Well,' said Atilec, 'we would like you to ask the permission of Wisimar. We are proud to be Tritons, we wouldn't desert, but this - if we land on the mainland - is too good an opportunity. We can walk home from there. We would like you, being an officer and all, to ask his permission for us to discharge.'

'Well,' I said, 'I cannot confirm what you have heard but if it does come about I will ask him.' I paused, looking for the right way to phrase it, uncertain of the reception it would get.

'More, if I can get permission for you, at the same time I shall ask release for myself. My thoughts have turned the same way for some time and now there are other reasons. If you do not oppose it, I would wish to join you for the journey north.'

There was silence for a while and then Lothar spoke up. 'Well, Lord, we would have asked, but we thought you here forever. You have been our eyes and have guided us from the prow for five years past. How would we find our way north without you? For me, welcome.'

There was a chorus of agreement from the others. At the word 'Lord' I had looked for signs of irony or mockery but I saw none. 'Thank you,' I said. 'I could seek no finer travelling companions. If we go to the mainland I will speak with Wisimar and will report back to you.'

After the ships were launched and it was plain the preparation was general, the orders came to store and rig ready for sea. I was working at this under the direction of the Gubernator when the orders came for the Captain, Tzazo and me to report to the Palace. And so, leaving the Celeusta in charge, we started for Byrsa Hill, to the Palace by the cathedral where Gaiseric maintained his rule.

Our summoning came without any reason given. I, for one,

felt my guts churn and my bowel loosen; my heart thumped at ramming speed. I feared punishment for some unknown misdeed, for why else were we summoned? If so, we were doomed, for punishment for misdeeds against the King was always fatal.

When we arrived we joined many already waiting in an outer chamber. We waited as more came in, swelling our numbers. At last the door swung open and we entered the room where the King received petitions and made decisions.

On the floor of the throne room were small piles of mud scattered here and there. Staring broodingly over them was our Master. Spare in stature, not a large man but with a tension that betokened great energy, even athleticism - until he moved to greet us. Then his dreadful lameness became clear for all to see. A fall from his horse when young, poor doctoring and badly knit bones had left him with the inability to ride or run again and great difficulty even to walk without a staff to support him.

It was plain, looking around, that we were the only ships' officers present. The others were the great men of the kingdom. Chiliarchs - leaders of a thousand - generals and advisers, all were there.

The King, vaulting along on his staff and dragging his right leg, heaved himself across the floor to meet us. He could wield this staff with deadly effect when enraged. Today he smiled a welcome.

'Greetings, greetings,' he said, his arm beckoning to show all were welcome. 'How do you like the shit pile they have made of my throne room?' He waved his hand at the mud and dust on the floor. He scanned the crowd and then stopped when he came to we three from the Triton. He frowned for an instant, not recognizing us at first and then, as if deciding between friend or foe, he relaxed his grip on the staff with his right hand and gestured towards us.

'And especially welcome to my good Trierarchus Wisimar, who has been promoted to Chiliarch, yes, yes,' he said, as Wisimar's eyebrows shot up in surprise.

'You will take command of ten ships of my fleet in a little enterprise I have planned, for I have work for you to do.

'This is your Gubernator, yes?' he looked at Tzazo. 'Well, he will now command the Triton and your Proreta will step up, I know how hard it is to replace a good Celeusta so find another Proreta.'

While I was still reeling from the implications of my sudden advancement, the King added, 'I'm sure you have someone in training.' And of course we had.

'Now my friends,' he said, 'gather round and I will tell you what the Fates are planning for us. And anyone who stands on or disturbs this,' he pointed at the earth and sand on the floor, 'I will personally strike down.' He rapped the iron-shod heel of his staff on the floor with a crash that caused chips to fly up from the marble tiles under his feet.

'Sometimes,' he said, when we all stood close around him, 'many things, each one great in its own self, happen together. This blending of great happenings leads to great tumult and great opportunity for those bold enough to grasp it.

'Let me list these things: Great Aetius, defender of Rome, is dead, slain by the very hand he served. Attila is dead and the Huns, who fought as often for the Romans as against them, are spent and dispersed. Theodoric is dead and for the moment our quarrel over his daughter is forgotten. On the throne of Rome is a usurper who, having murdered the Emperor, has dragged his widow to his bed through a forced marriage; the promise of the joining of the Imperial daughter to our prince has been broken and her mother, from her bed of shame, begs our help.

'And so, for the moment, Rome has no defenders other than the energy and courage of its citizens.'

A low chuckle passed round the room at this, even the King smiled. 'We have been invited by the Empress to save her and make good her promise to us. What can we do in honour, except go to Rome?' He looked around at his audience, now grave, the smiles banished.

'Well?' he said, 'What do you think?'

'I think the fleet at Portus Julius will cause many problems,' said Chiliarch Grimme.'

The King waved his hand scornfully. 'We are summoned by the Empress, a Flavian, of one of the great houses. How popular do you think this regicide - this rapist - is? The fleet will not sail, I am confident of that.'

'But Rome? How?' said another.

'The Empress' message had a bearer, a senior naval officer loyal to her and not to her abuser. This is he.'

One of the throng of servants standing behind the throne stepped forward. 'I am Droungarios Glaucon of Byzantium, at your service,' he said.

The King waved at the piles of dirt on the floor. 'This servant of the Empress helped me have this built. This is Rome,' he said. 'Look,' he pointed with his staff: 'the entrance to the Tiber, Ostia; the entrance to Trajan's canal, Portus; the Tiber; Rome; the Aurelian Wall. There are all the southern gates: the Portus; the Ostian; the Appian, the Latina; there the palaces on the hill and the Appian Way leading up to them. You see?'

The chieftains craned closer, looking with increasing interest and then awe as they realised that indeed Rome was laid out for them on the tiled floor.

The King spoke again, lowering his voice, speaking stealthily as if divulging some great secret that no others should know. 'I hear a rumour that if we will promise not to burn the city or engage in mass murder, we may be allowed in to loot at will. Of course, the Romans don't know that yet. This news is private to selected friends of the Empress; rescues of this sort are not cheap.'

The murmur of astonishment that had greeted his statement again turned into a chuckle, but this time in some disbelief.

'What if the rumour is wrong, what if it is a trap and the legions sally out to destroy us?' spoke another Chiliarch who was unknown to me.

'I will tell you my plan,' said the King, 'and you shall give me your thoughts.' He pointed to Portus, 'This harbour has much water and the canal is deep, no problem for our ships to enter and join the Tiber further up. However, Rome guards and defends it; they could trap our fleet and attack it before we even get ashore, both in the port and in the channel from the port to the canal.

'On the other hand, the entrance to Ostia is shallow and our stores ships may find it difficult at its worst, but there is a minimum eight-span depth and when the moon is new or full, given the right time of day and with the wind in the south, there will be fully three spans more. If we load lightly our ships should pass easily in eight spans, but we need more depth for the horse transports – the Hippogogoi. All can pass in eleven spans, however, even loaded with the wealth of Rome. The Tiber is not guarded and defended and is much wider.

'If we row to within two thousand paces of the city there is an ox bow here,' again he pointed with his staff, 'where on the south and west reaches we can beach our prows on soft mud and go ashore within a short walk of the gates.

'The plain is broad, if we form our battle line before the Ostian Gate, we can make a shield-wall with one flank on the river. We will take a Turma of light horse to protect our right flank. So...' he motioned with his staff, 'if it is a trap, or the youth of Rome overwhelm us,' he raised his hand to silence the jeers, 'we will fall back to the ox bow where we landed. A fighting retreat: the left wing will split and part will secure the flank between the river and this basilica or temple - or whatever it is,' he pointed to an upside-down wine flask by the side of the Tiber. 'The other part will base on the building and hold the position. The right flank will continue to retreat until it meets the river on the right and we have sealed off the mouth of the ox bow.'

He looked up enquiringly. The Chiliarchs gazed at the map, seeing the King's battle plan in their mind's eye. All nodded to show they understood.

He continued, 'Then we retreat into the ox bow with the line shortening as we re-board the ships, until only the rearguard is left. Then? Have at them with cavalry and bowmen. Make a brief counterattack with the rear-guard spearmen, then break off and run full tilt for the ships! We will lose many, but we should save most of the ships and the folk. The horses, in the event, would have to be abandoned I fear.'

The Chiliarchs agreed that the plan seemed sound.

The King turned to Wisimar. 'I have a special task for your thousand. This is what we will do if the gates are opened for us. The mass of the army will enter through the Appian Gate. You will enter through the Ostian Gate and then pass through the Vicus and up the road from the public fishponds and swimming hole, here and here,' he pointed, 'to rejoin us on the Palatine. You will need to cross the Circus Maximus, either taking your troop right around the Spina or to the right around the whole Circus. Then you will rejoin the Appian. If there is an ambush planned then the troops of Rome will be mustering there. If they are, then attack them, raise a noise and send messengers, we will hear and come to your aid and catch them from two sides.'

Wisimar nodded. Gaiseric reached into a small leather sack around his neck and drew out a tablet.

'Here, take this; these are the names of the ships of the fleet you will command. Word has been sent to the Captains; fly the Triton banner from your mast and they will form on you.' He looked around, 'Any questions?'

The Chiliarchs murmured; there were none, if they had doubts they were keeping them to themselves.

'Good,' said Gaiseric, 'then let us eat, for it is probably the last good meal we will have until the Domus Augustana.'

And so, for the first and last time in Carthage, I found myself sharing a meal with a King.

On the way back that night my head was spinning and my guts churning. Not from the wine I had drunk, for the King had served nothing stronger than water. It was the burdens of my new post, what I must do in the morning and the task before us that made my head whirl. After some thought I remembered that Captain Wisimar, now Chiliarch Wisimar, whilst in charge of a fleet would still be with us, for his flag would fly from the Triton, and Tzazo would still be with us, although as Captain, but both would be there for aid and advice and both approachable.

I felt a little better then and settled down from confusion to mere excitement. I had not spoken with Wisimar about our release in Rome and felt it best to say nothing and see how things turned out.

When we got back to the Ram my friends were all abed, so my news about my promotion to Gubernator and our mission to rescue the Empress of Rome must wait until morning. Before I could sleep, however, there was something I had to do that I could not avoid, though it made my heart ache in gloomy anticipation. I placed the purse that I had prepared in readiness for this day in my satchel and then started out for the Byrsa.

When I came to Elisia's house the soft light of the oil lamp was showing through the window. I peered in and saw her sitting under the lamp with her sewing. She looked up in alarm at first, then seeing me her smile lit up the room.

'Gewis,' she said, softly so as not to wake any sleepers in the house. 'What are you doing here?'

Without waiting for an answer she ran to the door and let me in. As I entered she looked closely at my face and with that seer's sight of hers read why I had come. Her smile faded and she drew me into the lamplight, placed her hands lightly on my shoulders and looked up into my eyes.

'Is it now then?' She gave a sad sigh.

I held her hands, taking them from my shoulders. 'Come with me,' I pleaded. 'If I survive I will come back and we can take a cargo ship to Massilia. I will be rich; you can ride all the way in a litter if you wish.'

She shook her head sadly. 'This is my place, Gewis. I could not survive in any other. Stay, be rich here, live like the King.'

Neither of us could agree anything here, this was old ground. We knew there was nothing we could change. I held her for the last time and we both cried a little. At last we broke apart. 'I must go. Tomorrow will be a long day and I must be alert.'

She nodded, 'Go then.'

I brought out the purse and handed it to her. 'This is so that you shall not want, now that Hilder is dead.'

I had thought that I might have trouble with her over this, but we were too long together and too close for any shows of false pride. Elisia took the purse gravely and as gravely thanked me. Then she turned, lifted the sewing from her stool and offered it to me. She had made me a shirt of linen, for she had seen with her seer's gaze that she must make a parting gift. 'I have just this minute finished it,' she said.

I thanked her, tears in my eyes, and then we pressed close together for a long time, both knowing it was for the last time. Then I took the work of her loving fingers, the shirt that I would never wear but always treasure, and I turned and left without another word.

My tears ran as I walked, but were drying on my face by the time I reached the Ram and fell into an exhausted and broken sleep.

The next day, while Wisimar sent for his Captains and discussed plans with them, I struggled to make sure I forgot nothing for the safety of the Triton and those who sailed her. I had walked to the harbour with my friends and reported the outcome of my night at the Palace. I had to confess that so rapidly had things changed I had not broached our requests for release to the Captain. Now it would have to be Captain Tzazo to whom I must go.

'Will you still come away?' asked Atilec. 'By the end of this raid you could be Trierarchus Gewis!'

I assured them that my promotion was unlooked for and that my intentions were unchanged. Atilec, walking beside me and out of earshot then said something I have puzzled over since.

'No matter,' he said, 'wherever you go you will always end

up in command of folk. You have a face that begets trust. Some are born to the purple but live short lives because they cannot lead, but those who beget trust will always lead, for folk look always to follow such. The trick is not to betray their belief. A man who is trusted and proves trustworthy will always end up sooner or later with a crown of some sort or other on his head. That is your fate.' He laughed, 'As for me, it would not matter if I was Alexander the Great reborn; with my face no one would follow me to the taverna even if they were dying from thirst.'

When we arrived at the Triton it was still dark, but Captain Tzazo was already on board and had told Hoamer of the changes. Good soul that he was, Hoamer showed no sign of ill will at being passed over and reported to me the state of all things on board that were the result of his all-night vigil. It seemed that all had been prepared and that while I slumbered the Celeusta had done my work for me. I thanked him and released him to catch some sleep before we set off.

I waited until he had curled up in his accustomed spot with his cloak drawn about him and then double-checked everything before ordering the food sacks and water skins passed out. I reported to the Trierarchus that all was done, all were present and the vessel was ready for sea. He thanked me and told me to stand by and await the arrival of the Chiliarch.

When Wisimar boarded, he ordered that we should sail at first light and wait off the Cape for our fleet to gather around us.

The following morning we sat in the water, ten ships in a group, on a fine, Fates-ordained sunny day, with a light southerly wind blowing and a rippled sea around us. Chiliarch Wisimar called the crew to listen then told them as much of the plan as they needed to know.

When he ended with an account of how rich this would make us all, there was loud cheering from the crew, already some of the richest seamen in Carthage. Similar sounds came across the water from the others of our small fleet as their Captains gave them the same news.

When the area fell silent, each vessel ordered rowing watches to their oars and we were off with the Triton leading.

I directed the helm to carry us north along the coast. We sailed north of Uttica until I brought the two headlands of the gulf into transit. This line I brought astern, I knew it would carry us south of Sardinia but towards the Italian coast. We would pass well north of Misenum where the Roman fleet lay, but close to Rome itself. Hilderic had taught me this and a number of other transits, in my learner days.

'Have you been to Rome?' I had asked when taught this one.

'No, never,' had said Hilderic.

'Where did you get this guidance then?' I asked.

He smiled, 'From the innkeeper of the Ram.'

I must have shown my doubt for he explained that the innkeeper of the Ram had Captained a cargo carrier and knew all the transits of this coast to every interesting place in the Middle Sea, from the Pillars of Hercules to Byzantium. When we took Carthage, and with it his ship, he had offered this knowledge to the King, who accepted and offered him either his ship back or the stewardship of the Ram forever. He had replied that the gods knew what they could do with the sea, and he took the Ram and was thankful for it.

'He taught everything he knew to every officer in the King's fleet at the Ram,' Hilderic told me, 'and made his own weight in gold from it in no time. He was able to offer to buy the Ram from the King, who being always a collector of gold was pleased to agree. Later, as the new owner of the Ram, he leased it to Wisimar for another bucket of gold. They say he may one day be able to buy the Middle Sea! He says he will not; not until he has enough money to pay to have it filled in.' Hilderic had laughed, 'He is a man happy to have left the sea.'

When we were on the heading for Rome, I set the shadow pin on the sun board so that the shadow crossed the mark for the month of Maius or Thrimilci to me. As the sun rose up in the sky so my young time-counter reset the board every five hundred strokes. In this way, by keeping the shadow of the pin on the mark, we kept the bow pointing in the right direction. It was not constant enough that we made the same coast landing every time, but it was better than sailing in circles and it somewhat made up for the loss of stars by day. It had always got us near enough to our landfall that the Proreta recognized something and corrected our course. Now we had on board the East Roman Admiral, Glaucon, who knew not only the coast north and south of Portus, but the Tiber itself.

Once we were on course, with a light south wind behind us, I had the standby crew set the mainsail, and then the spritsail to ease the work of the helmsmen, and then I stood the rowers down. I turned to Captain Tzazo, who had watched everything closely, and reported the situation. He dipped his head and then, surprisingly, smiled and gave a gruff, 'Well done, Gubernator.'

Chiliarch Wisimar, standing looking over the rail to check the positioning of the rest of the fleet, said nothing. That, in itself, was a compliment. As the pilot for the Triton I was also the pilot for the fleet and my failure would reflect on Wisimar. I knew if anything was wrong he would soon tell me.

The voyage was faultless, the rest of the main fleet soon drew together and with two hundred ships on the water the might of Carthage seemed endless. It seemed that our little fleet was the vanguard and when this hit me, that I, the newest pilot in the fleet, was the one conducting the whole naval might of the Vandal nation to war with the Roman Empire, I would have shivered in my shoes, had I been wearing any. It was only the presence of the Chiliarch and the Captain that saved me from collapsing with fright.

This was not the sort of fright that warriors get before battle. I spoke of it at a later date with Atilec; he said it sounded like the fright that scops sometimes get when singing a new untested song or singing before a great and unknown court. He himself had it many times when young and new to the performance of his art.

We cruised northward in fine clear weather with the southerly breeze behind us all the way.

At night I checked the heading by the stars, there is a box shape in the night sky made by three stars with an empty corner. When the spritsail is under that empty corner then the ship heads north. This seemed to be true, for every morning the sun rose as it should, broad on our steerboard bow.

By midday of the fourth day we raised the land. Droungarios Glaucon seemed startled and expressed his respect for my skill in directing the ship so close to the mouth of the Tiber. The land that showed ahead was, said Glaucon, the headland of Circeii and just to the south could be seen the white walls of Terrecina. The mouth of the Tiber was about half a day or less to the northwest.

This, whilst pleasing me greatly, was also a surprise and a great relief to me and I secretly thanked the good God Triton, protector of our ship, for guiding its keel to our destination.

I ordered the cloth Triton hoisted at the ladeboard yard end to show a turn in that direction and then, when the nearest ships repeated the signal, I turned.

I abandoned the sun-board and put it away. All that was necessary was to keep the coast to our steerboard side.

Just before sunset we arrived off the Tiber, relying on the memory of our East Roman to tell us. We dipped the cloth Triton to signal we had arrived. All the ships brailed their sails hard up and took in their spritsails. They manned half the upper bank oars and lit lamps on the bowheads as we prepared to wait for sunrise.

We waited well off the coast, for the water was deep right up to the bar, so we could not anchor. The Proreta and the Celeusta worked together to keep us in position off the coast by the lights of Ostia to our east and Portus to the north.

For two days now we had kept a sharp eye out for Roman naval vessels. We had seen none, nor did we see any cargo vessels. The sea was empty. It was as if our approach was expected, but no preparations made other than to keep well clear of us. I doubled the lookouts that night, fearing some trap, and they strained their eyes in the dark of a new moon to make sure no force crept up on us unawares.

The rest of the crews slept, for in the morning we could be fighting for our lives; a trade best worked at fresh.

In the morning the sun rose on another fine, calm day. I woke at first light and had not rubbed the sleep from my eyes nor rinsed my mouth with water from my skinbag, when the lookout called that a boat was approaching the King's ship.

A figure from the small rowing boat climbed aboard the vessel while the boat waited tied to the foot of the ladder. We could see the crew of the Gaiseric leaning over the rail and talking to the boatman who called back up to them, there was an outburst of cheering and then the boatman left the Gaiseric and rowed from ship to ship of the vanguard calling up as he passed.

He shouted that the Emperor Maximus was dead. One of his own soldiers had slain him and the mob had torn his body to pieces at the news of our arrival. The notables and leaders had fled the city. Only the common people remained.

The Gaiseric lowered a boat, which rowed across to us with a message: the King wanted the East Roman Admiral. He thanked us for what hospitality we had offered - poor though we knew it was - then the Droungarios departed and boarded the Gaiseric. The King raised his banner and we knew that it was his intention to lead us in.

First, a small boat from the King's ship rowed to the bar at the entrance to the river and started plumbing the shallows. This went on for hours and then the officer in charge waved his arms to tell us the soundings showed safe depths.

The Gaiseric ran out the full complement of oars for the upper bank and swinging round, she started to move with increasing speed towards the position of the rowing boat. Slowing to pick up the boat and drop an anchored floating mark, the Gaiseric then passed over the position of the bar and was clear into the river. One by one the rest of the fleet followed. We dawdled on the water, awaiting orders from the Chiliarch.

When all the fleet had passed, including the Hippagogoi with the horses, only then did Wisimar order the Triton to follow. We crossed the bar with little depth to spare, although we could see no bottom through the muddy water of the river.

The ship started to turn to ladebord, the helmsman heaved the steering oars to straighten the ship, but she only responded when the Celeusta increased the stroke. Then she answered the helm and resumed her proper direction. I knew from this that we had touched bottom and that the tide must now be falling, but all our little fleet, with greater or lesser trouble, managed to cross the bar into the river, thanks be.

After bringing the fleet here we now had nothing to do but follow and this we did, slowly; painfully slowly. The ebb tide ran against us and it is doubtful that five hundred strokes carried us one thousand paces.

The slower was our progress the greater our fear. For now we entered into a trap of our own making. We could not manoeuvre to fight or escape and divided as we were, we could be picked off piecemeal like fish in a slough if an enemy should come on us in the river. Truly, a fleet on a river is at risk: the longer we were there, the longer the Romans had to plan and muster. It was beyond belief that the masters of the world did nothing while we descended on them. But hour after hour that is what happened and hour after hour our misgivings increased until, by the time night fell and we were ordered to drop anchor, we were fit to scream and run berserk.

We did not know that the lead ships were already beached, which is hardly surprising given that an anchored fleet of two hundred ships in a line, with a ship's length allowed between each of them, is sixteen thousand paces long. The horse transports had also beached. There were fifteen of these, the Hippagogoi of Byzantium. Formerly used by the West Romans they had been captured in the military harbour with the rest of the fleet when Carthage fell. Like the citizens, most of the sailors were in the Hippodrome when they lost their ships.

The lead spearmen and the horse bowmen were already landing under the cover of darkness. I would have pitied the poor horsemen had I known; I am not good on a horse. The thought of leading horses off a ship and down a gangplank into thick mud and then onto firm ground in the dark, without getting kicked to death or losing half of them, filled me with horror when I heard of it. Like everything else about this enterprise, however, the soldiers carried it out with as little trouble as the best of wishes could hope; a few broken legs, nothing worse.

The injured horses, of course, had their throats cut and were passed to the Captain of the kitchens for preparation against the chances of a siege. A healer took charge of the injured men. Gaiseric was always very generous about that, he had, I supposed, a special regard for men with broken legs. When I heard of all this my thoughts went to my Alan friends who had been taken out of the Triton and put to the oars on one of the Hippagogoi.

Each old Trireme, for that is what the Hippagogoi were, was crewed by two crews of twenty oarsmen, ten each side upper bank only and five standby crew to tend the horses. The horses were positioned athwartships, one beneath each rowing bench and three more at each forward end, two at each after end. Thus thirty horses in each, with fifteen ships making an under-strength ala of four hundred and fifty horseback bowmen, with two hundred and twenty-five spearmen to protect the horse picket lines.

At first light we weighed anchor as ordered and resumed our crawling progress up river. We took our orders from a picket boat and beached our ship alongside the rest of the fleet.

When we were drawing abeam of the first of the beached ships, Tzazo ordered the helm hard over. As we turned, the water swept us sideways so that we drove crab fashion into the bank with our oars easily clearing the beached ship above us. As we struck, the stern started to cant in towards the bank.

I shouted to let go the anchor and calling the standby crew to follow, ran through the steerboard bulwark gate and jumped down onto the mud. Between us we carried the heavy anchor up the bank and embedded the fluke as best we could into the mud with the stock lying flat.

On the Triton, Tzazo's voice could be heard ordering the windlass crew to heave up on the cable and in a short time it started to draw up. When a tight bow in the cable between the anchor and the ship was drawn with the chain still in the mud, the windlass ceased its clanking.

No sooner had we clambered aboard when we saw the next vessel, the Annona swinging alongside about twenty paces off.

I asked the Captain's permission and then passed round the order to breakfast from our food sacks. I also ordered that, following our meal, we were to dress for war.

It was now the second day of Aerra Litha, or Iunius as the Romans called it. We rested, waiting for our orders to come, but not for long. Before midday a messenger came to the Chiliarch and we were ordered ashore to form up for marching to Rome.

The Chiliarch took the lead with us, his own company, following. Tzazo was in command and we - the new young Proreta, the old fat Celeusta and I, the new Gubernator - flanked him as the company of the Triton formed behind us. Then came the remainder of our fleet, Wisimar's thousand, although in truth it was nearer thirteen hundred, counting officers. Ours were the last in the column of the whole army and thus formed the rearguard, but when we drew up before the gates of the city there was no place for a rearguard. All twenty-five thousand of the war strength of the Vandal nation was drawn up in a shield-wall, five deep and six thousand paces wide, counting the cavalry on the right flank.

We were the left flank and close to the bank of the Tiber, straddling the Via Ostiensis, the Ostia Road. When I saw the size of the walls, both in height and where they stretched into the distance, I felt tremors in my stomach at the gall of our King in challenging Rome, the ruling city of the whole world.

We stood there, our hearts sinking down into our ball bags, waiting for the iron legions, conquerors of the world, to march out and kill us, the lucky ones that is. Those captured would die, at the least by crucifixion.

When nothing happened we were somewhat cheered. I thought then that perhaps only the angry citizens of Rome would face us. In that case we would probably be victorious, but there would still be deaths, perhaps mine, so I was not too cheerful.

The Ostia Gate opened and we each held our breath awaiting Fate's punishment for our pride … and breathed out a sigh, an unbelieving sigh of relief when all that came through the gate was an old man in long robes.

He was followed by another group of long-robed men singing. Yes, singing! Some sort of sad paeon to somebody, a god perhaps, the Nailed God almost certainly. They did not sound happy and they did not sound as if they were expecting victory. From their sideways glances while they walked and sang they looked frightened, which gave my heart a lift.

The King, on a litter borne by four of his bodyguard, followed by his Chiliarchs - who now all had mounts - made for a place in front of the advancing priests, not ten paces from where Tzazo and I were standing.

Bishop Leo, for such I took him to be, stood with his priests behind him. They regarded us silently, the horde of steel clad warriors facing them. He turned to the litter of our crippled King. This bishop had received his orders from the Empress and she had prepared his speech. Its delivery and consequences must have filled him with dread, but I guessed greater things were at stake. Approaching the litter he made the sign of the cross, which the King brushed impatiently aside.

I watched and listened, ears cocked like a fox, for on this meeting hung the lives and futures of many. The old priest spoke first in a ringing voice, trained, I thought, by the draughty hall of some great temple.

'Lord King,' he paused. Gaiseric said nothing, holding him in a steady gaze.

The priest continued. 'If you give your oath as a king and as a Christian that you will not burn the city or abuse or torment its people, I will order the gates open. From here the Ostian Gate to the Ardietan, and the Appian Gate all the way to the Latina Gate, you shall have access. The people will abandon the streets and take to their houses. You will be free to take all that you wish, for these are only things. God's people must not be harmed.'

Mouth agape, I almost staggered. The King, I knew, had hoped for this; perhaps this was the offer that came with the plea for help. If so, he had held the knowledge that it was more than hope and rumour close.

Silently, King Gaiseric surveyed the walls. I imagined he was numbering those who would die storming them and calculating for what extra advantage. Rape? Murder? Where was the profit in that?

For my part I mistrusted my ears. These people, I thought, how can they give up all they have? Give themselves into our hands when they have walls like these? I sighed my relief that we would not need the desperate plan for retreat the King had designed.

Whatever passed through the mind of Gaiseric, nothing of it showed on his face, which maintained its grimness throughout. He continued to wait in silence as if weighing the plea, then at last he answered.

'You have my oath. There shall be no fire, no avoidable torment and I shall take only those who summoned me, those promised to me or mine and such other of the people as shall be needful to me.'

There was silence as the priest considered this, and then, knowing he could do no better, he nodded and bowed in agreement. I am sure he felt relief that for the most part this was only plundering for wealth.

I knew there was contention between the Latin Church and the Arians. If I were he I would fear this Arian king: fear his destruction of the growing heart of Roman Christianity; fear he came to destroy the central rule that I had so laboriously constructed. For so I had heard it was: nothing would satisfy the Roman Church until all Christians bowed to it in religious obedience. I was sure the priest would give up a hundred cities to the flames and their people to death if it meant he could save their eternal souls through, as he believed, the one and only true faith.

Their god possesses these Christians and he must hate them, or so it seems, for there are many who bow to his will by hating themselves before all others. In Egypt they gather together, I have heard, in hordes in the desert. There they are not content unless they are starving or freezing or bleeding. They torment themselves greatly. That they must not kill themselves is the only rule. In each place there is one who rules, he is their master. They are worse than his slaves: obedience to him is all and they must obey every one of his commands no matter how vile or criminal. Great Mother! They make me shiver.

The priest and his retinue, who had resumed their mournful song, crept away through the poor shacks without to the towering city walls behind, to the centre of the world abandoned by its leaders and utterly powerless now to defend itself. As he shuffled away, the Bishop's mouth moved in silent prayer, perhaps in relief for his Church, perhaps for the helpless people of the city. Doubtless praying that the word of King Gaiseric could be trusted and that he had not made a great mistake in giving up the city to save the people and his faith. He had bared the breast of Rome to the power of us Vandals. Gaiseric had only to thrust in the knife and the centre of the world would be a dead husk; as was Aquileia to the north after the passing of Attila, or so I had heard.

As the priest passed through the Ostian Gate he signalled to the guards to open the gates wide. I watched him speaking to an officer, perhaps the master of the city guard. I hoped he was giving instructions that the other gates were to be opened, the city surrendered and criers sent to clear the streets of citizens.

Astonished, I watched as men rushed to carry out his orders. It amazed me that after the shameful death of the Emperor and with the mighty in full flight, this priest was the sole figure of authority left in the city capable of commanding obedience.

He knelt as the guards pulled the gates aside. I thought he despaired, but no, he was praying again. Well, truly now, the fate of the city, the Empire, his Church and the people were in our hands. If he felt his god had any influence on us, now was the time to ask. With the Senate fled and the people helpless with the knife at their throats, all were at dreadful risk.

I could feel the pull of temptation, the lust of absolute power, a thin echo of Gaul, and wondered at the mood of the rest of our army. By opening the gates, the priest had put his people in thrall to the whim of a horde of reavers. I hoped the power of the King could hold all in check. I hoped this priest shivered with doubt and fear - and not for himself – for I would have done, were I he.

As the storyteller's voice faded, the red glow of the embers lit only the nearest faces, for the fires had burnt down again and the rest were in darkness. All sat in silent contemplation of the fate of the city and all that they had heard that evening, knowing the proceedings were finished for the night.

'Yer,' said someone from the back, 'if Gewis is telling this tale ow duz e know what everyone be thinking?'

Bowdyn smiled. 'I am telling the tale, I am the Gleeman and I know what everyone is thinking, it's my tale.'

There was a muffled, 'Oh ah, roight, thankee,' from the back and the noise of scolding and some chuckles.

My father threw a bundle of twigs on the fire. It flared up, lighting the Cot so that the listeners could see their way out. The sudden crackle and spit of the flames broke the spell and the villagers got to their feet, the usual noise of shifting benches, coughs and curses all but drowned out by a swelling chorus of thanks. This was followed by a growing silence as everyone waited expectantly for what the Gleeman would say next.

He let the silence grow more absolute and then spoke with a query rather than statement, 'Tomorrow then, after Church?'

There was a chorus of enthusiastic agreement coupled with more thanks, before the crowd of what seemed to me like half the village, left the Cot and clamoured into the distance, their breath clouding the cold night air.

# Chapter 20

**AD 455**

**Gewis' Tale, the Long Road Home, Rome**

The nights were becoming raw and on Sunday, after morning service, my father made it my job to go with Bowdyn to chop and collect firewood from a fallen tree in the woods across the mere from the hill. It was too steep to take more than a light cart, but we sawed and chopped and filled that, and by dusk, with the light failing, we had built two fires against the wall in the Cot; far enough apart for Bowdyn's comfort, but large enough to heat everybody there.

At nightfall we made sure that the two fires were drawing well for we had the whole village to warm now. Even the village tavern, the Manor Arms, had closed so that the keeper and his family could attend.

Bowdyn sat in the Story Chair as the swelling audience arrived. They gathered comfortably around the twin blazes and settled in silence. Their faces turned to him in expectation and even the hushing died down, the silence massing in the warming air. Only then did he greet them and remind them where we were in the story.

He then sank back into shadow and resumed Gewis' tale.

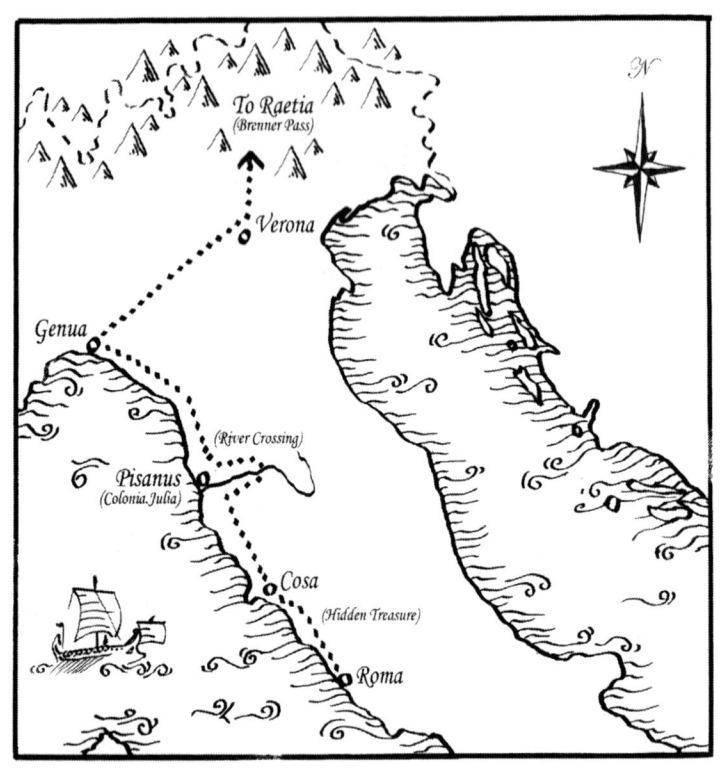

**Gewis' Tale – AD 455 Italy, The Long Road Home**

We stood to arms for a while, staring at the open gates and waiting for an enemy to emerge. When none did and after a wait of perhaps five hundred strokes, at the rise of the sun the word was passed that we were to enter as planned.

The far end of the army, the right wing, broke away from the shield-wall and company by company began to enter by the Appian Gate. We, the thousand of Chiliarch Wisimar also started to move. First the Tritons and then the remaining ships' companies broke away from the war-hedge and trotted towards the Ostian Gate.

We loped through the cluster of poor shacks, deserted now, that spread out like some rot from the base of the high city wall. The gates were double width to allow for the mass of traffic into the city from the port and so they slowed us not at all. On the other side were the poor houses of an area the Romans called 'the vicus', flanking the street that we were to take into the centre of the city. I guessed these houses had started life much like the hovels without, but were stone and brick built now. They were contained between an old set of walls and the massive outer walls.

We jogged up the road leading through this inner vicus, passing cautiously through a gate in the old wall, a stone tablet naming it the Porta Capena. There we turned into a road running to the right of the huge bulk of the Circus Maximus, the road of the public baths. These we could see to our right, in a building very much grander than the fishpond and swimming hole that it had started from if the name of the road correctly described it.

We slowed to a walk as Wisimar sent runners to look into the Circus Maximus for any signs of an ambush massing there. They returned, reporting the structure to be wonderful beyond all dreams, but empty.

We resumed our trot through deserted streets. Once or twice we saw children's faces at windows, but a swift closing of shutters followed the sound of angry voices. Other than this the city might have been a necropolis.

We trotted past the Circus Maximus to our left, where the road widened into a long and narrow paved area - where the crowds gathered before the entrances, I supposed - and then we were past it and our road joined the Appian Way, leading up to the vacant Domus Augustiana – the Emperor's palace.

Our main army having come the shorter way through the Appian Gate already thronged the Appian Way. They stood alert for any attack. We halted also and posted lookouts to the flanks and rear to keep a watchful eye for any approaching resistance. We sent a messenger to the King to report the Circus clear of hostile forces.

It was during this period, while we were still together and awaiting further orders that I decided to open what was on my mind to Tzazo. I faced him and hesitantly began.

'Captain?' he turned to look at me.

'Captain, you know that I joined the Triton with a party of friends?' He said nothing, waiting.

'Well ... we have been talking about our future. We have been here for seven years, which in itself is a long time. We should like to go home.'

Still he said nothing, holding me with a steady gaze.

'Also, Captain, we like our own gods, the gods of our people, we do not wish to follow the Nailed God of the Christians.'

The silence drew out and I feared he would not answer and then he spoke. 'I also do not want to become Christian, but I do wish to become rich and I would be happy to retire to an estate in Mauretania with a palace and many slaves and servants. You too could have this, you have the face and the luck for it; you could be Chiliarch one day. Are you sure you want to go?'

I nodded and he sighed.

'Well, we will have no trouble getting more crew. Already we are rounding up Greeks and Egyptians from Portus against battle losses. I will be sorry to lose you, but your friends, if you mean the axe man, the storyteller and the two bowmen, are easily replaced.'

He paused as if thinking. 'Here is the way it must be. If the city is ours, and it seems so, we will shortly break away to start the collection of the treasures. We must bring these to the Ostia Gate for transport to the ships. The sharing of the profits will take place in Carthage. You must take nothing out of the city that you do not already have, except horses that is. There is plenty of time, we must be here for fourteen days until the next high water or we will not cross the bar under the weight of treasure. But if you will take my advice, as soon as we break up to start the pillage, you go. Go north to one of the other gates and find a stable. There will be one for messengers' horses. Go while all is confusion and the night is full of screams.'

He scowled at my raised eyebrows. 'You do not really believe the King's agreement will be followed rigidly do you? This is an army: there will be pleasures to be taken, treasures to be wrung; slaves to be driven away.'

I nodded in understanding, wanting now to get away as quickly as I could. I did not wish to be involved. The thought of the pain and fear of the innocents sickened me.

I waited until the King's messenger came to us. He repeated what I had already heard from Tzazo. The city was ours. The King discouraged rape and torture and forbade fire on pain of death. Treasure was to be loaded on wagons at the Ostian Gate. The search was to be thorough and leisurely for fourteen days, following which the army would embark for Carthage. As treasure was off-loaded at the Ostian, so food brought off the transports could be collected. Water was available everywhere in the city.

And then the order to disperse came and with wild cheers the army broke into small groups, all going in different directions, except my band of friends who converged on me. I explained the rule Tzazo had laid down and although they grimaced at the thought of having no increase to their hoard from the sack of Rome, they each accepted it and none changed his mind.

'So,' said Atilec, 'when do we go?'

'Now,' I said. I had something of a plan for I had spent time discussing the problem with the Secretarius, with whom over the years I had become a firm friend as well as pupil.

'First we must find a great dome of a building called the Pantheon, from there we can find instructions for the way home.' They looked at me doubtfully, but said nothing.

'I am told it will be on the north side of the Palatine, the hill with the palaces on. I think we will need to cut between the Palatine and the Circus Maximus and then bear right.

'Lead on,' said Atilec.

I turned towards Tzazo, who had been standing some way off with the Proreta and the Celeusta. They had no need to pillage; they would receive their share in the apportioning to come in Carthage. I approached Tzazo and held out my hand, he clasped it in the Roman fashion.

'Goodbye, Lord,' I said, 'and thank you for everything.' He dipped his head and looked away. Already I was no longer part of his concerns other than needing to seek my replacement.

I turned to the Celeusta and grasped his arm. 'Goodbye old friend, take care, you have saved my life more than once, now take care of your own.'

He smiled. 'We will miss you, boy,' he said. 'You take care also, the hills are full of thieves - or they will be when you get there.' He laughed and with one strong clasp let go and turned away.

I briefly clasped the arm of the Proreta. I had helped to train him and he thanked me for it. Then I too turned away, a member of the Vandal army no more. It left a strange empty feeling inside me where being part of something so great had left a warm glow. This was coupled with the other cold emptiness at the certainty that now I should never see Elisia again. I had burned my ships. There was no turning back. This knowledge made me feel sad and lost as I returned to my band of friends.

They looked to me for direction and I realised that even without the authority of rank, I was now the leader of this little band of warriors. 'Follow me,' I said and started north between the Circus Maximus and the Palatine. In going thus we avoided the mass of men who streamed towards the palaces and temples intent on loot. There is an order to the sack of a city. Loot comes first, lust later. Loot was possessions: choice pieces to be secreted and withheld by those brave enough to risk the King's wrath. Lust could be satisfied at any time and slaves were there for the rounding up after greed and lust were satisfied.

Before long we came to the old city walls and passed through a gate marked as the Porta Carmentalis. We were now close to the river and followed the line of it between buildings until we passed the river island to our left. I struck out north from there, passing around a huge decorative pool and what I took as a bathhouse.

There, behind the baths, I saw a great domed building with a roof of gold, or at least gilded bronze. It was a dazzling sight and I knew this was the building I sought. As we approached the walls I searched for something I had never seen, but knew I would recognise. And then I found it: a wall covered with writing carved into its surface. This was it: the great Itinerarium of the Empire, a list of all Roman roads and their destinations just as the Secretarius had described.

I brought out my wax pad and stylus and started to search the Itinerarium, recording the gates and destinations of the roads north, leading to Germania. I told my group to sit and eat for I did not know how long I would be. It was at least two intervals of five hundred before I was satisfied I had what was necessary.

I turned back to my friends, 'I have it, we can go, we should make haste to clear the city before dark and be on our road.' I led them back towards the river looking for a bridge crossing inside the city walls.

I found two close together and we crossed the second, which was marked as the Pons Aurelius. I felt relief at reading this stone carving, for I knew we were heading in the right direction.

Once across the bridge we followed alleyways and backstreets south until we struck the main road west. This led to a gate set in the angle of the city walls, the Porta Aurelia, and I knew with certainty that we were on the way that would take us home.

We cast around inside the walls near the gate until we came to the stables for the post and messenger service. The area was strangely deserted, but horses were still inside and whilst Atilec kept watch, we saddled up five horses and loaded up three more lightly with panniers of horse feed. After some thought and talk we saddled a sixth. As Lothar said, horses can go lame or be slain in a fight. Better to have a spare for riding. The very last thing we wanted was for any to be on foot in dangerous country and with so far to go.

There was a breath of smoke on the air. I pitied the men who had lit it for they were dead men. In the distance we could hear the screams of torment and the crashing of masonry that told us the sack of Rome was well underway. Grimly we watered and fed the poor beasts. They drank and ate with such eagerness we guessed the ostler had fled the day before. We led them through the gate and out onto the Via Aurelia, the first of many stages of our long journey home.

Our first destination was a city called Genua, but along the way we were to pass many small towns and villages, all deserted. The dire news must have spread like brush fire from the city. The larger towns we resolved to bypass during the hours of darkness. There was always a risk when riding unknown ways at night, for one's horse might stumble and break a limb in an unseen pothole, throwing its rider in the process, but we agreed that the risks of this course of action were more than balanced by the avoidance of harsh justice from city watchmen or garrisons. It was wise not to forget that we were deserters from an occupying army in the midst of the unconquered countryside of the enemy. A very unwise and dangerous place to be and we had to be constantly on our guard.

Rome maintained way stations for official postmen or messengers where they could change their horses, also inns for non-official travellers where they could purchase food and drink. We found no innkeepers and so purchased nothing, but at least in this way we would get some plunder. We stuffed our panniers and sacks with food; mostly stale bread, dried out cooked meat and, when we were lucky, some cheese, and filled our spare water bags with thin, watered wine.

We did not hurry, but made steady progress towards our destination. The first nightfall we stopped at a deserted inn and taking it in turns to keep watch we slept like the dead until after sunrise. Following a leisurely breakfast we went on our way.

Whilst we slept, Skuld had twined new threads. She slid these into the weft and warp of the pattern of our lives changing our lot forever.

The road had taken us between pale, sand-coloured hills sparsely covered with scrub and herbs, and to the west the occasional glimpse of blue sea.

The time of year was a blessing, for the sun shining warmly on our backs was mild compared to the harsh sun of Africa, the colours less glaring. It was a pleasure to ride along this fine road in such pleasant weather. It was hard to keep our alertness in such conditions and so we took it in turns to take up watch-keeper duties.

As we rode north on the second day after we had left Rome, in the mid-morning when the shadows were sharp-edged the plans of the Wyrd Sisters started to enfold us. We were walking our horses near the sea on this stretch. There was a steep lofty island offshore, one I judged given over to the temples of the Nailed God, for from it, like wind sighing over the water, drifted a mournful singing such as the Christians make in beseeching favours from their tragic Freyr.

I imagined that news of the fall of Rome had reached them and that they were beseeching earthly rather than heavenly deliverance. Apart from the faint sounds of woe across the water there was no sign of life from the island or the bar that reached out to it, on which there were the buildings of a small, walled town.

We had been eyeing this for any signs of movement, for it looked about the size that would have a small tax guard or garrison. We would have circled around it out of sight, but to the right of the road was a further hill and by the light of the rising sun we saw, capping it, another town.

Any watch from the hilltop town would have seen us clearly on the road. To leave it would invite enquiry, so with some trepidation we carried on riding. As we drew nearer we were relieved to see that this town was in ruinous condition and deserted; whether forsaken through war or plague or changing circumstances I could not judge.

As we walked our horses into the shadow of the town-capped hill, such was the narrowness of our attention on both towns that we missed what was under our very noses, until Hunneric, the elder of the Alans, hissed in alarm and quick as lightning unslung his bow and notched a shaft.

We all, of course, reined in and had reached for our weapons before we saw in the shadow behind a brightly lit rock what he alone had seen.

# Chapter 21

**AD 455**

**Gewis' Tale, the Sword of Alexandria**

As we peered into the shadow we saw a figure: a man, dark complexioned, seated calmly on a boulder, regarding us. He moved and coming out of the shadow spoke in poor Latin.

'You will not need your weapons, I am alone and beg water, and if you will, your help.'

I translated to the others and saw the stranger was watching us with care. He marked that I was the Latin speaker; he also marked the reaction to his plea, as Lothar, the biggest and fiercest looking of us all, reached over to one of the pack animals and releasing a water skin hanging from a pannier hook, threw it to him.

I glanced beyond him into the shadows and then up the hill and to the back and front of us, but saw nothing to give the lie to his claim of being alone. I looked back carefully at the town on the shore and could see no movement. The drone of the singing continued in the background. I motioned to all that we should dismount and again I saw the quickness of the stranger's glance as he took in my leadership of the band.

'So what is your name and what is your story and why should we help you?' I asked.

'Please,' he said, 'come into my humble abode,' and he

bowed, waving a hand towards the jumbled rocks in the shadow of the hill.

'It is quite safe, there are no serpents here and the town has no soldiers.' At this his smile changed to a look of rue. He spoke now in the language of the Goths, one that we could all understand after a fashion. It was a tongue that had become the common speech of Africa, in which business and simple talk between warriors could take place, and was similar to the speech in common between my lost Elisia and me. As I heard it again I felt a pang of regret.

I regarded him closely: he was swarthy of skin, but more the colour of oil than the blackness of bitumen, perhaps a Moor, perhaps an Egyptian. He wore armour made from plates of ox hide to which were riveted long strips of bronze, no defence against a strongly delivered axe stroke. At his side was a long curved scabbard of leather-on-wood, decorated with gold and coloured stones in patterns that amazed the eye. The sword it held I could not see, other than that its hilt was leather bound and businesslike without adornment, but the scabbard was a work of art and fit for a king. From this, which would draw the attention and desire of many, and from the workmanlike sword hilt, I judged our Moor was a warrior swordsman of some skill, and so it turned out.

'First my name and station,' he said, when we were all settled in the shade and seated on boulders. 'I am Sefu, from Alexandria,' he smiled. 'My name means sword, so I am the Sword of Alexandria. No,' he lifted his hands in protest as we raised our eyebrows, 'do not laugh. Man must make a living and that is mine. I am a bodyguard to the wealthy; a swordsman. The Sword of Alexandria is my business name by which I am known amongst those who hire such as I.'

'So, Sword of Alexandria,' said Atilec, 'what brings you

here to the side of the road, begging water from strangers?'

Sefu looked at the ground and his face ceased its smiling, 'Failure brings me here to this sorry state,' he murmured. After a moment he lifted his gaze to us, 'If you wish I will tell you the story and you shall judge my fault.'

We nodded, settled ourselves comfortably and delved into our sacks for food, moistened our mouths with wine and prepared to lunch while the Egyptian entertained us.

In goodwill I offered him a leg of fowl, which he took with grace and I passed him my wine sack, from which he gulped appreciatively. We waited.

Sefu leaned forward and eyed us as though he was measuring the way in which he should tell his story to take our interest. 'My story is long; have you the time to hear it?'

'That depends, friend, on whether the garrison in that township comes to see us or not,' I replied.

He looked mournful. 'They will not disturb us. They are gone, for they already have a part to play in my story.'

'Then, Sword of Alexandria, we will rest here tonight and all our time is yours,' I smiled.

He bowed his head and spreading his hands in assent, began to speak. 'I was born into a family that dwelt always between the hell of the peasant and the heaven of the merchant. We were weavers and dyers of cloth, of both cotton and linen. If we could have made enough money to employ workers or buy slaves; if we could have travelled and sold our own cloth, then we would have been in heaven. But the merchants of Alexandria thought heaven was for them alone and made sure we were never paid enough to join them there. Christians were not welcome in their heaven.

'I was a quick and clever boy, more agile and athletic than most. I hated my life in the cloth trade, to me it was imprisonment. I was never happier than when I could sneak into the Roman Theatre and watch the gladiators practising. I soon learned all the stances, the attacks, the defences and practiced them endlessly with a line prop as staff.

'Only the professional gladiators of famous schools fought in the Theatre. Others, hoping for fame, sought to be discovered by the fighting-school scouts and fought in a small square in the backstreets of the city. These fights were always crowded with spectators and gamblers who bet small amounts on the skill of untried, unknown fighters.

'Those who survived developed a name, became a favourite of the gamblers and the odds against them were low. I entered this backstreet theatre as soon as I felt ready for combat. I fought other young fighters and won. I became an actor, for besides my solid grasp of stance and tactics, I threw in leaps and bounds and cartwheels that drew the admiration and applause of the audience. I fought against grown men and still I won. I soon became a favourite and my takings from betting on myself went down, which was bad. But a school scout discovered me, which was good, or so I thought.

'The scout came to me at the end of yet another win and offered me training, money and contests with the Rhakotis School. This school was one of the oldest and Egyptian rather than Greek or Roman, or so I thought. Although not the richest it had much to offer me, but only if I laid the staff aside and picked up the spatha. This now was serious business. With the staff if I was unlucky I would break limbs and if very foolish and unlucky could die from a broken head, but the spatha? Sword fighters lost hands and limbs. Sword fighters lost their lives. The lure of much money, much fame; the roar of the crowd in the Roman Theatre, attracted me like a fly to honey. But I was not stupid. I understood the risks. I agreed, but said that I would decide when the training was finished and when I was ready for the ring. There was agreement all round; we decided the money and made vows before God, on a Bible.

'When I announced that my occasional absences from the looms were to become permanent and told my family why, there was much weeping and hair tearing by my mother and sisters. My father was quieter; he asked many questions and then hugged me and wished me God's protection. He did not say so, but I felt he might have been a little proud of me.

'And so I entered the Rhakotis School and worked hard to learn my craft. Everything was to my liking except the man who owned the school. Not an old gladiator as I expected, nor an Egyptian, but a hard-eyed Greek moneyman, one Alcibiades by name. There were many stories about him. Rumour dubbed him a dangerous man with his hand in much of the vileness that bubbled and stunk beneath the surface of our great city. I wondered at the rightness of my choice, but continued to work. Eventually, when I had beaten all of my instructors into submission and they had nothing left to teach me, I announced myself ready for the ring.

'All was as I feared. It was not like the bravado and the tests of skills of the backstreet staff fighting I had so enjoyed. This was serious business: the sword kills. Before long, to avoid my own death I had to cause the death of others. The crowd called me a swift and elegant killer. I took no joy in it.

'I saved my winnings and added them to the staff fighting money until I judged I had enough to move my family into selling the cloth they made, instead of slaving to make it. I felt happy. I announced to Alcibiades my decision to quit. To my surprise he grew angry. He told me that he had invested more in me than I had won. That if I left now he would lose money on me.

'As I said at the beginning, I am quick with my brain as well as my body. I had added up his winnings from me and, without even counting bets, he had made much from me. I told him that I knew he lied. I bade him farewell and went to prepare my departure. That night he arrived at my room in the school with two of his instructors, all were armed. He gave me a choice. Either I continued fighting for his school until he - he! - gave me permission to quit, or his assistants would lop off my sword arm and throw me into the street. What could I do? They had put me in a position where I had no choice. After I killed the last of them I cleaned my sword, packed my clothes and some food and water, picked up my money and left.

'I went first to my parents' house and told them that I was leaving to fight in the city of Constantinople where the money was even better. I then gave my father the purse of gold, told him to take my family into riches and that I would see them soon.

'They hugged me with many tears and blessings and I left. I had to hurry now for if any partner of Alcibiades discovered the bodies I was a dead man. It would be easy for him or any other comrade in filth to arrange for a quick dagger in the back for me.

'I half walked, half ran to the port. A little bronze soon discovered the next grain ship out, leaving that night. I went on board and told the Shipman I was a gladiator bound for Rome. The clinking of my armour would have told him that, but given enough gold he didn't care.

'Rome was a wonderful city. Its walls and power had saved it from much destruction. Unlike Alexandria, many beautiful and ancient buildings and monuments remained. But the greatest of all was the Coliseum. To try out and to fight there was a great temptation to me, but one I resisted. I no longer wanted to be a gladiator.

'I went to the Guild of Protection. To belong to this Guild was essential to my getting work as a house guard or bodyguard in the city. At first they would not help. I was Egyptian and I came without references, my oath's worth was untried. I offered to slit their throats and eventually they agreed that I could be one of a troop. I must get someone respectable to vouch for me, until then I was on trial.

'I worked for the same householder for a year, for small wages. He was a senator who did not trust his slaves. We guarded the house from without and from within. He and I talked much in the night watches for he slept badly and he being Christian talked with me of Christ, for the other guards were pagan Germans. He asked me much of Alexandria, where Christ once lived.

'When I told him I was leaving and asked for a character, he was pleased to write one for me. I presented this to the Guild, they gave me full membership and straightaway I took up bodyguard duties under the name of "Sword of Alexandria." --- Rome, as you may already have heard, has fallen to the Vandals of Carthage,' he said.

We made a show of great surprise at this news.

'Yes,' he said, 'fallen. The greatest city in the whole world; the Emperor murdered by his own soldiers ….'

Sefu paused a moment in sad reflection before continuing. 'Well, the day the city heard that the Vandal fleet was off the Tiber and the Emperor dead, I received a message from …' he pursed his lips, 'shall we say an "organizer of services". It seemed that a banker of Rome, one Gaius Silvanus by name, wished to hire bodyguards of repute to accompany him and guard his person while he fled the city.

'And so, the money being good, and not wishing to confront the Vandal host, I accepted the fee, swore my oath of faithful service and in company with five others and the banker, Sylvanus, slipped out of Rome on the first day of Iunius. Word passed us on the road that the Bishop of Rome, perhaps on the orders of the Empress, had given up the city the very next day. We were glad to be outside the walls.

'The work promised to be easy, the banker a citizen of power and repute. The Huns had demanded his head and the Senate had resisted, what better proof of high status could there be?' Sefu paused again, swigged at the ale-skin and took a bite of fowl leg.

Chewing with much lip smacking and little grunts of pleasure, he swallowed and then continued his tale. 'Anyway, he carried all the right diplomata ...'

Atilec raised a hand, 'Diplomata?'

'Official vellum signed by a magistrate,' I told him, remembering my lessons with the Secretarius.

'Yes,' added Sefu, 'showing him to be about Rome's business and under its protection. With these he could pass freely and use the Empire's way stations. We were all practiced warriors for hire and six of us were enough to deter any normal numbers of bandits. Our horses were of good quality; should we have to flee then few could catch us. So I felt very good about the job ... until we got to here, that is,' he shrugged. 'Here it all went tits up like a dead pig ....'

Sefu stopped speaking, lost in thought. Atilec coughed to bring him back to the story from wherever he had gone and he resumed.

'With Sylvanus we numbered seven, mounted and with three heavily laden packhorses. We did not ask what they carried and he did not tell us, we were oath-sworn and that was all we needed to know. However, I noticed one thing that was an odd shape and it aroused my curiosity. Sylvanus, seeing this and knowing I was Christian, half pulled it from its sack and told me something of it.'

I interrupted, 'So what was it?'

He raised finger as if to say later, and carried on with his tale. 'When we approached this place, the road curving between the two hills made me feel uneasy. I said as much to Sylvanus and he, after some thought, ordered me to hang behind with the string of packhorses whilst the rest of our company went forward to check that the road ahead was clear. He was no coward, our banker; he went with them, his gladius in his hand.

'A little while after they had disappeared around the curve I heard much shouting and the clash of weapons. I reasoned thus: if my companions had cleared the way then they would return. If they were slain then there was little I could do on my own. As I sat astride my horse thinking this through, a figure in the armour of a legionary came into view at the curve around which my companions had so recently disappeared. He saw me and turning, shouted behind him then started running towards me.

'My duty seemed clear: to make off with the cargo and wait to see the outcome. I galloped away leading the string of pack horses, turned to my left and headed up the track to Cosa, the ruined city up there,' Sefu gestured upwards. 'I trotted up to the Arx, hauled off the panniers and hid the contents where they could not be found. I had just finished reloading the horses when five horsemen came cantering up the roadway.

'They were not my companions, although I recognized the

horses, so knew that all was over for the worse. I jumped onto the top step of the temple, positioned myself between two pillars and in the doorway drew my sword, prayed to Hermes for speed to my weapon and prepared to die as dearly as I was able. The legionaries remained in their saddles watching me and then one of them laughed. "Keep your sword, Moor, it is the horses we want," he shouted.

'And with that they gathered up all the horses, my own included, and galloped away. I puzzled over this for a while and then it came to me. These were legionaries, foot soldiers, mercenaries or foederati; they also had heard the news. They were deserters. Indeed, all they wanted were our horses, although I dare say they robbed the dead of their purses.

'I thanked my god for preserving me from the Underworld. I did not wish to be weighed in the balance. I was not yet ready. I waited all through the night in that town of ghosts, for so it felt. When the sun rose I walked down the hill and around the curve and there I found the banker, Sylvanus.

'Much good had his money and position and diplomata done him. Like his Emperor, he was dead at the hands of soldiers of Rome. He lay face up, his gladius spilled on the road, the pilum wound staining his brown travelling clothes with a black patch that had spread and dried in the sun.

'All my other companions were also dead, together with two of their attackers and two of the horses lamed in the fight, their throats mercifully cut, I supposed by the deserters. I had counted five on horseback, at least one on foot and two dead: eight against six; a fair fight as these things go. And now the survivors were all mounted and had taken the packhorses. I cursed them; they could have left me one. But then, they left me my life so I should not complain.'

Sefu had apparently come to the end of his tale. I had

listened carefully and felt there was something missing. This Egyptian was not telling us the whole truth. 'What was the cargo you unloaded and hid with such care?' I asked.

'Books,' he said, but his eyes failed to meet mine and I knew he lied. He must have seen my doubt, for he added, 'It was bankers' books, scrolls and codices, and a Christian cross. Have you any idea how heavy these things are? No wonder the poor horses were weighed down.'

It seemed to me that if the contents of the panniers were books then he would not have unloaded them so hurriedly. What use had deserters for books? They would have emptied the scrolls and codices onto the ground once they had the horses. Only the cross, perhaps, if gold, had value. I said nothing, for here was ground to be trod gently.

When I made no further comment, Sefu got to his feet and led us around the curve in the road to where his former companions lay in a bloodied, flyblown heap. We helped him to carry the bodies off the road and built cairns over them.

By then it was too late to go on with our journey that day. We were tired and needed to rest.

## Chapter 22

**AD 455**

**Gewis' Tale, Cosa**

This suited me very well. I suggested that while the town was probably harmless to us, as it seemed likely the whole garrison had deserted, we should for double safety hide out in the ruins above. The others agreed and in silence we climbed the road to the summit, for now even the Christians had got tired of their dreary singing and were probably sitting down for whatever foul feast such persistent virtue suggested. I had not learned then that, unlike the monks of the desert, Christian priests tended to live much better than their flocks.

We camped out in the citadel; we did not light a fire for the night was warm and we ate our food cold. And so we feasted, while the Hags cackled at the joke they were playing on us.

When we had found spots in which to make ourselves comfortable for sleep I volunteered for first watch. As the camp settled down for the night I touched Sword of Alexandria on the shoulder and beckoned him to follow me. He came, but unwillingly, I could see. We stopped in the forum of the old town and he looked at me, his look asking my purpose.

I wished there to be no misunderstanding so I spoke clearly. 'You lie about the nature of the cargo. We could torture you for the truth or we could kill you and search the ruins for your hiding place. We will not do the first, for we are honest men; we might drive you away and do the second. On the other hand, you could tell me the truth and maybe we can be of use to each other.'

He looked at me for some time, searching my face for the answer to some unspoken question. At length he said, 'I believe you to be honest and honourable warriors once you are oath-sworn, as am I. If I swear to be your man, will you swear to treat me fairly and to guard my life and well being as with the others in your band?'

'The warriors in my band are companions only and not oath-bound to me.'

He smiled, 'If you will answer my first questions honestly I will give you what you want, but then you will need to bind your companions to you. How you fulfil that is a riddle for you to solve. Now, will you exchange oaths with me?'

I considered for a moment then did as he asked. Sefu swore to be loyal and thus he became the first of my hearth companions. I, his Lord, swore in turn to match his loyalty with my generosity and protection. And so he told me what I wanted to know and when he showed me the hidden cargo, everything became clear. He went to his sleep and I to my watch, and then called the next, and watch by following watch the night passed.

When my companions awoke at daylight and we gathered round to take food I spoke to them thus.

'It is my wish to return to my home in the East Holding. I should also like to be rich and to help - and perhaps one day guide - my people or at least be held in respect by them. Please tell me, what do you wish for?'

One by one they spoke and all answered the same: to return to the land of their birth or at least to where their birth kin now stayed; to have enough riches to build a hall; to bring promising young into a Hearth Band; to be the protector of their folk and the ally of the ruler.

They each agreed that although they had sufficient for comfort, a lifetime with the Vandals would not have given them enough for their heart's desire.

Delighted with their response, I did what Sefu had suggested and said what I knew to be true. 'If I could make your uttermost wish come about would you become - at least until I reach the East Holding - oath-bound to me, to follow me, support me, fight for me; to support and fight for each other as a band of hearth-companions should. Also to take Sefu into the company, for he is already oath-sworn to me? If you will, then I will make your dreams come true and in turn will swear to release you when I am safely home.'

There was deathly silence following this, as all except Sefu looked at me in doubt. After a long pause, Atilec, always the quickest of the band, spoke up.

'I know you, Gewis, you speak what is true and we have always trusted your word. If you say you can do this then I know that you at least believe it to be so. Further, I have never since the Triton had cause to doubt your judgement. If you ask this of me and promise what you promise, I believe in it. You have my oath that I will be your Hearth Companion and you will be my Lord, although I would never have thought such a day would come all those years ago in Colonia,' and with this he smiled.

I regarded him gravely, 'I accept your oath and will always deal with you as a true Lord should and you have my oath on that.'

One by one the other three followed Atilec's example. At the end I had my own Hearth Band of five and was their Lord, strange as that made me feel.

They looked at me with eyebrows raised as if to say, What now? Make good your promise. And so I led them to the ruined Temple of Mithras on the hill and gestured to the bull pit. When they looked inside their eyes popped and gasps of amazement came all round.

'Great Wothan,' said Atilec, 'how much is that?'

At the bottom of the bull pit, where the worshippers stood for the blood to shower on them, was a heap of gold, silver and precious stones, all piled together as Sefu in his hurry had left it. The panniers of Sylvanus had contained his lifetime collection of treasure and many of his customers' collections too. Sylvanus, the crafty dog, had emptied his vaults and made off out of Rome with enough gold to buy a small town on an island and gild all the roofs with gold. I could not guess how much, but a horse could carry perhaps two hundred pounds, so between the three, all heavily laden, was perhaps as much as six hundred pounds of gold, silver and stones; perhaps fifty thousand solidi. Maybe eighty times one hundred solidi each if we divide it equally between the six of us, I thought, counting. I told them.

'Great gods! God's Mother and Jesus!' Lothar exclaimed. 'For seven years' work I have two hundred and fifty solidi. How long would I have to work to earn eighty times one hundred solidi?'

I did the work in my head, 'Over two hundred years my friend.'

He threw himself at my feet, this huge bulk of a man. 'I would give you my oath and call you my Lord for every day of those two hundred years, even if you were the meanest lord in the world henceforth and never gave a battle ring. In that two hundred years at Gaiseric's bench I would meet my death twenty times over, I owe you twenty lives. Here,' he said to the others, 'is the Lord of all ring givers,' and he bowed low. All of the others followed his actions.

I knew that in this display was much of humour and ancient fondness for me, the chick who had become an eagle, but I knew also that these men would now die in my service if needful and for the moment, knowing that frightened me. I resolved to show more care for them than I had ever shown for the Triton in my time as Proreta.

The treasure? It was very mixed. There were gold coins, a mixture of solidi, old aurei and others of roughly equal weight from the gods knew where. It seemed every little client tyrant had a mint and traded with Rome. As far as we could tell there was about a man's weight of gold coin. We divided and shared this first.

We set a guard against intruders and then we made a balance from two small gold plates of equal size and some harness leather and a stick. It was crude but near enough. We put a stone in one side and weighed it down with gold coin the other. Six times we did this and then repeated it until we had six piles of equal weight and only a small pile left. We dealt with this in the same way, using a smaller stone.

We then had the sharing of gold plate to carry out. There were golden dishes carved or moulded with designs or pictures, mostly to do with the faith of the Nailed God. There were gold cups studded with jewels and coloured stones of many sorts. We all understood what we must do.

The two Alans went out into the little town and came back with a large rotten piece of tree stump. We laid a plate on it and I took my axe and cut the plate into strips, which I then cut into pieces. We did this with all the plate.

Whilst this was going on, Sefu and the others had been

sitting prying the stones out of the various drinking cups and crosses. These they collected in a pile, passing the gold to me. The cups I crushed with the back of my axe and then cut in pieces. The crosses I hacked through, also into pieces.

Using the balance, I shared the mixed pile of pieces as evenly as I could. At the end everyone had about one hundred pounds of gold, both coin and metal, and an equal share by weight of the stones. In gold I reckoned seven thousand solidi each. The stones? We did not know, but could hope these would make up a thousand solidi gold-value for each of us.

There was one thing left. It was a silver case in the form of a cross, a forearm long and two spans wide, beautifully marked with whirling patterns confusing to the eye. Inside this case was a carving in black polished stone of the Nailed God. None of my companions wanted it; strangely, as it turned out, not even Sefu. Especially not Sefu, for he said it was a thing of ill omen. Nor did they want to carve up the case; the value would not be great, they said and it might bring bad luck.

As Atilec quite rightly said, crossing the land of the Romans and the Allemani to get to Cologne with our skins and balls in place, even without one hundred pounds of gold each, was going to need much luck; anything which made our store of luck smaller should be shunned.

But I? I was awed by the artistry, by the tragedy that enfolded the nailed figure and yet the love that flowed outwards from the face. How could a piece of stone say anything, let alone speak agony, love and forgiveness, even hope. And yet that piece of stone did. I knew my companions were right. We should leave the ornament in the Arx across the tiny Forum, but I could not; I wanted it. Suddenly, I had an idea. I turned to the others.

'Perhaps this can help us make our luck, perhaps it is our luck.' I explained. 'Rather than hide ourselves as we sneak across the land, perhaps we should not. If we held the cross in front on the end of a spear, thrust up high like a banner, we could be a wealthy pilgrim and his hired bodyguards; like the ill-fated Sylvanus, but a religious pilgrim rather than a banker.'

We would still avoid the cities, I told them, and most of all the priests with their awkward questions. From Sylvanus' body, newly buried along the road, we had taken the diplomata he carried. With these we should be able to pass any group of simple soldiers, illiterate Goths as they usually were, or citizens who would quail at challenging our armed band.

As for Christian words, we knew enough from our time with the converted Vandals to get by. At this point Sefu surprised us by reminding us that he was an Egyptian Christian and so it all fell into place: Saint Sefu of Alexandria, with his Decurion and guards, would take the road to Colonia and hopefully arrive alive.

Our 'Saint' said that such a course and pretence was sinful, but that if we all agreed to a vow to donate ten solidi of gold each to the cathedral in Colonia then we would be forgiven and bad luck would not follow us. So we all made this oath, had breakfast and loaded our gold. A little, perhaps twenty pounds of coin, we kept for safety on each of our horses. The remainder we loaded on the packhorses in bags I marked with our names, with the red-hot tip of my seax.

While we breakfasted I asked Sefu why he felt the cross to be of ill omen. It was not a feeling, he said, but a story, which Sylvanus had told him on the road. As we took our ease around the fire he repeated what the banker had told him.

'It is a tale involving the Huns and a Christian bishop,' he said. 'The bishop lived and ruled in Margus, a town in Roman

Pannonia up north by a great river.

'He was a man unsurpassed in his greed and with moral standards of which I, as a Christian, am ashamed. This bishop came to know where the Huns buried their kings on the other side of the river. He thought it good to cross over and rob these tombs of their golden and silver grave goods.'

Sefu sat brooding, looking into the fire as if the grave goods were there in the flames. After a moment he continued, 'He was betrayed to the Huns and he knew that he would die a very painful death if taken, so he sent a message in secret and it was agreed that if he could deliver up his town to the Huns then his sins would be forgiven.'

Sefu stared into the fire, 'And perhaps that would have been the end of the tale, except that he fled the city, leaving open a gate but against all sense taking the treasure with him. The angry Huns destroyed the helpless town. They sacked, raped, burned and enslaved, left the town a blackened ruin. But still they wanted their dead chieftains' grave goods. The bishop had fled to Sirmium for refuge and they followed him there.'

Lothar, who had been listening and tracing the whorls on the silver case, coughed impatiently. 'What has this to do with the cross?'

'Patience, patience,' said Sefu, 'I'm coming to that.' He shifted to a more comfortable position on the stony ground. 'The news of the sack of Margus came to Sirmium and the fleeing bishop was afraid, for he believed in God's punishment of sinners and knew that he had sinned very badly. You may not know, my pagan friends, that one of the better parts of my religion is that sinners can buy their way out of trouble if they give charitably to the church whilst telling their remorse.'

'So,' said Atilec, 'get on with it.'

'Well,' said Sefu, 'he thought to purchase indulgence by having a cross made for the cathedral in Sirmium. This cross,' he pointed, 'black in colour for his sins and shiny silver for his remorse and hopes of forgiveness.'

'So why is it a cross of ill omen?' I asked.

'I'm coming to that,' said Sefu. 'It happened that there was a young, unknown but wonderfully talented sculptor passing through Sirmium at that time who was looking for work. The bishop agreed the working of this cross and gave him silver from the grave goods to cast the case. See how beautifully he made it? It draws the eye, but the cross draws the soul…'

Sefu stroked the intricate carvings with his hand. He saw our impatience, and smiled. 'I know, I know, I talk too much. Anyway, when the bishop saw the cross he was delighted, but also overcome with the greed that had possessed his life and caused all the trouble. He sent gutter scum of Sirmium to fetch the cross. Bronze he paid them, but sent no gold for the sculptor. Having hidden the cross away, the young man, refused to give it up without his pay. The henchmen tortured him until he brought it forth. Even when they had the cross, excited by their power and sure of the bishop's protection, they raped the young man's wife, killed his child and gutted the sculptor, just for the pleasure of unbridled wickedness. As he died he cursed the cross that all who beheld it in awe should meet their doom.'

'That's it?' I said. 'Just the sculptor; not a god or even an elf?'

'That's it,' agreed Sefu, 'what more can there be? The young man poured his soul into the cross; it is beautiful; some part of his soul, his ghost, remains to carry out the curse. Also the case is made from grave goods.'

I snorted my disbelief. 'I believe in destiny. I believe in the gods and the Wyrd Sisters. They weave my fate. No cross, nor curse, nor grave goods can kill me unless they will it so. If it is their will then even a sprig of mistletoe will strike me down, as it did Baldor, the son of Mother Earth.'

The Egyptian shook his head in doubt for the names meant nothing to him.

'Hear me,' I said. 'Fate is all, I do not believe in curses. So, we will carry the cross before us as we agreed; it will save us trouble and questions along the way.'

'As you wish,' said Sefu, 'but this you should know. The Huns broke into Sirmium. They stuffed the thieving bishop with the stolen grave goods until he died, gutted him and brought them out. They killed all the monks and nuns of Sirmium so that they could wash the gold in their blood. The bishop of Sirmium had sent the cross and all of the cathedral treasures to Rome for safekeeping. Sylvanus said that the bishop's secretary had pawned it all to him and he had paid out gold coin for it. This coin was to pay any ransom for the bishop and some of his flock. When the secretary returned to Sirmium he told the Huns what he had done with the cathedral treasures, but he had no money from the pawn so they crucified him. Perhaps Sylvanus lied; perhaps he never paid over the gold.

'The Huns demanded Sirmium's treasures back from Rome together with Sylvanus. The Romans refused, but Sylvanus lies dead on the road anyway. Death follows the cross.'

We listened carefully to this tale, but I saw no reason to change our saintly procession and so we set forth, glad now of Lothar's foresight in bringing an extra mount, which Sefu took as his own.

Consulting the itinerary I had impressed on my wax tablet,

I told my plan to all. First we must circle the City of Colonia Julia, ancient Pisanus. Once we were past this and met up with the road north, then there should be no further dangers until Genua. There we had only to cut a quarter of the way around the city to find the Via Postumia leading east. On this we would climb over the mountains to Colonia Verona. From there the Via Claudia Augusta led north over a mountain pass to Raetia, a southern province of Germania.

'How long will this take?' said Atilec.

I read my writings from the Pantheon and did some figuring in my head. 'With these horses, and not forcing them, I think about four days to Genua, say six with the circling of the cities. Three days to Placentia and then, because it is summer and any snow will be light, I think perhaps seven days to Veldidina; then three more to Augusta. Past there I cannot say for there the Itinerarium stopped. But let's say three weeks or less to Germania and then we must find the Rhenus and a boat to Colonia Agrippina.'

The whole company sat quietly considering what I had outlined: three weeks, to arrive at some place off the edge of the Roman world.

We set off as soon as the sun had passed its highest and travelled joyfully with the heat of the sun on our shoulders, rich and happy men. We were seasoned warriors and did not neglect to keep lookout for the deserters from the town on the lake. In turns one of us scouted the road ahead, but they were far away for we never saw them. And so we continued easily on our way: sometimes walking, sometimes trotting but always watchful, always careful. We made a socket out of a water skin in which to carry the cross, and always aloft on its shaft, it went ahead of us. We passed travellers on the road and some bowed and some signed their respect to us in passing. Sefu raised his hand in blessing to all. If any stopped to watch us move away we speeded up, for the very last thing we wanted was a crowd of followers.

As we passed we cried, 'Rome is fallen!' This was enough to give them other things to think about than joining a religious procession. Soldiers going south moved with purpose and took little notice of us as we stood off to the side of the road while they passed. We continued happily in such fashion for two days until we came within sight of Pisanus.

The road - the Aurelia - was on the coast side of the town. To the west we could see the sea, to the east the walls of the city. Stretching in front of us from the sea and completely blocking our way was a river, wide and deep. There was a bridge at the edge of Pisanus crossing it and entering the gates. We sat quietly trying to see what plan would best cross us safely over, to continue on our road north.

At first we thought to carry on our pretence as a religious procession, a saint on a pilgrimage, but we could see a building with a cross on the roof peak; a cathedral probably, a town of this size would have a bishop. We knew that we would not pass without his attention and that he would see through us quicker than grease passes through a goose. Also, the bridge was guarded, there was a guardhouse, a search of our baggage was certain and that we could not allow.

We turned off the road and started to follow the river inland in the hope of finding a cattle or sheep track leading to a fording point. We rode all day. Off the road the going was slow. Up till now we had been following a good road leading through hill country, sometimes through bare hills dotted with scrub, sometimes through rich country with vineyards and olive groves climbing up steep, south facing slopes. Where the slopes were less steep grain was starting to ripen ready for harvest.

Now we were down from the hills into a broad river valley. As we rode alongside the river, looking inland for a way across, so our horses, heavily laden, slowed as they sank in mud up to their fetlocks. To help them we dismounted and soon our own feet and breeches were soaked and covered with mud. Buzzing swarms of insects rose and flew around our heads, landing and biting and leaving smears of blood as we swatted them. They flew into our eyes so that we walked, peering through slits and had to fan our faces continuously with our hands. The horses snorted insects from their nostrils and shook their heads vigorously to clear their own eyes, their tails thrashing wildly from side to side to clear biting insects from their rumps.

After a while of walking with our feet ankle deep in water, feeling pin pricks of pain I lifted a foot to find it scattered with great swollen leeches. I knew that if I pulled them off the teeth would remain and fester, so I left them sucking my blood until we reached higher ground. They looked full and so what they could take from me they had probably already taken. I looked at my companions and wordlessly we agreed, all turning away from the river verge to seek dry ground.

# Chapter 23

### AD 455
### Gewis' Tale, Crossing the River

Within a few hundred paces we found a low, tree-covered knoll where we tied the horses and threw ourselves down on the ground, examining the vile bloodsuckers attached to the exposed skin beneath our breech cuffs. There was dry kindling under the trees and Atilec soon had a small fire going. We each picked twigs with a glowing end from the ashes and touched them one at a time to our leeches and one by one they writhed and dropped off leaving the pink marks of their teeth in our flesh.

We doused the fire and then sat with our backs against the tree trunks discussing our plight. I did not know the river or how far it progressed inland, for all I knew there would be more cities along its length until we were high in the mountains again, days from the road. I only knew our way if we clung to the roads and I was unwilling to lose a road that fitted my travel plan.

Here was a good place to cross, but there was no ford, bridges were too dangerous, towns impossible with our happy burdens, which were too heavy for the pack animals to swim with. I stared at the water and the clouds of blue flowering weeds that grew between where we sat and the hell of the insect- and leech-infested marsh. And then it came to me, there was only one answer and we were resting against the means to accomplish it, but for one thing. I cursed my reckless lack of foresight. Why had I not thought to pick up rope when we took the horses?

I explained to my companions what I had in mind, but admitted I did not know how to accomplish it. At this Sefu smiled whilst Lothar eyed the trees and then held out his hand for his War Axe.

'You cut the wood,' said Sefu, 'and I will make the means to bind it together.'

In very short time Lothar, with Atilec and me helping, had felled and trimmed evergreens until he had assembled the pieces of a raft big enough to carry our treasure across the river.

'If we can find some way to fasten it, will it take the weight of the gold and our armour?' I asked.

'At least twice over,' said Lothar, 'had we only some rope.'

Sefu smiled for he knew something we did not. With the Alans' help, he started pulling up armfuls of the blue flowering plant growing near the water's edge. For the rest of the day he worked tirelessly at stripping the flowers and roots from the plants and twisting the stems into an ever-lengthening rope.

At our offers to help he shook his head, saying he valued his treasure too much to trust it to our clumsy attempts at rope making. I was not sure about his skill, although he seemed to know what he did and once again I cursed my lack of foresight in not securing some rope.

That night we slept in the grove of evergreens on the knoll and when we woke the next morning we found that Sefu had risen earlier and was still working at his length of rope.

'What is that plant?' I asked him.

He looked at me with amusement. 'Surely, Lord, your mother did not teach you much or you became a soldier too young. It has a word even in your tongue; you call it flax, in Latin, linum. As a boy I worked for a while making cloth from this. There is much more to that than rope making, but this will work, the thread is very strong.'

Comforted I again sat to wait. Having unpacked and stacked the saddles, bags and panniers the night before, we had moved the horses to spots were grass grew, pegging their reins so they could crop. Other than keeping lookout and attending the horses there was nothing to do while Sefu worked, so we slept.

In the afternoon, Gunthar, who was on guard, saw a boat in the distance. Quickly he roused us and we moved the horses behind the trees and out of sight until it had passed by. That night we slept again and by first light, when Sefu was finished, we started to lash the parts of our raft together. I tested his rope and found I was unable to break it with ordinary effort and so felt sure that with many turns it would be more than strong enough.

When we were finished we started to move it to the water. With all six of us we could lift and carry it, but only with the greatest effort. The horses would have made it easier, but there was nothing with which to fasten them and make towing traces. I was tired of lashing myself for my lack of foresight and so said nothing, nor did the others raise it. I suppose we each felt somewhat guilty not to have thought of it before. Anyway, grunting and straining for most of the morning we got the raft through the mud to the water's edge then carried down light branches and fronds of foliage to spread over the deck. Sefu had now made more lines sufficient in strength to secure the raft to a tree; tomorrow we would use them to tow our makeshift craft through the water.

Before sunrise the next day, when the hills inland were only just visible as dark masses against the lightening dawn sky, we loaded the raft with our sacks, panniers and armour, carefully distributing the weight so as to keep the vessel on an even keel. At each weight gain we moved it into deeper water with Lothar pulling lightly back on the flaxen tow lines to hold it in position.

Saddling two horses, we attached the tow lines to them and walked the animals into the water. Lothar and I grasped the bridles of the towing pair and by swimming ahead and coaxing drew them across the river towards the far bank.

We hurried to complete the crossing before the ebb tide started to flow and carry us down towards the city. With great relief we led the swimming horses into the shallows, but as their feet found the riverbed and they rose up out of the water the towropes checked them and they panicked. As the beasts plunged and strained, we heard a ripping noise and Sefu's ropes snapped. Lothar grabbed the end of one and hung on grimly while Sefu lunged forward and seized the bridles of the panicking beasts.

Using the flat of the war axe, I hammered into the mud the peg we had cut for the purpose and Lothar tied the frayed end of the rope to it. Carried by the floodtide, our raft swung on its rope and came gently alongside the bank.

The others came ashore with their horses and ours in tow and we secured them and quickly unloaded the raft.

We were across the river and we could at last breathe easily. We pushed and pulled the raft into a gap between rushes, hiding it as well as we could before loading the horses. That done, we rode away in a northerly direction until we were sure we were far enough from Pisanus for safety. Turning west with the sun at our backs we crept on, mud up to our knees, but watchful, until we came at last to the road. There we thankfully turned north again, once more raising Saint Sefu's cross before us.

The weather was good apart from summer rainstorms in the mountains, which made us both wet and cold. The roads between Genua and Placentia were more difficult than the old pass, which was an easy passage, but soon we had crossed out of Italy. At this point we had done with the pretence of being on a Christian pilgrimage, for here in Raetia there were still many followers of the old gods and such a course might have been dangerous. I took the cross in its silver case and put it with my gold on one of the packhorses.

By the time we arrived at Augusta Vendelicorum we had been nearly four weeks on the road from Rome. We found there was a road to Cambodunum and another from there to Brigantium. This last place was on a huge lake named the Lacus Brigantium, which feeds into the River Rhenus near the town of Constantia.

In five more days we were at Brigantium where we sold the horses and bought a large fishing boat for enough gold to buy the fisherman two more. And it leaked. We must have bailed half the River Rhenus through it.

The lucky laughing fisherman went with us as guide as far as Constantia. He left us there, but once on the Rhenus we just followed the river.

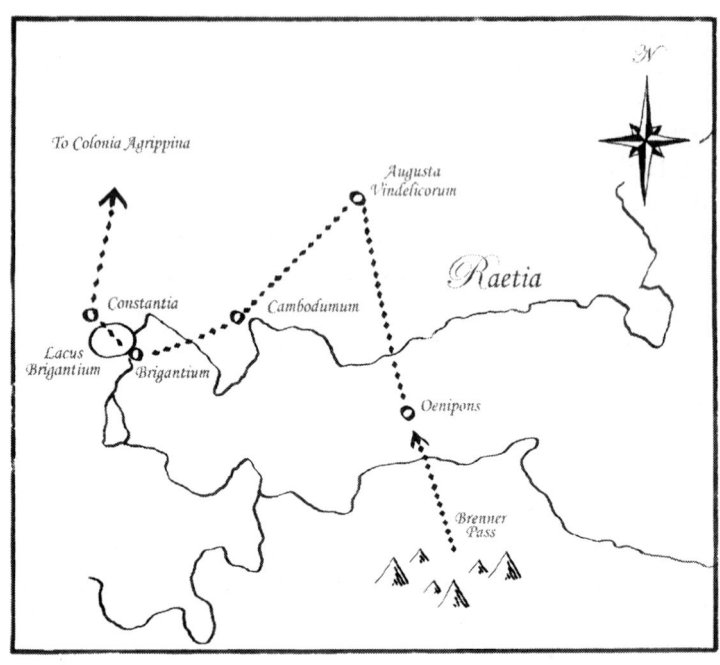

**Gewis' Tale – AD 455 The Return to Colonia**

# Chapter 24

**AD 455**

**Gewis' Tale, the return to Colonia**

It amazes me how fast a river flows. Of course, one thing we knew much about was rowing, but other than to keep from the bank there was little to do. In five days we found ourselves drifting up to the long bridge at Colonia Agrippina, back where we had started from more than eight years before.

This part worried me the most. I remembered how I passed through customs on my first arrival at Colonia. We had a great deal more to get into town than a few folles and no desire to mention the sack of Rome. I need not have worried, for there was no one on the bridge nor on the gate.

I hardly recognised the town as the Colonia I knew. Many buildings had burned down, charred timber and blackened rubble lay in the streets.

Of legionaries there was no sign, just a few Frankish warriors who took us for part of their own force. The town was sparsely peopled since I was last there and as I found out, had yet to recover from its sacking by the Huns four years before.

The two Alans and Lothar went to the horse market to try to buy nine horses. Looking at the town I doubted they would find a cooked joint of horsemeat to eat, let alone live fit beasts such as we needed. I had no cause to worry, for Lothar and the Alans returned within hours with horses of sorts. They were a sorry bunch, costly too and older than we would have liked, but at least not lame or sway-backed. Lothar said they were the best he could get and they had cost as much as prime cavalry horses, but I was relieved that at least we would be able to move on. First, however, we needed our old friend Harith, the Egyptian moneychanger, to turn our gold into coin. Even if he had survived, I wondered if there was enough coin in the whole city to satisfy us.

We camped beside our boat by the Rhenus, our horses tethered near the bank so they could drink at need. Atilec and Lothar went in search of Harith and since we had no idea of the nature of things in the ruined city, I allowed Lothar to borrow his axes from me.

They returned before nightfall with a greatly changed Harith. Gone were the bright outlandish clothes, instead he wore the dismally dull rags of the fugitive who seeks to escape notice. His eyes did not sparkle as they had when last we saw him - indeed he had lost an eye and over the left eye he now wore a patch.

We sat him down amongst us by the side of the fire we had lit as the sun was setting. He accepted gratefully the leg of fowl we offered him; we could see that meat was not a common meal in his life these days. We had renewed our stores from the land as we rowed upriver and now were glad of it. Foraging in this sad town we had found little food for sale. A fowl cost as much as if the carcase laid eggs of gold. I had, however, found rope - good oiled hemp - not wishing to be caught out by its lack again. I paid only a fair price, for in the ruins of Colonia sellers were out and desperate to sell anything except food.

We sat in silence as Harith told us his story. When we had left he had replaced Lothar and Atilec with new guards. As long as Roman law prevailed in the city he had no reason to doubt them. They reported on time, provided the protection he needed, were civil and dutiful and he grew to trust them.

When the Huns came to the city everything changed overnight. On news of their approach he had hidden all his money and specie and then himself. It was his guards who winkled him out and tortured him until they found his fortune; it was they who had taken his eye. They escaped the city by river before the Huns arrived and long before the city fell.

Harith had been abed throughout the siege and the city's fall. His slave moved him to her humble room and told the Huns he was her husband and that their master had taken his gold and left the city. By good fortune they believed her, and so poor Harith had escaped their torture to discover the wealth that must belong to the owner of so fine a house. Fine, that was, until it burnt down, for the Huns had fired the city before they left.

In the weeks after the sack, Harith had tried to make contact with his trading partners. They were either dead from the Huns' questioning or if young enough, carried off with their families into slavery.

He had no money, for his guards had left nothing, and he could not borrow for he had no friends left. Just staying alive was hard. He had some skills with writing and numbering and found just enough work to eat. He lived in the ruins of his house with the slave, for having saved his life and with nowhere else to go, she had stayed with him. He had thought of selling her, but she was old and of little value. Aside, she was loyal to him and he found that her company sustained him, even though feeding her was a further drain on his resources. He earned only small moneys as an occasional scribe to the not quite penniless poor and secretary to the newly poor; those who through cunning had escaped destitution.

There were no wealthy families left in the city. We had guessed true that there was not enough gold in the whole city to provide us with coin. A flash of Harith's old humour returned when he saw and tried to lift the sacks and peered inside.

'Why don't you buy the city?' he said. 'Give Rome some of her gold back for it. It will make a fine field of cut stone, to sell to someone wanting to build a city somewhere.' He thought for a while and life came back into his face. I could tell that scheming something more than how to get the next meal was bringing back the sharpness of his mind.

'I shall be your aurifex – your goldsmith,' he announced. 'There will be no coins, but in the street of the goldsmiths there will be furnaces and moulds, for they sell gold to each other in bars of the weight of ten solidi. I could melt down your plate and recast it into ten solidi bars. I can do it, for a price; I can do anything with gold, even make you all rings if you wanted. It will be easier to exchange. Any aurifex in a city will recognize it, but where will you find a city with that much gold? These are hard times my friends.'

We talked amongst ourselves. We believed him and decided to trust him. 'We will come with you and find such a place,' I told him, 'and for every one hundred bars you cast you may keep five for yourself. But you must test and mark the weight and value of the gold on each bar.'

And so we agreed and so Harith did. When we left the city it was with the coin we already had, but also with gold bars in our sacks, cast in pieces of ten solidi value. It had been slow work, for there were more than three thousand gold bars to make. The silver, and there was not much, we thought more trouble than it was worth there being twenty-five bars to one of gold. So we gave it to Harith. But over five days, during which we lived in the deserted shop of a dead aurifex, we melted and poured and cooled and counted until we were rich. And Harith? He had gold and silver beyond the dreams of any in the ruined city, enough to last his lifetime and to enable him, should he choose, to become the most prosperous banker in Colonia.

Our fortunes in gold amounted to over six and a half thousand solidi each. The worth of the stones we did not know, but Harith thought that in a prosperous city they would fetch around three thousand solidi. So my first thoughts of the value of the hoard had been a little high, but none complained at having only seven rather than eight thousand solidi!

We all still trembled with the understanding that we were rich beyond our dreams, also with the fear that such riches would tempt many to dare much. If we were not very careful all could be lost between here and my homeland, including our lives. I believe it was this that stopped any thought by the others of asking early release from their vows. No one would take the risk of travelling alone, the treasure made us huddle together for safety, doughty warriors though we all were.

If the neighbours, for such there must have been although we saw none, had wondered what we did in the shop of the aurifex they must have been as puzzled by our passing, for we left in the middle of the night, quietly. Harith stayed and fetched his faithful slave, for the shop and living quarters were better than the ruins of his house and, as he said, if any came to claim it, he could buy it from them.

There is a saying: he who builds a great hoard does so for

great thieves. Harith had suffered enough from thieves in his life. We knew he would be careful, but even so we urged him to hide his new riches well and be careful how he spent them. Then we wished him well and crept out silently - as silently as six armoured men leading nine horses could, but we saw no one.

On our way out of the city we passed by the cathedral and fulfilled our vow with the gift of one bar of gold each, which we left on the altar.

The gates were still shattered and the gateway watched by a pair of drowsy watchmen. They saluted us silently as we passed through into the misty night. The barracks and customs posts outside the gates were deserted: empty windows and shells, skull-like in the mist.

I led the way over the bridge and then up the hill down which I had slunk more than eight years before. Much had changed in ways that I could not have imagined back then. I remembered that I had found my way to the Rhenus by striking southwest. So, returning northeast and fording the small streams along the way we came to the Visurgis and there, following it to the north, found the ferry at Fabiranum and crossed, circling away from the little town and its prying eyes.

Water was plentiful and so we filled our bags at need. As the country was well watered and the grasses thick we let the horses forage. We were in no hurry so stopped five or six times a day to let them graze. As we travelled we stayed away from the sight of folk and only made contact through Atilec who, passing himself off as a poor warrior returning home from Gaul, sought food from hamlets along the way, and directions to the village of Hamm on the Albis River.

Atilec chose himself for this, for he said that it was his

country. Here he had wandered as a learner Gleeman seeking food for songs and tales. He had the dialect and folk would not think him a stranger. In the land of the Chatti they sought him as a murderer and Wolf's Head, but this was years ago now and many days' march away so the risk was not great.

No one had heard of Hamm, but they all directed us northeast to the river skirting the northern edge of the Leufana forest.

The food was poor, mostly flat rye bread and sometimes cheese or a rook or squirrel. We paid well and, said Atilec, when they saw the silver the fear melted from their eyes, sometimes to be replaced by greed and it was then that he loosened his spatha in its sheath.

We found the great river and eventually, by the number of banks and shoals, I thought I recognised the place where I had crossed before. If I was right, the village of Hamm would be on the far bank. From this point on, my having passed this way before, I took over from Atilec in making contact, and so, while the others made camp for the night, I unloaded my horse and with nothing more than my weapons on his back, I led him into the river.

Swimming alongside my horse in the gathering dusk it came to me that I was nearing my home and the power of my native gods was increasing. I thanked the Great Mother for the summer warmth that gentled the water through which I swam, for in winter I would have frozen. Then, slowing my mount, I trod water and drawing my seax made a small cut to the side of my palm, spreading the blood on the water and speaking blessings to any listening elves. I prayed to them to please not strike me with elf bolts while I swam, nor with the water-elf sickness when I landed. My prayers and blessings must have been enough for I made the crossing in safety.

Night was falling when I found a village on the riverbank, which I hoped was Hamm. I could not remember the name of the fisherman, but in one of the log-built houses was a tavern room, judging by the sound of the loud voices within. Tethering my horse, I pushed my way through the cloth-hung door and opened my hands to the gaping, silenced crowd to show I meant no harm. When I threw silver on the board and offered to buy for all, then explained that I had a party with horses wishing to cross the river, I was the centre of excited talk. I told them that my travelling companions would pay a gold piece for transport across the river. At this their talk redoubled in noise and speed. Then there was a satisfied silence.

The tavern keeper spoke up. There was, he said, a flat boat for taking timber to the shipyards at the river mouth. There were a number of fishing boats. If we loaded the horses and ourselves on the flat boat, the boats and their crews who towed the logs, would tow us across. They had done this before.

I thought this a good plan and told them so. I bought more drink for all and secured a place by the fire to sleep for the night. I paid the innkeeper for this and, showing that my purse was now empty, settled down to sleep, wrapping my cloak around me.

The next morning, true to their word the drinkers of the night before woke me. They had already tied the flat boat and the towboats to the riverbank. The day was warm, calm, dull, overcast.

Having checked my patient horse and arranged for him to be fed and watered, I boarded, and with two men rowing each of the two boats, we pulled easily across the river and then up against the ebb until we tied up by the overnight camp of my company, which we found by the smoke of the fire.

In no time we loaded the horses, split up my bags amongst them and re-crossed to Hamm. There I gave the leader of the boatmen an old gold aureus, which he recognized, having many years behind him. Our delighted ferrymen went off arguing. Where could they change the gold into twenty-five silver pennies? How much should go to the owners of the boats and how much to the rowers?

Once I had loaded my bags back on my horse again, we mounted, waved and left them to it. And that is where I took a wrong turn, so used to going northeast I continued in that direction when I should have turned north along the river. We travelled for one day and half the next before I knew we were lost. It was the water that told me. We stopped at a small lake for the horses to drink and they would not. I tasted the water and found it was salty.

When we came to the next hamlet I knocked at a door and asked the way to the western sea. The man of the house, spear in hand, pointed to the north and west. I thanked the householder for his advice and then he took my arm.

'Do not go north from here,' he said urgently. 'Go half a day west first, before you turn due north.'

I was puzzled by his obvious fear, but before I could ask what troubled him, his grip on my arm tightened. He lowered his voice, 'There is a white rock north of here, the flying mice of Hel come forth at dark-fall, it is known to be an entrance to her realm. A man from this place went there once and never returned. It is the way to doom.'

I prised his fingers from my arm, thanked him for his directions and his kindly advice and rode to rejoin my band. He stood watching us go and as we rode into the northwest he shook his head and re-entered his house where his family awaited his report.

As Gewis' voice ceased speaking there was a profound silence. For a long moment no one in the Cot stirred, as if waiting to find what it meant. So drawn into the tale had they been and for so long that they had forgotten where they were. And then someone coughed and it seemed everyone had been holding back, for there was then a multitude of coughing.

Bowdyn held up his hand and the villagers fell silent once more. 'The telling has been long this evening. I have gone beyond our usual time. My throat is dry and you, I am sure, are tired. Tomorrow is a working day and you will need your sleep. Let us meet again as we did today after Sunday church service, for starting early I can tell much before it grows too late.'

There was the usual hubbub as the crowd exchanged views. Getting to their feet and stamping life back into them, then stacking the stools and benches with much clattering, they called their thanks to my mother and father and to Bowdyn, then went on their way.

My parents were the last to leave. Bowdyn pushed himself out of the Story Chair, doffed his cap and returned their courtesies as they thanked him and bade him goodnight. Once they were through the door he stretched, smiled at me and flopped back in his seat. Wasting no time he raised his jug of cider and quaffed deeply.

I had many questions I wanted to ask, but could see that Bowdyn was finished with his story for the night. Resolving to ask them at the first opportunity I too bade my friend goodnight and went on my way.

# Chapter 25

### AD 455
### Gewis' Tale, the Bat Cave

The following Saturday, Bowdyn and I took the handcart, the saws and axes and returned to worry at the fallen tree from which we had taken wood to warm the Cot the week before. Whilst we chopped and sawed and loaded I asked the questions that were on my mind.

'Bowdyn …'

'Yes, Jo.'

'Creoda and Gewis are still riding through the forest aren't they?'

'Yes, Jo.'

'And so Gewis is still talking to Creoda as they ride and telling his story?'

'Yes, Jo.'

Creoda was much of an age with me and so I had an interest in how he felt and thought about things, for thus his story might shed light on my own future, which was obscure to me. And so I continued.

'Does Creoda have a future part in this story or is his part now only to listen to Gewis?'

Bowdyn laughed. 'Indeed he does, for soon his uncle's story will draw to an end and then the whole future of the story will be Creoda's. He has a very great part to play, greater even than that of Gewis. But as I told you, the story is long. Have patience, we will get to Creoda's tale again soon, when we get there.'

With that I had to be content, for he would say no more.

The next day, after church and our Sunday meal, the village began to arrive as the fires were starting to blaze up and heat the Cot. Once they were settled and my mother and father had seated themselves and were waiting, Bowdyn reminded folk where he had left off the week before.

'You will remember that Gewis had been given directions to the sea and warned against a white crag, which he was told was an entrance to the domain of Hel, Goddess of the Underworld. He rides to tell his companions what he has heard.'

Settling back in his chair, the Gleeman worked his magic and the voice of Gewis filled the room.

I repeated the man's advice and they considered it silently. Atilec spoke up at last, 'Flying mice live in caves,' he said, then he smiled. 'If we wander lost all over this land we are going to bump into someone a lot more powerful than we; there will be folk in larger villages than yours,' he looked at me. 'You have told me many times of your folks' wars with others. What if we wander into a war between your folk and those of Angeln or the Suevi? We will lose our lives as well as our gold.'

We waited; it was clear he was chasing a thought and had a plan to offer us. He looked around at our intent faces then said, 'What better place to hide our hoard than a cave full of

Hel's flying mice that everyone around here thinks is the entrance to Hel itself and avoids?'

I thought about this, looking for weaknesses. To be rich was new to me; I did not want to part with my wealth so quickly. I nodded slowly, thinking out loud. 'We could take a look. They may be too easy to enter or too difficult. Maybe what frightens these fellows around here is different there. Maybe there the children play in them. Maybe they are the entrance to Hel. Let us go look and decide.'

My companions agreed and so we continued north, looking for a white rock. We found it easily enough for it was a great crag rising out of the ground, perhaps as much as two hundred elbows high. Nothing broke the silence there. Truly it was an eerie place.

We searched around for water for the horses, for they could not drink from the salt water that lay in lakes in the ground here. We thanked our luck as we found a river running only about two thousand paces to the west of us, one I dare say that we had forded on our way northeast. They drank their fill there and we filled some of the skins we had added to our store in Colonia.

What we could not find was any cave. We spread out around the base of the outcrop, each within shouting distance of the next. Some showed concern to be separated in this way, in this place, but we were warriors and pushed down our fears.

At sunset, Hel's mice came flapping out of the ground and Sefu, who was stationed in the southwest, marked the place and called that he had found it, summoning us to join him before dark. When we came together he looked relieved and I understood what it had cost him to stay there as the dusk drew in. He was a Christian after all and had many strange beliefs about Hel and demons and devils.

We camped there for the night, tethering the horses loosely so they could graze; lighting a fire, eating from our food sacks and setting guard. As we fell into sleep, we could hear all around us the thin whistling of the mice, high and shrill as they swooped and circled above us. My companions slept closer to the fire that night than I had ever seen before, as if Sefu's fears were waking fears in them of wicked dwarves and elves in Hel's cave.

To calm everyone I cut my thumb and smeared it on a rock as a blessing to the cave elves, if such there were, with a plea that they protect us during our sleep.

The next morning we breakfasted at sunrise and built up the fire for we would need fire during the day. Then, having tended to ourselves, we advanced on the place from which the flying mice had come forth. After some searching we found it: a narrow flat cleft set deep at the back of a hollow beneath a shelf of overhanging rock.

It was too small for Lothar to enter and would be a squeeze for Atilec and me, but Gunthar, Hunneric and Sefu could wriggle in without much trouble. However, we decided that I should go first, with Atilec to help if something went amiss. I sent for the rope, pleased that I'd had the foresight to buy some in Colonia, and two flaming sticks of firewood such as we used to light our camp at night, wreathed in ivy stem soaked in the melted fat of our meat stores. I crawled into the hollow and poking my head and the flaming wood into the cleft, peered around.

The cave was large enough for giants. I could not see the other side, but the way in was a gentle slope from the cleft through which I gazed. There was a passage off to the right that was indeed like a passageway to Hel, for the roof was flat and the walls sloped in towards the bottom, making a narrow path on which to walk, but with widening walls rising to the flat ceiling. It looked as if it had been carved by dwarves. Wedged into the space between the ceiling and the walls were the sleeping mice, closely packed like thick, grey-brown serpents stretching away into the distance.

I wriggled back from the cleft and reported what I had seen. Knotting the rope around my middle and taking the flaming brand in one hand, I squeezed myself through the cleft feet first. Plummeting to the bottom of the slope, a slide of perhaps six arm lengths, I let go of the rope and it was withdrawn. Shortly afterwards I saw Atilec's feet come through the cleft followed by Atilec slithering down to join me.

With our two brands lighting the way we found that the cave was not one, but many: a maze of passageways that we were fearful to go too far into, afraid we should become lost. We did not need to go far, however, for about one hundred paces into the first passage I had seen was a side tunnel. There we found a place where rock had fallen from the ceiling of yet another, smaller, side cave. It was like a small rock room and in the floor was a pool, some two elbows deep, with water trickling down the walls to keep it full. It seemed to us that we had found as good a hiding place as any.

There was no sign that any other person had visited the caves, no signs of fire or spent brands, no scuffmarks on the rocks, nothing. The side cave was small, but the pool large enough for our bags of bars and coin, also for my cross, for I had tired of carrying it now that it had served its purpose. The roof fall would provide plenty of rock, not only to bury our treasure, but also to almost fill the pool in which it was submerged. Once we had hidden the hoard, all that anyone would see would be the side cave and a small pool filled with rocks from a roof fall.

We reported back to our waiting companions. Gunthar, Hunneric and Sefu entered and saw the place for the sake of memory. We all agreed that this should be the hiding place for our riches.

We sat at some length while our brands were soaking again in the fat, and explained the location to Lothar so that he could see it in his mind. He crawled in as far as was possible to him, saw the inside of the cave and understood which way to turn. He said that if he had to come and recover his treasure himself, he could mine his way in. The rock was soft; he would chip away at the cleft until it was big enough to let him pass, and so he also was satisfied.

We kept back only what could easily be carried and defended, about two hundred solidi each. The rest of the coin and all of the bars and the precious stones we left in the leather bags marked with our names. These we slid through the cleft. We placed them in the pool, covered them with rocks and left our treasure behind. That done, we cleaned the area with great care: we did not leave even the smallest piece of splinter or charcoal to show our visit to Hel.

Our lookout, for we had posted Lothar on top of the crag throughout this time, saw nothing and nobody. We were sure that the country folk gave Hel's cave a wide berth and that no one had seen us. If any had seen our fire in the night they would have put it down to elves or wights at the mouth of Hel, if not they would surely have come to see what passed and we would have seen them.

Nevertheless, we entered the forest and then leaving a lookout behind, withdrew far from sight. Four times a day the lookout was changed. If any had come near the cleft in that time we would have slain them and pushed them inside where the smell of death would have convinced any others of the authority of Hel. For five days we lay quiet and watched and in that time no one came near. We decided no one had seen us and none knew we had been there. Satisfied, on the sixth day we struck out north by west and came at last to the sea and to the East Holding.

And so my tale is done and there you have it. That is how we came by the treasure and now you know of my life during the eight years I was away from the Holding. Now, also, you know the true names of my brothers in arms. So that these are not spread to their enemies and bring trouble to our folk you must keep them secret in your heart, as we keep other things secret; things that are between you and me alone.

There are some lessons to be drawn from the tale. I hope you have drawn them. Reflect that had I not won the axes from Lothar, you would now be dead, killed by a Hun arrow. Fate is all. What they weave for us is what will be. The future is closed to us, but they see everything. The picture from the beginning to the end of all is plain to them as they weave the future. The hoard that we now journey to recover has a part to play that only they see and ....

Suddenly, the heavens opened and heavy rain started to fall into the Cot drowning out the storyteller's voice and hissing into the fires.

The day had been cold, damp and overcast, but the rain had held off until now. Gewis' voice halted in mid-sentence and Bowdyn looked towards the sky, then turning to the folk he shrugged. 'The vicar will be pleased that the weather wants a short story this Sunday night. It is telling us to go home and rest, for tomorrow the work may be hard in the mud.'

All those familiar with his storytelling knew he had come to the end of the story for that night. They stayed seated out of politeness, shielding their heads against the rain until he smiled in confirmation. Giving out their choruses of thanks they then got to their feet. The men drew their coats closer and the women pulled their shawls over their heads against the rain. All waited expectantly, their faces turned towards the Gleeman.

'Next Friday night then, weather permitting,' he said, 'and with the Master's permission.'

My father smiled and nodded, shielding my mother and standing under the shelter of the door arch, 'Of course,' he said. 'I also want to know what happens next.'

'At the next telling,' said Bowdyn, 'Creoda returns to resume his tale, for all that happens with Gewis now is under Creoda's eye.'

Again there was a chorus of thanks and then the clatter and cries of running folk, which faded away as the villagers hurried through the deluge to their homes and the farm folk to their beds.

Disappointed that the weather had interrupted the story just at the point where I had hoped to learn more of Creoda, I contained my impatience as best I could.

In my bed I reflected on this day's part of the story and was trying to imagine where it would take us next when I fell fast asleep.

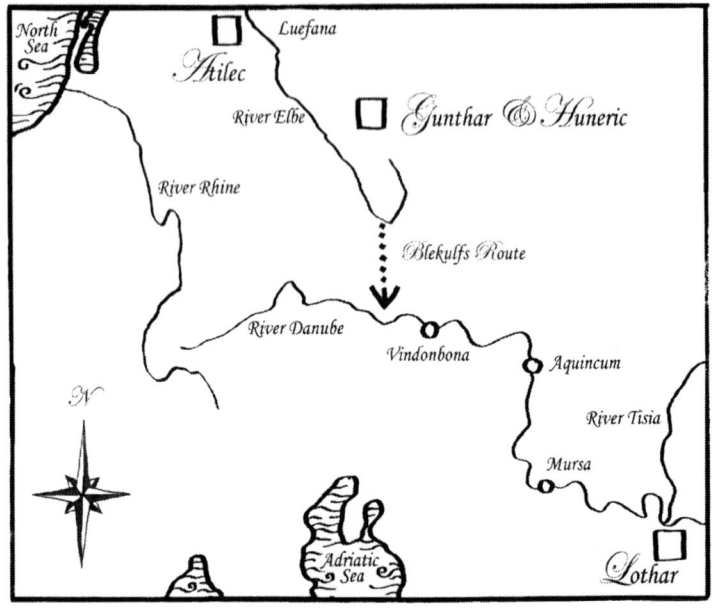

**The Homes of the Hearth Companions**

# Chapter 26

**AD 462**

**Creoda's Tale, oaths and choices**

When we all gathered before the fires on Friday night it was cold. Above the Cot towered great, swelling clouds lit up by bright moonlight. Following several days of drizzle and then rain there had been showers during the day and everything in the open was wet. Starting the fire had proved difficult until we soaked the kindling in old rancid kitchen fat. Now, however, the clouds had lost the great tops that looked like blacksmiths' anvils and the showers had grown less frequent. We hoped that no more would come to disrupt the proceedings. Risk of a wetting or not, the whole village arrived, as before. Perhaps they all had faith in Bowdyn's choice of day, for he seemed to have uncanny luck with avoiding the rain – or had until the last time.

When he arrived he acknowledged the villagers with a smile of greeting. Then, seated in his special chair, he launched himself back into the story, but this time as Creoda rather than Gewis, his voice changing once more to that of a much younger man.

As we rode, I cast back in memory to the time I first saw Gewis. He could say, 'And we came at last to the East Holding,' as if it were such an easy matter.

I was just a child at the time, still grieving the loss of my father and living under the love and protective arm of my mother. I remember the feelings of wonder and alarm that ran through the Holding when six heavily armed strangers, leading packhorses, came knocking at our gate one Freyaday morning in the month after midsummer. The watchman had seen them coming from far off and had called for aid to shut the gate and bar it.

The warband of Baeldaeg donned arms and came running, led by Wulfgar, his champion. The farmers and makers not out at work seized their spears and stood ready. The women pulled children into their homes and took up what knives or clubs they had. We waited for the word of Baeldaeg, as he mounted the step at the side of the gate to look over and judge the manner of these strangers. I could not hear what they called back and forth as I peered round the doorway of my home. I know only that Baeldaeg gave a great cry and jumping down from the step threw off the bar and dragged open the gate himself. He stood in the opening, arms open wide and as one of the bearded men walked forward Baeldaeg clasped him in his arms like some great bear and hugged him. We watched with amazement and then my mother, who was standing behind me and holding me back by my shoulders, gave a cry of delight.

'It is! It really is! It's Gewis, your Uncle Gewis!' And with that she flew from the door and running up to the two embracing men, took the hand of the stranger, tears coursing down her face. I dawdled towards them and wriggled my way through the gathering crowd.

My mother picked me up in her arms and said, 'See Creoda, it is Gewis, your father's brother; your uncle.'

This great bearded man, Gewis, took me from my mother's arms and grinned at me. 'A fine boy,' he said, 'as I would expect from my big brother and the friend of elves.'

He searched around him over the heads of the crowd. 'Where is my brother?'

A silence fell on the gathering crowd, my mother and grandfather looked at the ground in sorrow. Hearing no answer the man studied me, 'Where is your father, boy?'

I gaped at him in amazement, how could he not know? Everybody in the world must know; my father was a great man. I answered him simply, as I had been told.

'My father is dead, sir, he was killed by a Suevi spear.'

The man gasped, returning me to my mother. 'When? How?' he asked my grandfather.

Baeldaeg took a deep breath, 'It was some years ago, my boy, we will talk of it later; now is not the time, now is a time for celebration. For you, who we all thought dead, have returned and a fine man you are. Make these strangers known to us and then come and tell Elwine and me your story, all of you.'

He looked then at Atilec. 'Suevi are not welcome here, but I see you are my son's friend and that he wears the Suevi hair knot in friendship, so you also are welcome.'

'I am Suevi of the Langobardi,' said Atilec, and everybody hearing made murmurs of sympathy, for the sad history of the Langobardi was well known and they were not enemies of ours, the survivors having moved far away.

'Then you are doubly welcome and must rest in my hall. Tonight we will have a great feast, everyone must come, and you all shall tell your story again to the whole East Holding.'

And so it was, although I heard it not, for I was too young for the Feast hall and only heard the tumult as I lay in bed waiting for sleep to claim me.

After the tale telling, my grandfather settled land on Gewis, next to ours, and he built a hall for himself and his hearth companions. It was a good hall, for our men were busy with the harvest and Gewis sent away for builders and carpenters and woodsmen from the Frisian shipbuilders of Rungholt on the Island of Strand. He paid them well to cross the seas and work for him. He spent much time talking to these Frisians, for many had travelled far.

Once he left with one of their ships that had brought the timber from the Rhenus, and we did not see him again for ten days. Where he went he did not say or what had been his purpose, nor was I to find out for many years.

The men of our village said they had never seen a finer hall nor ever woodwork and jointing so fine, all fastened with treenails. Out of respect for his father, I believe, it was unadorned; no fine carving bedecked the eaves or the door pillars. It was the finest hall for miles around, but smaller and plainer than that of Baeldaeg, which one day, when his father went to the world of shadows, Gewis would live in himself.

He then took on the duties of an uncle, filling my days with pleasures I had never known, my father being long dead and I having no other uncle. He took me hunting, he took me fishing, he showed me the use of weapons; he told me many, many stories about the great world outside. He became more than a father to me, which is what an uncle is for. I had not understood what I had missed from my life up to that point. There were men who offered to be my uncle, I know, but my mother had refused them and sent them away. And then my real uncle came home. Him she greeted with open arms and soon they became friends, always making mirthful talk and telling tales.

In the beginning he asked her about my father's death many times until he knew every detail and then they never spoke of it again. He had decided, he told me later, that there being no blame to be found there was no punishment to mete out. I came to believe, thinking back to that time, that had there been fault he would have killed the guilty.

After that, as their friendship grew I saw my mother begin to laugh and be happy where before I had seen only a sadness about her. This I thought caused by the loss of my father. It was as if the morning he went out with the warband he had packed up her joy in a bag and taken it with him. I saw now that this was not true: her joy had been hidden away, ashamed to match itself against the sorrow that seeped into the home; a home damp with tears. Or so I thought. Much later I was to learn a hard truth: she had not cried; the tears were mine alone. To the young all things are simple, but life is not simple, it is more tangled than the young can know.

Six years and more had passed between my uncle's return and today when we rode out together, I proudly as a member of his band. I had seen this joy between Gewis and my mother and wondered about it. If they were so happy together, why could he not be my father as well as my uncle? The memory of my father had faded since Gewis' return and when I tried to remember his face, all I could see was that of Gewis. I do not know the answer to that question even now, why they left it so long. If they had not, they could have had more happiness than they did; more time together. But they did not. All that time Gewis could have become my father, but he did not.

Pondering on this, I rode beside him through the forest. Having finished his story and spoken to me of secrets to be kept, he looked a question at me, a long look, at which I nodded, understanding his meaning clearly and agreeing that all secrets would remain safe with me, as they were with him. He had also asked me to reflect on the lessons to be learned from his tale. Again I nodded, but doubtfully, for it seemed to me that what lessons were there for me in the story would take some thought.

I was still thinking about this when there was a cry from Lothar, who was riding in advance. He pointed and as we entered a glade we could see, over the tops of the far trees, a great crag of white rock.

My uncle sent Gunthar, who was little and lithe and deadly with his bow, who could kill silently and without fuss, to espy. If someone had found and now guarded the hoard and we blundered in and they killed us for our trouble, it would be a great misfortune. It was not a likely thing, as he said, but there are few old careless warriors: old warriors become so through being careful. This was a war saying for me to engrave on my heart, he said.

When Gunthar returned and said that the mountain was clear of life it was getting on towards nightfall. We gathered wood, chopped it and built a roaring blaze on the side of the hill, on a small platform in the rock. As the fire caught hold and blazed up Gewis spoke to all in his band, standing facing them across the fire.

'There is an oath,' he said, 'which, as I promised, could have been released at any time once we reached the East Holding. Yet in nearly seven years since we came here, none of you has asked release to return to his home, for which I am exceeding glad. However, tomorrow we will recover what is ours and I would remind you, my oath-sworn friends, that you are all free to go whenever you wish.

'When our treasure is once more in our hands we will be

pledge-brothers no more and you must decide whether to go or whether to stay. If you stay in my hall you are greatly welcome, but much depends on whether I can glean food from the countryside to feed my people. If we cannot live here, we must live elsewhere. I cannot promise you the life of safety and comfort we have all enjoyed these seven years past. There may be danger and the whole folk may be doomed and any who go with them.

'On the other hand, if you go, there is much danger in carrying such treasure through the lands to the south and east. There are still robber bands of Huns loose and the treasure is so great that many chieftains along the way would kill you for it. I cannot change that, but for those who decide to go, if you will keep together as long as can be I shall send a band of ten young warriors to ride with you for your greater safety. For Sefu I can do nothing,' he grimaced at the Egyptian and shrugged his shoulders. 'None of my folk would go to Egypt with you and I could not make them, not even for my father would they go.'

He looked ruefully from one to the other, for now his band of brothers was to disperse after many years - nearly half his lifetime they had been together.

'You must all rest in comfort by the fire and think what you will do.' He paused and then shrugged again. There was nothing more he could say on the matter until his friends were ready to speak.

He nodded to them and then, 'I shall take first watch and young Creoda the second. He will then wake Lothar, who is too big to enter the cave and therefore will have no work inside. It will then be morning and you must tell me what you have decided.'

As we settled down to our rest, each man in his solitary

place, I was aware that none slept; they lay turning over their possible choices in their minds. Only the two Alans spoke to each other in hushed voices until, as the eastern sky started to lighten, they came to an agreement and closed their eyes in sleep.

There were only two choices, to go or to stay. Why the heart searching, the mind racking? Surely, when it is this or that, the heart makes its choice and there's an end to it? And if it had only been as easy as that then no sleep would have been lost.

But even I, at my young age, could see it was not as easy as that, for there was the hoard for each man to worry over. If they stayed with us in the East Holding the hoard would be safe; but there was no land to take or buy, no place to raise a hall, no followers who did not already follow a Lord; and so where would their dreams be then?

And there was the homesickness. I had never been away from my home more than a few days, but I had heard in song the pain of it. I suppose after so many years the ache was dulled, but still in every man's mind must be the picture of how sweet it would be to return home as a wealthy man. To give help and ease to those loved ones left behind and to find land for the taking in which to place the family and become the ancestor of a new and powerful tribe.

But then there was the hoard. To move such wealth over unknown land was madness and almost certain death. Even hiring an army could not make it certain that the wanderer might arrive home safely. More likely the army or its chieftains would murder their employer for possession of the gold.

And so the choices were these: stay in safety, but remain a follower of Gewis, if a wealthy one. Stay as a follower of Gewis and if it fell out that the East Holding folk must find new land, hope that at that place a hall might be raised and warriors found to join the oath-sworn Hearth-Band of a wealthy warrior, a generous Lord.

Or choose to leave and risk the journey to find one's own people with all its dangers. And to do so would be to overcome the greatest difficulty of all, for none knew in which direction that home lay. Years of wandering over unknown lands had laid a maze between start and finish.

And so their hearts weighed two things in the balance: the love and trust of Gewis and our people and the safety they afforded, against the love of that home that was distant in time and place and the dangers of going there. Each felt the weight of these two things differently; it was only in the minds of each and the heart of each that the tilt of the balance could be felt. And having weighed these things in the balance each made his choice.

In the morning, when the fire had burnt down and we had wakened and refreshed our faces with water from our skins, we breakfasted and then the Hearth Band rose and stood facing Gewis.

'So,' he said, 'what is it to be?'

He paused and then raised his right hand and looked to the sky. 'Father Wotan, these warriors have faithfully carried out their oaths to be my pledge-brothers and now, in thanks, and at the end of the agreed task, I release them.'

He then held out his left hand, palm down and looked to the ground. 'Mother Freya, these warriors in my Hearth Band have faithfully carried out their oaths of friendship. Although they will always be in friendship held, I release them to go whither they will and will provide all help that friendship demands.'

My uncle looked around the circle, 'There,' he said, 'you

are all released. What will you do?'

Hunneric and Gunthar spoke up first. 'Lord, we have stayed for we feared to return to our home, but now the Huns are gone we would return to our people, but know not whither.'

Gewis nodded and smiled, 'We shall find the way.'

Then spoke Lothar. 'Lord, I also have heard that the Huns are destroyed. I can and must go back to my family, but I also find I am lost here, for I started from one place and ended in another and cannot join the two in my mind.'

Again Gewis smiled, 'Fear not, for we will hold a Moot for all travellers and find the best way before you set off.'

Atilec then spoke, 'Lord, I have no home to go to and a rope awaits me in my old land. I promised my master to gather new stories. So far, our story is one worth telling. I feel there is more and greater to come. If you will have me in your new warband I shall renew my oath and stay.'

'Any of this company who wish to stay shall do so as my true friends and shall always be seated on my right hand at the feast, at the head of the doughty warriors,' said my uncle.

And then spoke Sefu, our Sacramoor. 'Lord, I can never go home. If you will have me I will cast my lot with you and as you rise so shall I, and as you sink so I will sink with you, but my sword arm will be with you always.'

'Welcome, Sword of Alexandria, for the thanks of us all are due to you; from your trust and open-handed giving comes all of our prosperity. You shall always have a home with the folk of the East Holding, and there will always be food and ale and a place at the fire for you in my hall, and a place of honour at the feast.'

And so Atilec, Sefu and Gewis renewed their oaths and then we set about recovering the hoard.

I went in first with Gunthar, for we were small. Between

us we lifted and piled the rocks to one side and then hauled the heavy leather sacks from the icy pool where they still lay. We laid them on their side so that the water could drain from them and then one by one tied rope to them and we and the others pulled and pushed them through the cleft.

The bats hung in their ropes in the edges where the walls met the flat ceiling and we were careful not to disturb them for a cloud of bats in daylight would surely draw the curious.

When all the bags were out and in the possession of their owners, according to the marks burned in by the point of Gewis' knife so many years before, he turned to address us all.

'Here is what I suggest: we take all of the hoard back to the East Holding and put it in the store house at the back of the hall. We can pull up the boards and put it in the pit underneath and we will all take turns guarding it. I will find those amongst the Frisians or the Saxons who have travelled farthest and try to discover the best ways for Lothar and Gunthar and Hunneric to go. When they do go, I will ask for men from my father's warband, trusted men, who will be under oath to guide and guard. I would go with them as called for by friendship, but I have other tasks to perform for the safety of the folk who face starvation this winter.'

And so it was agreed, with much grateful speech from the three who were soon to leave, and we loaded the packhorses and with all of the hoard in our care, returned to the East Holding.

Bowdyn emerged from the shadows and smiled. The village sat in quiet reflection, no doubt thinking about so much gold and what even one tenth part of each man's hoard would do for their lives if it were theirs. With a collective sigh they came back to reality and with the now usual chorus of thanks and clatter of stools and benches and bottles, got to their feet and looked expectantly at Bowdyn.

He waited in silence, building the tension and then relaxed with a smile and said, 'Tomorrow night then, with the Master's consent and the rain's forbearance.' He looked at my father who smiled his assent.

As we all went home to bed, I for one wondered what would now happen to these folk with so much treasure in their possession - and wished that it was I.

# AD 463 – AD 464
# Thiatmaresgaho, Germania

# Chapter 27

**AD 463**

**Creoda's Tale, the Moot**

On Saturday night it was again cold, but with small, torn scraps of cloud blowing swiftly from the northwest. It was dry but with a brisk northerly wind that cut through clothes, and when the folk entered the Cot they were hunched over against the cold with much hand rubbing and stamping of feet. Once inside, however, they uncoiled and moved gratefully into the heat of the two great blazes we had fostered against the wall. Bowdyn was already sitting in the Story Chair against the wall and between the two fires, his forehead glowing pink from the heat. He showed no other sign of discomfort appearing to relish his closeness to the burning logs.

As soon as all were seated and it was apparent no more were coming – indeed, so crowded was the Cot I do not think there could be any folk left in the countryside nearby to come – it fell quiet and everyone looked expectantly at the Gleeman.

Then, suddenly, Creoda was amongst us continuing where he had broken off the previous night.

When we arrived back at the East Holding it was still dark.

We had camped close to the settlement and had arisen and moved out shortly after the middle of the night. The intention was to arrive at the village much before sunrise, when the watchman would be drowsy and all others asleep.

It was now Blood Month, when we would normally have sacrificed the flock we could not feed in the winter and salted the meat for our winter food. It was still dark and we were rested but cold when we called the watchman to open the gate for us. As we had thought, he was drowsy and took little notice of us and so we gained entrance with no disturbance and moved quickly to Gewis' unadorned hall.

We quietly unloaded the hoard and carried the bags of gold inside through the front entrance into the small entry room and on through the door into the hall. Anyone standing outside could not see in because of the positioning of the doors. We passed the glowing hearth, the servants having banked up the fire to keep the hall warm for its master's return. Gewis unlocked the small door at the back of the hall and we entered the storeroom where he stored food and drink, cloth and furs, against need. The room was not large, being a lean-to hut about nine foot-lengths long and six foot-lengths wide. Under it, to allow any rain leak to drain away and so keep the floor dry was a pit, perhaps four foot-lengths deep. Often the folk built huts such as this separately as stand-alone workshops. Sometimes, busy workers dropped tools for woodworking or weaving and they fell through gaps in the floorboards into the pit beneath. The builders of my uncle's hall had made a small hatch in the floor for the recovery of such lost tools and it was through this that we now lowered the hoard into the pit.

We closed the hatch when we had finished and took the goods that had been piled on top, which we had shifted to one side, and carefully replaced them in the same position so they looked undisturbed. The door into the store we latched back in the open position, at no time would the inside of the hut be out of the sight of the watchman in the hall.

Leaving Atilec sitting on the guest stool to take the first watch, we laid ourselves down in the softness of the rushes beside the hearth and on the warm wooden floor we slept.

One of the servants must have looked in and spied us huddled asleep for we were awakened at cock crow by the smell of food cooking in the cook house, the smell filtering along the small connecting passageway and into the hall where we lay.

I am sure I was not the only one who suddenly remembered his hunger, for soon we were all stirring and at a call from the cook, we took our customary place at board and were soon tucking into platters of fried sliced pork, fowl, eggs, cheese and great hunks of rye bread made from soaked and skimmed rye. All washed down with wooden cups filled with good ale. I felt that perhaps the cook was pleased to see our return for there could not be many meals of this sort left in the store, although what meat there was had to be eaten before the rot set in. Pig meat was now rare, almost as rare as that of our few remaining cows and sheep, even some of the horses must by now have disappeared into the stew pots.

When we had finished our meal, Gewis spoke of his plans. Atilec and Sefu were to stay and guard the hoard against sneak theft. Even if word got out about the riches in the cellar, Baeldaeg would guard them against attack. The work of sneak thieves amongst the servants was the only danger. Atilec and Sefu agreed that the store would be secretly under their gaze at all times of the day and night, while the two Alans and Lothar would set out with Gewis to seek directions to their homelands.

'What about me,' I said, with some fear that I would be left behind.

'Oh, you will come with me, of course,' said Gewis. 'Your mother has given permission for you to be by my side, we must make sure that she has plenty of time to get used to having a warrior son.'

Inside I was warm with pride when he said that, but I nodded and said nothing.

That very morning, after making our greetings and explaining our task to Baeldaeg, we went to see Elwine, my mother, to set her mind at rest that the gold was in hand to save the folk from famine. Then we set off southwest to the Frisian coast to start our search.

We were lucky, thanks be to our Lady Freya, for at the very first settlement we came to in the Frisian lands almost next to our own on the River Albis, we found a man who could help us. The settlement was enclosed with a hedge and built on a mound above the floods of the Albis; it was small and had no name, so for the good fortune we met there we called it 'Luckyworth'. After they saw a little of Gewis' gold, the folk there thought themselves lucky also and were amused at our naming of their hamlet - for all I know the name holds to this day.

The Frisians are very fond of travelling by water. They are so well known for this that some think they must have weak legs, for the other thing they are known for is the breeding of strong horses. So a Frisian moves over land on horseback if he has to, but will prefer any day to go by sea. Or so they say.

Anyway, in Luckyworth was an old man, a Frisian, one Bleikulf by name, who had travelled far. In his youth he had built himself a boat and carved a pair of oars. He had a great curiosity about what lay up the river he lived beside and so one day, to his mother's distress and his father's angry laughter, he had bade his family farewell. Taking his hunting bow, what food he could gather together and a keg of water, which his father, now calmer, gave him, he set off rowing up the river. He returned six months later, lean and fit and with tales of many places.

We sat in Bleikulf's hut as he told us this and we promised him gold if he would listen to the tales of Gunthar, Hunneric and Lothar, all of whom had lived by a river. We made him swear an oath to tell true what he had seen that might shed light on the whereabouts of their homes, but not to say any untruth that would send them off to be lost in the wilderness. He gave that oath and listened with care. When they had told him all they could remember of their homelands, he thought for a while and then spoke.

'This is what I remember,' he said. 'I rowed for many days down the Albis and indeed I did come to a stretch where it flowed from east to west, but all the folk along the shore on both sides were Saxon. Further south I came to a settlement on the north side of the river and these folk spoke a tongue I could not understand. Speak to me a little in your own tongue,' he said to the Alans. Hunneric did so.

The old man pondered and sighed, 'It could be, it could be, it was so long ago. There is one thing: there was a Goth with them who spoke a dialect I could understand. He told me they were subjects of the Huns and moved from place to place to their master's wishes. Most lived further east in marshy ground near another river, where the sheep were very good eating, so he said.'

Gunthar and Hunneric became very excited by this for they thought everything he said rang true and they were sure their homeland was east of the river. They resolved that they would travel up the river as soon as they could and seek their own people.

The old man then listened to Lothar's description of his homeland. 'I cannot say, I cannot say,' he said, 'for I am oath-sworn to guide you true, and in truth I do not know. Here is what I do know. After passing the land that these young men think might be home, I travelled south until I could go no more. When I returned I saw a smaller river on the west bank, into which I turned. It lies just south of where the Albis twists and turns like some small stream. I journeyed further south on this river and then, when it became nothing more than a stream, I hid my boat and carried on walking south. In a few hours I found another stream flowing in the same direction and I followed it.

'After about five days I found my way blocked by a great river, which flowed always eastwards. There was much traffic on that river and I hailed a passing boat that was rowing by. They held their place and asked what ailed me, I told them I wanted passage and would row, and so I joined them and went down the river to a great city that was built on either side of it.'

When he described this city, Lothar in turn grew excited, for it sounded to him like the very city of Vindobona where he had lived for two years as a Roman horse soldier. From there he said, he knew his way home.

Gewis offered the old man more gold than he had ever seen to act as guide to the homebound travellers, and once Bleikulf knew there would also be a guard of a chieftain's pledge-brothers, he agreed. It was settled that Gewis would hire him and a ship, which he, Bleikulf, would undertake to supply, and the travellers and their guards would meet him one week from that day at Luckyworth, where shelter and care for their horses would be given until the return of the guards.

All was agreed, except that Bleikulf said he could take Lothar only as far as the place where he had hidden his boat, for he was too old now for the five-day walk. Once he had reached the great city he had gone no further and after a while, tired of his travels, he had returned to his village the way he had come. He could find the way to the stream that ran south, but would go no further. And so it was agreed.

Baeldaeg was willing to release some of his warband to guard the travellers. He chose those men whose obedience and loyalty he would stake his life on and whose heads would not be turned by any tale of the hoard they travelled with and carried. And so, the day before the homeward-bound were to set off, Gewis, with Baeldaeg's permission, held a feast in my grandfather's hall.

The travellers were the guests of honour, Baeldaeg was at Gewis' right hand and my mother was the ale carrier. I and other young warriors, who had been in the fight against the Huns and survived, sat on the youngsters' stools, whilst Atilec and Sefu and the ten guards for the journey sat in the place of the doughties. In the guest seats facing Gewis and Baeldaeg and Elwine, sat Lothar and Hunneric and Gunthar.

My mother carried to the travellers the best drinking horns, their edges trimmed with gold. She poured strong ale then returned and filled the horns of my grandfather and uncle. She served in this order to show great honour to those soon to leave us.

When she had filled the cups of all those present, Baeldaeg raising his hand and said, 'Let all be well with us.'

This was the signal for the feast to commence. The music of the pipes led the food as the cooks brought it to the tables. Great bowls of bubbling stew. Stewed what, I did not ask. Whatever it was, my mother had flavoured it with herbs and garlic and thickened it with vegetables and roots, as only she knew how. The cooks had made a meal the smell of which made the mouth water. With it were great round loaves of bread made from skimmed rye, served with buckets of ale to wash it down. Mead there was also, in plenty, for the bee hives had been robbed for the wax combs to make the candles, which together with the fire filled the hall with a cosy glow. It lifted the heart to be in such company, in such warmth, with such food and drink. Truly, the hall as a place of feasting must be one of the great comforts of our lives, together with our kin - even though this life within the village binds us in ways that gall sometimes.

To be in the same hall to receive judgement must be another feeling entirely, I reflected, thinking back to the Goth we had judged here when a small band of thieving Goths had come this way before the Hun raid. We killed them all except one. Him we kept for Freya. Thinking to save his life, he had warned us that he and his hearth-companions were part of an army of Huns that had mutinied under Tuldila, their Gothic leader. Many were killed and the remainder, rightly fearing death at the hands of the Romans, had fled. A band of these mutineers was now in the lands about us, looting, raping and murdering at chance. Driven off by the Suevi to the south and the Anglekin to the north and with the Frisians on their islands to the northwest being unreachable over water, they now turned their eyes and the noses of their horses west, to us. He and the Goths we had just killed were their scouts.

We thanked him and then, before we sent the women and children to safety in the swamp and before we drew in our folk and allies from the out-holdings, we placed him in a marshy verge, covered him with a hurdle and stood on it until he ceased struggling. Thus we offered him to Mother Earth.

May she pardon him his many evil acts.

For a moment I was saddened that such things must be. To fight and kill when to feast was possible seemed such a poor choice. I wished my life could be one long feast. And then it came to me why to die well in battle was every warrior's wish, for such a death, the scop tells us, leads to the eternal feast in Wotan's hall.

Cheered by that understanding, I came back from my thoughts to the glowing hall in which I sat with my brethren, and gulped once again on the warm, nutty brew in my wooden cup.

Gewis had risen to his feet. 'Tonight,' he said, 'we feast, but it is a sad time for me. The warriors seated on the honour stools were lately my pledge-brothers. We rode together; we stood in the shield-wall together. We sweated together on the oars of the Triton, the finest ship with the finest crew that ever frightened the Romans from the sea. We were together at the sack of Rome, the most frightening and yet the easiest of tasks, and we fled together over the mountains to come to my home here in the East Holding. Together: to do what these men of honour swore to do, to bring me home. And they have stayed here for many years, guests of honour in my hall and guests of our folk. We have grown to think them our kin. Loved them like brothers - and I think in the case of some young matrons, as more than brothers.'

There was chuckling from the men's benches, although there was also at least one glare, for not all of the young matrons, widows all, had no other swains.

'But now,' continued Gewis, 'for three of my great friends it is time for us to part, perhaps forever. They have all hesitated to return home, fearing that the Huns might hunt them and their families. But we hear the Huns are broken and the remnants driven either east or far to the south. So my friends must needs travel home, to meet again their loved ones, sisters, brothers, fathers, mothers and maybe even long ago lovers.'

Gewis smiled, paused and then, 'I have already released my Hearth Brothers from their oaths. This I would have granted, had they asked, at any time after we came here. It is a mark of the love in which they hold our kin that they have stayed with us these seven years. Now, however, the Huns have left their lands and now my friends can return to their old homes without threat to their families' lives. So I release them again that you may bear witness. Also, I wish to give each of them a small mark of the love I hold for them.'

He left the board and with Elwine at his side, first approached Lothar. My mother filled Lothar's drinking horn and then that of my uncle. He raised it to Lothar and wished him health and luck in all his journeys and thanked him for the friendship he had received from him over all their years together. He then felt in his sack and produced an arm ring of glittering gold. He held it aloft for all to see and then read from the ring the Latin words cut into it, which he translated for those who had no Roman tongue.

'In grateful thanks from Gewis to his friend Lothar, a man of valour and honour.'

He held out the ring to Lothar who took it and slipped it on his right arm and then bowed his head and pressed Gewis' hand on it. When he raised his head, this giant of a man, I was surprised to see that his eyes were wet. 'Lord,' he said, 'I must return to my home and family, but if ever in time to come you need help, send for me, and if you ever need refuge come to me. For this,' and he held up his arm with the ring on it, 'many thanks. As long as this right arm wears this, that arm bears weapons for your bidding.' With that he bowed and returned to his stool.

I now knew something of Gewis' journey long ago with the Frisians. He must have gone to Fabiranum or even Noviomagus to have the rings made against this day. It was the mark of Gewis that he always looked ahead. Alas that he could not do so for himself and thus, knowing me for his bane, keep his distance.

He now moved to Gunthar and Hunneric and repeated the words he had spoken to Lothar. The pair of them each in his turn said similar things back, although there were no tears from the Alans. Gewis pulled an arm ring out of his wallet for each of them and they slipped them gratefully onto their arms. I wondered if he had two more hidden away for Atilec and Sefu, but I need not have wondered. Gewis was not the sort to offend a friend.

When he had finished with the three travellers he then turned and said similar things about Atilec and Sefu, but in their cases saying how pleased he was that they were to continue to be his pledge-brothers and he renewed his oaths to them; to be a generous lord to them, and always to protect them, fight for them and care for them. To each he gave also a golden gift ring.

Listening to this I found it hard to believe this was my uncle speaking, for he sounded the way I imagined a great king must sound, much more so than Baeldaeg had ever sounded. When she wasn't pouring ale, even my mother listened to him with her mouth open in surprise.

After the gift giving, Gewis sat back on the gift stool and the drinking and eating continued. The scop sang songs of heroes and gods. Atilec plundered his word-hoard for stories to entertain, and the whole feast went on joyously until about the middle of the night, when Gewis got to his feet, offered

Lothar and the Alans their weapons as a signal that the feast was over, and everybody went to their beds for welcome sleep. I have no memory of how I got to mine!

My mother woke me the following morning. Groaning from my sore head, I staggered out of my warm bed and rubbed my finger across my teeth, rinsed my mouth, splashed water from the pail on my face and stumbled out to witness the travellers about to depart.

The morning was crisp; the air acrid with the smell of wood smoke and dispersed fog; the ground frosted and hard underfoot. Mist from the horses' snorting breath gathered in the air. These, almost the last of our captured herd, not yet thin from hunger, pranced and milled joyfully at their freedom. The homeward-bound astride their backs were as joyful as their mounts. Their new treasure bags, many now, each light in weight for ease of carrying, were encased in store sacks loaded on the packhorses and hidden beneath food for the journey. With them were their guards, ten doughties. They were to collect Bleikulf at Luckyworth and board the ship he had provided for the journey.

Most of the village, those who were not working elsewhere, had come to bid good fortune and the gods' blessings on the travellers. With much embracing and good wishes from all, and with some furtive tears from some of the matrons, we bade our friends and their guards farewell.

Lothar stood in his riding cups, for all of the horses captured from the Huns had them. He looked back at us with a great beaming smile on his face. Then he waved and with a great cry of joy turned and joined the party as they trotted away. I and many others stood outside the gate and watched in sadness until they had passed beyond sight.

Gewis clapped me on the shoulder. 'Come,' he said, 'there

is serious business to be started today. You and I must search for food to buy, to tide the Holding over until next year's harvest, and for livestock to rebuild our herds. It will not be easy, we will need to travel far; collect some here and a little more there until we have enough for the folk to survive on.

'Go now, have breakfast and then take leave of your mother. Meet me by the horse pens at noon; we must select two of the remaining horses before the cooks get to them.' He smiled, but there was serious purpose behind his words, for with Lothar's departure the Holding's horses were reduced to only four.

I went to my home where my mother was waiting. She had already filled my pack with food for the journey and had laid out my leather armour, the helm that Gewis had given me, and my weapons: my father's sword and my spear. She helped me into the armour and to secure my weapons and then embraced me, her cheek warm against mine. She stepped back, held me by the shoulders her face turned up towards me. For the first time I grasped that my spring growth had overtopped her.

'Seek well, Creoda,' she said, 'for the future and safety of all of our folk go with you and Gewis. You understand that if we cannot buy food then all that is left is war? Many will die if we must steal to live. Such things are uncertain; if we try and do not win then the destruction of the whole folk might be our reward.'

I nodded, but before I could speak she added, 'I trust Gewis, he is a good man. I trust you too, my son. I pray that good fortune for us all go with you.' And with that she thrust me out the door and I set off to the pens to await Gewis.

We chose the two best horses and made ready for our journey. Gewis carried his axes, I my sword and spear. Gewis told me that he brought no gold for he did not want to tempt thieves nor to fight and kill on another's land. Our mission must be peaceful and was to find agreement to trade gold for food. Once we had agreed, so herdsmen and waggoners would bring the food. Warriors would then take the gold and make payment.

I had not wandered far from the Holding in the past, for to do so was dangerous and not to be done, unless at need. I had been north with Gewis to kill my attacker and south with Gewis and his friends to recover the hoard, but that was all of my travels. Now we set off to the east to find other halls and villages. At least, that was the plan, but once we had left behind us the farms that counted themselves part of the folk of the East Holding, once we had scaled the slopes of the eastern sandy hills, we found the land almost empty.

There were oldsters in some places who came out to speak with us. They told a tale of woe. The same murrain that had killed our flocks had struck down theirs; the same plague of the crops that had driven our people to madness and rot had struck theirs. The people were gone, they said, gone north to the Eider and thence to the sea to take ship to the west where there was good land.

We questioned why we had not heard of such a thing. There was no food, they said, and quick action was needful, so all who could fight had gone. So too had the women, the youngsters and the babes; all gone.

There were men of the folk who had gone a-raiding in the ships of the Angle people. It was with these that they had gone, for the warriors had returned to take the people with them to the west, where there was land for the asking and the winning. Land where the food that could be grown was greater than the needs of the growers since the Romans and their tax gatherers had left.

They feared us, these oldsters. They feared that we saw their weakness; that we would steal what food remained and with it what little life was left to them.

We told them our need without much hope. They smiled and said they could not eat gold, what they had was all they had to survive on and little enough it was. If we came to take it, they said, they would fight us, for better to die well and go to the Feast hall than to linger until the food ran out and then die a slow death. They were lonely without the people around them. Death would be a blessing.

We left them, who seemed to us to be living dead, and continued east, but the land was empty of the flocks we expected and there were no crops in the fields.

On the second day, as we passed through forest on this higher ground away from the coast, we were cheered when we came out of it to see before us a hall surrounded by houses. There was smoke rising and we could see movement. The settlement was not big enough to have erected a wall, so we knew there must be a bigger settlement nearby for protection in time of war, but we could see no sign of this. As we approached to seek directions to the hall of the chieftain, warriors bearing arms met us. Their leader came forward as we rode up to them and reined in.

We dismounted and sat on the ground, placing our weapons in front of us. He came and sat facing us, his spear also laid down. We greeted him and he replied agreeably enough but with a strange dialect, which we could make out if we listened carefully. He was not Angle, of that we were sure.

As Gewis explained what we sought the foreigner's head went back and he gave a shout of laughter, the curls of his beard shaking in time with it. His laughter became chuckles and then died away entirely and he looked at us most gravely.

'Where have you been Axe Man? This land is dead, the folk gone far away or buried in it. This is no longer Angle land; this is our land, the land of the Danings. We have come from the east across the sea to take it.'

Gewis told again that we sought food, not land. The stranger regarded us sadly for a while and then spoke. 'There is no food, this land has been stripped; although there was little here to strip I believe. Let me tell what I know.'

He thought for a moment as though choosing his words. 'As far as I know, the land here, the whole land by the sound of your tale, suffered from murrain and flood - even salt flood in the lowlands - and now famine. Many of the folk have left for lands to the west where there is food to be had for the taking. What could they do? The gods wish a folk to survive, do they not?

'We? As I said, we come from the across the sea. We are Danings, from Sweotheod. Our King is mad for he gives away land to those who serve him. Not lend, but give! Those he gives the land to have it forever; it is no longer his to give, so they pass it to their sons, who give it to their sons in turn. And so the landholders never change and the King no longer has land to give away. What is a warrior to do? How does he make a hall and raise children to be warriors to vie for the King's favour? How can the King be a gift giver when all he has to give are trinkets? Which is why we have come here, seeking to raise a hall and a family, but we find fine halls ready built and deserted. Most of the folk from these lands have gone and left their ruined land behind them. Those who cling and refuse to go will either fight and die or come to work for us.'

I shuddered, for by that he meant slavery: those who did not die protecting their land and families would become slaves. With their wives and children they would be at the mercy of these warriors from across the sea to use as they would. I thought of my people and knew that rather than let that happen, I would sooner kill my kin and die.

The stranger continued. 'The people from this place have gone to seek better land. For us, failed land is better than no land. We will work and make this land rich again. We will drain it and sow it and our beasts will graze it. Our folk across the water will feed us and our livestock while we prepare their new lands for them and for ourselves.'

He shrugged, 'Now, we have no food to sell, for here the land has fallen silent and even next year there will be nothing until the harvest. We will let the livestock breed until the flocks increase. They will eat most of next year's harvest, unless the winter is mild. Odin knows, there is plenty of grassland and it will be sweet if the rain washes it.'

He paused, there was no triumph in him and I saw he was an upright man doing what he must. 'I am sorry. I sorrow for your people, but there is no food here, what we have is barely enough for ourselves. Even for a place of honour on Odin's right hand, I have no food to give you.'

So his story went and was repeated elsewhere: no food in an empty land. In places, some of the Anglekin held onto their land, stubborn ones who would not go chasing dreams of plenty, but they hung on grimly, for the crops everywhere were spoiled and the murrain had killed many cattle.

We had taken our leave peaceably from the Danings and turned north towards the Eider seeking land still held by the Anglekin, but they could offer no help for us. These were tribes without ships, too small and too far inland, without alliances that would allow them to join those who had the precious ships. They said there had been more of the Anglekin left, but the Danings killed or drove away the smaller groups.

Those who survived had trekked to the coast and stayed and starved or found a berth as luck or fate would have it. These folk, striving to survive also had no food to spare.

Everywhere we went, the grim story was the same. And so our conversations with these desperate Angles turned away from food and towards where their people had gone. 'West,' they said, 'and we wish now we had gone with them, for what sort of life is this? West,' they repeated, 'to the Apple Islands long guarded by the Romans. The legions are gone now and there is land there to spare, good land with deep and heavy soil, not salt-soaked sand like this,' and they waved to include the soil around us.

'The coast that faces us to the west is the eastern land of those islands, is already finding room for our people. The land is flat like here and plentiful. The folk there are of our blood and tongue and when we come they greet us, or so we hear, for there is food aplenty, much food grown for the Romans who have gone back to Rome. The folk no longer pay taxes of grain to feed the legions and fields lie untended. Our folk live in peace over there, so we hear.'

We listened to their stories, bade them the gods' blessings and rode away in sorrow. It seemed that our happiness behind our wooden walls, on the borders of our Ingwine cousins' lands, had betrayed us. We had known nothing of these happenings in the lands to the east and the north. We protected our lands from them and they from us, and little speech had there been between us, least of all while we dealt with our disasters. In looking inwards, we had missed the world turning upside down so quickly around us.

And so, as we rode, the idea was born, and from the famine-struck land we moved west and crossed the water to Rungholt on Strand, where Gewis knew the shipbuilders who had built his hall.

Long talks had he with them about the islands to the west: about the cost to buy ships and the cost to hire ships, with crew, without crew; short trip, long trip. It was not a bargaining, but yet it was, and the more the jug passed around the more Gewis got into detail and into bargaining with the crowd of Frisians who came to talk - not so much in companionship as 'beership' - whilst we were paying. And then they paid also and the talk continued until we passed out from drunkenness and slept by the fire, comrades at the last.

But the next morning, Gewis had forgotten nothing and when we had crossed the water again he began to disclose his plan to me on the south road home, while I, my head splitting, became more and more sick in the stomach and stopped to spew.

I was frightened now at the way things were turning. I had spent my whole life in the East Holding. I loved the land: the heath; the meres to the west and beyond them the nearby seashore; our land of great bogs and waters. In idleness I had many times stood on the shore and looked west, but never had I wondered at the lands there, nor wished to travel to them.

Now Gewis was following through his thoughts of the various futures that faced the people of the Holding. They were all grim. He counted them off on his fingers as he rode and I jogged alongside, wishing for death.

He held up one finger, 'We could do nothing and starve, until we were so weak the Danings would take our land and enslave those who still lived.' He held up a second finger, 'We could fight and take food from others around us, but as we have seen there is little enough, so that a life for us would be a death for them; and so in the end it would be our village against the nation of the Danings.'

Finally, he held up a third finger and this is where Gewis saw our salvation and where my fear started, 'Or we could go over the sea to the land in the west, the new Angle land, and seek the help of our cousins there.'

I knew he did not mean for food, for with winter coming there was no time to seek food and bring it back by sea; no certainty that supplies of food, enough to last until next year's harvest, could be found in time, and while we searched so far away over the sea, the Holding might have starved. No, the hope for life lay in the whole folk going soon to New Angeln, seeking the help of our cousins already there, buying food, yes, but also buying land to raise the future crops and herds to feed the folk. What Gewis was talking about was settling our people in a new and foreign land.

Even so, he said, we had some luck, for we had the gold, and the hoard was the only hope in the beginning, for ships and Shipmen must be bought or hired, land must be got and grain and livestock bought.

I could see from the grim set of Gewis' face that like me he could see how badly our happy stronghold, so cut off from our neighbours, had betrayed us. We had relied on buying food when we should have known there would be none. We had left everything too late and it might be the death of us.

Gewis said that the Frisians, always keen to trade, had promised to bring what food they could find. Food they would sell us for gold, in the spring when the new sailing season commenced at Oestretide. But it would not be much.

Before we had set out from the Holding, Gewis had hoped there would be enough to fend off starvation until we came home with the food he had bought from the countryside. Now that we knew there was none to be had, he hoped there would be just enough left in the Holding to eke out and bring his new plan to ripeness, for in the end the choice for us was not war or peace. We, a village, could not fight the whole Daning folk. Our only chance of life lay in flight to New Angeln, and quickly. Or to lay our heads under the Daning Chieftain's foot and beg for Daning food in exchange for slavery.

It was with this heavy news and these grim choices that we returned to the Holding on a fine cold morning in the middle of Blood Month.

Yule this year would be very lean. No help would come before the spring. Nothing could put to sea, least of all a whole village, until the calms of the spring and early summer. But that at least gave Gewis time.

The folk would not believe in his plan. They would not wish to, it was too hard, the risks too great. But as their hunger grew, as they ate what little was left and faced starvation, it would help their minds to see clearly.

My fear faded as I saw with Gewis' words that all choices were bad; but to go west at least promised excitement and, if the Fates willed it, then a good death in battle for the survival of my kin.

Oh, the dreams of youth! So far from harsh reality. Later, in real battle, I learned what it was to shit myself with fear. For now, knowing no different I began to look forward to seeing what the Sisters had in store for me.

At the best, if our league cousins welcomed us, then perhaps we would find new and better lands. But Gewis needed time, to make the folk see what he could see and then to use some of his hoard to make it possible; to cast the dice for the survival of the Holding.

In place of that fear another dread came to me. In the remains of the villages to the east, the departing folk had left the oldsters behind to fend for themselves or die. In the

Danings' village I had seen no oldsters. I could not believe that we could do such a thing, to leave our old folk behind. But my head knew that we must, for the old and weak ate but could not fight. In a shield-wall their failing strength would be a dangerous weakness, a place where an enemy could break the wall. We, the young, the strong, would need all of our strength if we were to survive and all of the food we could glean to sustain it.

I asked Gewis about this as we rode back to the Holding. He thought long, and then said that I was right in my thinking, but that perhaps later, if all went well, we could send back for the old folk; but he had nothing of certainty in his voice.

When we arrived back at the Holding a noisy throng came out to greet us for they had seen us coming from far off. The noise dropped and then became silence as it was plain we brought no food with us; not even a sack of grain to show success in our undertaking. Gewis spoke to nobody, letting the grimness of his face tell all. He had said that only fear would cause the folk to make hard choices and now he started to sew the grim seeds of dread.

Inside Baeldaeg's hall it took some time for my eyes to see through the gloom after the bright sunlight of the day. When they cleared I could see that my grandfather had been awaiting us, sat at the high table. He pointed to the benches facing him as a sign that we should join him, but said nothing. Perhaps he read the news on Gewis' face, for he waited patiently for us to tell our tale, fell as he expected it to be. We did not disappoint his expectations, dashing any hopes he might have held on to.

He listened to our report as we described the empty land and the foreigners spreading across it from the east. As we continued, his expression, in turn, changed to match the bleakness of our own.

When we were finished he sat for a long time, eyes cast down as if drawn to some patterning in the grain of the board. Then, deeply weary, he drew his hand across his forehead and sighed. 'We are lost; we are lost and all is forlorn, what can we do?'

As Gewis began to speak and disclose his plan so the old man listened, at first with only part of his mind, which saw nothing but slow death and loss, and then with increasing attention until he listened with a look of fierce concentration.

When Gewis had finished Baeldaeg sat in thought, his brow deeply furrowed. I thought he would never answer he sat so long in silence, and then he spoke.

'Oh, son of mine, you bring me nothing but bad news and no way to escape our doom other than a throw of the dice with the lives of all at chance. And yet I see no other course with less risk and less certain loss. It is too weighty for me, I cannot decide this and if I tried none would follow. The change and the risks are too great, but do nothing and our doom is certain. This is too weighty, even for the Elders. We must put this before a full Folkmoot; perhaps amongst us is a vision for something better, some action that has less risk. If not, then at least all the folk can decide for themselves whether to die here or chance death in some foreign land. You are sure there is no food; perhaps the Frisians, the Jutes?'

'If,' said Gewis reasonably, 'the Anglekin had been able to beg, borrow or steal food from the Jutes of the North or the Suevi of the South they would have done so. They have been living with this, while we dreamed. They love this land as well as we, I think they would not have left, were there any other way for them.'

Baeldaeg nodded slowly and then stiffened as he made up his mind to action. 'Very well, we shall call a Folkmoot and as all are concerned then all shall come, except the children. All at an age where they can fight, men and women, must decide to stay or to go. I will send out the word to all in the Holding and to all the hams and hamlets that cleave to us.

'What you have told me must stay secret until then. That there is no food is plain for all to see. Tell them nothing of your plans. I do not want the rabble-rousers setting up camps, all pulling in different ways. What you plan is the only way; I see no other, unless something comes of the Moot. To my mind there is only go or stay. This is what we give to the Moot to decide. I will announce the gathering for Tiwsday, for if we must make war to survive then we will need Tiw's help.'

This, by my count was the next day. Even I could see the wisdom of cutting short the rumours that would now abound, with or without news from us.

We bade Baeldaeg good day and as we left I asked Gewis about my mother. I could not see in my mind the possibility of not telling all to her. Gewis agreed, and amongst the calling of questions, which we waved away, we went to my house for a trial Moot with my mother. She was the wisest person I knew. If there were any other way to escape the doom that approached us, she would know it.

Alas, she did not. She listened with sad attention and then opened her sack and withdrew the casting stones. I had seen her use these many times before. I could see nothing in them and wondered at the ease with which she drew wisdom from them. To me they were just stones. In my heart I felt the magic was in my mother and the stones only the steadying point, whilst her mind flashed hither and yon until it saw the truth and fixed on it.

Now she cast them and examined the pattern they fell in. She knelt watching them until I began to worry that she was ill from the bad tidings. Then she sighed and her gaze, still sad, returned to us. 'I can see no way out; we must do as you say. But,' and here she gripped Gewis' right arm fiercely, 'we must do it with all our hearts. We must not half do it. All must stand ready to fight. You must arm and train the women, those with hearts and arms strong enough to carry a weapon. We cannot win our way as a village with only our warriors. We must be a people in arms; an army. All boys with twelve years must join the youths in the second row, all women the third.'

Gewis turned these thoughts over in his head and nodded. 'Baeldaeg calls a full Folkmoot, will you cast your stones there? It may help the folk to make up their minds, for they reverence your nearness to the gods and the vision they give you.'

My mother agreed and so it was set and she and Gewis started to plan for the Moot and the training of the women and the young boys that must follow it. I had no place in this, but they instructed me that my role was to swell fear throughout the Holding by spreading tales of the desolation of the land, the absence of our Anglekin cousins and the terrible might of the Danings. Whatever I said would be changed and made one hundred times worse as it passed around, said my mother, so I was given a free hand to tell as tall a tale as I wished, within limits that folk could believe in.

By the next day there was panic in the Holding. Fearful looks were everywhere and even the children were silent and stayed and played quietly with the old women who oversaw them, whilst the adults gathered in Baeldaeg's hall for the Moot. The very young seemed to sense the ill omens for they cried a lot. The anxious oldsters, the silent children and the sobbing babes huddled together and all seemed to cry out fear and threat.

Inside the hall, dread was in the eyes of all gathered there. The reality of starvation, of almost certain death or slavery had sunk in to even the dullest mind. Indeed, those who worked the land and fed the Holding had known of the risk of starvation since the flood and the murrain. The news of the leaving of the Angles and the coming of the Danings only added to the bad tidings they talked of daily. Much hope had ridden with Gewis and me as we set out to buy food. Our return empty handed had stunned everyone until the fear took over and now turned to horror.

When all had gathered, pressed shoulder to shoulder, the hall was full to groaning. There were more than three hundred present. We doused the fire. My mother commanded this, but not to prevent accidents, as I soon found out.

Baeldaeg came into the hall from his one room at the end. This had been a greeting room and a waiting room at one time, away from the Chieftain's living rooms. These, Baeldaeg had given over to the comfort of his Hearth Band; such a generous Lord was he and thus well loved. He said one room was enough for him, his sons no longer lived with him and he was alone. This was easy for him to say, for he was a warrior with few needs for comfort; his wife had died of the water-elf disease years before. I had never known my grandmother on my father's side.

Baeldaeg moved through the silence that had fallen on the hall and sat in the Lord's chair. Gewis sat at his right hand in the place of honour and my mother, as befitted the friend of elves and our way to the mouth and ear of the gods, dressed in her very finest and whitest wool dress with the golden shoulder clasps, stood on his left.

Baeldaeg began thus, 'We are kin, we are one folk; there is none amongst you who does not know all others. When one stubs his toe all others feel it, when another cuts his hand we all bleed for him. I have grim tidings, which because we are one folk affect us all.

'We all know the lack of food and the dangers for the coming year. Gewis and Creoda have ridden through the land to east and north, for we thought we could buy our way through these troubles, that if our neighbours could not help us for pity they would certainly do so for gold. But,' and he held one finger aloft, 'our neighbours have had the same troubles as we and so our neighbours are gone.'

Mouths gaped, heads turned to each other in confusion and there was a gasp from many mouths and a mumble of disbelief. Baeldaeg continued.

'The Angles and the Jutes have long been ship folk. We, with abundant crops and herds, with fish and eels, needed nothing more than boats to fish from and so did not take that way. We did not need to raid or steal; we lived at peace and only showed our war face when folk came to steal from us.

'Our cousins, the Anglekin, have taken to their ships and gone. Danings from over the Eastern Sea have taken their lands. Those of our cousins who have chosen to stay have lost their lands and been taken into bondage by these foreigners, so great in number and fierce in war.'

Indeed, although I had been singing the same song, I did not believe the Danings were any fiercer than we. We knew they had taken some land by force, but only from old men and women for the most part. If they were that fierce why did they not come whilst the warriors were still at home? I could see, however, that feeding the flames of fear would make unhappy choices easier and so said nothing.

My grandfather waited in silence while these facts, already spread abroad but now confirmed, sank into the minds of the listening, glum-faced throng, and then he began to speak again.

'These are the three things we can decide to do. We can starve and protect our land until we die or lose it through weakness.' There was silence throughout the hall.

'We can bow to the Danings, give them our land and place our heads under their feet in exchange for food.' There was a growl of disapproval at this.

'Or we can follow the Anglekin. We can take ship and join them in New Angleland across the sea to the west where there is said to be good land for the taking and ample food to sustain us, until the earth yields to us of its fruitfulness and we can live again as free men should, by the sweat of our brows.'

There was a chorus of approval at this, but then the questions started.

Why, if we had to move, did we have to go over the sea? Why, if we were to go to war for land, could we not take the easier course over the land to the south? If we were to go by sea, where were the ships to come from? Our wealth lay only in our beast herds and flocks. Now that the sea and the land had destroyed them were we penniless paupers?

Baeldaeg answered all questions except this last. Then he reminded the folk of Gewis' heroic history. He reminded them how Gewis had fought alongside the Alans and the Vandals, how he had fought against the might of the Romans and had been in the army that sacked Rome, how he had been Under-Captain of a Vandal Galley. He then called on Gewis to speak.

Gewis got up from his chair and stood silently regarding the folk. He was young; younger than most there, but his legend gave him age. His air of stern command brought him respect, so that all listened with care as he started to speak.

'My brothers, cousins, kin, here is my plan ....'

He laid out for them the tidings he had of the new lands across the sea, protected for so many years and now abandoned by the Romans: the plentiful soil, its depth and fertility; the cleared and ploughed land planted to crops for the Roman taxes that were now unpaid; the rolling forests that could be cleared with sweat to make new lands without stealing from others; the old folk of the eastern edge who spoke a tongue akin to ours; the new folk, the Angles who had gone before, who were our cousins; Ingwines, who being kin of sorts would not war on us or turn us away.

He then turned to ways and means. He told them of his talks with the Frisians. They had promised to bring food in the spring. He would pay for this with gold. The Frisians' word was good in matters of gold. When we had recovered our strength the Frisians would supply five ships to take us to the eastern shore of New Angeln.

Gewis made it known that he, as son of the Chieftain, would pay for all: the food, the ships and any weapons that we must gather before we set off.

He ended by saying, 'You are my folk, my kin, I have the means to get the things we need for this undertaking, but only you can bring forth the courage and the spirit to make it thrive. This you must ask of yourselves. If you tell me that your courage is enough for this, that you will fight rather than die, then I will make all other things come about.'

When he had finished there was a long silence. Everyone there mulled over the possible choices, looking for other, easier ones, but there were none.

Then a farmer from an outlying holding spoke up, addressing my mother in tones of the greatest respect. 'Please, my Lady,' he said, 'these choices are beyond me to decide for all seem black. What action will receive the blessing of the

Great Mother? That at least will calm my heart, for she knows where she would have us ditch and delve to bring forth her fruitfulness.'

The whole room went silent, for the support of the Mother would give some hope of the rightness of our action.

Elwine stood and looked upward to the roof and to the sky beyond it, to where the smoke usually curled through the airway in the roof. Now it showed a patch of blue against the dark, smoke-blackened beams of the hall. She took kindling from a sack that she must have brought with her for this purpose.

The crowd melted apart in front of her as she moved to the hearth and knelt. And now I understood why the earlier fire had been doused. She piled the kindling and taking a fire iron from her girdle and a flint from the sack struck sparks until the dry kindling caught. Reaching inside once more she produced dried herbs, which she scattered on the flames and a wholesome, aromatic smoke spiralled upwards and swirled through the vent hole.

Rising to her feet, my mother cast her arms to the sky and cried aloud, 'Great Mother of all that grows and lives, nurturer of all living things, we bow to you and beg for guidance, for without your help we will surely die.'

Every head in the hall bowed in respect for Freya, the protector and lover of all life. My mother pushed gently through the sea of bowed heads until she had mounted the platform at the front on which stood the seats of honour and the high board.

She looked around the room as those heads raised and the faces turned towards her. Making sure that she had the attention of all, she drew her casting stones from the seemingly bottomless sack and held them aloft to the sky as if to make it easier for the Mother to enter them. She then cast the stones onto the table.

A hush fell over those within the hall while, with her eyes shut as though she was listening, my mother turned her face to the small patch of sky. After a moment she opened her eyes and shifted her gaze to the fall of the stones, seeking the meaning. Raising her head to regard us all, she again spoke in ringing tones. 'To the north and east is death, to the south is death, and here there is death and shame all about. Only to the west is life.'

She stayed with her head erect in a listening attitude, then gasped and staggered as if hearing shocking tidings. Then she spoke again, 'But only for the saplings of the forest. Those great trees with roots deep in the soil of our nurturing must stay to shade and honour the mounds of the ancestors, that they in turn may live with them in the shadow world when they pass over.'

When I heard this, I knew that Gewis and my mother had decided the outcome of this speaking with the gods before the Moot had even started. But then, who is to say that my Lady Freya had not put the thought into their heads in the first place? Mysterious are the ways in which the gods do what they want to do.

My mother finished talking with the gods. Then Baeldaeg stood and told the Moot that they had heard the plan and why it was the only way. For himself, he was convinced and would call 'Aye' for Gewis' plan, for with all its discomforts and risks, it was the only one that promised survival of the folk as a whole.

Slow and reluctant as a landslip, the people spoke. The 'Ayes' mounted in volume; the avalanche gathering pace until all the folk were carried to agree. In the end there were no nays, though the reluctance of most was plain.

'What then,' cried someone from the back of the hall, 'is to become of the oldsters?'

Baeldaeg again rose to his feet. 'I shall stay. Any who still carries weapons for the folk shall go. Those who have laid their heavy weapons aside will stay with me. To sustain us we will have all the land and any of the Frisian flocks to come. If the Danings come, we shall fight and die, and live in the Joyous hall of the battle-slain forever.'

With that, oldsters all around the hall, men and women, called out that they would stay with him. I believe there was some relief in their voices. I think that the idea of living out much of their remaining years in a familiar place and with familiar company was more comfortable for them than the thoughts of a journey to a strange land, with all its discomforts and dangers. And who could tell, perhaps all would be well?

And so, under the weight of an understanding of the true state of the land, the folk decided to follow Gewis' plan and seek a new home across the sea.

Only one thing remained to be decided and here Atilec rose to his feet. 'I am a guest in the Holding,' he declared, 'and so have no voice that must be heard; you have just been told by your Chieftain that he will not come to the new lands. You must decide who will lead the folk. I have Gewis as my Lord. He has always been a good and generous lord since I first laid my head on his knee. He it is who has planned your future, he it is who pours out his wealth for the sake of all, he is the sole remaining heir of your Chieftain. Choose Gewis as your leader and you will choose wisely.'

Baeldaeg got to his feet. 'What Atilec, who has become a brother to us, says, is true in all points. There is no better man, good, kind and generous, thinking always of the well being of others, no better battle proven warrior, no more experienced a man in the whole land to lead you on this adventure than my son, Gewis.'

Then Elwine rose and spoke. 'My heart and my mind and my feeling for what the gods accept as right and proper tells me that what has been said is true, I will say aye to Gewis as my leader.'

The folk roared, 'Aye.' Gewis had made many friends since he had returned to the Holding. Their chorus was strong and heartfelt for all held him in great respect.

And so the greatest Moot in the long history of the Holding - history that melted into legend so far back did it go - was over. We had made our decision to change our land and our leader, to cast ourselves adrift and at risk on the ocean.

Only the Fates would decide what was to become of us, for the weave was still unfinished and how and when and where it would finish rested in the hands of the Three Sisters as they moved from one thread to the other in passing the weft over the web. Even the gods, even the Great Mother, could not alter that. Even their fates were in the weave between now and the end of the world.

The voice of Creoda faded in the shadows and there was a heavy silence in the Cot whilst the villagers considered the choices facing that other village so long ago. Perhaps, amidst all their grief at what was happening around and about them in their own lives, they felt a shiver of thankfulness go through them that they were spared such stark choices.

Bowdyn regarded them steadily and when, as if awaiting more, none rose to go, he spoke.

'We now near the end of the first part of our tale. The night is fine, the Cot is warm; few have fallen in ale-calmed sleep.'

There was a laugh at this for, in truth, there were no sleepers.

'Shall I go on and finish this part of the tale, for tomorrow is the Sabbath and if this work tires you, then you can rest?'

A mighty chorus of ayes rose from our own Folkmoot, and no nays, and so Bowdyn continued as Creoda.

Thus it was that in the middle of that bloodless Blood Month we started to make ready to go from our land to that of others, to buy land with gold or to win it with blood. We knew we could hope for the first, but must prepare for the second.

We sent parties out into the emptying land to make contact with those left in the abandoned halls.

Their purpose was to buy weapons, for although all warriors were armed we had need to arm the young and the strong womenfolk. The smith scoured the countryside for iron. What little he found we bought for silver and he turned into spearheads.

In the abandoned land there was now little use for hedge trimming and few to do it, and from this we were able to arm the women. Every farm and every hall had billhooks for pruning trees and trimming hedges. These could be fearsome weapons. Gewis held a warriors' Moot and it was decided that the women should be in the third row of the shield-wall as my mother had thought best.

Most did not want them placed in danger at all, but my mother spoke strongly and angrily that the women were at risk as much as the men, or more and so had the right to defend themselves and, given the time we had, should be trained to be part of a deadly and practised war-hedge.

Whether everyone agreed or not, I cannot say, but she was so fierce in her anger that none opposed her and the warriors decided that the women were to be in the third row behind the youths. They would be armed with billhooks and light staffs, nine foot-lengths long, and would train to probe beyond the shield-wall with these. They could hack with the side blade or catch enemy spears with the hook. All of these things would take the attention of the first row of the enemy shield-wall and perhaps create openings through which our doughties, or the youths behind them, could strike.

Gewis set in hand the training of the youths and the women in spear and bill-work, giving the work to those he felt best able to carry it out.

Atilec undertook to oversee the training of the women; with whom he was a favourite for the stories he could tell, notwithstanding his ugly face. He it was who worked out a shield, broad at the top, narrow at the bottom with a strong leather sling that could be slung over the head. This shield protected the front from shafts great and small and left both hands and arms free to handle the bill, for few women had the strength for one-armed work.

Gewis and Sefu undertook the training of the youths in spear and knife work. Few had swords and whilst the shield-wall held, could not use them from the second row. But all had a small seax; and if the shield-wall broke, could perhaps use these against intruders to help seal it up again. So, while Gewis worked on axe, spear and shield to break the enemy shield-wall, Sefu worked on the really close-quarters work of saving a breaking shield-wall.

Three things happened during that time, before and after

Yule. The first was the hunger. This did not happen at any point in time, but was with us always. As time went by, we slaughtered the remaining beasts and doled out the meat more and more meagrely. The unused spoiled grain was beyond washing so we burned it: better to hunger than to rot to death. The air grew so cold that the fish and eels went deep into the bottom weed and were harder to catch and so even fish could not help much with the hunger.

The first snows came and the meres froze over. Ice had to be broken for water; hands froze on weapons at practice, for the cold was great. Many of the hungry folk took with the water-elf sickness and huddled around the fires shivering, sweating and coughing up great gobbets of snot. The oldest of the folk took cold and could not be warmed and shortly after, some passed into shadow.

My mother took over nursing those who had fallen sick. She gave orders and the folk obeyed. She said that what they needed was food and warmth and she directed all efforts to the first. She halted the weapons training and the fishermen doubled the time spent seeking food in the sea and the meres. They brought back everything living that they caught. These things we made into stew. We used what herbs and vegetables we scraped from the empty storerooms, but vegetables were few for our time for growing them had passed.

My mother, held by all to be the kindreds' Wise Woman, sent the children out far and wide seeking chickweed, winter cress and onion grass, which they brought back in great bunches. These went into the fish stew along with any garlic she could find in the storerooms. This stew she gave only to the sick. They lay shivering by great fires, wrapped in furs which all gave on loan. One thing we were not yet short of was wood and another was open-handedness.

She next sent the children for pine needles, which she heated in water to make a fragrant smelling drink, the steam of which was to be breathed in as the liquid was swallowed. Within days the worst was over and the sick began to recover and none, except the very old, died.

This was not the end of this pestilence, however, for as one became well so new ones fell sick. By Yule, many of the folk had suffered from this and been saved by my mother.

The second thing that happened just before Yule was that Lothar returned to us with his escort and his treasure. He was on foot and led his horse, his escort following behind. When his lone figure trudged to the gate and was let in with joyous acclaim I felt sick in my stomach, for the Lothar who came back through the gate was not the smiling warrior who went out, on his way home to his family. That smiling Lothar was gone forever: I never saw him smile again.

People standing near me were saying that perhaps his home was so far he couldn't find his way; but I knew it was much more than that. His escort was surrounded and questioned by curious folk and the talk was serious with many a glance in Lothar's direction where he stood staring at the ground by Gewis' hall.

Someone called Gewis from weapons practice. Looking troubled, for he too noticed the difference, he took Lothar by the arm and guided him, for he seemed deep in thought, until they entered the door and were lost to sight within Gewis' hall.

Later, Gewis told me the tale of what Lothar had heard of his family's fate. How can anyone ruled by the Fates plan a life, when the greatest effort can sometimes yield nothing and at another time the merest unthinking act can doom thousands? For that is what Lothar's axe throw had done. The Huns had killed his entire family. They had used his mother and sisters then, mercifully, cut their throats. His father they had leashed by the neck to a tree while they built the wood from his yard in a circle around him. When they fired it, no matter where he ran, and he ran in many circles, he was roasted. The leash was too short for him even to leap on the fire and shorten his pain. The Huns stood around the circle and laughed at his antics until he ceased screaming and fell bubbling to the ground.

When he was well done, the father and other relatives of the youth slain by Lothar's hand, feasted on the roasted flesh and thus relished their blood price.

Valimar, the King, could no longer restrain the Goths, hitherto allies of the Huns. When they heard this fell story, the whole Tisia river valley burst into revolt. The Huns and the Goths fought many battles without final success on either side. The Gepids, seeing the Huns faltering in the north, brought them to battle on the Nedao and destroyed them. Thus it was that many thousands were slain by Lothar's axe throw.

When he returned to the shipyard, found his family gone and heard the tale, he made to cut off his axe arm with his battleaxe, but the neighbour who had given him the grim news struck him down with a balk of timber and tied him until his anguish died down.

'Do not destroy yourself,' said the neighbour. 'Slay Huns and all like them who would torment and enslave.'

Lothar gave his oath that he would no longer seek to harm himself and the noble neighbour untied him. He must go, said the neighbour, for all the Goths were trekking to Pannonia. The Gepids were taking the Tisia Valley, they had won it. The Goths, who had been the allies of the Huns, were not welcome no matter how they had suffered.

Lothar, oath-sworn not to harm himself, had nowhere he

wanted to be more than with his friends and so he and his escort, their duty done, had come home to us. Always formidable, now there was deadliness in him, a merciless, dangerous quality that would, I was sure, add the strength of ten to our shield-wall. And for this, I think, as much as for the love and the pity we felt for him, Gewis welcomed him.

The third woe was desertion. In the beginning, many folk slipped away with their families in the night, seeking a place where they could settle and avoid the dangers that the future held for us all. This did not last long, for while there are always doubters, hunger is a hard teacher and doubts were banished in the cold light of day away from the Holding. All who left returned cold, hungry and sorry. Their lessons taught the others and so, very shortly, desertions ceased and everyone did what they could to make ready.

Gewis, seeing this and understanding that fearful folk should be kept busy, had the idlers put to work under a Frisian builder, to build a mock ship so that all could practice the use of the oar and rowing in general. As he said, the Frisians relied on oars to drive their ships, but the ships would not carry a large crew for there must be room for the passengers. Our people must, therefore, be able to help in an emergency.

He handed over his training of the warriors to Lothar, who otherwise sat brooding, and undertook the rowing training himself. He had always, he said, wanted to be Celeusta and had never had the chance before.

And then it was Yule.

# Chapter 28

**AD 463**

**Creoda's Tale, the last Yule**

Both Gewis and my mother had insisted that whatever the state of the stocks there could be no scrimping on the Mother's Night celebrations.

There would be no Yule boar, for the one surviving boar of the folk would sail with us to father our new herds, or so we hoped. But there could be a Yule Log and Gewis explored the higher ground until he found a fallen ash tree that would be the fuel for our Yuletide flames. There would also be singing on Mother's Night, when we celebrated the Goddess birthing the new sun of the New Year. With this in mind, Gewis gathered together Baeldaeg's old scop and such players of music as there were amongst the folk. One could play the sacpipa of the Sweotheod; others had bone chanters; there were leg bells too and, of course, drums both big and small.

My mother spoke with other mothers, and they spoke with their daughters and when there was no weapons practice we heard strange noises faintly on the air, coming from the far woods. Lothar and Atilec became involved and had many long talks with Gewis, with much sandbox drawing and waving of hands.

Gewis was everywhere, as was my mother and it was plain

to see that they planned some great entertainment for Mother's Night.

Another of the horses was missing from the pens and I knew that with the grass no longer growing and no grain, we would soon slaughter them all before they became too thin to be worth eating. The women had been collecting salt from well before Blood Month, so they were ready. I thought it likely that the last of our horses would be gone soon after Yule.

Gewis took us young men of the Holding to the forest and chose the Yule Log. It was our task to plan how to get it to the hall and into the hearth, without breaking anything. It was a plight, he said, for us to deal with, but we must do it in addition to weapons practice.

He left us to it. It was heavy and thus ponderous. Moving it was possible only if all seized hold, lifted and worked together, with one to direct. If we did all of that with a will, with best effort and with frequent stops to rest, then it was easy. I think this was a lesson that Gewis wanted us to learn and I believe it was lost on none.

With the Yule Log at the hearth, ready to lift into place, and with wood stacked ready to burn around it, it was the turn of the maidens to decorate the hall with pine branches and holly. These never died in winter and so connected the life of the old sun to the newborn sun to come. Because of that there was a special kinship between man and evergreen, for the Mother also favoured us with long life.

As for ale, there was plenty, but to make sure the feast should not run dry there was also much beer. During the spring and summer we had made beer from anything that could be brewed, such as elderflower, forest fruit and dandelion. The folk vied one with the other to produce the strongest and best tasting beer from the oddest growing things and just before Mother's Night they prayed for icy nights so that they could strengthen their beer in the moonlight. With the cold we had all through Yule, I looked forward to the strongest beer ever.

On Mother's Night all would bring their tuns to the feast. This year they would not bring food, for there was none. Baeldaeg held, guarded and doled out the last of the food in the Holding. He it was who donated the horse that would make the thin stew for the feast.

On the eve of Mother's Night we ate nothing and because of our weakened state we did not work, although weapons practice for the matrons and the young men continued.

Strange sounds were still to be heard from the distance and the maidens of the village seemed to be gathered together for some kind of making or weaving in the small weave houses of the Holding. It was all very mysterious. Something was to happen, that was plain, but although each knew her part in it none would speak of it outside her group. And so the warriors and the wives - and the makers and growers, the part-time warriors, of the Holding - knew nothing.

On the morning of Mother's Night I was starving and cold. I went to the hall to help with the Yule Log. When we had heaved it into the hearth it started to crackle, for the days it had been laying by the fireside had dried it out. We heaped the logs from the waiting piles around it and stood warming our hands as the flames started to rise.

The meat-thane and his women helpers came into the hall with pots of stew, which they hung from the hearth chains so that the rising heat from the Yule Log would bring the stew back to bubbling heat by the time the folk assembled.

We left the great board in the hall, for the Chieftain, his

family, guests of honour and the doughties, but moved it towards the wall to clear a space. The other boards we removed and replaced with benches and stools brought in from all over the Holding and also from store, where we kept some all year for special feasts.

Gewis appeared and ordered the benches laid out so that a space was left in the middle. A small passage led from this space to the door of the Chieftain's room at the end of the hall, which also had a door from the outside. Baeldaeg had emptied the room and I knew that his things were now in Gewis' hall. It seemed that it was from here that the mystery entertainment would come forth.

The final task was to bear our great boar, the last of our herds, caged and squealing into the hall and place him on a dais at the end of the High Table. He should have been feeding us, but tonight we would be feeding him, and hopefully the God Ing would smile on us for so doing and allow our new herds to grow in a foreign land.

I ached with hunger, but sitting by the roasting Yule fire at least I was no longer cold. By the time the last of the drab, brown wool-clad men and womenfolk arrived at Baeldaeg's hall, the smell from the pots on their iron rails above the fire was maddening. My stomach rumbled endlessly while my mouth filled with spit.

The long stone fire-pit set in the middle of the floor and flaming around the Yule Log, added dancing rosy flickers to the steady golden glow from the many oil lamps. The walls of seasoned, oiled wood glowed red and honey-coloured in the light. The pine-scented billows of wood smoke rose through the great blackened beams of the hall. It gathered in clouds, misting the underside of the roof trusses before escaping out of the vent, through which, between swirls of smoke, we could see the wavering stars.

We were waiting, holding our hunger in check, when Baeldaeg, Elwine, Gewis, Atilec, Lothar and Sefu took their places at the High Table.

I slid on my bench as I felt a push on my right shoulder. Swinging round to see from whence it came, I nearly fell off the bench from a push to my left. Laughing, my two shield-wall flankers, Aglaeca and Grindan, slipped into place on either side of me. I grinned with pleasure. We were training together and were friends, as indeed we must be, for in war I would depend on them, and they on me.

'I've never been to a feast before,' said Grindan, bouncing his skinny body with excitement as usual and brushing his dark curly hair out of his eyes as he peered around the hall.

'Nor I,' I admitted.

Stolid Aglaeca smoothed his beefy hand across his mouth and his warrior face hair, which was fair, sparse and baby-soft. 'I'm starving,' he grumbled, 'when do we eat?'

'You're always starving,' I said, 'you're just a bag of guts on legs with a mouth always open like a baby bird.'

Grindan laughed. 'Then he will fit in with the other monsters in the place we go to. Is it true what they say, that there are giants and tiny folk who walk the land? If the gods bid us go, as they spoke through your mother, will they walk amongst us when we get there?'

I had my own feelings about whether our Lady had really spoken to my mother at the Moot, although I accepted she may have spoken to her before it. 'I do not think the Great Mother will ever be far from the folk,' I said, 'but I do not think she will come amongst us, other than through the mouth of her priestess.'

'By the Great Mother, when will they feed us?' Aglaeca

said. 'My guts cry out that I have lost my head. They think someone who hates them has cut my throat. They ache for something, anything. I could eat the floor!' And with that he bent to pick up a handful of the rushes that covered the floor, but then, catching the smell of them for they were not fresh, he threw them down.

'Why do you throw good food away?' I mocked. 'They are rich with the piss and shit of those caught short at the Moot.'

'Rot your ballocks,' laughed Aglaeca good-naturedly.

'At least he has some,' squealed Grindan in a high voice, 'you ate yours as soon as the hunger started!'

We all laughed and then turned to pay attention to what was happening about us.

At a wave from my mother some of the older matrons of the Holding moved between the benches passing out wooden cups. Others followed these matrons, two at a time, carrying large bowls of ale from which we all filled our cups.

We sat waiting. The hubbub silenced. My mother, in her white robe of priesthood, her long, blonde hair gathered respectfully back, stood and called out.

'We drink to our Lady, may she have an easy birth. May we be warmed by the new sun in peace and plenty, as is foretold! All hail the Mother!'

We lifted our cups and roared, 'All hail the Mother!' and drank. With my stomach empty, the ale went straight to my head.

The bowls passed again and we refilled our cups. This time Baeldaeg, my grandfather, stood. Grey-bearded, tall, his ornate tunic patterned from the brown and yellow wool of our now dead flocks, the gold torque of chieftainship glittering at his throat. Horn held high he cried out in a loud voice, 'Good health to all here!'

We matched him with our ringing shout, downing our ale.

By now I was feeling dizzy and saw, thankfully, that the matrons were reaching across the flaming Yule Log and with hooked yokes were lifting out the food pots and placing them on the ground. They ladled our bowls full with big gristly chunks of Hunnish horsemeat, boiled roots from dried Yule stock, and delicious smelling broth. Then, on the direction of the meat-thane, they passed the bowls along each row and when all to the left had theirs so then I had mine.

I lifted my bowl to my mouth and took the permitted two swallows, groaning as the salty taste flooded my mouth, the broth sweeping over my tongue and down my throat, scalding as it went. Then, as called for by custom, I waited for everyone to be served. A bitter burden!

Aglaeca, after his two swallows, held the bowl beneath his nose breathing in its savoury odour and groaning in mock misery, watched with mirth by those sat around us.

When all had their bowls, Baeldaeg and my mother rose again and gave the hoped for orders.

'Eat well and be merry!' called he.

'Thank the Lady for her bounty!' cried she.

'Thank the Lady!' cried we, secretly wishing her bounty a little more full than tough Hun horse.

I regretted the small piece of meat that I must leave for our boar. We passed the boar bowl along and each tipped a gift into it. By the time it reached the cage it overflowed. My mother pushed it through the hatch and Ingvi's beloved thrust his muzzle into it and ate mightily, the squealing soon replaced by contented guzzling.

Ingvi, son of the Great Mother and brother of my Lady Freya, was the patron of our Ingwine League. I hoped he knew the greatness of our humble gift and so would help us in our venture.

We, being famished, bolted our food like wolves. Again we filled our cups as the ale pot passed. I was starting to feel quite warm and cheerful by now.

Baeldaeg's scop walked before us and I saw that the entertainment was to commence. The scop was old and his voice fading with the weakness of wind that old age brings, but we all held him in great regard and Baeldaeg would hear no other.

The scop picked up his age-blackened harp and briefly tuned it and silence fell, for to speak would spoil the magic that he was still able to spin about his listeners.

He looked at the ceiling as if calling things to mind and then he spoke to the folk. 'This is the song of Atland the Lost, our first home, a place of plenty, of love and justice, lost beyond time beneath the sea, but remembered by us all in verse and song. Now we must seek such anew. I will tell the tale, and the men, if they will it, will sing the sea. We have remade our home in the past and now we shall again.'

My mother stood and spoke for the women. 'And shall the women sing the storm as they did in times gone by?'

'Aye,' he replied, sharp-eyed and quick, 'they must, for now is the time coming when all must act together.'

He plucked a chord on his harp and then began to sing, in a voice of such loss that tears came to the eyes of the oldsters who had heard this many times before, but now knew not when they might hear it again.

Between verses the deep-voiced men made slow falling and rising notes like that of the sea surf crashing then hissing in ebb on the pebble beach, and the women sang the high cry of the wind moaning over the waste. The two sounds, low and high, sung in the age-old manner, came together in a tone of such desolation and woe as would freeze the heart. Thus we sounded our common sorrow at our present loss as the scop sang that of old.

> 'Where are the dew-dampened, dawn-dappled lithe deer?
> Where the sun-gold glowing, great seeded grasses?
> Where the sweet waters with white-capped waves weighted?
> Where are the great grunting, gorge wetting, gore-beasts
> Dipping to drink at the dun-darkling deluge?
> Gone, lost forever, beneath the salt sea.
>
> 'Where the wise women with wisdom and counsel?
> Where the just Mothers, fair, sitting in judgement?
> Where the fleet seekers for fare sought in freedom?
> Where the glad home hearth, heating and lighting,
> Preparing the food for the famished the frozen?
> Gone, sunk forever, beneath the salt sea.
>
> 'Where is the Peace when folk prospered in plenty?
> Where for the poor many meals of plump meat?
> Where sits the safety where surfeit sustains folk,
> Where the urge of the thief is to share not to steal?
> When folk lived with freedom, fairness and justice?
> Gone, sunk forever, beneath the salt sea.'

And so he continued, until first one, then two, then a multitude joined in the mournful legend of change and loss; of the golden age of ease and freedom and justice, before all was overwhelmed by the sea countless years in the past, and for those who survived a hard life of struggle and conflict took its place.

When all verses were finished all sat in silence with many a tear shed at the unfairness of life, for now even what was left to us was to be lost, and the thought of parting with loved ones, to venture the gods knew where to make a new life, filled many with anguish and fear. A pall of gloom hung over the feast; all were brought down whilst cheer seemed to flow out of the door

And then, into the silence came the drone of a Sweotheod sac-pipe, followed by the soft beating of a drum. A wild tune from pipes and chanters joined the drone and the drum changed to an urgent rhythm. Then came the jingling beat of bells as the pipers with bells around their ankles stamped in time to the music.

From the Chieftain's room, which they had entered quietly from the outside and then stood awaiting the signal, came a troupe of young maidens dressed as olden day priestesses of the Mother, with their long hair and string skirts swaying to the beat of the drums. As the maidens danced to the wild music, the pipers and drummers also entered the hall, which rang with the skirl, the drums and stamping feet, the carefree cries of the youthful dancers.

I, my war brothers and many others, shook off our sadness and, uplifted by music, energy and youth rose to join hands around the fire and dance. Just as Uncle Gewis had planned, the wake became a party and ale and beer flowed freely, the pain and fear ebbed away and a new feeling of hope inspired those soon to sail into the unknown.

When the maidens left the floor to the cheers of the folk, the beat of the drum became loud, insistent and harsh and the pipes changed to the wailing notes of the battle song. With feet stamping in time, the new young of the war-hedge, in two ranks, ten wide, came onto the floor of the hall. In their arms they bore spears and shields and when they reached the centre of the floor, the front rank turned to face the rear rank. To the martial beat of the drums and the uplifting wail of the pipes, they followed the routines of war training. First one line with offence and the other with defence and then with counter to be met by defence, and so on, until all of the moves of the spear had been followed and their skill with the weapon had been shown to the folk.

To the sound of the pipes and the drums they left the floor followed by the applause of the warriors and the doughties.

As the watchers, thinking all was over, turned to their cups, so the drums beat their harsh war music again and the pipes once more picked up a forceful and angry tune. But this time the two lines of armoured and armed dancers were the young matrons of the Holding. As with the youths, they were in two ranks but longer, for there were more matrons than youths. They had arrayed themselves with the teardrop body-shields devised by Atilec, and carried the long, spiked billhooks. The two ranks faced each other and again went through all the movements of the trained warrior, but this time made especially for the long bill, both hands to the weapon, the shields hanging in front from a broad strap, as judged fit for the third line of battle.

Their job was to push aside or to hook the spear points of the enemy and pull them down, push them up or to one side, so that the doughties in the front row could strike a mortal blow whilst the enemy struggled to recover his weapon. They carried out their moves with grim care and bloodthirsty intent. No one watching their deadly two-handed bill-work doubted the heart of these women warriors or their will to fight and win.

When they had shown the limits of their instruction from

Atilec over the weeks gone by, they left the hall, stamping their feet in time to the drumming. The folk, emboldened, cheered proudly, and long.

## Chapter 29

**AD 464**

**Creoda's Tale, the leaving**

After the Yule feast there was a new spirit in the folk. Before, we had seen the famine from which we suffered as our doom. We beheld the plan that we followed with dread. Now we replaced dread with a new eagerness. Now the folk, who before had doubted, began to believe that what we planned could thrive, that perhaps new land and a better life awaited us over the sea.

The warriors in training, including the young women, returned to their practice with a will. The old women, given the task by Gewis of weaving into long bolts of wadmal the stores of wool from the fleeces of our slaughtered sheep flocks, set to in the weave houses as if they were weaving their wedding dresses. This was unusual, for Gewis did not even tell them what they wove, only that it should be strong and that pattern did not matter.

It became hard to find Gewis, where before Yule he had been everywhere, governing everything. He spent nearly all of his time with the Frisians of Rungholt. What he did there he did not fully explain to anyone as far as I know, although he had many conversations with Atilec and Lothar. What little I did glean was that the shipbuilders of Rungholt, whilst very skilful in the working of wood, were not able to provide ships of a design that suited my uncle's plans.

When questioned, he would say things almost as if he was talking to himself. Things like, 'If the crew is many then passengers will be few ...' Or, 'We do not have time to make warriors and sailors ...' and then walk off deep in thought.

Anyway, what I learned afterwards was that as a Gubernator of a Roman-built war galley, he knew a lot about the details of ships even if lacking the skills to build them himself. He made a bargain with the Frisians: he paid for the shipbuilding changes; they kept the changed ships. Gewis paid them for the use of these ships for our needs and at the end of that time they could undo the changes if they wished, for the ships were theirs.

I know as truth that they never did and I heard they were building new ships with the same changes twenty years later. But that is another story. I know Gewis made them pay us for the cloth we wove for the five he had them change.

At Oestre, when the horses were all gone and when all of our remaining food stores were emptied; when we were living on thin fish stew and herbs from the woods, and everyone had become a fisherman; when fear was turning to panic, the Frisians came, as they had promised.

By then Gewis had shortened the weapons practice, for the warriors and the shield maids were thin and pale, listless from hunger and lacking the energy to fight, even in practice. Everywhere there was the sound of crying children and although Atilec, Baeldaeg and my mother did their best to cheer us and feed our belief in Gewis and that all would be well, dread had returned in full force. What if the Frisians did not come? We no longer had the strength to go raiding. And so, when the sea watch in the watchtower shouted that ships were coming, we took to our weapons, closed the gates and prepared in our minds for death - which is how we were when Gewis came striding to the gates, driving two fine bulls.

'Open up,' he called, 'come out and meet tonight's feast!' When we on the fighting steps heard his voice, saw the cattle and recognised our salvation, the relief was very great. Dread turned to tears amongst our warrior maids and laughter amongst our men.

We threw open the gates and gathered round our leader. My mother embraced him and startled by the uproar, the cattle protested and pranced away.

'Everyone to the beach,' Gewis said, 'your food awaits you there, bring it home. Slaughter these two beasts and start the cook fires burning. Tonight, with Baeldaeg's leave, we will feast in his hall. I see you thin as autumn leaves, now we will start to fill you out again.'

At the mention of food we started the long walk to the beach. Before we had gone far into the marsh, even from ground level we could see five beached ships, their prows drawn up on the sand. When we drew near we could see they lay in perhaps only three feet of water. From each ship stretched both anchor cable and a broad gangplank, and gathered on the beach were cattle of various sorts: cows and goats, pigs and sheep. Also piled up were bales of wool, more stock for spinning and weaving by our oldsters.

Sailors were already walking up and down the planks, carrying baskets, which we found to contain good wheat. Grain stored from the last year's harvest in some plump country more fortunate than ours.

I can tell you, there was no lack of volunteers to bring the food home, weak as we were.

When all the baskets of grain had been put into the grain

stores, from which all traces of the addled rye had been scrubbed in hopeful readiness; when all the beasts had been penned; when grain had been portioned out to my mother to supervise the bread makers; then and only then could I look over the ships that Gewis had brought us.

Beached as they were, I could see that the hulls were rounded on the bottom and the walls were high, for the side of the ships rose at least a man-height from the water. The hulls were perhaps - I say perhaps, for lying in the water as they were I could not pace them out – twenty-five big paces long and seven paces wide.

Near the bow and the stern were rowing points, not many, four at the bow, three at the stern, fourteen oars altogether. In the forward part was a strong, stumpy mast crossed with a stout spar. This I found out later was one of the changes Gewis had demanded. As he explained it to me, the folk were the cargo, and so space had to be cleared for them in the middle of the ship at its broadest point; they were not bales of cloth or barrels of ale, they needed room. They needed air about them, they could not crouch like jars of wine below the rowing benches, with oarsmen pissing and shitting above.

Also, we had to shelter the women with small children or the babes might die, so at each end the builders had decked the ship over to create a small space or under-deck, away from the cold salt spray and the breaking waves.

With the cleared space at the middle and the decked over ends there was then only room for a few oars, seven each side as it happened, four each side at the bow, three each side at the stern. This was not a raiding ship and had no need of the normal rowing crew of eighty. Reducing the oars to fourteen - the least possible for rowing – allowed more room for passengers and was made possible by training some of the folk to row, which Gewis had done.

Of course, the fewer the oars the slower the speed and also, protested the Frisians, the pull of the oars would not be enough to hold the bow up into rough weather. To this, Gewis replied that double manning could increase the rowing power, and so that the oarsmen would be fresh when needed, the ships should have a sail for fair weather sailing.

This caused much fear amongst the older seamen for it was not done this way, they said. So Gewis spent time telling them of his experiences with the Vandals in the Middle Sea, and so knowing was he about the ways of the sea and of ships under sail on the sea, and so tempting was his gold that he made them agree to what he wanted. Thus the ships were altered for the purpose of carrying our whole people to a foreign land, to thrive or die as the Fates willed it.

There were two hundred and seventy folk to go now that eighty of the oldsters were to be left behind. Each ship would carry fifty-five passengers, ten under shelter at each end and thirty-five in the waist. It would be cramped, Gewis told us, but of those who were to go, there were fifty children all below fighting age, some of these were babes in arms who would take up little room, and some little ones who must be under the care of their mothers.

Those active children, who lacked the strength and size to bear arms, say between the ages of five and twelve years, would nevertheless be useful on the sea, for they would help with the bailing, a constant task in an open ship, Gewis told us.

My mother, with her counting stones, and Gewis, with his writing wax, worked out where everyone would go so that each ship had its fair numbers of sheltered mothers and young; so that husbands, wives and children were together and families were not parted; so that every ship had its needed numbers of trained rowers - this was very important if the sailors were to work the sails, for someone had to keep the ship moving through the water – so that the Shipman at the steering oar could keep direction.

In the days that all this was being decided we fed on the stocks brought by the Frisians. Those who followed my mother's advice and ate with care thrived. Those overcome with greed or who thought they knew best, over ate and sickened and were sorry. The Frisians, on the other hand, seemed to spend much of their time emptying our stocks of strong ale. There was little trouble though, for their Shipmen kept order and they were, I think, aware that we were a Holding on a war footing with all armed who could carry arms and that there were some great warriors amongst us.

If they molested any of the women it was of the women's choice. I am sure there were some sly meetings, for women, I am told, are utterly drawn to the new. But if so, they were careful not to create friction between Holding men and sailors. I think my mother kept a close eye on the chances of rub-stick fires and was quick to advise where needed.

The Frisians split into watches, one to stay and watch the ships the other to sleep or to take food in Gewis' hall. We handed over those of our storerooms that were empty to be little guesthouses for them, and they were happy enough, drunk or sober.

Gewis set the date for our leaving our old home and our venture to the hopes of a new, for the end of the Month-of-Three-Milkings. Our grass had never grown so lush for us that we ever had this happen; our lost herds had mostly given only one milking a day, but we would have been glad to have it, could we but have them back. However, this date gave us six weeks of good eating in which the folk could recover their health and their strength.

As soon as the colour started to come back into folks' cheeks, then so the weapon and rowing training increased. We worked hard and we fed well and our belief in ourselves returned.

I could see that in six weeks we would not eat all the cattle that Gewis had brought and he explained that some of the livestock were to be slaughtered and salted for the passage. The remainder were to be set aside for the old folk to give them a chance of surviving until we had made our home and could support them. Then we would send two ships to fetch them, for three of the ships were to stay with us for one year. This had been paid for, so that if we could not buy or grow food where we landed, we could send for stores from elsewhere.

I was glad that we had Gewis; the Vandals had trained him well for he planned for all the things he foresaw the Fates might send us. I was glad of his treasure also, for without the luck of that we should surely have perished. My uncle's hoard had doubled with the coming of Lothar. Gewis confided to me that Lothar had given his share to him, saying that he no more wanted his own hall and hearth-companions as only death and destruction followed him, for always his choices proved bad. And so his treasure lay, held in trust should he again change his mind, but ours to use if we wanted.

The Fates favoured us, or maybe they favoured Gewis, for good fortune seemed to follow him and it spilled also over those who were with him: us, the lucky Gewissae as we became - for a while at least - until much later. Then, for me, all became misfortune piled on misfortune and I learned to scrape the last cold, sour, soul-sickening leavings of grief. But at the time of our leaving I had no knowledge of what the Wyrd Sisters had in store for me and so I looked forward to my future. I was young and strong and for me, life was filled with promise.

When the day before our departure dawned it was grey and overcast with a light easterly breeze blowing. Gewis and the Frisians took this to be a good omen, for such a wind, if it held, would blow us direct towards the new lands of the Anglekin and our Ingwine allies almost without the need to row - at least until we reached the sand banks that stretched north and south protecting that coast.

There, said the Frisians, there were fierce tides that swept now south now north and, without oars to power us, would sweep us onto the shallows of those banks. Many ships were lost there until their crews learnt to deal with them. Once again we thanked Gewis' foresight for hiring not just ships but the expert crews to guide them.

That night, the last before we left, there was no big feast. Each family, each house had its own ration, its own fire and its own cook pot, for this was a time for family goodbyes.

My mother's folk being long dead, Gewis, my mother and I went to Baeldaeg's house where my mother had started the cooking of our last meal together.

There was stew, with vegetables and herbs from the countryside; I remember the sharpness of the nettles against the savoury meat. Whenever I smell nettles growing, the fresh, sharp smell of them, I always bring to mind the smiling face of my noble grandfather. The mood was sad but he it was who tried to lighten it.

He was happy for us, he said, that we would make our way in a land that must be richer and happier than our own. He counted the disasters that had struck us: Huns and Suevis stealing our stock; the flood and the drowning of what remained; the ruin of the harvest; the blight and murrain of that which we salvaged; and now, the Danings pressing ever closer.

We had made no contact with them at the East Holding, but we had sent out scouts to spy out the countryside and we knew they were closer than we had seen them on our food-finding trip into the East.

Baeldaeg said that the old folk would probably live out their lives peacefully long before the Danings came to the Holding. If they came sooner, then there were still enough folk, old as they were, to man the walls. If the Danings wanted the land so badly that they were willing to storm wooden walls for it, then maybe a bargain could be struck: the Holding in trade against a life of peace on the shore, for they were too old to be much valued as slaves. We knew in our hearts that this was all nonsense, but we loved him for it.

The old loved to fish, said Baeldaeg, it was peaceful. A good summer's catch could be salted and barrelled and would provide food for the winter. Perhaps they could have enough land near the shore to raise a few salt-marsh sheep, the most delicious of all. And so Baeldaeg breathed hope on us to lighten the mood, but the more he did so the more sad we became, that we should leave behind this brave old man and all the oldsters like him; old folk, who through their boldness and hard work had raised us who now deserted them.

And yet there was no un-knotting the problem. There was now no room on the ships, but even if there were, there would be the babes and the old, one hundred and thirty of them, who produced little, to be defended and fed by two hundred and twenty, in a new land where all must start from nothing. To take the old was to face disaster. We knew it, but knowing it did not help, and so we shed our tears of parting, my mother and I, while Gewis sat with moist eyes staring into the far distance.

There, facing us in the flickering firelight, as I tried to force the food down, Baeldaeg comforted and tried to cheer us; his wind-burned face, strong, calm and wise, smiling gently as he told us again that to take the old would bring misfortune on the whole venture; that they would be happy in their own homes surrounded by life's memories.

He then bade us rise from the board and we set off around the Holding to bid goodbye to all. He, still towering over me, walked by my side and laid his arm around my shoulders clasping me to him as if he would pass his strength to me.

Everywhere we stopped the tale was the same and by calling we broke up the grim mood. Each family had its own old folk, but every house had brought in others. These were the old and lonely; kin from families long dead. All did this, so that none should pass this night of sad parting and gloomy leave-taking alone.

It was like a bad dream: the getting ready had been exciting, but now it was no longer the game I had felt it to be. Now I waited for the dream to end, so that I should awake and find that life would continue in the way it always had in my childhood; with my mother and uncle, my grandfather and my kin all together, carrying out the simple tasks of living in the warm summer sunshine. Or perhaps the grownups would say that it was all a game, a practice for a day when disaster might strike. But they did not, this was all real, we were all to go the gods knew where, and the old folk and my grandfather, our Chieftain, were to stay.

At last I accepted the grim reality of what we did and planned to do. It was at this point that I finally threw off my childhood and accepted the manhood that first my killing of the Hun, and now the needs of our people, thrust upon me. It was on that night that I put off self-pity and discovered grim determination within myself. If we were to die then I would die fighting to survive. Perhaps that is what growing up demands, the acceptance of the possibility of death and the courage to fight against it, not just for oneself but also for others, and to be ready to die for them.

That is what came to me that night as I watched the good cheer and courage with which that grand old man faced parting and the likelihood of death in battle - for I had seen the Danings and felt their resolve. In my mind, I pledged that my sword, which was my father's, which my father's brother and his oath-brother, Sefu, had taught me to use, would be at the service of our folk. If I died in their service then that was my doom.

At the end of that gloomy last night in our homeland, few slept easily, but it was needful that we should be as fresh as we could be, for the following day we sailed.

I woke at dawn with the first light creeping over the distant eastern trees. I did not feel fresh and for a while at least my manly resolve faltered. I felt like crying and, looking at my mother's doleful face as she packed the last vital possessions in a spare cloak, I could see she felt the same. Strangely, her weakness strengthened me. It had always been my mother's strength that supported me; now, for the first time in my life, it was I who supported her. I laid a hand on her shoulder and as she looked up I smiled.

'The wind is still from the East, it is a good day for it.' I reached my hand to take the bundle she had wrapped. She gave me a long look and then, as if something gave her satisfaction, she smiled in turn and the tearfulness was banished.

'Then let us go, before the Fates change their minds,' she said. She stood and took my hand, and we walked the long walk down to the ships. We did not spare a backward look at the house with its cold hearth.

The ships were high and dry at this time for the tide was out but the moon had been full during the night, a lover's moon as they say, so I knew that the tide would be very high by midday.

At the beach, where I had expected that all would be confusion, I was surprised to find order and quiet. The folk themselves were more muted than I would have believed possible. I supposed this to be due to lack of sleep, and some fear, for reality sometimes can be stunning when finally grasped. I judged that like me, many thought that this day would never dawn, that something would happen to rescue us, to make our own efforts needless. Finally, like me they had realised it was happening and their future and that of those they loved were in their own hands, as well as in those of Gewis and my mother, our unchallenged leaders.

Gewis had his wax tablets with all the workings that he and my mother had spent so long over. From these he was calling names and mustering the folk into five groups, one for each ship. My mother took some of the tablets from him and went to each of the five in turn. Each of these she made into three groups and pointing, showed each gaggle of mothers and little ones where they must go to take their places under the sheltering deck, which of them at the bow, which at the stern. The men she pointed to the waist. Also to the waist went childless women or those with grown children. With them also were the 'bailing gangs' of boys and girls, all laughing and giggling with excitement.

All of the women and young children trudged carefully up the gangplank at each ship. They clambered and inched over the structures in their way and got themselves at length to their appointed places. Here they sat, as best they could, on their bundles of spare clothing. Those with weapons now bundled them and laid them, shields on top, under the decks. The food stores, dried meat, bread and water in skins, had been packed beneath the bow and stern decking under the eye of my mother before the Yule feast, and the ship's tun, enough for seven days, filled with fresh water.

The men and grown children remained on the beach for they had an important task to perform. The Frisians drew in the gangways and threw over the boarding nets so that they draped the sides. The sailors left on the beach lifted and carried the anchor stone to under the bow of each ship, where it was hauled up into place and secured.

Then we waited, while the women leaned over the rails of the ships' sides and watched, and called back and forward worriedly with their menfolk. They feared they would drift away and the Frisians then would enslave them. We waited, as painfully slowly the water crept up the sides of the ships.

At a time understood only by Gewis and the Frisians, my uncle gave the order and each group on the beach put shoulders to the bow and pushed. At first nothing happened and then, with a grating noise from the gravel beneath, the ships started to move, first inch by inch and then, as the water deepened, in a rush.

The Frisians on board put out a pair of oars to hold the ships from drifting off in the soft east wind, whilst we all waded to the sides and started to scramble up the boarding nets, tumbling over the side into the waiting waists of the ships chosen for us.

Across the inside bottom of my ship, and I supposed the others to be the same, was a partial decking laid along the keel and across the frames of the hull. I say partial because the bilges to the sides were open for ease of bailing. The space available for the thirty-four of us was not enough for us all to stretch out to sleep, only for sitting and standing. Those men and women without babes were fortunate for they were able to snuggle together against the cold that soon gripped us, regardless of the early summer weather. It seemed as if the sun that warmed the land did not do so to the sea, for the ship was cold and I for one could not get warm. At the Holding in such chill weather we would have lit the fire, but here we could not. I missed my home already!

As the ship made its way through the low waves with an easy rocking, so a light, mist-like spray flew up. It misted the clothes of those nearest the edge. Their woollen cloaks and mantles were soon damp from this and they felt even colder.

We single men envied the couples who kept each other warm. I would have given a great deal, as I drew my dank cloak tighter round me, to have had a warm girl to cuddle into.

It was plain that when it came to sleeping we must make some arrangement to take turns to lie on the deck. For those not sleeping, standing to the side and leaning on the shell of the ship was not possible without standing in the water-sloshing bilge, but for one thing: fortunately there was a wooden beam that ran the length of the ship at the turn of the bilge and it proved possible for me to sit on this and put my feet on the edge of the planking that formed the deck. With ten of us each side perched on these beams, there was plenty of room for the remaining fourteen to stretch out on the deck. And so we quickly agreed to change places at sunset, midnight and sunrise, so that everybody could have some comfort during the day. That was the plan, but little comfort had we from it as it turned out.

The Frisian sailors manned their oars and slowly our little fleet pulled away from the shore and followed it until clear of the offshore sand bar, turning then to the West and slipping quietly through the gap where the water flowed out from the Eider.

Our land is flat. From that, I suppose, came our troubles, for the sea could not have roared across a land of hills, destroying our livelihood as it went. I, and many others, clung to the side and looked with longing at the dark shoreline of our homeland as it thinned and merged with the sea. Because it was flat there was not much to see. We could see nothing but the trees. Of the East Holding, or the surrounding farms, or the old folk, there was no sign. We had said our partings: the old had foregone the heartbreak of coming to wave us off. There were many on the ships who could not have stood that pain and would have got off and stayed behind.

As the ships slipped slowly and quietly west, blown by the east wind on the sails, even the trees slipped from sight and then the sobbing started all around. Later, the sounds of chattering teeth overtook these soft sobs, for the cold was a constant misery that beset us.

As the last glimpse of our land, the Thiatmaresgaho, passed over the sea edge I returned to my perch on the ship's side above the stinking, sloshing bilge. Folding my long, cold, stiff and aching body as best I could, I ran my fingers through my matted, yellow hair and my thin, new beard, gritty with white salt from the spray. Now I understood why the Frisian Shipmen plaited their hair. I wondered whether to copy them, but to do so would lose me my trophy, pride of my fifteen years, the warrior topknot; my reward for killing the Hun.

Gewis was on my ship, I saw him on the afterdeck as the seamen were raising the sail. The old women wove the wadmal sail. It was wool, part brown, part yellow. He had told them not to pattern the cloth, but he should have known better than to try telling an old woman anything, for she will have her way. To make the sail, they had sewn the long strips of wadmal together. The Frisians had strengthened it with a rope pattern set in squares, but the old weavers had patterned the wadmal in squares of brown and yellow, just like my cloak. It made a brave show, bellied out and filled with the cold easterly breeze.

I went to join Gewis but he had no time for idle talk. He set me to work visiting the women and babes under their shelters at bow and stern and had me report back to him on how they fared.

We who stationed ourselves in the waist did not know how lucky we were, spray or no spray. There the air blew free and we men and women mounted the sides and hung our arses over to use the sea for our daily needs. Not so under the sheltered spaces: my stomach heaved at the noisome smell I found there. Babies empty themselves when they want. They make up for the smallness of their size by the smell of their guts, which would do for a giant.

There were hanging pails into which the mess could be scraped and the smell came from these and the soiled swaddling, which gathered in piles awaiting washing. All that could be said for the shelter was that it would keep the breaking waves from soaking those living there, but it was no warmer than the waist and although some planks had been positioned to make seats or beds to lie on, it lacked much in the way of comfort.

I was sorry I went there, for as soon as they saw me the mothers pressed me into work, emptying the stinking shitty buckets over the side. This I did, holding my breath and thanking the gods for the rope on the handle, which allowed me to dump the bucket into the sea and wash it clean. As soon as the women saw this, they wanted that I should empty all the buckets, wash them and bring them back filled so they could wash the foul-smelling cloths that the babes had soiled. Not that they would ever dry. I looked at the squalling stinking mites and decided there and then that I should never want such a thing in any house belonging to me!

When at last I had attended to the needs of all the women, both at the bow and the stern, I spoke to Gewis about it and my feeling that emptying and washing babies' shit-pots was not fitting work for a warrior of the second row. He laughed and then agreed.

At the waist, where the men and women sat, the bailing gangs were already busy. These children, between the ages of six and twelve, were scooping salt water from the bilge, climbing with their buckets to the ship's rail where I had emptied my pots, and emptying the water back into the sea from which it came.

Gewis pointed out to me the ship on which my mother sailed. I was shocked, for I had thought her with us. Each ship, he said, needed to have someone from the Holding who knew something of the ways of ships under sail. For this reason he had placed Lothar on one, Atilec on another, my mother, no sailor but a leader, on another and Sefu, who knew nothing of ships, but was a loyal oath-brother, on the last.

My uncle opened his thoughts to me, 'I do not wholly trust the Frisians; they are great slavers. Should a ship be lost from sight, the folk will need a leader to make sure the sailors do not deceive them.' He shrugged, 'It was the best that I could do.'

Most of our folk were farmers, with a few fishermen mixed in. Gewis' hearth-companions and my mother, on the other hand, were worldly and respected, so I understood why he had split them in this way.

'I have a job for you,' he said. 'You can be in charge of the bailing gang for this ship. Break them into watches but do not let them go away from your sight except when, at change of watch, you send one aft and one forward to repeat the shit-pot duty you have just performed.'

I was pleased to receive his orders, in part because it relieved me of the unpleasant task of baby tender and also because it gave me a post of responsibility suited to my dignity as a warrior of the second row.

And so it went. There was no relief from the cold, although everyone undid their bundles and donned what clothes they had so that we all looked like mounds of cloth. The Frisians laughed at our landsmen softness, but I noted that although their arms were free to ply the oars when needed and to handle the sail, they each wore a fur upper garment and had warm woollen breeches wrapped about their legs. Also, there is a great deal of difference between keeping busy in cold weather and sitting doing nothing.

As the land faded from sight I discovered a truth: to put a distance of water between oneself and that that is lost, turns the mind to what lies ahead. The sobbing fell away; the teeth chattering began, but also a constant hubbub about where we went. As the ship hissed and creaked through grey, wave-scattered water; as the wadmal sail, so stubbornly patterned by our deserted old women, bellied shuddering under grey skies, and as the cold wind whined through the cordage of our mast and sail, so also were our people now adding to the noise with excited, cheerful, uproar.

The level of sound was amazing. All around came the noise of my charges, my bailing children, who seagull-like, skittered endlessly up and down the ship's sides, calling their high, thin cries. Before me, the folk each made noise as if every head had two voices. They called one to the other, their voices echoing between the wooden walls of the ship, chiming as if they had a cracked bell on every tooth. Beneath the raised decks at the ends, seated dry on our piled war gear, were the mothers and very young. From there came the noise of joyful childish shrieking, but also that of infants' woe as mothers sought to occupy unruly little ones and comfort swaddled babes.

The cold wind and spray had not yet subdued the folk in the least, but I feared it soon would. For the present, though shivering, nothing seemed to dampen their spirits. It was the magic of Gewis and my mother, Elwine, which worked this change from fear to hope. My memory of the Yule feast of their making, where they had spun their spells of togetherness, was still fresh and I, shivering and wistfully recalling it, shut out the cold, wet, grey day.

On we sailed, the Frisians well pleased with the sail for the moment as it saved them from rowing. Our folk huddled up in the cool east wind, thinking and talking, calling and shouting, mostly about what welcome our Anglekin cousins would offer us when we reached their new realm.

We were told that with the wind so behind us, in two days we would be breaking out the oars to skirt the sandbanks and making landfall north of the great river mouth.

Two days. With only that before us the discomfort did not seem too great to bear.

Creoda ceased speaking. The fires had burned down during

this telling of the story, which had gone on longer than usual. The listeners shivered in sympathy with the poor folk setting off on the cold sea and leaving their land behind.

'Surely this is not the end,' cried out the butcher's wife. 'Surely you will tell us what happens to them?'

'Indeed I will,' said Bowdyn, 'for this is a very great story and I will continue as long as the master permits and you have patience to listen.'

He looked around with a twinkling eye, 'But, for now, your bums must be as cold as mine. Go home and God bless you. Sleep well; work well; eat and drink well, and if God wills it and you wish it - and the master permits it - we will continue next Saturday night.'

And so we all went home, our minds churning with the problems of the East Holding and so immersed in their troubles that, for a while at least, we forgot our own.

# Chapter 30

**AD 464**

**Creoda's Tale, the Frisian Sea**

The week leading up to the appointed day with Bowdyn was a gloomy autumnal time. The leaves were in full fall and the black, bare bones of the trees were starting to appear, stark against the grey of the sky. The rain fell, not heavily but steadily until everything felt damp inside and soggy without, with squelching footfalls on anywhere not paved. By Wednesday, the rain relented somewhat and turned from a steady downpour to a drizzle that lay somewhere between rain and fog and seemed to penetrate, like cold steam, beneath the warmest clothes.

By Friday, we could see great towering clouds everywhere, and from them hung skirts of heavy rain that swept across the already sodden countryside. Unable to find refuge in the ground, the water filled the ditches that drained into the swollen streams. These in turn drained into the swollen rivers, which overtopped their banks and flooded across the water meadows before running south at last to drain into the sea.

In these flooded meadows patient cows stood in lowing confusion. We had plenty to do, driving the worried herds and flocks to higher ground where they turned their attention back to cropping the glistening grass, forgetful of their recent troubles. We poor things waded cold and shivering, knee deep through floodwater until all the beasts were safe.

By Saturday, though, in keeping with Bowdyn's weather luck, the skies were clear of all but broken clouds streaming from the southwest in swift rags across the sky.

Bowdyn and I, with my father's permission, again took the wain and collected timber for the fires from the woods on the other side of the swollen mere. We laid and lit the fires well before sunset to give the wet wood plenty of time to catch, so that by the time the first folk started to appear at the Cot door there were two good blazes warming the air within.

When all had arrived and were sat waiting, we sent word to the house and as soon as my father and mother had slipped into their chairs, Bowdyn entered. He smiled his greetings, sank onto the Story Chair and without more ado, for everyone knew what had gone before, he worked his magical transformation and Creoda resumed his tale.

When the water between our old home and our ship grew wide, long after the home coast had faded from sight, our heartache at leaving our homeland, which had for a time been hidden beneath our excitement, became fear of what lay ahead. This we eased by talk amongst ourselves, until we were calm as a fish taking a bait worm and the hubbub of previous days subsided, although the babes in their damp swaddling seemed never to cease their thin wailing.

With the soft, but bitter east wind pushing us along at a steady pace, though we shivered with the cold we lost our fear of the sea passage, which seemed to become easier as we grew accustomed to the conditions. All went well until, on

Thunorsday at sunrise, the Shipman passed the word that the next morning we would see the shores of our new home.

As we breakfasted and chewed loudly and thankfully at that tasty news, the Wyrd Sisters must have chuckled, for the first little puff of wind came from the north and set the sail to shivering.

As the day neared its middle, the cold wind increased and moaned through the ropes. It stirred my thin beard. White-capped waves began striking the sides of the ship, breaking against us with a thump and a rush and a rattle of spray. Sometimes, when a wave overtopped us, green water and spray broke into the ship, soaking those in the waist and adding wet to the misery of the cold. I saw Gewis in grim-faced talk with the Frisian Shipman. Then out came the oars and we altered course towards the northwest. He called men from the waist to help, so that a Frisian and one of our folk manned each oar.

In the afternoon, the moaning of the wind rose to a shriek. The seas combined together into great watery slopes, in lines topped by waves breaking in welters of foaming white. The ship's rolling increased, and then, as the wind strengthened, shrieking in the rigging like some dreadful chooser of the dead, the rolling became lopsided. The ship swooped further away from the wind than towards, dipping the lee rail and scooping water. More men were called from the waist to take over the oars. The Frisians, staggering, even on their sea-fast legs, struggled to heave on the brail ropes to bring the sail right up. For a while this worked; the ship halted its lurches away from the wind and I became aware of the awful misery around me.

While I had watched the Frisians and the rowers, deafened by the wind and the crashing of the waves, the passengers in the waist had been spewing. The lucky ones, on their hands and knees, hung over the surging waters in the bilges whilst they heaved and emptied their wasted food into the seawater soup. Others, not lucky enough to find a bilge-side spot, knelt and slid in spew, emptying their stomachs over their fellow warriors. The stink was foul.

Thus my infant gang, my first command gifted by my uncle, took charge of our shield-wall. In their childish wonder they seemed, like me, proof against the sea's movement, but also proof against the fear of it and the fearful noise. To my orders, they worked as if whipped. They scuttled up the lurching ship's sides like spiders, redoubling their efforts to empty the bilges. As they bailed the slop the level fell. Then they passed water buckets down for the warriors to wash the stinking slime off the deck.

Not that the sickness had passed; indeed I know that for some folk it only ends with the passing of the body into shadow. It was just that our shield men and maids had nothing left to give. Those on their knees with their heads in their hands still heaved, their throats dry as summer dust.

'Wulfstan, take two girls and go help the mothers,' I ordered one of my charges.

'Do I have to? Those babies stink.'

'Yes you do. Go. Quick!'

They three of them staggered into the bow and stern spaces, re-appeared, careered downhill and struggled uphill with the rolling of our ship. They held their noses and carried pails, these they threw into the sea, heaving the full buckets back on board to take to the women. They returned, miming spewing.

'Smellyyyyy!' they chorused.

'Think of the mothers,' I said. 'They and their seasickness

are with that stench all the time.'

I looked around. Those at the oars seemed to suffer less from the sickness than the idlers as the ship endlessly soared, hovered, swooped and rolled, and they struggled to keep stroke whilst the helmsman and the Shipman clung to the steering oar.

The Frisians took to the halyards and with great difficulty, lowered the yard to our deck. There they fought to control its charging movements from side to side, as they wrapped the sail tight about it and lashed it down with light line.

As the daylight started to dim, the ships, which against the odds had thus far stayed within sight of each other, were all brought round, bow into the sea and held in that position with steady strokes of the oars. The rolling eased, but the ship increased its pitching, the bow now pointing at the sky, now burying itself deep into the sea, shearing off to one side and then threatening to turn back broadside to the swell.

The noise did not abate, all around was the crashing and rushing of the waves, the pounding of the bow into solid water, the creaking of the ship, the shrieking of the wind, the hammering of the oars on the thole pins, and the hubbub of frightened voices. All the oarsmen, Frisians and Gewissae, now took turns at rowing. Dark patches of sweat formed on their backs and their arms shivered with the cold and the effort.

As time went by and the sky darkened, it became harder for the oarsmen and helmsmen to keep the bow into the sea. It was clear that the press of the wind on the mast and the high prow, both being forward of the waist, forced us away.

We had started to fear that we would be blown broadside and swamped by the sea in the night, when the bow lookout gave a great shout. As the sun set behind the clouds the western rim of the sea had lightened and now, against that light, the ragged edge of land could be seen.

Again, the Frisian Shipman and Gewis brought their heads together, with much pointing and grim looks. I heard later from my uncle that the land, towards which he thought we headed, was very flat. The sight of that more rugged coast showed the Shipman that we had been blown much further south than planned. It was clear that the oars, even double-manned, were losing against the strength of the wind and tide and the weight of the sea.

I watched our leaders with some dread. Their heads nodded as they reached an agreement. The Shipman cupped his hands and shouted above the shrieking of the wind.

'Steerboard oars pull together, strongly now.'

'Ladeboard oars up and hold fast.'

The helmsman rammed the grip of the steering oar towards the steerboard rail and the ship turned to the west and then spun round to the southwest as the wind caught the mast and the prow.

Again the Shipman bellowed. 'Up oars,' and then, 'Give way together.' And the rowing started again.

I looked to the east to the other ships of our little fleet. The pale rounds of faces watched us over the rails and then disappeared from sight. One by one the ships followed us until we were all five safe around and blowing towards the southwest.

Now the stern rose high in the air as the swell and the waves overtook us and passed under us, and then down into the trough we went, and the next great following sea towered over us as the bow climbed up to the sky. These seas were terrifying, threatening to crash over us and drive our poor ship, with all on board, to the bottom. In the night I clenched with fear at each one, but each time, as the wave towered and the stern rose, the mountain of water slid underneath us.

The motion of the ship in the following sea was somewhat easier. The sufferers in the waist had ceased to dry-heave and the fear-filled hubbub increased. In the dim, cloud-shrouded moonlight I saw that some lay exhausted on the bottom boards, with husbands and wives, or lovers, in pairs to give and receive comfort. The hardier, single warriors found themselves perches on the wooden stringers that stretched along both sides of the ship above the turn of the bilges. They shouted their worries back and forth across the deck.

I sent the children for water from the tuns. They came back with full goatskin bags, these they passed amongst the sufferers, who gulped brackish water like finest ale.

Staggering and hanging on, ducking the salt spray, I went to see our leaders, to report. It made me feel important, like a doughty, despite my fifteen years. 'Uncle, the bilges are emptying, the passengers are watered, the babies cleaned. The stink is terrible.'

Gewis laughed. He looked me over, leaning close, inspecting for damage.

'Are you all right, Creoda?'

I knew he meant are you frightened? I was too old for such a question and did not answer. The Shipman, listening, shouted through the strain of bracing against the movement of the steering oar. 'I am glad you are here, Creoda,' he said, 'I need you to take our words to the folk.' He staggered as the stern came down with a thump.

'Tell them that the storm forces us towards the narrow sea between Britannia and Roman Gaul. Now we run before the wind. Tell them calm days will come and then we shall return. Tell them all is well.' He grunted as the steering oar kicked against his grasp.

I nodded, proud that our leaders should trust me to speak for them at such a frightening time. I took his words to our folk in the waist. The frightened clamour faded once they knew there was a plan.

Daylight brought relief that our little fleet was still together, for we could see them and count them as they rose up on the swells. Daylight also cast doubt on the wisdom of his words.

'Land ahead,' bellowed the lookout.

The northeast wind still shrieked past the mast and the mast stays, but aided by the tide set us fast to the west. Great white cliffs rose out of the waves ahead of us and then slid past to the north. Jutting out from their base, unmistakable in the growing daylight, a dark line of shore stretched across our bow. The wind and tide carried us towards it at a fearful rate.

The Shipman and Gewis still stood together. I was not surprised; I doubted if many had slept much during darkness. Our warriors crowded to the rail and watched silently. The Shipman bellowed, 'All oarsmen to the oars, NOW. Row to break your backs!' The rowers from the waist jumped to help the Frisians.

The Frisian Shipman and the helmsman together put the grip of the steering oar hard over, towards the steerboard side. The rowers dug deep and rowed, grunting, for they knew that death and the foundering of all our hopes was rushing towards us.

Yard by painful yard we clawed out to sea, but slower than the wind and tide that carried us west. Now we could hear the waves as they broke in great clouds of spray. We could hear the roar of the pebbles on the beach as the sea threw them up. We could hear them as the sea dragged them back down with the hiss of the seaward rush.

To my eye, we were doomed and my heart hammered, as I looked ahead to what I should do when we struck the strand...

There was silence in the Cot. We all looked at Bowdyn, waiting for him to continue. 'And there, for today, we will stop,' he said, smiling as everyone groaned.

He held up his hand until the clamour ceased and he had our attention. 'Those of you who meet in the tavern will no doubt wish to discuss what happens next, but it is fitting that we pause here, for the story changes. So far we have been in Germania, Gaul and Africa. Now the story shifts to our own country. Think about this. Does the ship hit the shore? Do all perish? Surely not, for where would our story be then? Perhaps only Creoda, or maybe Gewis, save themselves. Do they become slaves of the Britons?

'At this point in the story there are many possibilities. The Fates will weave whatever they need, to make the greater story. You may be sure that the Fates have something in store for the folk of the East Holding.'

He paused, thinking, perhaps remembering that my father had ruled that no high-church man was going to dictate on what day we could hear our Gleeman in our own story house.

'Weather permitting, we will start the new story tomorrow after church,' he said.

We thanked him and having tidied up the Cot, wended our way to our beds, everyone trying to guess what was to come. I for one could not wait, for in my mind I was Creoda, facing possible death... and yet I remembered that in his story he had talked about the future, so I knew he at least must live, but what of the folk? I lay awake thinking on that doomed ship of a thousand and more years ago and when I slept it was restlessly, with nightmares full of screams and crashing water.

I woke tired and I confess that next morning in church I found it even harder than usual to concentrate on the minister's sermon.

Afterwards, we walked briskly home and I noticed that even about Mother there seemed to be an unusual urgency as we ate our Sunday meal. I finished first and waited impatiently until it was time to go to the Cot and at last Bowdyn was settling himself into his Story Chair.

And then he began, in Creoda's voice, to tell us what happened next....

# Author's Note

This volume concludes the story of the folk in Germania. It continues in Part II, *The Axe, the Shield and the Halig Rood*, where the action takes place in Britannia.

The wonderful thing about historical fiction is that it doesn't have to stick to the facts, and the wonderful thing about the Dark Ages is that with the exception of the archaeological and DNA records, there are few facts. They are the Dark Ages because there are so few written contemporary records. Men with an axe to grind wrote those that there are.

This, of course, is only a thought of mine and I am sure any scholar of the period would say that I have taken diabolical liberties with what we think we know about the times.

That the mutiny of Majorian's Hun auxiliaries led to bandit bands of Huns and Goths fleeing from that confusion and tumult seems probable, after the leading mutineers were killed by loyal Roman troops.

The Bagaudae revolt was one of several, although the landowner, Pulcher, and his terrible revenge are fictional. That Aetius supported the great estate owners of the time in putting down the revolt is undisputed, as far as I can tell.

The Vandal occupation of Roman North Africa is of course factual, as is their piratical raiding of Roman coastlines. The ships they used were, originally at least, those captured in Carthage at the fall of that city while the citizens were literally 'at the races'.

The details of ship types and ship names I owe entirely to that most excellent book Ships and Seamanship in the Ancient World, by Lionel Casson, any misunderstandings of the subject which have crept into my stories of the Triton are my fault entirely.

Roman dates are taken to be reliable; the sack of Rome by the Vandals commenced on the second day of June, 455 AD and finished two weeks later. The Vandals sailed their ships up the Tiber, which was notoriously shallow over the bar at the entrance to the river. It is interesting that a consultation of NASA's records of moon phases for that year shows that spring tides started on 2nd June and occurred again two weeks later. The two weeks that the Vandals took to sack the city may be more a testament to their informed seamanship than their greed.

The political reason for the invasion may have been pretence, but the Vandal fleet departed with the rescued Eudoxia and her daughter on board, together with many leading Roman citizens taken into slavery. I suppose the Empress would have said, 'Serve them right,' insofar as they had connived at her loss and humiliation.

The cursed cross, which is introduced in the story and which carries on its baleful way in the sequel, The Axe the Shield and the Halig Rood, is not pure invention. A mystery Christian cross was unearthed on a hill in Somerset in the 11th Century as a result, reportedly, of a dream of the village blacksmith.

The cross was taken by oxen, left to wander at will, to Waltham in Essex, coincidentally also owned by the Danish noble to whom the cross was given. The present Waltham Abbey was eventually built to house it.

The battle cry, 'Halig Rood,' at Hastings, by King Harold's army, called on this very cross. This later reappearance of the malign cross forms part of volume III of the Ancient Freedom epic entitled Edith, Fair as a Swan planned to appear in 2012. The story of the curse is pure invention on my part, but the wicked bishop of Margus is not.

The treasure of Sirmium existed, as did the mercenary and treacherous grave-robbing Bishop of Margus; the prudent Bishop of Sirmium, who sent the treasure to Rome and the Roman banker, Gaius Silvanus, to whom it was pawned. That he fled Rome with all the contents of his vaults, including that from Sirmium, and that this treasure was buried in, and then recovered from, Cosa, is fiction, although the ruins of Cosa exist and were deserted at the time of the story.

The Bat Caves of Kalkberg are real and are a tourist attraction, the entrance having been re-discovered during the Twentieth Century.

The founders of the Kingdom of West Seax (Wessex) were a nebulous group called the Gewissae (the trustees or trusted ones). The eponymous Gewis appears on family trees tracing his origins back to Wothan. I have dispensed with all that and tried to put human rather than mythical flesh on the bones of the Gewissae. This is pure invention on my part, as is the East Holding, in what is present day Holstein.

The mythical original homeland of the Ingwines I mention briefly in my story as Atland. This I see as sited in what we now call Doggerland, under the North and Wadden Seas, for which there is ample evidence of a land teeming with wildlife. The time of peace and plenty remembered at the final Yule I envisage as folk memory in song of a 'hunter gatherer' lifestyle based on co-operation between free roaming groups. This part of the story, Volume I of the Ancient Freedoms epic, is planned as a 'prequel', oddly, this will be the last in the series to be produced, with a provisional title Atland the Lost.

In attributing famine as the trigger for the migration of the East Holding there are many precedents for this. The Langobards are an example of a nearby tribe forced to migrate by harvest failure.

As for the flood that caused the famine, this is not an uncommon event historically. The land bordering the Wadden Sea is low-lying. The present name for the northern part of the area, Dithmarsch comes from the Saxonian name Thiatmaresgaho that I understand to mean 'Land of large bogs and waters'.

North Sea storms have caused great loss of life and property in recorded times. The island of Strand was torn apart and the town of Rungholt sunk beneath the sea in one of a series of floods caused by a combination of spring tides and North Sea wind storms creating storm surges (the Grote Mandrenke - great man drownings - the first of 1219 with 36,000 deaths and the second of 1362 with 25,000 deaths, the third in 1634 with 15000 deaths. The most recent occurred in 1953 with 2400 deaths). I imagine the severity of the flood and loss of life is inversely proportional to the efficacy of protective seawalls, dykes and the like.

My ideas for the origins, collapse and migrations of the tribe were stimulated by my readings of Jared Diamond's thought provoking books: Collapse and Guns, Germs and Steel. If I have misunderstood his reasoning that is entirely my fault.

To any of the serious scholars and students of this period of Dark Age history who may read this work of fiction and be horrified at the liberties I have taken with accepted views based on their careful research, I apologise, tongue in cheek. It is just fiction after all.

James M. Hockey, Bristol, January 2012

# Place Names, Ancient and Modern

Albis River --- River Elbe
Antissiodorum --- Auxerre
Aquincum --- Budapest
Arelate --- Arles
Atland the Lost --- Legendary land lost beneath the North Sea now rediscovered as Doggerland
Augusta Vindelicorum --- Augsburg
Baetica --- Province in the south of Spain from which the Vandals crossed to Africa
Barcino --- Barcelona
Barneek --- Modern Benghazi, Libya
Bishopston --- A fictional village in Somerset during the reign of James II at the time of the Monmouth Rebellion.
Bosa --- Harbour town on west coast of Sardinia, north of Tharos
Brigantium --- Bregenz
Byzantium --- now Istanbul
Cambodunum --- Kempten im Allgau
Carthage --- A city in Tunisia, first Carthaginian, conquered by the Romans, captured by the Vandals.
Colonia Agrippina --- Koln --- Cologne
Colonia Mursa --- Near Croation city of Osijek
Constantia --- Konstanz
Domus Augustana --- Palace of the Emperors of Rome
Durocortorum --- Reims
East Holding, Thiatmaresgaho --- Now Ditmarsch, Northwest Holstein, just south of the present-day Danish Border
Ebussus --- Ibiza

Eider --- River between Denmark and Holstein, north of
    Thiatmaresgaho
Fabiranum --- Bremen
Hamm Village --- the first settlement of Hamburg
Hlawdun --- Batcaves at Kalkberghole, Segeberger, Holstein
Icauna --- River Yonne
Ivelbridge --- Fictional Town near the village of Bishopston
Lacus Brigantium --- Lake Constance or Bodensee
Leptis Magna --- Vandal port in North Africa west of
    Carthage.
Luckyworth --- Fictional village near position of present
    town of Gluckstadt
Luefana ---- Luneberg, Germany
Margus --- A city in Roman Pannonia, now Serbia
Massalia --- Marseille
Mosae Trajectum --- Maastricht
Namuricum --- Namur
New Angeln --- Anglekin colonies in eastern Britannia
Noviomagus --- Nijmegan
Oenipons --- Innsbruck
Ostia --- Silted up port at the mouth of the Tiber
Pannonia --- A Roman province in the area of present-day
    Croatia and Serbia
Portus (Augusti) --- The great harbour north of the Tiber
    mouth, connecting to it by canal.
Portus Julius --- Roman naval HQ at Misenum near Naples
Rhenus --- River Rhine
Rome --- The progress of the Main Vandal Army, the
    Chiliarchs 1000 and Gewis and his companions
    can be followed by any wishing to do so on Platner
    and Ashby's Map of Ancient Rome, discoverable
    on any Internet search engine (Platner, Ancient
    Rome Maps)

Rungholt --- Port city on the Island of Strand sunk beneath the Wadden Sea in a storm.

Saldae --- Early capital of Vandal North African kingdom, now Bougie, Algeria.
Sirmium --- Capital of Roman Pannonia now Serbia
Sparrowhawk Island --- Small offshore island on southwest coast of Sardinia.
Strand --- Island in the Wadden Sea destroyed by a storm, the remains of which are the islets of Pellworm and Nordstrand.
Sweotheod --- Sweden
Taunton --- County town of Somerset
Tharos --- Harbour town on the west coast of Sardinia
Thiatmaresgaho --- Present day Dithmarsch in Schleswig Holstein, Germany
Tiber --- River connecting Rome to the sea
Tisia River --- Tisza or Theiss River flows through Hungary and joins the Danube in Northern Serbia.
Tolossa --- Tolouse
Vindonbona --- Vienna
Visurgis --- River Weser

# Weapons in use in the 5th Century AD

Axe (Bearded) --- As in war axe, but with one long blade extension for hooking shields.
Axe (War) --- One- or two-sided, long-handled, heavy blade
Bill --- Long-handled weapon with hooked blade on one side, axe blade and spike on the other, also usually with a spike at the end. This weapon was used by English infantry from 5th to 17th century.
Cataphract --- Armoured, applied to ships or horses
Catapults --- Common in legionary use, sometimes mounted on ships.
Fire pots --- Clay pots filled with inflammables, fired by catapult.
Gladius --- Roman standard short sword
Hammer (War) --- Single or double, long-handled, heavy blunt instrument
Hand Ballista --- Early crossbow
Hunnic Bow --- Laminated from wood and horn in a double bow, short but powerful.
Javelin --- Light short spear carried in bunches behind shield
Langseax --- Longer, more sword-like, one-edged blade.
Liburnian --- Fast double-banked galley.
Pilum --- Infantry throwing spear, wood half shaft, other half shaft and head of metal.
Pugio --- Dagger
Seax --- Short, knife size, one cutting edge, stabbing blade
Spatha --- Long, heavy, Roman cavalry sword
Spear --- Metal head, wooden shaft
Trireme --- Refers to the numbers of rowers (3) to each oar. Usually double or triple banked oars.